Acc
His U
An Erotic Anthology

"*His Underwear* is one of the best collections of erotica I've read this year. There's something here for every kind of underwear fantasy imaginable. Two thumbs up!"

—Paul Willis
Editor of *Dangerous Liaisons*
and *View to a Thrill*

His Underwear
An Erotic Anthology

HARRINGTON PARK PRESS®
Southern Tier Editions™
Gay Men's Fiction

His Underwear
An Erotic Anthology

Todd Gregory
Editor

Southern Tier Editions™
Harrington Park Press®
The Trade Division of The Haworth Press, Inc.
New York • London

For more information on this book or to order, visit
http://www.haworthpress.com/store/product.asp?sku=5756

or call 1-800-HAWORTH (800-429-6784) in the United States and Canada
or (607) 722-5857 outside the United States and Canada

or contact orders@HaworthPress.com

Published by

Southern Tier Editions™, Harrington Park Press®, the Trade Division of The Haworth Press, Inc., 10 Alice Street, Binghamton, NY 13904-1580.

Reprint - 2007

PUBLISHER'S NOTE
The development, preparation, and publication of this work has been undertaken with great care. However, the Publisher, employees, editors, and agents of The Haworth Press are not responsible for any errors contained herein or for consequences that may ensue from use of materials or information contained in this work. The Haworth Press is committed to the dissemination of ideas and information according to the highest standards of intellectual freedom and the free exchange of ideas. Statements made and opinions expressed in this publication do not necessarily reflect the views of the Publisher, Directors, management, or staff of The Haworth Press, Inc., or an endorsement by them.

This is a work of fiction. Names, characters, places, and incidents either are the products of the author's imagination or are used fictitiously, and any resemblance to actual persons, living or dead, business establishments, events, or locales is entirely coincidental. This novel may contain scenes of graphic sex and/or violence. It is not the intention of The Haworth Press to condone any particular behavior depicted within this fictional work.

Cover design by Jennifer M. Gaska.

Library of Congress Cataloging-in-Publication Data

His underwear : an erotic anthology / edited by Todd Gregory.
    p. cm.
  ISBN: 978-1-56023-624-5 (softcover : alk. paper)
    1. Gay men—Fiction. 2. Fetishism (Sexual behavior)—Fiction. 3. Erotic stories, American. 4. Gay men's writings, American. I. Gregory, Todd.

PS648.H57H58 2007
813'.0108358086642—dc22

                                                                2006034873

CONTENTS

Introduction

Todd Gregory

I love underwear.

I remember the exact moment in my life when underwear became sexualized for me. Prior to that moment, it was just another part of clothing to me—you know, what you put on before you pulled on your pants. But in one instant, that changed forever, and from that moment on underwear became an object of fantasy for me.

I was thirteen years old, a freshman in high school and an unwilling member of the freshman football team. I was probably the most uncoordinated pubescent teenager in the world; clumsy and unathletic and much more interested in spending my time lying on my bed reading a book rather than wearing pads and slamming into other boys on a practice field every afternoon after school. The only saving grace to football practice was showering afterward. Although I was immensely shy of my own body, I would sneak looks at other boys in the showers or as they paraded about in the locker room either naked or in some state of undress. I was always amazed the other boys had no shyness about their nakedness; some were unmistakably voyeuristic as they paraded about stark naked, stopping to bullshit with friends at their lockers or snapping towels in the communal drying area.

The star of the freshman team was a guy I didn't know. His name was Jim, and while he seemed like a nice enough guy, he was one of the elite to whom I simply didn't exist. Not only was he our best running back, he was also our placekicker; and since he stayed on the field after wind sprints to practice kicking, I'd never

His Underwear: An Erotic Anthology
© 2007 by The Haworth Press, Inc. All rights reserved.
doi:10.1300/5756_a

seen him in the locker room or the showers. This particular practice day it rained, so we ran plays in the gym (in those sexist days of the mid 1970s the football team preempted the girls' volleyball practice), and he didn't have to stay later. I was carrying my towel and stepped outside of my row of lockers and there he was—two rows away from me, standing in the aisle wearing nothing but his briefs, talking to another boy, his back to me. His back narrowed from his broad shoulders to his small waist. His perfectly round, hard ass was outlined perfectly in his almost too-white briefs. Drops of water glistened on his lower back just above the waistband. His legs were strong and muscular. He was laughing, and his wet curly reddish-brown hair bounced as he laughed. I just stopped and stared for a few moments, until he half-turned and saw me standing there. He nodded at me, still smiling, and realizing I couldn't just keep standing there, I mumbled a "hey" as I started walking into the showers.

The image of him standing there, so effortlessly beautiful and sexy in his underwear, was seared into my mind. On the bus ride home, I kept playing that scene over and over again on my mental video camera. My dick was so hard it ached, and I half-ran home from the bus stop, heading straight into the bathroom where I jacked off.

Every chance I got from that moment on, I spied on Jim. My nascent gay sexuality, which up until then had been completely absorbed with looking at cocks and asses, changed. I found the thought of underwear much more exciting, much more mysterious, and much more thrilling. I started watching the other boys, rather than in the shower with water cascading over their nakedness, while they changed, seeing them pulling on their underwear—or their jocks as they changed for practice—in order to replay the images later in the privacy of my bedroom as I masturbated. I always preferred the briefs to jocks, though. Perhaps it was the lack of exposure; the jockstraps were put on fast and covered up and later were stripped off quickly. The guys never seemed to walk around and hang out in the locker room in their jocks the way they would in their briefs. I loved the way their packages looked, all wrapped up in their white cotton covering—almost like a Christmas present. And how I wanted to tear that wrapping off!

As the years passed, my fascination with underwear never abated—rather, it grew as I discovered there were more kinds of underwear than I could have possibly dreamed up. The International Male catalogue introduced me to the thong, for example—a delightful yet uncomfortable looking contraption that exposed both ass cheeks with just a tantalizing triangle of material poised at the confluence of butt curve and lower back. I remember being disappointed when picking up a hot stud in a bar only to discover, on getting him home, that he wasn't wearing underwear beneath his jeans. I loved the idea of meeting a hot guy and having him strip down to his briefs in front of me. And I have yet to meet a guy who'll say no if you ask him to flex his muscles for you while in his briefs.

The pinnacle of my underwear fascination, of course, was the Marky Mark ad campaign for Calvin Klein. Of course, I'd already fallen madly in lust with him watching him on MTV. He had this delightful predilection for dropping his pants and walking around in his underwear, revealing his magnificently chiseled body and a very nice package, yet somehow managing to seem somewhat innocent—an "aw shucks" quality and youthful exuberance. You just knew he'd stay hard all night . . . and grin.

I used to slice those ads out of *Vanity Fair* and frame them, hanging them up around my desk at home. When I was stuck on a short story or whatever I was writing, I could look up at Marky Mark grinning at me, his huge bulge provocatively exposed, and draw inspiration. I even bought the issue of *Penthouse* when he did a Calvin layout for them. (Of course, in most of the pictures he posed with a bleach blonde with huge bare breasts, but his masculine beauty trumped her.) I still have all those ads in a folder in my filing cabinet, and every once in a while I'll pull them out and take a look. I'm still a fan of his, even though he rarely appears shirtless or in underwear anymore in his films. (Perhaps my biggest disappointment was the remake of *Planet of the Apes*—I was really enjoying the thought of him running around in a loin cloth for two hours.)

So, when I decided to make the move from merely writing erotic stories to editing an anthology, it was a no-brainer what the theme would be—it had to be underwear.

Enjoy!

Red Briefs, Blue Briefs

Greg Herren

To me, Americus might as well have been on the moon.

It was actually in Kansas, a sleepy little town of about 700 people. Ten miles away from the county seat of Emporia about two miles southwest of the Neosho River, it was surrounded on every side by cornfields. I could look out my bedroom window and see rows and rows of corn, wilting and shrinking in the heat. It was also so quiet, especially at night when the stars came out in the velvety bluish-black sky. Cars rarely if ever passed by our house, and every once in a while a car would zoom by on the county road down at the corner.

We moved there the summer I turned fifteen from Chicago, with its hustle and bustle of police sirens, fire engines, cars, and people. There wasn't much for me to do. Out there we didn't get cable, so we only were able to get the CBS station out of Kansas City. The town library consisted of one room and was only open one day a week. The first week I was there I went through it book by book and discovered nothing more recent than 1968. I found myself reading books I had already read, time and again.

The only break in my daily routine was walking a couple of blocks to the post office to get the mail. Every morning after *The Price Is Right* Showcase Showdown was over, I would leave the house and walk down to the corner where the next paved street intersected my street and turned left. The next corner was where that

His Underwear: An Erotic Anthology
© 2007 by The Haworth Press, Inc. All rights reserved.
doi:10.1300/5756_01

road met the county road, the crossroads that was the hub of the town. That was where the blinking red light, suspended over the center of the intersection, swung in the breeze. On one corner was the town park; directly opposite was the Americus Bank, then across from it was the post office. The final corner was an old two pump Shell gas station. I rarely saw anyone on my daily trips. It was almost as though it was a ghost town during the day. Every so often I saw a woman in a house dress hanging laundry on a line in her yard. I knew there had to be other kids my age in town, but I never saw anyone. There would be plenty of time, my mother said, to meet kids when school started in the fall. I really didn't mind.

One morning I came out of the post office with a couple of credit card bills and the bank statement. It was especially hot. The sign hanging on the bank said it was ninety-eight degrees. The post office was air conditioned and my soaked tank top had dried while I had been inside. The heat hit me like a brick. The sky was blue, not a cloud to be seen anywhere. I wiped my forehead and stepped down onto the sidewalk and was immediately blind sided. My vision was a kaleidoscopic explosion of stars, the sky, the roof of the post office overhang. I landed on my back with a bone-jarring crash that knocked my breath out. I had perhaps a half second of respite before something landed half on me. I had tried to grasp at a breath but it was knocked back out of me.

"Fuck!" A voice very near my ear said. As my eyes swam back into focus and air filled my lungs I became aware that it was a person lying on half of my body. The pressure on the left side of my body was gone and I turned my head to try to see the person. I lifted my head. He was standing with his back to me. In a quick glance I determined that he was blonde with golden tan skin. He was wearing a pair of cutoff jeans with threads dangling down his thighs. His back was broad and thickly muscled, and his legs were sprinkled with a dusting of faint blond hairs that were almost invisible to the eye. The shorts were tight and hugged a round, hard butt. I started to get up as he turned around.

"Are you okay?" he asked, reaching out his hand to me to help me up. He pulled, muscles in his arms, chest, and shoulders contracting and shifting beneath the skin. I scrambled up to my feet. He was beautiful, maybe my age or a little older, with grayish-blue eyes, a strong nose and chin, and the faint outline of dimples in his cheeks. His hair was damp, and lines of sweat streamed down his face. All of his exposed skin was covered with droplets of water.

"Yeah," I said, still trying to get control of my breathing. My head ached a bit, as did my ribs, but nothing felt broken.

"I'm so sorry," he sighed. "I guess I was running too close to the building because you stepped right out in front of me."

"I should have looked."

He laughed. "Like there's ever a reason to look!" He looked both ways and then back at me and grinned. I could see his point. Although cars were parked at forty-five degree angles to the side-walk, there wasn't another living soul in sight. "My name's Kevin."

"Dennis. Dennis Whitsell."

He looked me up and down. "You look pretty strong. You going out for football?"

"Yeah."

"What position?"

"Guard."

"You're small for a guard, but I bet you're quick." He grinned. "I'm a halfback. Well, I should probably finish my jog. You jog?"

"No."

"Get in shape early." He winked at me. "I'll stop by your place tomorrow and you can come with me." He started off.

"But you don't know where I live!"

He turned and ran backwards for a few steps. "Yeah, I do. The town ain't that big."

Sure enough, the next morning at ten forty-five, our doorbell rang for the first time. I had on my gym shoes and my old white gym shorts from my old high school. My mom made me wear a White Sox baseball cap ("No sense in getting heat stroke," she said in her slight Southern twang). Kevin grinned at me as I stepped out into the shade of the porch. He was wearing a pair of green cotton shorts. "I've never jogged before," I said hesitantly. I hadn't. I had to run laps and sprints in football and baseball practice before, but that had never been my strong suit. I couldn't run fast and had no endurance.

"It's just jogging." He punched me lightly in the shoulder. "It's just a little bit faster than walking, is all. You work up a good sweat, and before you know it you'll be running for miles."

I doubted it, but we started at a slow pace. We hadn't gotten to the foot of the driveway before I started sweating, and I was breathing hard by the time we got to the stop light. My legs were getting heavier with every step. I had never been past the intersection before. On the next block was a big old school that looked like it had seen better days. A big faded wooded sign read AMERICUS GRADE SCHOOL, HOME OF THE INDIANS. Another block past there was another cornfield with trees shading the road. I was having trouble breathing by the time we got that far. My shorts were soaked, and water was running down my body. Kevin didn't really seem to be breathing hard. When I glanced over at him the sun shone on his wet skin. We reached a driveway with a mailbox at the end of it. Kevin slowed down and bent over, putting his hands on his knees. I did the same, feeling like I was going to throw up.

"Want some water?" he asked between gulps of air.

Unable to speak, I nodded. He motioned me to follow him up the driveway. The name on the mailbox read HANSEN. My legs felt rubbery. I followed him up to the house and then around to the back. He grabbed a hose and turned a spigot. He let the water run for a few minutes, bent down to drink from it, then handed it to me. I swallowed and swallowed the cold water down. I handed the hose back to him. He took a drink then held the hose over his head, the water cascading in sheets down his chest, over his heaving stomach, over and through his shorts, and down his legs. As the shorts got wetter, they darkened and clung to him even more tightly. He handed me the hose back, and I took another drink. I wasn't seeing the dark spots anymore, and I was starting to catch my breath. I held the hose over my head as he did, and let the cold water cool down my skin. I then put the hose down. He turned off the spigot and climbed up on the back porch. He came back down

holding two white towels, handing one to me. I started rubbing it
through my hair and over my face. I was going to start wiping
down my arms when I noticed him slipping his shorts off.

"What are you doing?" I asked.

He grinned at me and finished removing the shorts. He was
wearing a pair of white underwear that was so wet it was completely see-through. I could see the dark blond hairs, the outline of
his genitals. He wrung the shorts out, and then slipped off his underwear and did the same to his underwear. "Can't go in the house
wet." He shrugged. "Don't worry. Mom and Dad are at work and
my little brother is at my grandmother's. No one is going to see
you."

I took a deep breath and, my hands shaking a little, slipped off
my shorts and underwear. I wrung them out the way he had done.
He was already drying himself with the towel. I put my shorts and
underwear down on a rock in the sun.

I had never been alone and naked with another boy before. Sure,
at my old high school I had been naked among others in the locker
room in the showers after gym or practice. I had long since gotten
over my modesty and shyness in that environment. But I had
never been alone with another naked boy before. I was always
afraid that I would get an erection in the locker room, but it had
never happened, no matter how attracted I was to any of the other
boys, no matter how many surreptitious looks I had snuck at my
classmates. I watched Kevin dry off out of the corner of my eye as
I rubbed the towel over my body. Rather than being embarrassed
or self-conscious about his nakedness, he seemed to revel in the
sun on his bare skin. Just below his navel the golden tan stopped.
The contrast between the bright whiteness and the tan was almost
intoxicating. The whiteness stopped a few inches down his thighs,
giving way to the gold. He wrapped the towel around his waist and
smiled at me. I did the same.

"Come on. Let's get out of the heat." I followed him up the
stairs, watching his hard butt working beneath the white cotton.
We walked through a screen door into a plain kitchen. There was a
big old white gas stove next to a counter with a white porcelain

sink built into it. The old white refrigerator hummed. The cabinets were all fronted with glass so that you could see the contents. He opened the refrigerator door and handed me a Coke bottle. I used the opener on the counter and took a healthy swig, suppressing the belch. Kevin felt no such compunctions. He opened his mouth and let out a healthy burp. We both grinned at each other.

"Come on." I followed him up through a door and up a staircase. At the top of the stairs were a couple of doors. He opened one. "My room."

I walked in. There was a single bed in one corner, beneath a window. It was open and the sheer blue curtains moved in the slight breeze. There was a makeshift bookcase of plywood and bricks against one wall and a desk next to it. In another corner was an old stereo. Kevin walked over and started going through the pile of albums next to it. I looked around at the posters he had hung up. George Brett of the Kansas City Royals. Bruce Lee with the three lines of blood on his left shoulder. Linda Ronstadt lit from behind and pouting slightly at the camera. Farrah and her orange one piece with the huge nipple clearly visible. Kevin put an album on the turntable and started it. It was Fleetwood Mac, *Monday Morning*. Lindsay Buckingham's unique voice filling the room. "I love Fleetwood Mac, don't you?"

"Yeah." I had the album myself. I bought it because I had loved the song "Rhiannon," and had been pleasantly surprised with the rest.

He air guitared a riff for a moment, and then opened a bureau drawer. He tossed me something made of blue cloth. I caught it. It was underwear, navy blue with red trim. I looked at it. Only a couple of boys at my old school wore underwear in any color but white, and I had found it incredibly sexy. I stood there staring at his back. He dropped the towel, revealing his round bare white ass. He slipped on a pair the opposite of mine, red with blue trim. I pulled mine on.

He walked over and sat down on the bed. "How do you like Americus so far?"

"It's quiet." I stood there for a moment and then sat down on the opposite end of the bed.

"Boring," he agreed. He scratched his balls. I took a drink of my Coke. Condensation was beading up on the bottle. The slight breeze couldn't cut the heat in the room. I was starting to sweat again. "You did pretty good for your first time."

"Thanks." I felt my face getting warm. "I thought I was going to die."

He laughed, "It gets easier." He stood up and walked over to the mirror. He started striking muscle man poses in the mirror.

"You look like a pro wrestler." I said. He did, sort of, in the colored underwear. I had seen someone on a late-night show earlier that week wrestling in red underwear. He was lean and muscled and blond, like Kevin, and he had beaten a balding guy with a big gut in black tights.

He turned around and struck a double biceps pose at me. "That's me. World Heavyweight Champion Kevin 'The Crusher' Hansen." He growled at me, "And that makes you the challenger, Dennis 'The Loser' Whitsell."

"The Loser?" I said, standing up and posing myself. "I don't think so."

He smiled and stepped closer to me. "I do."

I stepped closer to him. We were about the same height. Our chests were barely a half inch apart. We stared into each other's eyes, neither making a sound or moving. An eternity seemed to pass as we stared, our bodies so close that I could feel his breath on my chin. I could feel my cock starting to harden slowly. He leaned forward slightly so that his hard chest touched mine and then rocked back a little. "Yeah?" I said, my voice low.

Our chests touched again. "Yeah."

"I can take you."

"Try it."

He moved so fast that even had I the slightest inkling of what he was about to do I couldn't have blocked him. His right leg slipped behind my left and his arms went around my waist as he pushed forward. The bed groaned as both of our weights landed on it. He locked both of his legs around mine and squeezed them together. He forced both of my arms over my head and held them down. His body stretched out over mine. I could feel his hardness against my stomach. *I'm not the only one,* I thought to myself crazily as I struggled against him. He was too strong and had me locked up. I couldn't move. I couldn't do anything.

His face was above mine. He smiled. "Looks like I'm still undefeated."

"Cheap shot. I wasn't ready."

"Everything's fair in wrestling. Don't you watch?" He smiled. He brought his face down close to mine. He let go of my arms and legs but didn't get off of me. "And what's this?" He touched my hard-on.

"You've got one too," I said quickly.

He laughed. "So I do." He rolled off of me and got up on his knees. He ran his hands down his chest and over his stomach, finally stopping at his erection. He held it with one hand while he cupped his balls with the other. "So now what do we do?"

I sat up slowly, trying not to look at his hands. "I don't know."

He slid his underwear down on his legs. His cock was longer than mine, but mine was thicker. "Well?"

I swallowed, and slid mine down.

"Nice," he grinned. He reached out and put his hand on mine.

No one had ever touched mine before, and I moaned a little bit. It felt nice, even though all he was doing was touching it.

"Lay back down," he instructed me. I did as he directed, my mind whirling. What was going on here? I had always dreamed of this, but now that it was happening, with a nice guy, a sexy guy, I was scared, nervous. I was conscious of him pulling my underwear off completely; the blue briefs tossed on the floor. He stood up, and kicked off his. I stared up his legs at his beautifully muscled and tanned body. He seemed almost like a giant. He spit on his hands, and then knelt down and spread his spittle on my cock. I shuddered again. He squatted down over me, grabbed my cock, and directed it into the crack of his ass. He paused for a moment, closing his eyes, and then slowly began to lower himself on my cock. It was tight and hurt a bit, but then it began to loosen a little as he slid further down it. His eyes were still closed as he began to stroke his own. He stopped when he got all the way down and I could feel the pressure of his ass on my balls. He stayed there for a few moments. The only sounds were our breathing and the friction noises from his rubbing himself. He began sliding back up. It felt so good, so much better than when I was locked in the bathroom and beating off, visualizing the boys in the locker room, their wet bodies glistening.

I moaned.

I felt hot drops pelting my chest.

I opened my eyes. Kevin's cock was raining white drops on me. His eyes were still closed, and he kept pulling on his dick. He kept working his way up and down my cock, still slowly. I closed my eyes and felt the burning sensation starting, my balls starting to work to pump my own come up through the head of my dick. He started moving faster, his eyes still closed.

I opened my eyes as my entire body went rigid and moaned as I started to come, harder than I ever had in the bathroom. Kevin started to whimper and kept moving. It felt so good, so amazing, and it just kept rushing over me, wave after wave of pleasure, my body shuddering with each shot out of my cock. Kevin whimpered louder and a stream of come shot out of him, thicker and ropier drops than the first time.

I shuddered again.

Kevin stopped coming and smiled at me, settling down onto my cock, which was softening. He sat there for a moment, staring into my eyes. Then he got up on his knees and I slid out of him. He got off the bed. "Come on, let's get cleaned up." He reached out his hand and took mine. Holding hands, he led me into a bathroom and turned the shower on. He pulled me in behind him.

The water was hot but felt good. He began running a bar of soap over my chest, lathering it up. My dick started to get hard again. I took the soap from him and ran it over his torso, and then running it over his dick and balls. His dick was getting hard again. I took it and started stroking it. He moaned and took mine, doing the same.

He used his free hand to start playing with my right nipple, stroking it, pinching it, flicking it with his fingers. It felt amazing. I put my free arm around him and pulled him close to me, our wet soapy torsos slipping against each other and I kissed him. He opened his mouth and slid his tongue into my mouth. I sucked on his tongue and then worked mine into his mouth. He was still stroking me.

I could feel it coming again. I started stroking him harder and faster. Both of us began breathing in shallow gasps as our hands moved faster. We looked deep into each other's eyes and then his closed and his body began jerking as he came. A few moments later I came.

He grinned at me lazily. We rinsed off and climbed out of the shower and used the towels from outside to dry off. He walked naked across the room and tossed the blue underwear at me. "I'll loan you a pair of shorts to walk home in." he said. I pulled on the underwear, watching as he slid the red ones back on. He gave me a pair of blue gym shorts that I put on, and then socks. He pulled on a pair of jean shorts.

I finished my Coke as I followed him downstairs. I put the bottle on the counter and walked outside, putting my shoes on. My clothes were still damp.

"I'll be by tomorrow at the same time," he said, winking at me. "Be ready."

"Okay."

He flexed his arms. "I'm still the champ."

I laughed. "Only because of a cheap shot. Tomorrow I'll take the title away from you."

"We'll see." He punched me in the arm. "See you tomorrow."

I walked down the driveway. I looked back. He was watching me. I waved, and he smiled and waved back.

Maybe I would like it here after all, I thought to myself as I walked back into town.

Backstage with the Bulldogs

Aaron Travis

The lights go down in Ringside Coliseum. The fans go wild.
The announcer barks into his microphone, "And now, ladies and
gentlemen, the match you've been waiting for, the main event of
the evening: The Lightning Kid versus Leo 'Hit Man' Logan!"

The Lightning Kid is already in the ring, soaking up the crowd's
adoration. Tonight he wrestles solo, but he's usually part of a
team, one half of the Baltimore Bulldogs. His partner, Lanny Boy
Jones, stands outside the ring playing manager tonight. Both Bulldogs look fantastic. They've been training like devils, pumping
steroids and iron, hardening their short, stocky physiques to join
the upper rung of wrestling superstardom. Even the TV announcer
can't contain his enthusiasm: "Get a look at the superb physiques
on these fine young athletes!"

Despite the fact that they could almost pass for twins, the Bulldogs have never been billed as brothers. The only logical alterna-
tive, from the way they casually touch each other on the rump and
embrace before and after every match, is lovers. Lanny Boy is obviously the top; he's a little chunkier and smoother, with huge slab
pecs, massively muscled shoulders, a big boulder ass, and just a
trace of a gut. Something in his swagger tells you he's got an enor-

---

This story appeared originally in *Tag Team Studs,* Clay Caldwell and
Aaron Travis, 37-44. New York: Badboy, 1997. It appeared again in *Full Body
Contact,* ed. Greg Herren, 329-335. Los Angeles, CA: Alyson Publications,
2002. Used with permission of the author.

mous clubcock between his legs, which the Kid loves going down on after a hard match in the ring.

The Kid's the bottom, with his etched-in-steel physique and hard round ass. He suffers more beautifully in the ring than anybody else. And he gets plenty of chances to suffer when they pit him against Leo "Hit Man" Logan. As the crowd boos, Logan swaggers in wearing a black tank top that clings to his pumped-up pecs and sporting his trademark mirror shades and a smart-aleck smirk.

The bell sounds. Logan proceeds to put the Kid through his paces. Slamming him against the boards. Throwing him clear out of the ring. Following him out and yanking him to his knees by a fistful of hair. Calmly dragging him back into the ring for some more punishment of that godlike young body.

Logan wraps the Kid's outstretched arms in the ropes, then steps back and gives his bound half-naked body a leering once-over. He makes a fist and pummels the Kid's iron-banded stomach, slaps his face, and knees him in the groin. They've done this routine before—in private, with both of them naked and the Kid begging through busted lips for the privilege of kissing Logan's donkey dick.

The crowd starts screaming—it's Lanny Boy bounding over the ropes to come to the rescue, breaking every rule. He does a quick take-down on Logan, then rushes over to check on the Kid. The Kid lies there, glistening with sweat, breathing hard, his face screwed up with pain. Lanny Boy helps him up and out of the ring, but the Kid can't stay on his feet. Lanny Boy cradles him in his big arms and carries him up the aisle, one hand under his shoulders, the other firmly holding his rump. The audience goes wild— hands reach out to grope a fleeting touch, flashbulbs spark. The Bulldogs disappear backstage.

Alone in the dressing room, Lanny Boy starts getting hot and smoochy—kissing the Kid's bruises, stroking his hard buns. "Pull down your tights," he says, his voice deep and breathy. The Kid hangs his head. He strips for Lanny Boy, and underneath his tights he's wearing nothing but some Frederick's of Hollywood black satin panties, stretched so tight across his hard bubble butt they're about to split.

Lanny Boy likes the idea of the Kid wearing those panties under his tights when he's in the ring, getting the shit beat out of him by the Hit Man. "Good boy," he whispers. "Now take off your panties."

Sure enough, there's a puddle of cum staining the front panel. The Kid couldn't help it—it happened when Logan had him bound up in the ropes, slapping him around. That wasn't agony on the Kid's face—it was pure, helpless lust.

"Guess the Hit Man worked you over pretty hard," says Lanny Boy.

"Yeah," the Kid answers, hanging his head.

"And I had to come in and rescue you," smirks Lanny Boy. "Just like always. Shit, maybe you ought to at least say thank you."

"Thank you, sir," whispers the Kid, staring downward.

"Maybe you ought to *show* me instead of just saying it." Lanny Boy pulls down his tights. His massive dick flops out.

"Yes—please—let me," gasps the Kid, dropping to his hands and knees and crawling toward Lanny. The Kid's own cock presses rock hard up against his belly. It's a little dick, despite all those big polished muscles, not more than four inches—just a weenie compared to the plump forearm of meat hanging between Lanny Boy's muscle-bound thighs.

The Kid takes the whole thing in a single swallow and starts fucking his face on it while Lanny Boy settles into an easy chair for a long blow job. There's a knock at the door. The Kid jerks, but Lanny Boy holds him in place and yells, "Come in."

It's Leo Logan all sweaty and pumped up after the match. He's wearing a skintight tank top, faded jeans, and mirror shades; he's got a twisted grin on his face. "Already at it," he sneers.

"Go ahead," sighs Lanny Boy—the Kid really knows how to deep throat a guy—"take a piece. You earned it."

"Sure." But first Logan grabs his belt buckle. The long leather strap slithers through the loops and cracks in the air as he pulls it free. Logan stands behind the Kid, staring down at his hard pale

ass and the way it juts up round and plump above the silky small of
his back. He swings the belt and lays a stripe across the Kid's
rump.

The Kid squeals and chokes around Lanny's meat. "Shit, that
felt great," sighs Lanny. "Do it again."

"Hell, they don't call me Hit Man for nothing," Logan smirks,
drawing back his arm and laying on another blow. He proceeds to
crisscross the Kid's ass with welts. Every blow makes the Kid
squeal around Lanny's cock. The vibrations drive Lanny wild.

Finally Logan's had enough; he wants his dick up the Kid's ass.
He makes the Kid stand up for it, bent double so he can still suck
Lanny's cock while Logan slides his greasy pole deep inside the
Kid's guts.

They double dick him until the Kid can hardly stand—Logan
really pounded him out in the ring and he's exhausted. But Lanny
and Logan are fired up and ready to go on for hours. They change
places and double dick him again. Then they settle back for a
breather while making the Kid mince around the room with his little cock pushed out of sight between his legs, taking cracks at his
ass with the belt. The Kid's so shaky he can hardly stand. He's
covered with sweat and breathing hard.

There's a rattle at the door, and in comes Larry McMasters, with
his slicked-back hair and hand-tailored polyester suit. McMasters is
the Bossman, head honcho, lord and master of the wrestling cir-
cuit. He locks the door behind him. "Having a party, boys?" Logan and Lanny Boy laugh and nod.

McMasters stares at the Kid, who's standing stock-still, quivering and blushing deep red from head to toe. He looks at the Kid's
crotch where there's nothing but naked flesh and a frazzled tuft of
pubic hair, the smooth sweaty muscles of his hard belly and thighs
curving into a deep pocket of flesh that begs to be fucked but
can't.

"Well, well," McMasters booms, "my favorite piece of Baltimore ass." He walks over to the Kid and runs his hands all over his
hairless muscular flesh, pushing his middle finger between the
Kid's legs, filling his hands with big hard pecs and pinching the

Kid's nipples. Finally, he pushes the Kid to his knees. McMasters pulls his cock out of his pants.

The Bossman is number one in the dick department—his foot-long tube of meat is one of the ways he keeps his boys in line. It's as thick as a man's forearm, plump as a family-size sausage. He rudely shoves it into the Kid's mouth, but the Kid can only take about a third of it without splitting his lips and choking to death. The Kid wraps his hands around the rest of it—his fingers and thumbs hardly meet—knowing that's the way the Bossman likes it. McMasters fucks face for a while, but it's not easy for him to get a good blow job; Tommy Dakota's the only one with a mouth and throat that can really satisfy him. He pulls the Kid back to his feet.

"Hold him," he says. Lanny and Logan each take one of the Kid's arms. The Kid loves taking the Bossman's cock—eventually. But every time, for the first five minutes or so, he fights like a hellcat to get off it. McMasters walks around behind him and lubes up his dick—he's still wearing his suit, just his cock and balls hang free—and abruptly pushes the whole thing inside the Kid—who lets out a howl that even the screaming fans out in the auditorium can hear. Then he starts blubbering and whimpering, begging the Bossman to take it out. McMasters ignores him and starts pumping away, holding the Kid by the hips. He's a hard fucker. The Kid keeps begging nonstop, pleading with McMasters to *please* take it out—it's all he can think of, getting away from that monster up his ass. McMasters even teases him a few times, pulling all the way out—but before the Kid can catch his breath, he shoves it back in and fucks harder than before.

Finally, after five or ten minutes of sheer torture, something breaks inside the Kid. He never stops begging, but now he's begging the Bossman to fuck him harder and never stop. He goes crazy for the cock up his ass, rotating his hips and fucking back against it. McMasters pulls it out with a laugh—the Kid gyrates his greasy ass in lewd circles, searching for the Bossman's cock until the blunt tip pokes his swollen hole. The Kid opens wide and squats back on it, sucking the whole thing inside.

But not for long. McMasters laughs and pulls out of the Kid's ass with a loud liquid plop. He reaches for the Kid's Frederick's of Hollywood panties and wipes off his drooling, rock-hard dick. "Sorry, Kid, but I can't give you my load. Gotta keep it hot and ready for my date tonight with Tommy Dakota!" He stuffs his cock inside his pants, gives the Kid a hard swat on the ass and heads for the door. "You boys put on a great show in the ring tonight," he calls over his shoulder. "Have a good workout."

The Kid's a sobbing, quivering, sweat-drenched mass of muscle on the floor. His face is pressed against the carpet. His ass sticks straight up, making circles in the air. He reaches back with both hands and spreads it wide open. He's drools on the carpet and whines, "C'mon guys, fuck me. Fuck me! Fuck my ass, please!"

Meanwhile, Lanny Boy and Logan rummage through the Kid's footlocker. Lanny pulls out a pair of handcuffs, a leather paddle, and a braided whip. Logan smirks and pulls out a wicked-looking pair of tit-clamps, an official Baltimore Bulldogs dog collar, and his favorite sex toy, a bona fide Larry McMasters–size dildo. . . .

Relic

Jeff Mann

Not golden, not bejeweled, nothing like the reliquaries
of Munich's Residenz, Vienna's Hofburg,
those ornate receptacles for the flotsam and jetsam of saints.
Only a cardboard box in the storage room
of my father's house in Hinton, West Virginia.
Inside, amid occult tomes, rests what I retain
of you. The scrawled, seductive letters you sent
after moving with your husband to Massachusetts.
A thin album of photos, a few bottles of German wine we emptied.
The leather teddy bear you bought me in State College,
the silver pentagram ring you mailed me from Framingham,
a few flirtatious valentines. And—most intimate keepsake—
the last thing I asked from you, mere weeks before we parted—
a pair of your white jockey shorts.

What did I expect? That something precious could be saved?
Your taste, your scent? The mourning dove's dirge?
The way I felt, those larcenous afternoons?
The first pair of underwear you gave me,
cloth still moist from the gym, I slipped inside
a Glad bag, hoping to preserve your sweat.
Fanatic's error. The crotch-musk soon turned to folly,

His Underwear: An Erotic Anthology
© 2007 by The Haworth Press, Inc. All rights reserved.
doi:10.1300/5756_03

the faint smell of mildew. Sheepish, I asked again.
The second pair? FTLs, tattered a bit. Folded neatly still
inside a box there is no reason to open any longer.

These briefs are scentless after fifteen years,
evidence not of beauty but of failure.
Something for my survivors to throw out
after I am over, souvenir meaningless to all
but me. I would like to lie here, say that once,
when I had you naked and bound, the way I loved you most,
I gagged you with this very garment, your own sweaty shorts,
then wrapped my arms about your hairy chest and,
as I entered you, relished your muffled moans, but

no, that never happened, that was only another ecstasy
our hurried time together did not allow,
one of many revelations we never got to share.
You gave me a pair of white jockey shorts,
you gave me what was easy to give,
reserving the rest for another. What I have left of you
is cotton white, stained by none of rapture's sap.
No longer a fabric I press to my face, no longer
a history of musk to breathe deep.
Flesh will never revisit the saints' finger bones.
Scent and warmth will return to this garment
no more than youth will, youth shared for six months,
then squandered apart. White as the heron
picking low tide for scraps, white as the skin
of buttocks beneath their fine coating of fur.
White, the waves' unscrolling epitaph.
White, the paper remaining when words run out.

Martin Tyler's Class Reunion

Max Pierce

Martin wondered what the heck had possessed him to fly 1,500 miles just to attend his high school reunion. On the crest of forty, he lacked the Oscar, Emmy, and Tony Awards he'd planned to wave in everyone's faces after he graduated from Pleasant Valley High School. He didn't even have a boyfriend; his last interesting date was six months ago. Such was life in New York City, selling shirts at Saks and still struggling for overnight stardom.

"Look," said Carleen, interrupting his thoughts. "There's Kirby Thompson. I had such a crush on him from the third grade on. I heard he's a trainer or something for the Dolphins."

"Who?"

"On the left. The Panthers won state because of him. How could you forget that?"

Martin strained his eyes. In the corner, among the former captains of the Pantherette drill team, stood a tall, square-shouldered man with his back to them.

"We all took Speech class together. Don't you remember?" Carleen added.

As far as Martin was concerned, these names and relationships were all a blur. He'd moved to Pleasant Valley his junior year, and in a class of 300 upper-middle-class white kids, it was easy to get lost. Carleen, in her duties as student council social chairman, showed him around and they became fast friends. If he was in

His Underwear: An Erotic Anthology
© 2007 by The Haworth Press, Inc. All rights reserved.
doi:10.1300/5756_04

Speech class with Kirby Thompson, Emma Thompson, or the Thompson Twins, he didn't care then or now. Martin's focus that spring of 1984 was getting out of Pleasant Valley and to Manhattan.

In hindsight, it had been for nothing. Unlike these Stepford students, who laughed as if it had been two weeks instead of twenty years, Martin had no fond memories to relive.

"Try and be happy. Or at least fake it, like everyone else is," Carleen said, as she blew an air-kiss at an overweight woman and grabbed a handful of grapes.

"Who's that?"

"Our homecoming queen. How times change. At least we're not fat."

If Martin had it all to do over again, he'd have pursued romance rather than concentrating on good grades and acting, and maybe he'd have a better life now. He was here tonight because Carleen, still his closest friend, begged him to escort her and he had yet to learn how to turn her down.

Carleen continued talking the entire time. "Kirby was never like those other jock goons. Oh listen, we're singing the fight song!"

This was it. They'd been here an hour and while Carleen enjoyed her travels down the nostalgia trail, Martin had not. It was too warm in the school cafeteria, and that was another thing— watered-down drinks and party platters from Sam's Club. Couldn't the reunion committee have afforded the Pleasant Valley Ramada Inn? Yet he was the only one looking bored. He had nothing in common with these people back then and nothing to offer now.

"Let's go outside. I'm sure you're ready for a cigarette," Martin said, but standing up from the table, he became light-headed. He should have eaten dinner and not drank that third cocktail. He turned to Carleen, but while her mouth moved, there was no sound and bright colors swirled around her head—just like in an old disco movie. Then the lights went out.

"You okay? Hey!"

Martin opened his eyes, the strong smell of Jovan Musk Oil invading his nostrils. The Texas sun blazed overhead. He and Carleen arrived at the reunion at 8 p.m.; now it was daylight. He had been out for a while. And who was this young guy with the Pacific blue eyes studying him so closely?

"What happened?" *Mrs. Rester's voice*, Martin thought. He blinked twice. Good old Mrs. Rester, looking just like she did in high school; wearing that kooky purple paisley shawl and the crazy crystal around her neck that she claimed was her lucky talisman. She never attended a speech tournament without it.

"Gosh, Mrs. R, you don't look any older."

"Martin Tyler. Did you eat before you got here?"

"Only a martini."

Mrs. Rester's eyes widened. "I see you haven't lost your sense of humor. I think you're excused for the day. Thank the Goddess this happened after you delivered another excellent reading. I know you're going to place first again. Now, I can't leave the team; Larry and Michelle haven't competed yet. Are your parents home?"

"I can take him, Mrs. Rester. He lives near me."

"That's awfully nice of you, Kirby. You're—"

"I'll do it, Mrs. Rester." Carleen's voice. "Marty, what happened?"

Seeing her, he covered his eyes. "That afro never looked good, and why the braces again? Weren't six years enough?"

"You squirrel! How dare you!"

"Carleen, he doesn't know what he's saying. It must be a record heat and we're not even near the solstice. Kirby, would you mind getting him out of here?" The teacher pulled five dollars out of her tooled leather wallet. "Get some lunch on the way home."

Martin got up without assistance, wondering how the Banana Republic khakis he'd had were replaced by the brown polyester slacks he'd tossed out years ago. Carleen disappeared, and he was on the back lawn of Pleasant Valley High School, where they waited during speech tournaments for the winners to be posted. Martin decided he must be dreaming—still unable to escape the past.

The tall boy with the intense blue eyes stood before him shaking his head. Martin noticed the soft cleft in his chin, and how his tousled brownish-blond hair fell over his ears and forehead. He wore a three-piece suit just like everyone at speech tournaments used to. Broad shouldered, this one, and with an annoyingly confident attitude. They walked in silence to the parking lot, filled with American made cars.

The young man removed his tie with one motion. "I'm glad you fainted. I—"

"I did not faint." Martin said, irritated. That sounded so . . . gay.

"Hey, don't sweat it. Practice in the summer sun in full uniform sometime. I've passed out lots of times. I hope I can get some extra credit for taking you home. My speech grade could use a boost." He unlocked the passenger door. "Okay—hop in."

"This Trans Am's in great shape for an old car."

"Excuse me, jerk, but it's brand new. I got it for Christmas. For winning state."

"State what?"

"Football, of course. Man, I think you hit your head bad. We'll drive through Jack in the Box and get you some food."

Martin leaned his head back and looked out the window at Pleasant Valley High. It looked unchanged, as did the neighborhood. As the Trans Am sped down Westmoreland Road toward town, the young man turned up the radio. A Pat Benatar song ended and The Eurythmics began singing. Martin grimaced. "Must be another 'Totally 80s' weekend."

"What do you mean?"

"It's a sure indication of bad times when this old music is still so popular."

Martin glanced at the driver, who looked at him like he was crazy. Maybe so—he never had a dream that lasted so long and employed so many senses. He waved him off. "You're too young to understand."

"Screw you. When's your birthday?"

"October 10."

"You're four months older than me. Big whoop."

Martin laughed, "I didn't think kids talked the same way we did."

This ticked off the young man more. "Who are you calling a kid, pipsqueak? Just because you're the star of the speech team doesn't mean you can boss it over the rest of us who aren't so talented."

A Chevron gas station sign caught Martin's attention. "Ninety-five cents!"

"Sucks, doesn't it. I'm going to have to get a better-paying summer job just to keep gas in my car."

The Trans Am pulled in the Jack in the Box drive thru. Martin scanned the menu; he couldn't remember the last time he had fast food, but right now fried anything would hit the spot. "Jack Burritos! I'll have two. I didn't know they'd brought those back. And a large strawberry shake. Look at those prices; it's so cheap!"

The young man gave him a tired look. "Would you mind just shutting the hell up?"

"Did your mother give you enough money?" Martin said, reaching for his wallet.

"My mother?"

"I saw her hand you a five, frankly I didn't think that'd buy—"

"Mrs. Rester is not my mother. Hold on—" he yelled his order into the speaker and then stared at Martin. "You must be the only person in school who doesn't know who I am."

Martin could tell this was a blow of sorts to the tall boy. Martin felt sorry for him, in his polyester suit and permanent press shirt that nonetheless accentuated his wide chest and long muscular legs.

"Here you go, Kirby," the girl at the window said, handing the food and winking, but not taking money.

"Thanks, babe."

Kirby tossed the bag into Martin's lap, who said, "That looked just like Leanna Floyd. She always gave people free food."

"That *was* Leanna. Man, you may need a doctor. I'm planning to study sports medicine in college." He looked over Martin again. "Maybe I'll minor in psychology."

Martin flipped down the visor and studied his reflection in the mirror, blinking his eyes twice. The old wire-rimmed glasses he'd tossed the minute he got to New York were back, as was that bad haircut, courtesy of Pleasant Valley Mall's Regis Hairstylists. . . .

He looked at the young man. Indeed, they were the same age, though this guy was filled out better. The speakers broadcast an update on President Reagan's visit to China. Martin turned off the radio. "What's today's date?"

"Saturday, April twenty-eighth. Four weeks to graduation. Duh."

"April twenty-eighth what?

"1984. Man, you are out of it."

Martin took a bite of the burrito; delicious. He didn't recall being able to enjoy taste while dreaming. "So, who are you?"

"That's more like it. Kirby Thompson. I sit behind you in speech and advanced English. Last year in geometry and chemistry."

"You did . . . do?"

"Let me ask you, is there something wrong with me that you can't say hello? Do I smell?"

"Huh?"

"I know jocks and brains don't usually mix, but you've always been kind of snobby."

"Me, snobby? I . . . just don't think we have anything in common."

"Maybe you're wrong," Kirby said, looking out the window.

They had pulled into a driveway in front of a rambling brick house that Martin didn't recognize.

Kirby said, "This is my house. I want to change out of this stupid suit. It'll only take a minute. Besides you just live a couple of streets over."

"My parents sold their—never mind. How do you know where I live?"

Kirby shrugged. "I know lots of stuff about you, Marty."

"I hate being called Marty. I prefer Martin."

"I think Marty suits you better, but whatever. Come on in."

They walked into a spacious kitchen with harvest gold appliances and an Amana Radar Range the size of a high-definition television.

"Anybody home?" Kirby called out. Receiving no reply, he opened the refrigerator. "Want a beer?"

"Aren't you a little—no, thanks."

Kirby closed the door. "Me neither. I think I drink too much as it is."

"Why?"

Kirby shrugged. "I don't know. I have stuff on my mind. Who I really am."

"That's very adult of you, for a football player, I mean." Martin said.

"Football's not my entire life, dude." The mask of defense went up over Kirby's face. "I will have an apple, though." He picked up two. "Want one?"

Martin shook his head.

"Watch me sink this." Kirby launched the apple toward the bowl of fruit on the counter but missed, knocking the strawberry shake into Martin's lap.

Martin jumped up. "Damn it!"

"Sorry, man. I really am . . . ," Kirby said, and then started laughing.

Martin grabbed a roll of paper towels and began wiping the pinkish mess off his crotch and shirt. "This is just great."

Kirby jerked his chin. "I have a pair of shorts you can borrow. Come back to my room."

If the dream continued, Martin knew he'd get a lecture from his mother about dirtying his suit and he didn't want to experience one of her tirades again. He followed Kirby to his bedroom, a standard eighteen-year-old's—totally trashed. Kirby rummaged through a half-opened drawer and pulled out a pair of denim cutoffs and a Fleetwood Mac T-shirt. "These should fit you. I outgrew them."

"Where can I change?'
"Right here, stupid."
"In front of you?"
"I see guys naked in the locker room the whole time, it's no big deal." He paused. "Uh, unless you're chicken, then the bathroom's down the hall."

Without waiting for Martin to answer, Kirby removed his jacket and shirt with what appeared to be lightening speed. Martin Tyler was not about to be pegged as chicken. He tried not to look at Kirby, but it was difficult not to stare at the well-developed back and chest muscles, the sparse line of hair above his waistband, and the long legs that tapered into slim hips and a narrow waist. As Martin pulled off his soiled trousers he made another awful discovery; the sexy Calvin Klein boxer briefs he loved were replaced by Fruit of the Loom underwear—another staple of high school. This wasn't a dream; it was a nightmare. Turning back to Kirby, he laughed out loud.

"What is your problem?" Kirby said, sounding irritated again.

"You wear a jockstrap under your suit? That's so . . . football player stupid."

Rather than clock him, which Martin half-expected, Kirby blushed and looked embarrassed. "I always do. What's wrong? Are you some god of clothing laws?"

Martin started to answer, but the blood had rushed down to his waist. Aside from Kirby Thompson's casual attitude about nudity, and his playful behavior that hid a sad loneliness, the sight of the athletic hero in such a vulnerable position was making Martin think about those opportunities he had never pursued. This was a dream, right, so what would it matter what he did?

He pointed to Kirby's crotch. "You're getting a boner, Mr. I-See-Guys-Naked-All-the-Time."

"Screw you," Kirby replied, but there was no mistaking the stretching in the natural-colored fabric. "It just does that. I can't help it. Stop looking if it makes you so weird about it."

Martin wished his own Fruit of the Looms could be magically replaced by some of the raunchy underwear he'd seen for sale in Greenwich Village but never bought.

"It looks like you've got a big one," Martin said, wishing he could come up with more clever dialogue. "You screw a lot of girls?"

Kirby's sturdy face turned red. "No. And talking about it just makes me hornier, so shut up." The pouch of his jockstrap was now quite full, and he gave a quick tug, while staring directly into Martin's eyes, then down at his waist.

Martin sensed the white fabric of his own briefs had filled up. He glanced in the mirror and frowned; all those years in the gym training, counting each thick chest hair as they grew in, yet in this incarnation he possessed the undefined and hairless body of his youth. But there was a wistfulness to this reflection that he'd lost over the years and, seeing it again, he wanted to regain it. That loss had made him a bitter adult, and he wanted that determination and youthful confidence of invincibility back.

He looked at Kirby, still wearing only his jockstrap. Kirby: so available yet no doubt confused about his sexuality. It had been all about experimentation at this age. Martin couldn't go on with the dream. "Wake up," he said aloud.

"I'm awake, and I know what I want," Kirby said in a low voice, crossing to Martin. "I've had my eye on you all year." The football player extended his hand and brushed it against Martin's chest. With a tug, he pulled Martin's briefs down. "I just didn't think it would be this easy," he said, leaning over and placing his sensual lips on Martin's.

Martin drank from Kirby's mouth, and their tongues met. He reached out and touched the fullness of Kirby's jock, noticing how the texture of the mesh fabric moved as it protected the power of the flesh hidden underneath. Next, he moved his hands to Kirby's ears, flicking the lobes and with a gentle motion. Martin placed his little fingers in the openings and steadied Kirby's head as they lip-locked.

"Wow, you're terrific," Kirby said, breaking his mouth from Martin's.

"Wow is right." Martin replied. Sensations he hadn't enjoyed in years flowed through his body, and feeling more alive than ever, he explored Kirby's body without fear of rejection.

While continuing to look deep into his eyes, Kirby massaged Martin's erection, squeezing his testicles and running his finger underneath. "Marty. . . ."

Martin decided he didn't care what he was called, as long as this fantasy continued. How sexy Kirby was with his wavy hair, his firm muscles—created by exercise and not by pills and powders—and an easy masculinity affirmed by a simple jock strap.

They flopped onto the bed, a mass of entwined legs and arms. Kirby removed Martin's underwear with his mouth and tossed the briefs on the sheets beside them. Martin ran his hand through Kirby's hair, inhaling the mixture of Dial soap and musk, while the taller man probed Martin's mouth deeper with his tongue and nibbled his neck. Kirby still wore his jock, and Martin felt it press against his own hardness. He reached down and, with a deft pull, released Kirby's erection from its safety net. Dropping his right hand underneath the fabric, Martin located where the cotton straps were sewn together. From there, he traced a line just beneath the base of Kirby's scrotum, and directed his finger across the athlete's firm buttocks. With new confidence, Martin manipulated Kirby's anal opening, navigating an entrance, and then with a swift push, entered the quarterback.

The look on Kirby's face was one of surprise at the realization, then of complete surrender. He leaned back, closed his eyes, and began to scrunch his face. Martin saw the large balls of the athlete draw up, yet Kirby continued to pump Martin's own cock faster without hesitation. With one great thrust, both experienced orgasm together, Martin ejecting white globs of semen onto Kirby's jock, while the football player coated the front of the white briefs.

Martin had forgotten how quick he could get off when he was younger. But an advantage of youth presented itself in his mind.

"Want to do it again?" he panted, noticing the swift recovery of Kirby's excitement.

Kirby reached down and kissed Martin on the mouth, then jerked his head to the left. "Crap! My parents are home."

"What?"

He scrambled off the bed. "I heard the car in the driveway. Quick—in the closet."

Martin had only time to grab the denim shorts Kirby offered him earlier before he was shoved into a narrow space littered with clothes and packed to the ceiling with sports equipment and a dozen board games. Flailing for the light, Martin struck an object and before he knew it, boxes from a shelf tumbled down on him. A Ouija board struck him square on the head, and he fell to the floor, hearing the Pleasant Valley Panthers fight song grow louder.

"Hey, you okay?"

"What happened?"

"He's coming to . . . Martin . . . Martin . . . drink some orange juice. There you go."

Martin looked up into the careworn face of Mrs. Rester. The crystal on a chain hung around her neck, but her purple shawl was gone. She looked old.

"You're all right. Thank goodness Kirby Thompson saw you fall."

"Let me help you up."

Martin blinked again, looking into clear blue eyes, with tiny crinkles around them. His blond hair was short, with a hint of gray, and a slight cleft remained in his chin. A familiar hint of musk and soap entered Martin's nostrils. The crowd dispersed and moved away.

"You'll be all right. Steady up," Kirby said, lifting Martin to his feet. "Say, I don't think we ever officially met in high school. You were too busy winning all the speech tournaments to notice me."

Martin looked around. They were back in the cafeteria.

Kirby whispered, "Truth is, I'm glad you fainted."

"I did not faint. I—"

"Passed out, then. I was looking for an excuse to get out of this boring reunion." He paused. "I don't suppose you'd like to have a cup of coffee?" Whispering, he added, "Away from here."

Martin shook his head. Was he dreaming again?

"I guess not. Well, glad I could help anyway."

Martin clutched his arm. "You're Kirby Thompson."

"You do remember me." He blushed. "I didn't—"

"I'd love to have coffee with you. And call me Marty."

Heat of the Moment

Jordan M. Coffey

Even now I wonder if it was some deity's private joke or maybe just a peculiar convergence of circumstances—a coincidental twist of fate where everything slides into place perfectly, albeit a little hesitantly and somewhat awkwardly. The mundane giving way to something spectacular, considering that it stemmed from a borderline obsessive preoccupation with underwear, and was compounded by a bout of extreme weather, until one morning I found myself, in a weird way, at the goal line with one hand in the end zone.

It had been hot. Much, much hotter than it usually gets in this area. And not just hot, but humid. An unpleasant combination of too damned hot and too fucking humid—the clammy, stifling effects making it difficult to breathe the thick air day in and day out. Worse was the fact that in the old building where I worked for a small law firm, the air conditioning had maliciously breathed its last. After a few days of suffering, I had latched on to the idea of the local mall, stealing moments at lunchtime along with countless others that flocked there, forgoing their usual outdoor meals in order to beat the heat.

Home wasn't much better. My apartment faced toward the bay, but the occasional breezes that drifted in over the water that week were so heavy with heated moisture that they brought no relief. In-

His Underwear: An Erotic Anthology
© 2007 by The Haworth Press, Inc. All rights reserved.
doi:10.1300/5756_05

side, the fan did nothing more than sluggishly move the oppressive air around in the enclosed space like slow-shifting atmospheric blocks. Even so, it offered an advantage over my stuffy office, and I tried to slip home as early as possible, where I could get paperwork done in near-naked comfort.

My roommate, Casey, had been disappearing, supposedly to the university where he was doing some postgraduate work, to take advantage of cool, quiet alcoves in the various libraries. I speculated that he was really lying naked somewhere while some willing acquaintance rubbed ice all over his sweaty body. In fact, I probably indulged in that little fantasy a bit too much, more often than not picturing myself doing the rubbing. Regardless, he had been pretty scarce, so I would strip down to almost nothing, lie out on a cool, clean sheet on the living room floor, and guzzle glass after glass of cold water while I read notes on my cases.

One morning, near the end of that incredibly hot week, Casey and I crossed paths in the well-worn passage from our respective bedrooms to the kitchen and he literally made me sweat. He stumbled from his bedroom just as I was leaving the bathroom (the constant side effect from drinking all of that water), and I was simply unprepared for the sight of him.

I met Casey at law school in a class on economic justice. He was only a year behind me, but at twenty-one, he was six years younger and worlds apart. Unlike me, he spoke up regularly in class, voicing his opinions with open-minded intelligence. I liked how he used his whole body to express himself and how he never seemed intimidated or afraid. Often, I sought out opportunities to talk to him, and the outcome of one of those occasions was that we ended up as roommates.

But, in the three years that we'd lived together, I had never seen Casey without his various combinations of layered clothing. It was as if he were self-conscious about that lean, muscular build he'd acquired as a result of both his strict eating habits and his tendency to bicycle everywhere. Even coming from a shower, he emerged from the steamy environs of the bathroom with a towel around his waist, another draped around his neck (the ends covering his chest), and, more often than not, rubbing vigorously at his hair with yet another.

The first morning that Casey woke up in the apartment during the heat wave, everything changed. His wild, sleep-rumpled black curls, the weirdly unfocused blue-eyed look of forced concentration, and the dragging before-coffee pace as he made his way past me were normal enough. What was different was that he was wearing a pair of boxers and nothing else.

Faded old boxers. A washed out plaid, worn thin, with a stretched-out waistband and stretched-wide leg holes. Almost permanent wrinkles formed in the material at that crease where leg meets groin, from years of being scrunched up by him sitting, or maybe sleeping curled over into himself. It was one of those various pairs of underwear that Casey wore to bed or under his sweats when bumming around the apartment—information that I had obtained in the course of handling laundry duty.

I should explain. According to those that know me, I'm a neat freak. I think I'm just . . . orderly. Towels hanging in the bathroom don't have to be lined up just so, but I do prefer them to actually *make it* to the towel bar. And while I have the habit of kicking my shoes off as soon as I walk through the door and of leaving stacks of files tossed on the coffee table, eventually, I get around to straightening it all up.

Casey's hit-and-run style of habitation had been an adjustment. In the beginning, I bitched about him helping out with the domestic upkeep, but after the first time he offered to do my laundry along with his own, I couldn't quite resist the urge to refold everything. Exacting though I may be, I was also reasonable enough not to expect him to actually take *folding* lessons, and it seemed petty to complain, so instead I simply started doing his laundry along with mine. His response was to take over the cooking. And since I was constantly doing load after load of towels (as if a family of six inhabited our apartment, rather than two grown men), I felt it was an even tradeoff to sit down to a meal that I didn't have to prepare.

The first time I separated our clothes, automatically folding Casey's just as carefully as I did my own, I noticed the half-dozen or so old pairs of boxers. They weren't ratty or torn, but just *worn*. So much so that I wondered how they ever made it through the vigorous cycles of the washer and the dryer. And, even after the agitated action of a warm water wash and the tossing tumult of a spin-dry, they still seemed to retain an odd lived-in look as if Casey had just stepped out of them.

I asked him about it, turning it into a joke about them being a waste of soap and water, teasing that even a poor public interest lawyer like him could afford new underwear. Though the image of how he would look wearing nothing but such soft, threadbare fabric had haunted me. He told me that it was just an old habit to set aside older pairs to wear in relaxed moments at home, saving the newer ones for out in the world.

I understood about old favorites. I have a pair of sneakers that have seen better days and a certain T-shirt that's usually the first one to be worn after the laundry was done. And one pair of jeans that I've had forever, that I'm pleased still fit me just right in all the right places. So, without commenting, I simply handed over his stack of clean, folded clothes and tried not to think about the various shapes, front and back, that had served to wear thin the boxers in question in the first place.

Over time, as I saw underwear come and go—newer pairs becoming old, older ones disappearing—it soothed me in a strange way. It showed the passage of time, while underscoring Casey's continued presence in my life, prolonging the day he would decide to strike out on his own, most likely without ever knowing all that I kept hidden and why.

Then came the sudden appearance of the boxer briefs—a baker's dozen in an assortment of colors. My reaction to their existence made me face a series of truths, not the least of which was how far gone I actually was.

I had been around Casey enough to imprint the unique scent that I associated with him, and for the most part I tried not to focus on it. So, it was the occasional whiffs of perfume that would capture my attention as I laundered his T-shirts, indications of intimate contact that I didn't want to acknowledge. I had always been sure that, unlike me, Casey dated women. I'd seen him with them, smelled them on his clothes. But, the first time that I tossed those · boxer briefs in the washing machine, I was struck by the sharp spice of a cologne, or some sort of aftershave—scents that I knew Casey didn't wear.

Different underwear giving off a different smell—something different to consider about Casey's life. Of course, theoretically, the prospect didn't bother me, but still somehow I felt like I had taken a hit below the belt.

I grew to dread the sight of those pieces of navy, or gray, or black material. Even, months later, when they no longer came out of the hamper with that distinctive scent clinging to them, and I figured that whatever relationship Casey had been in was over. I hoped I never had to hear the story about "James the visiting Anthropology Professor" or whoever it had been, and his thing for the way Casey's ass and thighs looked in form-fitting black cotton.

And no matter how enticing a vision that made, stirring my blood as the picture vividly implanted itself in my head, I was glad that Casey didn't have a pair of them on that hot morning as we passed, giving our customary nodding, grunting, first-thing-on-a-lazy-morning greetings.

Besides, the genuine article was enough to get me to abruptly alter my course. Where a few minutes before I had been planning to head back to my bedroom, instead I followed Casey to the kitchen. I busied myself getting a glass of juice, and watched him plug in the coffee-maker. He put a filter, coffee, and water into the appropriate places, a prelude to that first gurgle and burst of aroma.

The air in the room seemed to grow almost unbearably thick. It had nothing to do with the weather, but everything to do with the waves of longing that flowed from me, so that the very atmosphere grew heavy with need and heated with arousal. All one-sided, I was sure. The pull that I felt was so strong I couldn't imagine how Casey could be unaware of it. But he just stood with one hip against the counter, a mug near his hand, watching as the coffee pot slowly filled.

I would have sworn time slowed down. I could feel my temperature begin to rise. Fresh layers of sweat covered my body, the moisture gently squeezed from my pores, sticky under my arms, trickling down the middle of my back, building up steam between my legs. I was impossibly hot and getting hard; my dick rearranged itself inside of the gym shorts that I wore, wetness collecting at its tip.

My vision wavered, and I felt high, drunk from the force of my own desire. So intoxicated that the wild, rebellious thoughts that were raging through my mind all coalesced to make perfect sense. That I could walk the few feet that separated us, reach out and palm the contour of Casey's ass, and everything would be all right.

Casey, I concluded, liked men, or had been to bed with a man, or at least had permitted some sort of masculine attention below the waist. And I believed the two of us had become more than simply roommates. Though we obviously both had secrets, we had built up a friendship and shared a lot over the years. Why couldn't we share an intimate moment, even if it was just once? Even if it was destined to become a close-kept memory and not a repeated occurrence. What would be wrong with allowing our lives to intersect that way, in that instant . . . just that one time?

As Casey poured himself a cup of coffee, the scent of the fresh brew was almost orgasmic. From my vantage point, leaning back against the table just behind him and to the left—with my glass forgotten—I watched . . . and wanted.

Wanted to touch—to find out if his balls were hairy like his legs, to see if it the stretch of skin that ran down his spine was as smooth as it looked, to know if each cheek of his ass was equally firm, to explore the hardness of his cock, the wet heat of his mouth, which would be even wetter and hotter after a first sip of coffee.

As if on cue, he took that sip, sighed, and then took another, shuddering a little. Probably from the kick of caffeine, but I still briefly considered that maybe it was from the strength of my stare and the incredible heat that had built up in the space between us.

And before I knew it, before I could stop myself, before I could listen to the inner voice that was saying even once would be too much and not enough, I was there . . .

. . . reaching out, one hand shaking as it covered half of Casey's rear. And I realized that I hadn't known the true meaning of heat. My palm burned, branded by the contact with his body through the thin layer of cotton. I squeezed slightly, my fingertips catching in the crack of his ass as I grabbed hold.

With so much of my brain power concentrating on what my hand was doing, and what my dick was doing inside my shorts, both seemingly of their own free will, I didn't know what to make of the fact that Casey had gone completely still. He didn't rock back into my touch, but he didn't jerk away from it, either. He just stood motionless, as if not surprised, but unsure which way to go.

Maybe he had already come to certain conclusions about my sexuality based upon such circumstantial evidence as my lack of girlfriends. Regardless, after a lifetime of hiding my nature, right there in my kitchen, my closet door swung wide open. I had made my move, Casey wasn't stopping me, and my body knew exactly what it wanted, unleashed as it was from my usual heartfelt fears and rationalized restrictions.

I relaxed my grip, sliding my hand across his hip in a slow caress until my fingers curved around the warm skin of his inner thigh. Snaking my other arm around his middle, I pulled his yielding body back as close as I could get it, fitting his ass against the solid bulge in my pants. Casey let out a little groan then and that sound set me free.

Free to inch a hand up inside the stretched leg of the boxers to fondle the tightening sacs of his balls, registering that they were slightly fuzzy to my touch. Free to grasp the stiff length of his cock under the soft material, massaging it with a friction-filled stroke. Free to hump against the fine, fine flesh of his ass, setting a rhythm, and creating a sensation that was so much better, so far beyond all of the sex I'd had in recent memory. And, joyfully, Casey was there, matching my motions, stepping the tempo up a notch, one hand gripping the counter, his other reaching back to clutch at my hip, while he made little hissing sounds that caused the head of my dick to twitch.

The moans were mine. I didn't even realize that I had been making them, until the second that I pulled myself out of my shorts, shoved my dick into the humid space between Casey's thighs, and noticed that the moans had stopped, because I had started cursing in some strange, breathless voice. I wasn't just hot anymore, I was about to go up in a burst of flames, and I didn't want to go alone.

I paid attention to every sensitive area that I could, trying to bring Casey closer to the same fragile place I found myself occupying. Leaning down, amazed that I hadn't taken a taste before, I licked the salty patch of skin behind his ear, nosing into the damp, sweaty strands of his curly hair, filling my senses so completely that I was coming almost before I was aware of it. So startled that I couldn't even cry out, I just bit down on the side of his neck, my hips pumping uncontrollably as I erupted over and over.

Awareness came with the sudden, rushing return of a rich coffee scent, a wet warmth coating my fingers, and the realization that I was falling because my legs refused to hold me any longer. I ended up on the floor with Casey in my arms.

For a few long moments, we sat quiet and still, Casey leaning back slightly into my embrace, and I wished—hoped against hope— that we could just stay that way forever. But Casey moved, turning a little so that he could look into my face. Despite the churning in my stomach, apprehension easily slipping into the space so recently taken up by postorgasmic bliss, I met his gaze, noting with dread the questioning look in his eyes. But he seemed to rein it in, coming to some sort of conclusion on his own. His features relaxed and he smiled the tiniest of smiles.

"Pierce, you know we're going to have to talk about this, right?"

I could only nod, closing my eyes, trying not to notice the faint smell of smoke that I knew was simply the imagined side effect of fearing that I had just burned too many bridges in too short a time. When I felt the pressure of a strong grip on my knee, I looked at him again.

"I mean where you actually have to *say* something."

And that calmed me more than anything else Casey could have said, because it seemed so utterly normal. That difference in our personalities addressed with a slight touch of humor. I nodded again, forcing myself not to look away, desperately hoping that all I felt showed plainly on my face and clearly in my eyes as insurance against the fumbling turn our conversation might take later on. Despite my earlier internal monologue, I wanted more than just one time, wanted an involvement deeper than just getting each other off. But, I'd learned that while it's easy for me to come up with the right words in a professional capacity, I always struggled whenever personal matters were concerned.

Words were the last thing on my mind when, a minute later, Casey stood up, eased off his messy boxers, and used them to dab at himself, wiping up the creamy smears that I had left on his thighs. I stared, not even worrying about the fact that my dick, still hanging out my shorts, was showing renewed interest. I checked him out, front and back, touching with my eyes those places that my hands had so recently explored.

He smiled down at me, tossing the wad of cotton into my lap, and said, "I need a shower," before turning and leaving the room.

I was smiling too, as I tucked my soft, sticky flesh back inside my shorts and closed my eyes, visualizing him moving around naked, the sway of his cock as he walked, the same cock that had made the wet spots in the boxers I now held to my nose to catch the fresh, potent scent of him.

When I heard the whooshing of the shower starting, I was gripped with a wave of panic. I wondered how I could ever explain myself so that he would not only understand, but want me, as well. If he did want me, would we want the same things and be able to move forward without screwing up our friendship.

A hand landed on my shoulder, and although I hadn't been aware of Casey's return, I didn't flinch. His presence quieted my inner turmoil, and instantly I felt the panic recede. There was a tug on my arm, and I opened my eyes to see him holding out a hand. He helped me to my feet, and then turned and pushed me in the direction of the bathroom where the shower was still running.

I dropped Casey's underwear in the hamper, stripped down and tossed mine in on top, and felt a tremble in my muscles as he came up behind me and placed a kiss between my shoulder blades. Our lips touched for the first time as we got under the blessedly cool spray. I knew then that I would do or say whatever it took to work it all out, because there was no way I could go back.

Later, as we were rinsing off, after more kisses, another heart-stopping climax, and ultimately getting clean, I realized that, along with everything else, I was on the verge of obtaining the answer to one of the mysteries of life—Casey's Multiple Towel Phenomenon.

Casey arched an eyebrow at my grin, smiling back. I shut the water off and kissed him again, making it long and full of promise.

That day, I became part of a team, instituting a new game plan for my life. It was an important victory for me. In the ten years since, I finally came out to my family, moved on to a job I love, and have happily stayed with Casey. I still do the laundry, he still does the cooking, and I haven't regretted one single moment of us being together.

Even now, the sight of him in old, worn boxers can make me sweat. And, every year, we go someplace hot to celebrate.

Caught by a Jock

Christopher Pierce

I was on the track team in college. It was hard work but I loved it, being around all those hot, sweaty, athletic men . . . it was heaven.

I'd often fantasize about my teammates, wondering what it would be like to suck their dicks or get fucked by them. Frequently I'd find that by fantasizing while I was on the field, I'd get just the extra boost of adrenaline I needed to complete the course in record time. The other guys would cheer me, clapping me on the back and slapping my ass playfully. I'd just smile at them and think, *If only they knew what helped me along . . . it was the thought of them naked.*

One of my best friends on the team was named Daryl. He was big and strong, sort of lanky while being muscular at the same time, a little taller than me. He had really light blond hair, almost white, with sexy light blue eyes.

Sometimes I'd imagine what I would do if Daryl ever showed any sexual interest in me. I knew I'd take him somewhere private where no one could find us. Placing my hands on his shoulders, I'd just look at him for a minute, my dark brown eyes gazing deeply into his, their color so different from mine. One of my hands would rise to his cheek, which would feel soft but at the

---

This story appeared originally in *Indulge Magazine,* 67 (1997). It appeared again in *Straight 2,* ed. Jack Hart, 12-19. Los Angeles, CA: Alyson Publications, 2002. Used with permission of the author.

same time a little rough as his beard grew back in from his morning shave, growing too slow to be watched but fast enough to be noticed.

Daryl might start to say something, but I'd put a finger on his lips to stop him. Shaking my head, I'd show him talking was not necessary. Then I'd pull him near me, and leaning up on the tips of my toes, my lips would meet his. I'd kiss him gently at first, not wanting to scare him with my passion, at least not yet.

My arms would encircle his body, and I'd feel his doing the same to mine, wrapping around me and holding tightly. He might even lift me slightly off the ground, being both taller and stronger than me. Our kiss would start heating up—his hands would start gripping me kneading the hard flesh of the small of my back, his fingers moving down to squeeze my butt cheeks.

My own hands would rise, taking his face in them, as if holding him so he wouldn't pull away. Daryl's hungry, curious tongue would dart in and out of my mouth as we kissed harder, and I would boldly answer his curiosity by forcing my tongue deep between his lips. Little moans of excitement would squeeze out of the sides of his mouth and I would lift his loose-fitting tank top off his back and over his head.

Our kiss would be broken for a second when the fabric passed between us, but I would hold his arms up in the air, my mouth moving to one of his exposed armpits. The hair I'd find there would be as light as the hair on his head. I would breathe in the wonderful masculine smell of Daryl's armpit, and then move my face down to one of his nipples. The slightest gasp would escape him as I gently mouthed his tit, massaging it with my lips and tongue.

With my hands I'd feel his body—his hairless pectorals, down to his abdomen with its hard abdominal muscles. When I reached his waist, I'd see that his gym shorts were tented—his hard cock poking through the fabric. Dropping to my knees, I'd feel the organ through the shorts. Daryl would grunt in pleasure, and I'd pull his shorts and jock strap down.

The jock's dick would stand free, full and erect and fantastic. It would be surrounded by dark hair, the ballsack hanging beneath it large and plump. I'd take his balls in one hand, cradling them in one palm, loving the feel of their weight and strength. His shaft would be only inches from my face, and I'd breathe it in as I had his armpit, for that moment satisfied by the smell alone.

The pink head of his smooth penis, with only a few veins, would be just visible through the protective foreskin. Above me Daryl would rumble with approval as I close one hand around that erect cock. I'd jerk it gently, massaging this stiff rod that grew from between my friend's legs.

Then I'd put my face in his crotch, thrilling at the sensation of his pubic hair tickling my nose and cheeks. I'd inhale deeply, taking in as much of his scent as I could. I wouldn't know if this experience would ever be repeated so I would want to enjoy it as thoroughly as I could. I'd start licking the jock's balls, my tongue absorbing the salty taste of the bag of flesh. My friend would make noises, letting me know he was enjoying this as much as I was. Opening my mouth wide, I'd actually get one of his balls into my mouth, and carefully, lovingly caress it with my tongue.

When I released it, I'd lick his cock, running my tongue along its length starting at the base and ending at the head. Daryl would shudder with pleasure, and with my hands I'd gently turn him around so his ass was facing me. Pulling his butt cheeks apart, I'd put my face between them and start lapping at his tight asshole. He'd exhale with a big sigh of pleasure and move himself back toward me. Pushing in as deep as I could, I'd actually start mouthing him with my lips, trying to bring him maximum sensation.

At the same time we'd take hold of our cocks and start jerking ourselves off. I'd continue rimming him as I stimulated myself and I'd feel his body quiver as he did the same. Within seconds the feeling of my tongue in his ass would be so intense that we couldn't hold back anymore, and fantastic orgasms would shoot through us as our balls emptied the cum out of our cocks in big spurts.

And when we'd recovered, we'd start all over again.

This was only the beginning of what I imagined doing with Daryl. But let me tell you what *actually* happened. . . .

One night after practice I was in the locker room, toweling myself off and getting ready to head out. I liked to take long showers, so by the time I finished up most of the other guys had gone home already. That suited me fine.

Sometimes I'd even jerk off in the shower stall when I knew I was alone. It was the only way to work off the steam that would build up in me every time I worked out with all those hot hunky guys.

That particular night I was feeling especially horny. Daryl had been unusually chummy with me all day, rubbing up against me and horse-playing rougher than usual. It was sexy, damn sexy, but I knew enough not to think too much of it. These guys were my teammates, not my fuck-buddies. It was important to maintain our distance, or so I thought.

So Daryl was on my mind that night as I dried off. I thought about his blond hair, his square-jawed face, his ice-blue eyes, and his strong, muscular body. I might've jacked myself off, but I had an exam the next day and had to get home to finish cramming for it.

As I hurriedly rubbed the towel over my body, something caught my eye. It was a flash of white on the edge of my peripheral vision. I glanced over and saw the something half-in and half-out of the locker Daryl used.

It was a jockstrap.

It was one of *Daryl's* jockstraps.

I dropped the towel and walked over to the locker. This was the first time any clothes had been left out. Normally, the guys locked everything up in their lockers before they left.

Gently, reverently I picked it up. Now, I didn't have a thing about jockstraps. At least *before* that night I didn't.

But when I lifted that piece of fabric and elastic to my nose and breathed in its aroma, all that changed. As the ripe musky odor of Daryl's crotch sweat permeated my nostrils, I could feel my cock stiffen up. It smelled so good—I fucking loved it.

What a treasure to find unexpectedly! It was so wonderful to have that jockstrap against my nose and mouth . . . it made me feel like I was a part of Daryl somehow, like I was in some way connecting with him. . . .

My daze was interrupted by the sound of the locker room door slamming open. I whirled around, totally surprised—I thought I was the only guy who'd stayed late that evening.

It was Daryl.

Just my luck. We stared at each other for a couple seconds without saying anything. I felt like a kid with my hand in the cookie jar, but it was worse, way worse—standing there with one of my teammates' jockstraps in my hand, having just been smelling it deeply . . . .

"What the fuck are you doing?" Daryl asked me, his handsome face contorted in disbelief.

"I . . . um . . . ," I stammered.

"I knew I forgot something down here," he said, walking toward me slowly. I backed up, not knowing how he was going to react. My back hit the wall of lockers, and I realized I was trapped. "But I didn't think I'd find anyone . . . especially someone playing with my jockstrap."

He grabbed it out of my hand. The sudden move startled me and I flinched like a junior high school wimp.

"That's what you were doing, wasn't it, man?" he asked, his voice rising. I couldn't tell if he was angry or excited or both. "You weren't just playing with it, you were *smelling* it, weren't you? You were *smelling my goddamn jockstrap!*"

Daryl put his hands up to the wall of lockers, fencing me in. My burly teammate had me trapped between his muscular arms, and I still didn't know what he was going to do with me.

"Come on, Daryl . . . ," I said. "Take it easy. . . ." I felt like I was alone with a hungry lion—one false move and I'd be dead meat.

"Well," he said. "If you like smelling it so much, here!" He put his jockstrap against my face, holding it there with one hand. I whimpered and tried to struggle out of the way, but Daryl pinned me against the lockers with his other hand, holding me still.

"Come on, man," he said. "Breathe deep! Take it in! Take in that smell you like so much. The smell of *me!* The smell of my crotch all hot and sweaty after a night of practice on the track. You know you love it, so just take it in."

Fearing to disobey, I followed his orders and took in another deep breath. Again, the intoxicating odor of Daryl's groin coursed into me, filling me with his essence. I was a little scared, yet at the same time there was something exciting about being held in place like that, about being in another man's power, the same man whose delicious scent I was devouring through my nostrils.

My cock betrayed me then, hardening up between my legs and standing out, begging for attention. I was still naked, not having had a chance to dress since getting out of the shower, and my erection was painfully obvious. Daryl saw it and his eyes bugged out.

"You *do* like it!" he said triumphantly, as if there'd been any doubt. "Look at that. Look at that dick of yours gettin' all hard from smellin' my jockstrap. . . ."

Then he was putting his hands on my shoulders, pushing me down.

"That's it," he said. "Get down on your knees, man. That's what you want, isn't it? To get down in front of me and worship me? I knew that about you from the first day of practice. I knew what you were then, and I know it even more now . . . you're a *cocksucker,* aren't you?"

He grabbed the waistband of his sweats and pushed them down. His cock popped out, and was I surprised to see that it was already half-hard! He was getting off on having me in his power like this.

"I know what you want," Daryl said, grabbing his pecker with one hand, gripping it around the thick base. He squeezed it and the head bulged, its plum-shaped corona turning dark pink and squeezing out of the foreskin. "You want *this* don't you? Admit it, man. Admit it!"

Without thinking, I nodded my head. I was too strung out to lie.

"Yes, Daryl, I want to suck your dick!" I said. "I've wanted to suck your dick since the first time I met you!"

"Well, why didn't you say so?" he said, pushing his cock toward my face. I opened my mouth and took the fleshy rod inside, loving the feel of its masculine strength.

"Ooohhhh. . . ," Daryl groaned as I stroked his meat with my tongue. At my touch it completed its erection, hardening in my mouth like a steel spike. It felt so good to have it in there. I immediately started sucking it, running my tongue up and down its length, caressing and stroking the head with my tongue. I know he liked it because he moaned and rolled his head back.

"Mmmmm, that's good," he said. "You're a good little cocksucker, ain't you?"

"Mm-hmmm. . . ," I mumbled around the meat in my mouth. I was happy I was making him feel good, maybe now he wouldn't be mad because of what he'd caught me doing.

If I'd thought smelling Daryl's jockstrap was hot, it was unbelievable to have him right there in front of me in all his glory. He'd just come in from practice so he was still all grimy and sweaty, his body giving off a plethora of odors. It was heaven . . . olfactory paradise!

While I sucked his dick I thought about the jockstrap, about that clingy fabric, about how it clung to his balls and cock—the same cock I was sucking. I thought about him running on the track, how the jockstrap kept his jewels safe and protected, cradling them and wrapping them up in a cocoon of warmth and safety.

My mind was so entranced with these thoughts and images that I hadn't noticed myself sucking faster and faster, going up and down on my teammate with a ferocious energy.

"Oh yeah!" Daryl rumbled above me. "That's it, you got it cocksucker! This is was you wanted to do since the first time you saw me. . . ."

He was babbling, more to himself than to me. I continued my endeavor, trying to give him the best and hottest blow job he'd ever gotten. I hoped he'd always remember this one. Maybe I'd even get another chance sometime!

But I was getting ahead of myself and had to concentrate on the here and now—his cock was flexing, I knew it was going to blow soon. The big guy started face fucking me, grabbing me by the ears as if I would try to get away and he had to hold me in place.

As if! No way. This was a dream come true, and I was going to ride it out to the end, like a surfer on a wave. But a minute later he stopped and pulled out of me. I looked up at him, and he was grinning down at me.

"What's wrong?" I asked.

"Nothing's wrong," he answered, "I'm just thinkin' that if you're a cocksucker, then you probably like getting fucked in the ass, don't you?"

I didn't answer immediately.

"Don't you?" Daryl asked again.

"Yes," I said.

"Yes, what?"

"Yes, I like getting fucked in the ass," I said.

"Then ask me," Daryl said. I could tell he was really getting off on this power trip.

"Please, Daryl," I said.

"Please, what?"

"Please fuck me in the ass."

"Louder!"

"Daryl, please *fuck me in the ass,* man!" I said, "I need you to fuck me! Come on, take that big old horsecock of yours and shove it up my butthole! I *need* it, man! Fuck me!"

"Oh yeah!" he said. "You got it, cocksucker! Get me my works from my bag."

I reached into his gym bag and pulled a condom package and a tiny bottle of lube. I wondered who else's ass on the team had been fucked by him. Daryl took the stuff out of my hand and got himself ready.

Then he put me against the wall of lockers and lined up his cock with my asshole. Usually I like a guy to warm me up with his fingers, get my hole ready for penetration, but that time I knew we had to hurry. Everyone was supposed to be gone, but there was always a chance of being discovered by a janitor or security guard or someone.

Daryl shoved his cock in my ass. Even with lube it hurt, and I let out a little yelp of pain. The jock put one hand over my mouth as he started fucking me.

"Shhh, cocksucker," he whispered in my ear.

It was quick, dirty, and fast; he thrust himself into me, then pulled out, then thrust into me again. Within a few moments, his breathing sped up and I knew he was ready. I grabbed my own cock and pumped it in my fist.

"I'm coming, cocksucker," Daryl said. "Can you feel me come?" And he took his hand off my mouth.

"Yeah, man, I'm coming too; can you feel me?'

"Oh, yeah!" we both said, and we blew our loads together as our orgasms bloomed inside us like explosions of pleasure. When we were done, Daryl pulled out of me gently and threw away the condom. I got some paper towels and wiped off the lockers where I'd shot my spunk all over them. When I was done I tried to stand up but lost my balance and almost fell.

"You okay, man?" the jock asked me.

"Yeah," I said, "I just got two workouts today, one on the field and one in here. I'm pretty tired."

Without a word Daryl walked over to me and picked me up, cradling me in his arms. It was amazing—a gesture of such tenderness from a rough jock dude. He carried me to the showers and lovingly washed me and himself. When we were all done, dried off, dressed, and ready to go, Daryl pushed me against the wall and got up in my face again.

"If you *ever* tell anyone we did this, I'll tell them what you were doing when I came down here, cocksucker," he said.

"You got it, man," I said seriously.

"Good," he said, and grinned. "I don't want to have to share you with anyone." And with that he kissed me.

When he took his lips from mine, he gave me another grin, then slung his gym bag over his shoulder and headed for the exit.

"You coming?" he asked me.

College Jock's Bikinis

Jay Starre

Kenny was in a rush when he returned to the locker room for the books he'd forgotten. He found the college basketball team changing after practice and was forced to elbow his way through naked and half-naked jocks as he made his way to his own locker. That's when Kenny spotted the tall dude in the corner. Already sporting a growing boner just from being around all that bare flesh, Kenny's dick leaped to full mast as he gawked at the lanky jock.

Opening his locker and pretending to be busy there, Kenny stared. The guy was very tall, at least six inches taller than his own five feet eleven inches. The long, lean body was naked, except for a pair of underwear covering his butt. Long, creamy flesh was bisected by those tight briefs, a dark navy blue that only accentuated the full butt cheeks Kenny's eyes were glued to. The underwear themselves were bikini small, which seemed out of place on the tall jock. The globes of his rounded butt stretched out the skimpy bikinis, and when he turned toward Kenny, the crotch was packed full of balls and dick, swollen to what looked like the tearing point.

Kenny blinked, bit back a gasp at the sight of that bulging package, and then let his eyes slip upward, just in time to meet a pair of cloud-grey eyes staring back at him. The jock grinned, and Kenny flushed and nodded. The guy pulled a T-shirt over his head and Kenny stole one more greedy glance at that bikini-clad crotch be-

His Underwear: An Erotic Anthology
© 2007 by The Haworth Press, Inc. All rights reserved.
doi:10.1300/5756_07

fore slamming his locker shut and fleeing. The dude had caught Kenny checking him out!

Kenny hurried home through the December chill of an eastern Washington State night. He couldn't get the towering jock out of his mind. On the college hockey team, Kenny was careful not to be obvious in the change room with his teammates. He was a senior, not some blushing freshman, but he didn't advertise his gay inclinations. If he had met the sexy basketball player outside the locker room, he would have chatted him up.

Kenny bypassed his roommates and closed the bedroom door behind him, tearing off his clothes in a heated frenzy to jerk off, the basketball player's half-naked body dominating his thoughts. Kenny stood naked in front of the wall mirror, his hard cock in hand. Kenny looked at his own stocky body, perfect for hockey with broad shoulders and muscular hips, and couldn't help comparing it to his mental image of the long-limbed basketball player. He'd always had a thing for taller dudes. Kenny stroked his fat cock, his face flushing to match the deep pink of his excited rod. He moaned out loud, the feel of his own fingers pumping in a flailing beat bringing him up on his toes. In the mirror he glimpsed the beds behind him. One was empty; his roommate had just moved out. Kenny imagined the basketball jock his new roommate, sprawled out on that bed.

Kenny spit down in his palm, sliding the wet fingers up and down his hot dick. His imagination ran wild, picturing the basketball player on the empty bed. The dude's skimpy bikinis covered his bulging crotch, dark against white. His dick strained hard against the tight material. The basketball jock grinned, the smile broad in Kenny's memory, before he rolled over and spread his legs, displaying his cotton-covered butt cheeks. Navy-blue bikinis outlined the perky mounds, accentuating the deep divide. The jock rolled his ass to tease Kenny, humping the mattress in a raunchy heat that had Kenny gasping. Kenny wanted to see that butt, to rip off those tight bikinis, and feast on what lay beneath.

"Take those fucking underpants off before I tear them off for you," Kenny gasped out loud to the imaginary image in the mirror.

Kenny's fantasy lover laughed, then reached behind himself and hooked both thumbs in the waistband of those dark, tight bikinis. As Kenny whacked off furiously, his imaginary roommate slowly pulled down his underwear, revealing inch by inch the creamy butt and deep crack.

Kenny blew a load that splattered the mirror in sticky gobs. Staggering to the bed he fell asleep with the image of dark bikinis, and a naked white ass underneath floating in his mind.

It had snowed during the night and the next day was brilliant. Blue sky met the white landscape as Kenny hustled to class still thinking of the basketball jock and his bikinis. Why would a big, tall jock like that wear something so skimpy and tight? Was he advertising the goods? Kenny couldn't get him out of his mind.

Three more days of sun and cold followed. Kenny was as horny as ever with the basketball jock and his bikinis on his mind. Kenny hadn't been that hot for a guy since the summer before when he'd met Todd. Todd had been tall too, and had a dick to match. They had moved in together with two other guys in a little house close to campus. But Todd had been a jerk, even though he was good-looking and sexy. He had just moved out, and Kenny and his roommates were looking for someone new to share the rent. Kenny was supposed to be looking for that roommate but all he could think about was the basketball stud and his tight underwear.

Four days had passed without Kenny running into his fantasy lover. The days were short that time of year, and it was already dark when Kenny headed for hockey practice. Something made him detour into the basketball court, which was adjacent to the ice rink. The basketball team was at practice too. There he was! Kenny hovered in the shadow of the bleachers staring at the team as it raced back and forth across the floor. He wasn't any taller than his teammates, but his pale skin and golden mop of gelled hair marked him out. Kenny noticed the name on his tank top. Maclean. He had a name.

Kenny watched Maclean as he trotted back and forth, imagining those bikinis under the basketball shorts, tight and clinging to his sweet ass and full package. His dick and balls would be sweaty, his crack too. Kenny would love to lick them off for him, after he tore off those tight bikinis!

Maclean spotted Kenny and nodded. Kenny was only slightly embarrassed this time, nodding back. He'd just been fantasizing about licking the jock's ass and balls, but Maclean didn't know that. Kenny watched a few more minutes, then raced to his own practice. If he was lucky, he would run into Maclean in the change room.

Practice was a blur. Afterward, in the large locker room both teams shared, Kenny took his time changing and showering, hoping against hope that Maclean would show up. The basketball team had filtered in a few at a time and then left, but Maclean hadn't showed. Kenny soaked in the shower for a long time, then returned to the change room. It was emptying out and still no sign of Maclean. Kenny leaned naked into his locker, searching for his own underwear and thinking of Maclean's. Without warning, a warm body pressed into him from behind.

"Hey, buddy. See something you liked earlier? I know I did. You're cute as hell and packed with muscles. I like that in a guy."

Kenny froze, feeling a bulging dick, encased in cotton, press into his naked butt, and hearing that sultry whisper in his ear. It had to be Maclean! A shiver of lust ran up and down Kenny's spine. He turned his head to see two big hands pressing into the locker on either side of him as Maclean leaned against him from behind. The dick pressing into his butt crack stirred and stabbed at his ass.

"I liked what I saw then, and what I feel now," Kenny hissed back as he craned his head around to see it really was Maclean. The smile was crooked, big white teeth between pursed, thin lips.

Maclean abruptly pulled away and strode toward his locker as a couple of other jocks rounded the corner, laughing and joking. Kenny's eyes followed Maclean's ass. Tight bikinis, this time a dark forest green, outlined his globular butt. Kenny leaned into his locker and grabbed his underwear, in a hurry to hide his stiff dick. Maybe that's why Maclean wore those tight bikinis, to trap his boner in the locker room whenever it threatened to flare up.

Maclean was dressed in what seemed like seconds and returned to pass by Kenny, who was still shaking from that momentary encounter. Seated on a bench while putting on his shoes, his body felt like it was on fire as Maclean strode by him and winked.

The tall jock leaned over and growled in a sexy whisper, "Meet me under the bleachers outside in five minutes."

"Sure," Kenny answered, his eyes again following the long-limbed jock. Kenny imagined those giant arms wrapping around him and those long legs up in the air as Kenny ploughed Maclean's ass hard and deep. Kenny was so flustered he had to retie his shoelaces twice.

The bite of the winter night was sharp. Frozen snow crunched underfoot as Kenny made his way behind the bleachers of the football field, his dick hard in his jeans and his heart beating rapidly in his chest. Where was Maclean in the darkness?

"Over here, bud, with a hard-on about to tear a hole in my underwear."

The husky whisper pulled Kenny into the deeper shadow of the bleachers. He couldn't see shit but felt long arms pull him close. "Hey," Kenny whispered back, the smell of freshly showered jock in his nostrils as he leaned into the tall basketball player.

"I've only got a few minutes right now, but I couldn't wait to feel your hard body in my arms. You are so fucking sexy," Maclean growled down into Kenny's face.

"We might as well get to it then," Kenny growled right back.

Kenny was burning up with desire. He dropped to his knees right then and there, tearing at Maclean's belt and fly. The feel of the cold ground against his knees was a shock, but the warmth of Maclean's thighs against his chest was much more meaningful. He wanted to get into those underwear! Right now!

The fly parted and Maclean's jeans slid down to his knees. Kenny pressed his face into Maclean's crotch, opening his mouth in the darkness and searching for the prize—jock dick! He found it immediately, a long tube trapped under tight cotton bikinis. Kenny clamped his lips over it.

The jock was giggling, almost hysterically. "Hey! You don't have to do that right now, but, fuck, it does feel awesome—your lips on my dick!"

Kenny was acutely aware of the smell of Maclean's crotch with his nose pressed against it. There was the clean scent of those bikinis, almost like lemon or something, probably the dryer sheets he used, or his Mom used or whatever. Kenny rubbed his nose in those tight bikinis as he chewed on Maclean's stiffening cock, which strained against the cotton material.

Kenny reached around Maclean and clutched at his butt. Again it was underwear, clinging tightly to flesh, that he felt. Maclean's globed cheeks tensed and jiggled as the jock gasped and reached down to grip Kenny's shoulders.

"So nice, buddy, so fucking nice."

Kenny worked his mouth over Maclean's cock through his underwear, soaking the material with spit as he found and captured the bulbed cockhead. Maclean thrust into Kenny's face, his ass cheeks clenching under Kenny's groping fingers. Kenny squeezed that compact butt, working his fingers toward the crack as Maclean humped Kenny's face and gasped loudly in the darkness.

Kenny chewed with focused concentration, while his hands zeroed in on Maclean's ass crack. Through the tight bikinis, he managed to shove a hand into Maclean's deep divide, but the smooth flesh was still elusive with the underwear blocking access. Kenny was intent on dick, though, and when Maclean dug his own hand into his underwear and pulled out his long bone, Kenny dived over it, inhaling the meat with a snort.

"Oh, fuck! Yeah! Eat that meat! I can't believe it! You are so fucking hot!"

Maclean was on his toes, driving into Kenny's mouth. His ass cheeks were clenching and relaxing under Kenny's fingers. He was feeding his long dick in and out of Kenny's slurping lips, faster and faster. Kenny tasted cock against his tongue and lips, long, hard cock. He sucked and slurped as that stiff tube wildly plunged in and out. His fingers pushed deep into Maclean's cotton-covered butt crack, managing to find and press against the jock's puckered butthole.

Maclean shuddered all over as Kenny's fingertip stabbed at his asshole through his underwear. "I'm gonna blow!" He yanked his dick out of Kenny's mouth just in time. Cum fired out in spurts past Kenny's ear as the pulsing rod pressed against his neck.

Maclean pulled Kenny to his feet, laughing breathlessly while wrapping his arms around the stocky hockey player. "That was awesome. But I really gotta go. Something important. My name's Danny Maclean. I'll see you real soon."

Kenny's hand was still pressed into Maclean's ass crack, but in the darkness Maclean squirmed around to pull up his jeans, still laughing as he broke away. "What's your name?"

"Kenny," he called to the back of the disappearing jock. The taste of cock was still on his lips, the smell of cum lingering in his nostrils. He recalled vividly the feel of that tight ass, the cotton underwear encasing them like a second skin, and that tantalizing butthole protected by the same underwear. Alone, under the bleachers, Kenny almost pulled down his jeans and jerked himself off, but the cold suddenly hit him. Instead, he pulled up his hood and ventured out into the night.

Kenny walked through the cloudless night, a sliver of moon and sparkling stars brittle in the cold sky. After the brief but intense sex, he was feeling a strange mixture of emotions. He was elated on one level—Maclean had obviously enjoyed it and asked his name. But he had rushed off, something more important than Kenny on his mind. Maybe the dude was just selfish, only concerned about getting off. With Kenny on his knees and jock cock in his mouth, Maclean had gotten what he wanted and that was enough for him.

Kenny thought of Todd, for some reason. In aimless circles around the small college town, Kenny walked and thought. Todd had been so fucking sexy, with that long snake of his. He'd fucked Kenny willingly, and eagerly, but afterward had always pretended nothing had happened, ignoring Kenny until he was horny again. Then Todd would jump on top of Kenny in their bedroom and they would hump like wild animals; Todd's long, hard bone slithering in and out of Kenny's willing asshole.

Kenny had finally had enough, after four months of undeniably steamy sex but emotional emptiness. Todd had just laughed when Kenny asked him to move out. He had been gone the next day, which was only two weeks ago. Kenny halted in his tracks. Fuck! He was supposed to be home to interview a new roommate! He'd forgotten all about it in his heat to meet Maclean.

Kenny rushed home, realizing he was two hours late already. Coming in through the back door, he stopped in the laundry room to take off his snow-coated boots and coat. In the dim light streaming in through the doorway from the kitchen, something caught his eye as he leaned on the dryer. A small pile of dirty clothes huddled inconspicuously only a few inches from his hand. Strange clothes. Not his, not his roommates. On the top of the pile was a pair of dark green, bikini underwear.

Kenny froze, his heart pounding, staring at those underwear. A voice called out from nearby kitchen.

"Is that you, Kenny? What the fuck happened to you? We got a new roommate without you. It's your tough luck if you don't like him. Fuck if I'm gonna even tell you his name, you idiot. He's in your room."

That was Trent, his nasal twang unmistakable. He was mad, but he'd get over it. The important thing to Kenny at the moment were those underwear. With shaking hands, he picked them up. In the quiet darkness, he pressed them to his nose. That clean lemon-dryer scent, and at the crotch, the raunchy stench of dried cum. Cum that Kenny had sucked out of Maclean's cock!

After inhaling deeply, a grin of sheer pleasure growing on his face, Kenny set down the underwear and headed for his bedroom, whizzing past the disgruntled Trent with a hasty "sorry."

At his bedroom door, he lingered before opening it. What would Maclean be thinking? Would he even know he had Kenny as a roommate? Kenny hadn't told him his last name.

Kenny braved the door, pushing it open quietly. The small bed stand lamp was on. Todd's old bed was occupied. Long bare thighs, a naked back, a head cradled in long arms. A perky ass, maroon bikini underwear clinging to the rounded cheeks. Kenny's · heart leaped in his chest.

Kenny looked up from the semi-naked body on the bed. A picture of Kenny and Todd still stood on the bed stand, the lamp illuminating it. Maclean would have seen it and recognized Kenny. What was Maclean thinking? Was he happy to be Kenny's new roommate, or was he going to pretend nothing had happened earlier? Memories of Todd's insensitive behavior popped into Kenny's head. But the sight of Maclean's perky ass, encased in maroon, seized him by the balls. Kenny's head reeled and he was · breathless as he pressed the door shut behind him.

The sound stirred Maclean. The long-limbed jock lifted his head from where it was cradled in his arms. He craned his head around and looked at Kenny. He broke out in a crooked smirk, his big teeth glinting in the light of the bed stand. Maclean laughed lightly as he deliberately rolled his tight butt in a slow lewd circle.

"Thanks for getting me off under the bleachers. Now it's my turn to repay the favor. My ass is all yours!"

Kenny's heart pounded against his chest. His own grin just about split his face in two. Without a word, tore his clothes off in a heated frenzy. Maclean giggled on the bed; he was up on his elbows and wiggling his butt in nasty circles as he watched the crazed hockey player who was his new roommate.

Kenny's hard-on reared out from his crotch as he leaped on the bed between Maclean's long thighs. Maclean's blond eyebrows arched as he took in the sight of Kenny's blunt, stiff boner.

"Fuck me with that big stick! Rip off my underwear and drill my ass," Maclean urged Kenny between giggling bursts of laughter.

"I'm going to," Kenny gasped, his face flushed and his body on fire. The feel of Maclean's naked thighs pressed into his. His hands whipped out to take hold of Maclean's lush butt cheeks, squeezing greedily.

Although it had been less than a week since he had first laid eyes on Maclean and that bikini-clad butt, it seemed as if it had been a lifetime. Kenny couldn't wait another moment to see what flesh lay hidden under those tight cotton bikinis. He seized the waistband with both hands and yanked down. Maclean laughed and wiggled his ass in the air, but the underwear were so tight, they only rolled down to just below his butt cheeks.

"Oh man, fuck, oh man," Kenny muttered, staring at the pale pink expanse of naked ass. No hair, no blemishes, a deep divide, and lush, firm flesh. Kenny lunged forward, burying his face in that exposed crack.

"Hell, yeah! Eat my ass before you fuck it!" Maclean cried out.

Kenny used both hands to spread open Maclean's ass, burrowing deep between the firm mounds with his tongue out like a slobbering dog. He tasted and smelled, his senses on fire. Jock ass! Kenny burrowed for the target, silky ass flesh surrounding his cheeks as he stabbed deep into that crack. He found the hole; this time no cotton underwear protected it. Kenny lapped and licked and probed, Maclean's moans encouraging him to delve deeper, and deeper. Maclean had lifted his butt in the air, pressing back into Kenny's face. His asshole flowered outward, the lips parting and the inner flesh exposed as Kenny tongued it and sucked it.

"That feels so fucking good, your tongue up my ass, but I want your cock. Right now, Kenny!"

The shaky need in Maclean's voice was undeniable. Kenny pulled his mouth out of Maclean's crack and grinned, spit on his lips and his eyes burning. One look at Maclean's heaving, wet ass crack, and Kenny lunged again. This time he covered Maclean with his own stockier body, his hard dick driving down between those heaving, warm butt cheeks. His cock struck right on target, wet butt lips parting for the blunt head. Maclean's deep grunt matched Kenny's explosive sigh.

Kenny's cock wormed deeper, the force of his powerful hips behind it. Maclean pushed up to meet the driving rod, sucking in inch after fat inch in a greedy lust for hot poker up the ass. Kenny felt Maclean's entire body convulse and spread outward, opening for him like no one had ever before.

Kenny's thighs were shaking as his cock sunk deeper and deeper, the column of meat burning up with tight anal lips clamping over it and torrid hole surrounding it. Without thinking, he reached under Maclean's belly and found his cock. The tight cotton bikinis still clung to it, trapping the boner. Long and hard, it pulsed under Kenny's fingers. Kenny released it and wrapped his hand around it, squeezing fiercely to Maclean's deep groan.

Kenny pumped that stiff meat while he drove his own cock to the balls in Maclean's willing asshole. The two jocks heaved and moaned and gasped as they fucked themselves to a gut-wrenching orgasm. It only took a few minutes of deep pounding, and they were spurting. Kenny felt Maclean's dick pulse in his fingers, lengthen and then shoot onto the bed covers beneath them. His own cock erupted in a stomach-churning explosion, filling Maclean's squirming ass with spurt after spurt.

Kenny collapsed on top of Maclean. He was sweating from head to toe, the slippery body under him just as sweaty. His cock continued to unload inside Maclean as he lay there and caught his breath. As his head cleared, he thought he should maybe pull out and get off the big basketball jock, but he just didn't want to. Not yet. Not ever.

"You feel great inside me. But you're heavy as shit," Maclean finally murmured with a giggle added at the end.

Kenny rolled to the side, his sticky dick sliding from the tight hole it had just fucked. That perky ass was wet with sweat, the dark maroon underwear bunched down around the cheeks. Kenny giggled too, elated to have finally revealed what the bikinis had hidden.

"I was hoping my tight underwear would catch your attention," Maclean smiled into Kenny's face as they lay side-by-side on the bed. When Kenny looked at him quizzically, Maclean explained. "I noticed you months ago in the locker room but you never even looked my way. Maybe you had someone else on your mind. I decided to advertise the goods and bought a dozen pairs of the tightest, skimpiest underwear I could find. Did it work?"

Kenny laughed and laughed. His hands slid down to cup Maclean's ass cheeks. "It worked. Boy, did it work."

The picture of Kenny and Todd disappeared from the bed stand. A few weeks later it was replaced, a smiling basketball jock in his bikini underwear standing beside a hockey player in his boxers staring out from a bright new frame.

Keep It Clean

Adam McCabe

The whole thing started as an accident. I'd only reached into the drum to get out the day-old clothes from the sole dryer in our apartment complex. I threw the clothes on top of the dryer, resisting the urge to pitch them on the ground. After all, it was Christmas week, so I was feeling more charitable than normal.

I moved my clothes from the washer to the dryer, the last batch of laundry before going home for the holidays. I'd had to locate and clean the clothes I'd worn last Christmas. No one in Wichita wanted to see my skintight shirt and button-down jeans. I had to find the sweaters and corduroys that proclaimed my midwestern wholesomeness.

I dropped a sweater on the floor and bent down to pick it up. As I brushed off the lint and dirt from the cement floor, the contents of the last load caught my eye. The thin black line of a G-string stood out against the pristine whites of the towels. I pushed the sweater into the dryer and picked up the underwear by one of the strings. It was still warm; I brought it close to my nose to smell just a hint of the manliness in the fabric.

I put it down quickly and looked around, embarrassed to think that someone might catch me. However, it didn't stop me from examining it closer as I put in a dryer sheet and inserted my quarters into the machine. The underwear's pouch was still pushed out, making me wonder how big the guy was who wore these. I started to get hard just thinking about it. I grabbed my laundry bas-

His Underwear: An Erotic Anthology
© 2007 by The Haworth Press, Inc. All rights reserved.
doi:10.1300/5756_08

ket and sprinted upstairs to jack off thinking about a hot, hung man in a G-string.

After my return from Wichita, I twice saw the same G-string in the laundry. Each time it was lying on top of the dryer, and I had a chance to touch the smooth fabric and fantasize about the man who wore them. I imagined his lithe, smooth body and the curve of his big balls that barely fit in the pouch. I even rubbed it up against my own crotch, thinking about how good it would feel to have him next to me.

I had just finished my laundry for a late January ski trip when I ran into a man in the laundry room. He was tall, blond, and everything I'd dreamed the G-string guy to be. His long hair obscured his eyes, so I couldn't see if he was checking me out as well. He wore tight jeans and a T-shirt that said he hadn't been outside lately. He was carrying a basket of clothes.

"How ya doing?" I asked as I folded up my long johns. Not exactly the underwear choice to inspire passion, but it would hold frostbite at bay on the slopes.

"Good." He slid two quarters out of his jeans pocket and pushed them in the slots. His hand dove deeper into his pocket a second time, but came out with just some lint. "Hey, you wouldn't have an extra quarter to spare? I could drop one off later."

I pulled a coin from my shirt pocket and handed it over, careful not to touch his palm. "Don't worry about it. You can drop it off any time. I'm in seven D."

"Eight A." No wonder I hadn't seen him around the building. Different floor, different wing.

I slowed my folding to check out the black G-string, but he didn't remove it from the basket. I was almost done with the load, when he dumped the rest of his laundry into the washer without pulling it out. I tried a smile and he nodded. He threw down the basket and walked toward the stairs.

I quickly opened the washer lid and rummaged around looking for the G-string, but it was nowhere to be found.

I had given up hope when I noticed he was standing in the doorway. I tried to act cool, but there seemed no good excuse.

"I just spilled coffee on my shirt, and I wanted to wear it out tonight." He pointed to a dark spot across his right pec. "What were · you just doing?"

"I think I left something in the washer. I was trying to see if it was there or if I misplaced it." I couldn't think of a better lie on short notice.

"Oh, let me help. What were you missing?" He pulled a few soaking shirts out of the washer but saw nothing, of course.

"A G-string," I stammered, not sure that I'd even said it. His underwear was about the only thing on my mind at this moment. My face grew hot as he looked at me. Blood rushed to other parts of my body as well, creating a bulge in my pants that I knew he could see. My cock ached against the fabric.

"What color?"

"Red." Like my face.

He pushed through the damp clothes in the washer. Of course, he found nothing. "Sorry, nothing like that here. Glad it's not in here. Wouldn't want all of my clothes to end up pink." He smiled at me, and I momentarily forgot my embarrassment at rummaging through his underwear.

He pulled the bottom of the T-shirt from his jeans and pulled it over his head in one fluid motion. He made a mock basketball shot, and the shirt sunk into the washing machine's drum.

At the close range, his body impressed me. He had well-formed pecs that curved up into his bushy arm pits. A thin line of hair ran down from his stomach into the jeans. I wanted to find out more about where the hair led to. He crossed his big hands over his chest as he watched me, biceps flexed

My dick hadn't subsided with our conversation. If anything, I could feel its demanding pulse more. I pulled myself closer to the dryer to avoid discussion about my erection. I could feel the sticky material of my own underwear against its pounding shaft.

"You're hard." He smiled again and shifted closer to me. "I'm getting there too. Watching your dick pound like that is getting me hard." He let an arm drop to his side and a hand slid under the unbuttoned band of his jeans. I wanted to be those fingers as they slid inside his waistband.

The agitator was the only sound in the room as he removed his hand from his jeans and moved it to my throat. I wasn't sure what to expect, but he slipped the roaming extremity under my shirt. My own lightly furred chest tingled as he managed to find a nipple and tweak it. I caught my breath and realized he was enjoying the scene.

I helped him along by unbuttoning my shirt. The cool air felt good against my skin as I threw the clothes on the floor. Now we were even, man to shirtless man. I could see him admire my tight waist and muscled chest.

"Looks like I might not be going out tonight after all." He pulled me toward him and our mouths met. A tongue pushed between my lips and darted back and forth inside. Little licks along the corners of my mouth made me want him more.

I cupped a hand around his neck and refused to let him pull back. I wanted him too much for that. Our mouths clung to each other like leather clings to skin on a hot day. His hands wasted no time in exploring me. They started at the neck and quickly slid to my arms. As if synchronized, they dropped to my armpits and tickled the fine hair under my arms. He gave the hair a quick tug and went for the nipples. The attention made them change to hard balls of flesh on my chest, as he tweaked and pinched them. We still kissed deeply but with more urgency. I could feel the desire in his mouth.

He slipped a hand into my pants and his fingers probed the end of my dick. He flicked my piss slit and quivers ran down my shaft. It had been days since I had a chance to whack off. I could feel the tingling of my balls as his fingers slid down the length of my seven-inch cock. He knew all the moves to turn me on.

I pulled his body to mine, and I could feel the heat of his crotch against my dick. He slid his hand out of my pants and around my waist. His fingers explored my butt crack as I ground my hips to his. I kissed him again and let my lips slowly trace down his cheek and neck. My mouth found his shoulders, biting the tan flesh and leaving red marks.

He put his hands under my arms, but it didn't stop me from dropping to my knees. I bit at the rough denim, getting it wet with my saliva. The jeans were unbuttoned, so a quick flip of the wrist had the zipper down. The jeans went down to his shoes. He was wearing one of the G-strings I'd seen in the past weeks. The pouch hung low with its load. His ass was firm and muscular with the slightest curve to it. I grabbed a cheek in each hand. I slowly pushed the pouch to one side and uncovered his thick cock.

The man was hung. He had about eight inches of solid man flesh. He thrust upward as my tongue found the head of his cock, and I almost choked. It filled my mouth and throat as I took all of it. The thick veins pulsed under my lips as I started to suck it, moving my mouth up and down the shaft.

I reached up and found his nipples. The smooth skin around them puckered into gooseflesh as my fingertips worked around them. The nipples balled into hard lumps of flesh under my touch. He moaned softly, his throaty call echoing throughout the laundry room. His voice urged me on as I continued to suck his dick, holding his cockhead just inside my lips. My tongue circled the ridge under the purple head.

My hands left his chest and slid down to his waist. I played with his ass as I sucked him, squeezing the muscular globes of flesh. He contracted the muscles, so all I felt were the hard mounds of his ass. My fingers found his tight hole and one digit explored the puckered opening. His back arched away from me and his dick came out of my mouth, slapping me in the face. I tried to catch it with my lips again, but the finger fuck seemed to have touched a nerve in him. As I went in to the second knuckle, the moans grew louder.

My cock throbbed inside my pants as I kept up the pressure inside of him. He started a rhythm on my finger and squeezed until I thought it would come off inside of his ass. I started to insert a second finger, but he caught my wrist with his hand and pulled me to my feet.

"I gotta have the real thing now, man. Take me." He grabbed me by the belt and pulled me closer to the washing machine. He unbuckled my belt and tugged at the button to free me. I was wearing boxer briefs, but they only lasted a second before he had them around my ankles. My cock pulsed as he found it and teased its head between two fingers. Juices flowed from my cock's head as he ran a finger along my piss slit. I knelt to grab a rubber from my pants and put in on hurriedly.

His pants still hampered his legs, but he bent over. His arms hugged the sides of the machine, which pounded in a steady rhythm that only served to make me harder. I bent over him and bit his back, tiny nibbles across the broad shoulders and muscular frame. He moaned louder this time and pulled his cheeks apart for me to enter.

I pushed inside of him. It was a tight fit between the muscular cheeks and he squeezed as soon as I was in all the way. I slid an arm around his waist and grabbed his cock. It was already slippery and I used his own precum to lube him up. My fingers barely touched my thumb as I waxed his shaft with his own juices. He released his ass muscles and I started a quick thrusting rhythm, which he matched immediately. The slapping of my balls against his firm backside was the only sound besides the occasional guttural noise coming from him.

I put my hands on his back to get better balance. His back was covered with a layer of sweat from our exertions. I watched my cock as the shaft moved in and out of him like a piston. As his excitement grew, I pulled out to the tip and pushed in until all I could see was my groin against his ass.

He tightened his ass muscles again as I thrust in. With the insistent pressure from his sphincter, I knew I couldn't hold out much longer. I felt the swell of cum in my balls and knew nirvana was coming soon.

I pulled out of him and yanked the rubber off. A few swift strokes later, I shot my load across the hard plains of his back and ass. Tiny drops slid down his legs and into his jeans.

Having come, I dropped down to my knees so that his dick was just above my face and chest. I watched as he stroked himself, · slowing moving his hand from his balls to the tip of his cock. His meat quivered with each hand motion and from my vantage point, I could see the thick veins in his dick pulse. His balls still hung low and I craned my neck to pull one of the shaved orbs into my mouth. The taste of sweat filled my mouth as I rolled his ball in my mouth.

His hand moved faster now, rapidly whacking his dick as I sucked his ball. I felt it grow tight, and I let go of his ball as he shot a load down the length of my chest. His cum warmed me as it · snaked through the hair on my upper body.

He practically pulled me to my feet and held me close. His cum smeared across my chest as we ground our bodies together. He smiled at me and stepped back. He pulled up his pants and looked at me again. "I've got a half hour before the next load." He blushed. "Laundry, that is. I have another load for you any time you want it. Want to go upstairs?"

Matthew's Total Fitness

Troy Ygnacio Soriano

"Not every guy looks good with ripped abdominals—look at those dudes. They each have that six-pack, but way too skinny in the legs. That's my opinion anyway, what do you think Troy? Troy, you're not looking."

Matt was on the bench press, lifting the heavily loaded bar up and down in a slow, smooth groove. I watched him from behind, engrossed in his effort. His words were only slightly strained. I felt his breath go across the hair above my knee as he exhaled forcefully, setting the bar up on the bench, completing his repetitions.

"I couldn't look at them, because I was spotting you, M. Where are these guys?"

I could lift a lot of weight, but not as much as Matt. I thought of his workouts almost like a series of wonders or astonishments, and there was a lot to like about having his face between my legs in a room full of busy people, my eyes trained on him only, his warm labored breath going up my shorts. I reluctantly shifted my attention away.

"Maybe they have different fitness goals though, Matt."

"Hmph. Really. Bodybuilding used to have a certain aesthetic to it. If your chest is overdeveloped, and then you're too skinny in the legs—well, that doesn't look right, does it? Doesn't look natural. But maybe that's changing."

His Underwear: An Erotic Anthology
© 2007 by The Haworth Press, Inc. All rights reserved.
doi:10.1300/5756_09

He laughed softly as if the easiness of his laugh had proved his point, and left me to contemplate it as he lumbered, and I merely walked, to the men's locker-room.

"Well, they are young," he winked at me with a dazzling smile, "they'll learn."

Right and natural were the words to describe Matt physique. There is a certain newness to young men's bodies that Matt had left behind as something inarguably useless to him now, like footed pajamas.

Matt had a body which was notable because it was so clearly not growing or developing, but gloriously built and lovingly maintained. At the gym, he came in like an SUV to everyone else's bike. His body described both the scope of his ambition, and his flair for follow-through. It was also very lived-in and without even a bit of awkwardness. I had seen very muscled men just walk by a young woman struggling with her couch on the sidewalk, but that wasn't Matt. He was nice, friendly, helpful—yet somehow intimidating. He was out of the wilderness of his twenties, truly in his prime. Truly enjoying his prime.

"You're young too, Matt."

"I don't know, man. I'll be thirty-one this year, Troy!"

I had to laugh at him and his mock-seriousness.

He grinned with sincerity and rubbed his chest, "Born in year of the pig."

"Year of the what?"

"Year of the Pig. In, uh, Chinese astrology." He laughed exotically.

"Oh yeah? Does it mean something?"

"Well, supposedly it means I'm playful, helpful, and sensual."

"Really?" My eyes were sort of frowning, but my mouth was in an accepting smile. "I'll be thirty-one this year too, Matt."

"Then you must be the same as me then. Two pigs, I guess."

"I guess," I said, and we went into the locker-room.

Here is Matt undressing: floppy brown hair hanging straight down over his blue eyes, and his round, muscled butt bouncing slightly when he walks. Without a word, he advertises the best that can be achieved from heavy squats on the Smith machine. This was no thirty-inch waist; he was built like a football player.

He had what I call a "cheeks together" butt, his ass cheeks built up high against each other, his scented hole buried deep between them, like a good secret kept for a lucky few.

I knew even if a man was lucky enough to be with him, getting to his asshole, physically getting to it, wouldn't be easy; you couldn't just bend him over or lay him down. I knew getting to that warm spot would require a man to use his muscles, to pry those mounds apart with force. I thought this was a good metaphor for Matt, the great work and challenge of getting close to him, and what I imagined would be the even better reward for bothering to do so.

As if that were not enough, there is the dick that cannot be ignored, always tumescent, always half-ready, a long, fat sausage in a room full of starving carnivores. His dick hung down, meaty and uncut, the very definition of well-hung.

Whenever we were changing in the locker-room and I got a look at his dick, I always felt like there was suddenly another person in the room. It's like his dick had its own personality; it was bold. No man who had it in his field of vision could keep his eyes from it, and no man who looked at that dick, straight, gay, or unaffiliated, could look away from it right away. I loved that about him; he made everyone his admirer, almost against their will. They were hopeless against his charm; it wrestled them down.

But we were friends, so I was only sometimes intimidated by him. I undressed slowly and watched him; he met my eyes from time to time, giving me a humble smile. He grabbed his towel and went to the showers; I was still in my boxers.

I looked over at his pile of clothes on the bench with interest.

First there was his sleeveless black tee, then his nylon running shorts. At the very top of the pile were his jockey shorts, his very bright, tight, white shorts. I instinctively put my hands on his pile of clothes, which were still warm and damp with sweat. I noticed there was another man changing not too far away, watching me feel up Matt's clothes, but I didn't care much about that guy. What would he say to me? I wasn't as big as Matt, but I sure as hell was no slouch either. I dared him to interfere, as I was literally crazed with lust.

I picked up Matt's jockey shorts and walked toward the toilet area of the locker room. I went into a stall and closed the door behind me, my heart beating harder than it ever had while lifting weights. I turned Matt's underwear inside out and pressed them into my face inhaling the scent of his balls and dick and asshole deep into my lungs. Heavy, damp, sweaty, sweet, soapy, it was the best smell ever; it was Matt. I wrapped his underwear around my thick dick and almost shot my load right there. I put the head of my cock right where his asshole would be and oozed my hopeful precum there. Three minutes later, I was back at my locker, with Matt's underwear in my hands. Maybe I looked pitiful, I didn't fucking care. I was happy.

"Hey! Where's my underwear?"

Matt was already there. I heard his voice before I saw him and was a little freaked. I had worked out with Matt, hung out with him as a friend dozens of times, but I had never made a pass at him. Coming back to the locker holding his underwear was pretty shady. Matt stood there, naked and confused, and I noticed the guy who had seen me feel up Matt's clothes standing there too, now fully dressed, arms crossed disapprovingly.

"That's the guy that took your underwear."

I felt it was a pretty dumb thing to say considering I was holding them.

"What were you doing with my underwear, man? Huh?"

I choked, not able to speak, sensing my actions had ruined our bond. Matt approached me closely, face to face. He looked like the ultimate bully.

"Were you bringing them to me? Like my little slave boy?"

He had a hard look in his eyes, and I was unsure of what he would do.

"Were you sniffing my underwear, man? *Were you?*"

I backed up a step or two. I didn't know where he was going with this, but a very subtle change happened then. Though his words remained stern, I recognized a playfulness in his eyes.

"Did you rub my underwear on your dick, guy?"

Okay—I got what he was doing. He didn't care; he just wanted to make me sweat. So now I would try to wrestle *him* into discomfort.

"Yeah, hell yeah I did! I went into a stall and smelled, sucked on, and jacked off with your underwear, Matt. There's a big salty load in there; enjoy sloshing around in it, bud."

If Matt had had anything in his mouth, he would have spit it out, he was so shocked. He visibly held back his laughter.

"Okay, well. Hahahh. Just checking. Can I, uh, have them back now? Thanks."

The other man who was witness to my crime, walked away slowly, his eyes clearly judging us both. Matt addressed him as he walked out of the locker room.

"You got a problem, friend?"

We left the gym and marched into the Boston summer day. We didn't say much, the mood was uncharacteristically serious. He stopped and turned to me, putting his hand on my shoulder. His thick eyebrows were raised, and he was very earnest.

"Can I come to your place right now, Troy?"

What was this feeling?

"Uhh . . . sure, sure," I said softly.

"Good."

I didn't live far from the gym. We stopped for some beer, a sixer, and then walked to my apartment. I again noticed how his beefy butt moved, how he kept looking at his feet. At my house we relaxed, drinking our beer.

"Your shower was kind of useless, Matt," I laughed, swigging. "You got all sweaty, took a quick shower, put on the sweaty clothes you worked out in, and, just in the walk over here, are already . . . sweaty again."

Matt swigged his beer, smiled and shook his head no in a way that said, leave it.

"You haven't showered at all, bro."

"Hahahh, how embarrassing. You're right."

"No, it's fine, you smell great. You're great," Matt laughed nervously, smiled, and finished his beer in one long gulp. "But, Troy. You know what's not fair?" He was speaking in a quiet, intense tone I never heard before.

"What's that, M?"

"Well. You got to feel all around my underwear, and I didn't get to touch yours at all."

I looked at him for a long time, recognizing this basic injustice.

I finished my beer, took off my shoes and nylon shorts, and stood there in my tighty whities and T-shirt. I was ready for whatever.

Matt approached me slowly, directly. I am strong, weigh 170 pounds, and stand only five foot seven, but I am all muscle. Matt was three times my size, easily, but somehow we were equal. I felt a deep vibration of respect from him—and attraction.

Matt fondled my dick through my underwear. He caressed and cupped my balls lightly through the humid, white cotton. He swallowed hard and pushed me back onto the chair I had been relaxing in.

Using his huge hands and forearms, Matt held on to my thighs and went down on his knees, leaning in, nuzzling my balls with his nose, and inhaling. He didn't look at me; his eyes were trained on the bulge in my jockey shorts. I was seriously bulging. Matt looked up at me then with a sober expression, and ran one finger along the inside strap of my underwear, pulling it away, so that my hard dick popped way out of the leg hole. I wasn't as thick or as long as Matt, but I had a bigger dick than most guys. Between us, we had a lot of dick. A lot of everything, I guess.

"This looks—" His expression became overwhelmed with wonder and lust for a second, but he continued, "—so good to me, Troy. Wow. It's really nice. I knew it would be."

"Thanks, man," I said, concealing my great surprise.

"I've never given a guy a blow job before. I'd like to try it with you, though."

He seemed to be talking to my penis, not me. My first idea was that he was probably lying, but as he grabbed my shaft with his

right hand, I noticed his left hand shaking uncontrollably with
nerves.

"Have you been with many dudes, Troy?"

"A fair few."

He barely listened to my reply, because he was giving me the
best blow job of my life. His big mouth was a great place for my
outsized dick to be. My dick didn't fit my body; it was large, and I
was built-up, but still small framed. It did fit nicely, however, in
Matt's big, square-jawed mouth. He backed off me, admired my
saliva-coated manhood, and then with the tip of his tongue, licked
his way from my asshole—he had easily lifted my leg over his
shoulder—to the tip of my dick.

My main thought after that was that I couldn't reasonably complain about anything in my life ever again. To do so would just
anger the gods. Clearly, I just had the peak human experience. I
could die a happy man.

Matt gave enthusiastic head and looked like he was relishing his
first time with a man. He kept swallowing me completely, and
then taking it out of his mouth to hold it in his fist; he would admire my dick, with a grin. He was giddy. Now I knew he wasn't
lying. Matt was still on his knees in front of me, this huge attractive guy, with everything going for him in the world, going out of
his way to thrill me, and himself.

"Troy, this is making me so happy. You were the right guy to
have my first experience with. I want to do this a lot with you, is
that okay?"

Matt dived down on my dick again, and I reached down his
back and slid his tight soft jockeys over his ample ass. He was giving me head. I was massaging his ass and running my fingers
down and into his butt crack. He was asking *me* if it was okay?

"Yeah, Matt, let's do this a lot, all the time."

"Mmmm, Troy, it's *good*. It's so fucking good."

Matt's dick was very hard now, but with the way I had pulled
down his shorts, only his big muscle ass was exposed and his dick
was fighting the top elastic in front. He reached with one hand to

pull his shorts down and free himself, but I wanted in on that action.

"Here. Let me help you out there. How's that, man?"

"Mmm. . . ."

I pulled down his jockeys completely and now had his size XXL dick in my hand, stroking its soft-yet-very-hard length back and forth, running my thumb along the piss slit in front, and finding the clear, glossy drops of precum hanging there. I licked it off my thumb and, with the other hand, kept kneading and massaging his giant, white muscled ass. I smelled the hand that had just worked over his ass, and it smelled like the underwear I had made off with, earlier. It all became a little much for me. I squeezed Matt's shoulder and moved backward.

"Careful," I laughed nervously. "You'll have it all over the place soon."

"I like this. I like giving you head, Troy."

"I like you giving me head, Matt," I said tenderly.

"I can't believe I've had this fucking dick in my mouth, Troy. It's looks just. . . ." He shook his head, amazed. "You have a porn star's dick. Nice and thick. I feel so good!"

"Thanks. You're a god-on-earth, Matt. And . . . so nice too." I ran my hand through his hair; it fell into his face again.

"Hey, Troy, can I try something?"

"I think we can try anything, Matt."

With that, he stood up, leaned over, and kissed me softly. It was just a peck, but it was perfect and very gentle. Then he laughed boldly, lustily, loudly.

Suddenly, with great force and show, Matt came right up against me, and with one arm grabbed me to his chest, and with the other started jacking me off with slow, firm, rhythmic strokes.

The hand that had me pulled to his chest came up to my head, in a motion designed to make me lean back, and I did intuitively. He was kissing me hard now, and I knew I would come.

"Troy, grab my ass. Grab my ass *now!*"

I leaned forward and grabbed his ass and rested my head against Matt's hips, right next to his giant dick. I kept my eyes on it, while he leaned over and stroked me off. When he bent over to kiss me again, I let loose ten days worth of the white stuff all over his hand, down my legs, all over the carpet, and all over his toes. I had shot in seven big liquid convulsions and was laughing into his mouth, joyously.

"We're in sync with each other," Matt laughed softly.

"It's from the gym, Troy, spotting each other, working closely together."

"Well, we have another set left, looks like," I said, looking at his dick which stood next to my face, just inches away. *Nice to meet you,* I thought, looking at it.

My cheeks were soon full like a chipmunk who had found the biggest nuts. I loved the way his dick filled my mouth, but I did struggle with it, I admit. I came off his length and admired him now.

"Maybe I could fuck you sometime. I've been watching you do squats for so long Troy, fantasized about it." His hand went down my back. He kneaded my butt roughly and his serious expression told me he was already doing that in his mind.

"Yeah, I mean whatever. We can do each other" I said breathlessly.

I stood up and hugged him, and he jacked, looking at me with a smile.

"I'm really attracted. Have been for a while, Troy."

He leaned backward slightly, released his grip on me somewhat, and started stroking himself very hard and fast. I was snapping digital pix in my head. He kept looking over at me, and then down at his massive meat, and once in awhile closing his eyes in bliss, with a huge smile on his face. But I wasn't about to let him come without my help. I got down on my knees to run my tongue very gently around his ball sack, and all around his balls in wide circles. All my previous gay experiences were not to be in vain.

"Oh my god, Troy, what are you *doing*? That feels *fucking great*! Ohhhh! Aww . . . FUUUCKK!"

My face was soon blanketed with essence of Matt, and I had to close my eyes to keep it out. Matt was laughing, but after he went, he helped me over to the sink. We rinsed me off, him running his huge hands over my face, cleaning me thoroughly with the water.

"I'm so glad you stole my underwear today," he laughed a big booming laugh.

I looked at them lying heroically on my floor.

"Yeah, that turned out differently than I thought."

The whole next year after that day turned out differently than I thought, as Matt and I continue to get together for great times. We don't call each other boyfriends or lovers; we don't label it, really. The relationship tells us what we are to each other, not what we call it. And, as for having the peak human experience and dying a happy man, I am learning that there are many peaks, and I won't so much die a happy man, as live as one.

Mushroom

Trebor Healey

We called him Mushroom. Well, actually, we just called him
Mush. For short. And it didn't have anything to do with oatmeal or
fungus. It was his hair. He had an afro. If you were walking behind
him, he looked like an atom bomb that had just gone off. That's
how he got the name.

Social Studies class fifth grade. TJ, the wise guy—who always
sat in back—blurted it out as the teacher tried delicately to explain
the tale wherein America dropped Little Boy on Hiroshima in 1945.

"Wow," TJ suddenly said as Mrs. Edelman ran the film and we
all watched the A-bomb go, like the speeded-up photography of
bean plants and flowers a year ago in science class.

Larry—that was Mush before the nickname—was sitting in the
front row directly ahead of TJ, who was four desks back.

History is a collection of moments. So it is with our names. And
TJ said it:

"Holy shit man, Larry's head looks like a fucking mushroom
cloud. Check it out!"

"TJ, you'll have to leave if you can't be quiet. And I won't have
that language in my classroom!" Mrs. Edelman commanded.

But as the cloud rose on film, TJ added: "It is the lesson, Mrs. E.
We got an atom bomb right here in our class. And look," as he
pointed at the film, "it's getting taller, just like Larry! His whole

---

This story appeared originally in *Addictions,* 7 (April 1998): 9-10. Used
with permission of the author.

fucking body is it. He's a walking atom bomb, a fucking mushroom cloud!"

"Stop it!" she screamed. And he did, and so did the projector. "This is no laughing matter!" she shouted.

"It sure ain't," TJ added as she led him out of the room.

And the name stuck. Like mush to the bones.

Larry was a cute boy. I knew I wasn't supposed to feel that. But suddenly I did. All 200 megatons of him. I felt it all, drop, detonate, explode.

It was a powerful crush that kept getting worse. And this was sixth grade. It occurred to me one day that I'd be in junior high next year with these guys, and we'd have to take showers during PE. I was terrified. I was larified. I wanted to see Larry, but I was afraid.

Of course I ended up in the same period of PE as Larry. I had pretty much avoided him, and all the others, all summer. They didn't understand, so they called me Sometime. "Where's Sometime at?" TJ'd call out. I was hard to find. But I hung there like a bomb dropping out of the sky. If I'd had a nickname for TJ, the busybody that he was, I'd have called him Ground Zero. Point of Impact.

Physical Education. Like a soldier, I took it a day at a time. Hoped I'd make it through that locker room alive. The steam and the skin of it. But I didn't, as a hell of a lot of soldiers don't. I fell apart that first day of PE. I ran out of the locker room when it happened. Like a nuclear wind I blew. I ran into people in the doorway, I was moving so fast. I could have planted their shadows on the wall. I was blind with fear, with power, with love. I was on fire. Fireball.

I'd seen Larry. It all hit me at once, like they do.

Larry took off his shirt, Larry took off his pants. Larry stood there in his jockstrap and he looked at me next to him. I hadn't begun to change out of my clothes. I had just stood watching him, wondering what the hell was happening. I wanted nothing more than for him to be naked next to me. I wanted nothing more than to get naked and be with him naked too that way. I didn't know if to cry or to shout or to roll up in a ball with fear and terror. I just stood there with his gaze fixed on me.

I'd heard of homosexual panic. What was this—homosexual paralysis?

"You wanna see it don't ya?" Larry said softly. And he grabbed the front of his jock and plumped it with his hand. "Don't ya, you wanna see my cock?"

I said nothing. He turned around to get something in his locker. I saw his beautiful ass then, all strapped in to that jock. He grabbed the straps and snapped them.

"Well?" he said.

I was struck dumb, stupefied with beauty, fear, and surprise. What was Larry doing?

And then he pulled off his jock, and I swallowed. My mouth must have dropped open. Larry had a beautiful, big mushroom-headed cock in a mess of hair as black as an oil refinery fire.

He plumped it again.

Then he threw the jockstrap in my face and walked away, tying his towel around his waist.

That's when I ran. Blind and driven as the wind. Knocked a kid over, smeared his shadow on the wall for good. My head full of fusion, fission, fire, and Larry. This side of crying, that side of a scream. Somewhere in that maw in between.

Hit daylight with his cock in my mind, his body wrapped me like a sky. All the trees in the courtyard beyond were mushroom clouds, people were missiles about to explode.

I was a *Big* Boy now. A big boy.

His cock was that way too. His cock like a mushroom. Standing up, I knew it would be the bomb.

I ran all the way home. I gobbled a bottle of my mother's valium. She found me. I survived. Missed a week of school.

I wouldn't look at Larry. Larry ignored me.

I got a locker somewhere else.

I feared him.
Then TJ said it: "Fuckin' faggot."
The truth.
Like mush.
Sticks to your bones.
The bombed-out crater of being a teenage queer.
Japan lived; so will I.
And a mushroom grows from death.

Vestments

Max Reynolds

I want you to touch your cock while I tell you the story, that is if you're sure you want me to tell it to you. Well, since you asked how a priest, "A good Irish priest," is what you said, got to be such a randy bastard always after other men's cocks, I'll tell you if you want to hear the tale. But I want you to take off your vestments first. Yes, everything—the surplice and cassock—right down to your underwear. Leave that on. Yes, of course it's perverse, but you wanted the story so we have to set the scene, now, don't we? No, I'm leaving my vestments on. One of us has to maintain the decorum of the sacrament here, and it might as well be me since I have what—a year on you? That makes me your elder, does it not? Plus it *is* my parish. You are merely the assistant rector. So you should assist me, should you not, Thomas?

Well here it is, then, the story of how I came to be getting after the cocks of other priests like yourself. I remember it so vividly. Surprisingly vividly, given how many years have passed—what is it, nearly twenty now? It was Holy Week. Really cold and rainy. It still felt like winter, and it had been a particularly hard winter that year. It was bloody cold and wet alright, even though it was April. We would come in through the parish house in a rush, and then run into the vestry, all wet from the rain because then none of us ever carried an umbrella. Umbrellas were for old men and wankers, not toughs like ourselves. We were like a pack of wild, wet dogs, shaking off in the vestry, trying to be quiet. We were supposed to

His Underwear: An Erotic Anthology
© 2007 by The Haworth Press, Inc. All rights reserved.
doi:10.1300/5756_11

be silent once we entered that part of the church, so close to the sacristy, so we'd all be nudging each other, all elbows in the gut and back and sometimes between the legs trying to get someone to laugh out loud or squeal. But there we were, the six of us, stripping off all our clothes and getting into the nice dry black cassocks and crisp white surplices, like the ones you just took off. We knew Father Casey, the parish priest, and Brother Flynn, the choirmaster, were waiting for us to start. And of course, them not knowing we were all standing around there in our underwear, or better yet, stark staring naked.

Yes, I remember it very vividly. So vividly it makes me hard just thinking about it, and it's all I can do to keep my hands off my prick or keep from putting your hands on it for me. You have to understand that the memory of it is the memory of my first of real arousal, real intense sexual awakening. I know it sounds ludicrous now, when I'm thirty-three and have been running my own parish for years, and spent so many of those years endlessly breaking my vows of chastity with you, and other men before you. But back then I was just a poor lad from the outskirts of Dublin with nothing but my desires. They were both what I had and what I had to give up—my desires were what I owned, nothing else, but they were deep and true and even then I knew they were something of value. A gift—from God, to God.

That week was such an intense one—all the sense of urgency that goes with that age added into the intensity of Holy Week and the approach of Easter and the end of Lent, because in Ireland we actually gave things up for Lent. There I was, getting ready to sing for Holy Week and make my Mum and Da proud, all the psalms and plainsong and alleluias vying in my head with tunes from the Pet Shop Boys and U2 and the like and me standing there with some of my best mates wanting nothing more than to grab them each by their wet, white underpants, drop to my knees, and suck their dicks. That's a different kind of passion play, is it not?

I know it's different in America, but you do understand how it was for me, right? The sexual charge and heat that went with those moments? It wasn't only what should have been the guilt and sacrilege of it all, because there was certainly that—except in retrospect it was surprisingly guilt free. Wanting to suck other boys' cocks during the holiest week in the Catholic calendar, and not just wanting to do it but wanting to do it under the very eye of Christ himself as you are standing there almost bloody naked with your mates. Well, that's something.

I'm sure you'd already done it by the time you were sixteen. Had it off in the shower at school with some other boys, am I right? I mean look at you—who'd take you for a priest even now? You look like a cowboy or a sportsman or at the very least someone's personal trainer. Without the vestments no one would guess you were a priest. Lying there, like you are, in nothing but your underwear, you look sleek and sinewy and very, very sexy. That hard-on—so wonderfully big, I might add—certainly isn't the hard-on of a priest. Or shouldn't be. Who'd have thought when you were a teenager that you'd end up in Ireland in this poor parish with me above you during the day and at your knees sucking your cock by night, or laying beneath you with my legs in the air and your stiff prick up my arse? Tell me—you never have told me—what was it like when you first did it?

Okay, let me finish my tale. My Holy Week recitation. No, don't—don't be touching me yet. I want to feel it build, don't you know? I want to feel my prick tight and hard in my underwear, just like ours were then, just like yours is now as I look at you, all stripped off except for those black Y-fronts of yours. What is that about, the black? Is that some American-Catholic fetish? No, I'm not saying to give it up—I like it, I like that black underwear stark against your skin. You could be Irish, you know, with that creamy skin, your black hair, and those gorgeous blue eyes that are the same as all those silly portraits of Jesus that we grew up with, as if Jesus had blue eyes. My God. No. I love you lying there in nothing but those black briefs, especially while I'm still sitting here in my vestments. My but we Catholics do have our rituals and fetishes, now don't we, Thomas? And mine is most definitely about and for other men's cocks.

What if I just stroke you a bit while I tell you this story? I'd like to take it in my mouth, of course, I'd like to run my tongue over the tip and down the sides and take you deep into my throat and let you feel the heat of my mouth and my tongue close over you, let you feel me suck and lick and tease and bite your dick and finger your arsehole, rub against your balls, stroke the inside of your thighs and pump your dick a little with my hand while I suck you until you spurt into the back of my throat, and I come in my own underwear just from listening to you come, feeling you come, tasting you come. But I can't talk and suck your cock at the same time—not and give my story or your magnificent prick their due.

You want me down to my underwear as well, now? Out of my vestments? You want to see the outline of my cock in my pants while I tell you what it was to finally have the revelation of who I was that night in the vestry? Shall I strip for you then? No, I haven't changed much since, despite the twenty years. I was just as tall, but not built at all like I am now, from the weights. None of us worked out then. We didn't have the time nor the inclination. I was just a soccer hooligan, like every one of my mates. My legs were very hard and strong but the rest of me was just a tall lanky pole of a boy—that's what my Da would call me when I'd drag him home from the pub. His arm over my shoulder, he'd say that, "My tall lanky pole of a boy, get me home to your mother and my bed."

My hair was very black then—they called me the milkman's son because the rest were all redheads. I got my mother's eyes—the black coals of the Downeys, she'd call them. Either a saint's eyes or Satan's, she'd say. I'm not sure what she'd think they were now if she saw me here with you like this, two men together—two *priests* together—all stiff cocks and hard bodies and ready to fuck at any moment.

Okay, now it's nothing but the briefs—and no, I'll not be changing from white to black with you. I like the contrast. Why don't you lay on me for a moment while I talk to you. Yes, lower yourself onto me. Harder. Press your cock against me. I want to feel it through the underwear. Yes, it *is* very hot—I like it when there's something between us like this—something keeping me from your cock and you from mine. Teasing us both. I know you · always laugh when I say this, but really, Thomas, this is a sacrament to me. Men, priests, vestments, the Church—they are all part of my worship of Christ, though I believe the Vatican takes a different view of it.

See it wasn't like it is now—all sex scandals and the like. The priests I grew up with offered comfort to the *women* of the parish, if you know what I mean. Boys played with boys and men played with men and priests played with needy women. I've no doubt that there might have been other things happening, but I didn't know about it. We aren't very sexually aware over here, you know, even now. Ireland is the land of late bloomers and closet cases, so even if we knew about ourselves, we'd not know about anyone else. And that was why that night was so important to me, so eventful, if you will. Because I don't think I ever consciously *came* before that week—I mean beyond the waking up in the sticky sheets of a morning. I hadn't touched my own cock till I came, I always stopped before that happened. So that night in the vestry with those other boys was the most monumental of my life at that point.

Come here for a moment and kiss me, Thomas. On the neck. Bite my nipples just a bit. God, you make my prick hard, you make me so hard, you make me want you so much. Put your hand on your cock inside your briefs and stroke yourself against me, against my cock. Just a bit, get yourself good and ready. Tease yourself. Tease me with your hard cock, with the stroking. You want to take me up the arse now? No. Not yet. Almost, but not yet.

So there we were. Six of us—we were choir and altar boys and curates in training, all of us. Jimmy was the youngest. He'd just turned fifteen and Will was the oldest at seventeen, with Donal right behind, and the rest of us—Frankie, Seamus, and me—no, they called me Johnny then—in between. We were all footballers—all hooligans. We all had the voices of angels and the pretensions of our age. I'm not sure why we were all in such an altered state that week, although I am sure none of it would have happened had we not been. Donal's sister had just had to get married a few

weeks before, and we had been sticking up for her and him all over
town, as the gossip flew about. Will's Da had been killed in a
factory accident that March and Will was going to have to leave
school, and he was the smart one, so it was killing him. Seamus's
Mum had gone a bit crazy during a snowstorm in February,
had tried to run away from home, and hadn't been right since. And
there were other things that had pulled us together, things like that—
personal and tragic, really. They had made us close, without us actually telling each other how we felt, in the way kids do now. The
bad things had pulled us together. Tight. We were like a pack—
Donal at our lead. Donal was the sexiest of the lot, though we were
each sweet little toughs in our own way. But Donal was a lean
blond boy with a hard edge; you wouldn't want to meet him in a
dark alley. I don't think I ever wanted anything like I wanted to
bed him. You can't imagine how I wanted him. He tossed his underwear at me one day when we were playing about after a game,
and I kept them, wouldn't give them back. They stayed under my
pillow for weeks until my Mum found them and, thinking they
were mine, washed them. I'd rub those briefs against my cock at
night and imagine what I am feeling with you now. The head of
your cock's wet; it's pressing through my underwear from yours.
I'd take Donal's briefs and smell them and rub them across my
chest and down onto my dick and rub and rub. But I'd always stop.
I never came in those briefs the way I'm going to come in yours.
Maybe we won't wait till I finish the story. Maybe I'll put my legs
up for you right now. . . .

Oh, so now you want to tease me? You want me to finish my
story or finish wanking off your dick? My cock is so hard—touch
it, will you? No—outside, through the briefs, through the cloth. It
feels so forbidden like that, so very forbidden. Sinful. Like you.

So that image—that almost haunting vision—of all of us, standing there, cold and wet, our balls tight to our bodies like we'd been
swimming in a too-cold ocean. A bunch of Irish boys all looking
just a little blue at the lips, and those of us who were naked having
our dicks bright red at the tips, from the chill. I remember all of
it—how we looked, how we acted, how we smelled, how rough

we all were. Just a little pack of wild dogs, young thugs we were then, except Will, who had a bit of the toff about him.

My sixteenth birthday fell three days after Easter that year and I was really full of myself, really feeling the whole grown-up thing, you know? You remember how it was then, how we were so sure we knew everything, even as we were totally clueless about anything? I knew I had been picked to be the priest of the family and I was ready for it. Wasn't resigned. Didn't feel the calling per se, but I felt the pull of the Church and I certainly felt the pull of being with other boys all the time. Nothing ecumenical about Ireland— the women are allowed to arrange the flowers and feed the priests, and that's all they have to do with the Church. Well, that and fill the pews with their drunken husbands.

I'm not sure when my mates and I decided what it was that we were going to do that night, or even if we actually decided it. It was Holy Thursday, and there had been the washing of the feet and the repetition of the Last Supper, like we do here. We had sung the plainsong psalms and Mass, and we had sounded beautiful enough to make our mothers weep. We had stripped the altar bare and removed all the flowers and covered the crucifixes with black cloth. It was all very spiritual and very spooky at the same time, and I think we were all a little in awe of it. Even Seamus, who was the one I'd have said was the most likely to become an atheist, had been taken aback by it.

We were the last in the church, the six of us. We were charged with setting everything up for Good Friday and with preparing Father Casey's vestments, laying everything out. Father Casey— he was an old man by then—had gone off to eat and sleep, Good Friday being a fast day and an arduous one at that. It was a howling rainstorm outside—you could actually hear the wind in the church. After we were done doing what was expected of us, we all just sat down in the vestry, each of us still in our cassocks and all, no one wanting to put on our still-wet clothes and go out into the drenching night. No one talked. All we could hear was the wind and our own breathing.

It was Donal who got up first. It was still all quiet, you see. And he got up—you can't imagine how beautiful he was then, seventeen and everything about him was striking from his blond hair to his strong jaw to his eyes, which were this sharp cat's-eye kind of green. And he just stood and stripped off. Hung his vestments up—all neat and everything—and then he turned toward the rest of us. He was just there in his white underwear, briefs just like the ones I had kept that day that, then, were still home under my pillow. And he had this amazing hard-on. Just huge. And he turned toward us, grabbed his own cock in his briefs, and started to wank it. Not very fast and not very hard but he was doing it alright, and he wasn't stopping.

Now if it had been any one of us but Donal—he was the toughest of the lot and every bit the leader, even Will who was a bit older than Donal would do what he said—we might have laughed or tossed something at him or wrestled him down and pantsed him, but as it was Donal and as it was such an eerie state, we were all in it was like a directive. Frankie stood up and took off his things. He wasn't wearing any briefs, and his cock was stiff, I guess from watching Donal. He leaned against the cupboard, where we kept our things, and started wanking off, although he was doing it with less of a tease than Donal—you could tell he was after coming, and rather quickly, if he could.

I'm not sure why I was the last. I was dead in the middle, agewise, but I think it was all so new and actually really shocking, that I just got into it slow. You have to know that still and all, none of us were talking. It was just the sound of us slapping our own cocks and the wind whipping round the church and the hollowness of the stone ringing back on itself in the storm.

I was close to Donal because he was next to where I put my things, and so when I stood back after I had stripped off, I brushed against his dick. That was when I thought I would come before I ever put my hand to myself. And I guess that was also the action that inadvertently took us all to the next step, because that was when Donal reached for my hand and put it inside his underwear, right on his cock. I thought I would die right there in the church vestry.

He was the first of us to speak after Father Casey left us. All he said to me was, "Pull it, Johnny. Pull it fast, pull it hard." His voice was softer than it usually was, soft and a little short of breath. I could feel just a bit of something spill out of my cock into my briefs, and I wanted nothing more than to give him exactly what he wanted. I'm not sure what prompted me to say what I said to him, because I didn't know about blow jobs or really even understand exactly what fucking was; but there I was, his big, hard cock in my hand—this dick that I didn't even know I dreamed of having in my hands—and I said to him simply, "Is that all?"

They were all watching us then, the rest of the boys. And Frankie, always ready to follow anything Donal did, took Will's hand and put it on his cock, which was too big for his underwear. Will turned toward him and reached over and just pulled the underwear down, releasing Frankie's cock. And then Will dropped to the little bench, and he took his own underwear off and with one hand he was wanking himself and with the other he began to stroke Frankie's balls. And then his fingers moved up the shaft, and then he did something none of us had ever seen; he put his mouth over Frankie's cock and started to suck.

Seamus and Jimmy were off to the side a bit, and they just turned toward each other and traded dicks. Seamus took his hands off his own and took Jimmy's and Jimmy did the same and they were both pulling on each other and feeling each other's balls.

I was there, my hands all over Donal—his thighs, his balls, the thickness of his cock. I said it again, this time almost a whisper. "Is that all?" He was very hot, you could tell, and his hand was hard on the back of my neck, and he kind of pushed me toward his dick and said as he took my cock in his hand, "Let me wank you while you do *that*." And nodded his head in the direction of where Will was sucking Frankie off.

We all heard Frankie come before we knew what was actually happening. I don't think I knew for sure at that moment what it was I was hearing, but I have never forgotten the sound of it and how it echoed through the vestry. If ever I need to get myself very hard very fast I remember that sound—the pure, unencumbered pleasure of it, the sound of experiencing sensual delight for the first time in a guiltless way. I felt Donal's cock stiffen in my mouth when Frankie was coming, and I watched what Will was doing to make that happen. Will never took his mouth away, never stopped sucking, never did anything but lick and suck and swallow and make Frankie come better than he might ever do again in his life.

Seamus and Jimmy wanked each other off to coming almost immediately after Frankie came and the spunk shot onto their stomachs and thighs. If you could say to me, was there a single moment in my life when I knew that I was going to be going after cocks for the rest of my life, it would have been then because I was exhilarated by it. Imagine the chill, harsh weather outside and the frightening feel of the absence of God that comes when we prepare in that week for Jesus' crucifixion. There is real unease among those of us who believe, as I have always done, never wavered in it, that Christ died and rose again. Christ who always seemed so wonderfully accessible to me, who seemed like the kind of man I'd want to know, be close to—not in a sexual way but in a deep friendship kind of way. So there we all were—fearful and uneasy in the manner of the days of Christ's dying—and here is the most explicable example of his love for us, our bodies, our temples of the Holy Spirit. It is not a perversion of either my religion or my sexuality to say that what I felt that night was very much the presence of God and the sure knowledge that God exists. I never felt for a moment that what we were doing was wrong or evil or sinful or any single one of the things that had been inculcated into me. I felt as I do now, that to feel this pleasure—to feel you, Thomas, on me, feel your strong, stiff cock pressed so hard against me right now—is a gift. And I received that gift for the first time on that night.

After Frankie had come, I think his gratitude took over and he bent down to suck Will off in kind, but Will did something none of us would have imagined. He lay down on the floor—right down on the hard wood of the vestry—and pulled Frankie on to him. He spit in his hand and rubbed his arse with it and put his legs up over Frankie's broad shoulders. "Put it in," he told Frankie, and the mere suggestion set Frankie's cock hard again. My hands were still all over Donal, and he was wanking me while I licked and sucked. But we both stopped for a moment to watch this thing we'd never seen before. None of us thought to wonder how Will knew about these things—the sucking, the fucking—we just knew he was the smartest of us and it made sense he would know such things. I—we—never seemed to consider if Will had done any of these things before.

Now, I know the expert way Will opened his arse to Frankie's thick cock means he had indeed done it before, but I don't know with whom or how often, and we never spoke of any of it after. But the excitement I felt as I watched Frankie on his knees, holding Will's legs up over his shoulders, and ploughing his arse, and the intensity of Will's pleasure, the look of ecstasy on his face, were immense. I'm not sure what made Seamus walk over to the two and reach for Will's cock, but he did. It was all Will needed to get off. Frankie up his arse and Seamus wanking his dick, he was coming in a second. His dark red hair thrashed against the floor, and his eyes shut tight as he breathed, "That's it, boys, that's it."

That's when Donal spun me around against the cupboard door and pressed himself against my arse. Not in me, just against me. He reached around and had my cock in his hand and was rubbing his own dick hard between the cheeks of my arse. I don't know if it was what I wanted, or the way I wanted it, but the surprise of it, the feel of Donal's whole body pressing into me, the feel of his hot spunk in my arse as he came so hard into it, was thrilling, and I came almost as he did. He was pulling so fast on my cock while he came that I could hardly stand the pleasure; it was so intense. I'll never forget the sensation of coming in his hot, sure grip on my dick.

It ended much as it started, although this time it was Will who led us. He just stood up and began dressing. We all followed. Nothing was said. As I pulled on my pants, I spied Donal wiping is cock on his underwear, and then sticking the briefs in his back pocket. I had such a desire to grab them and take them with me—a souvenir of that evening, of his touching me, him coming on me, him making me come for the first time.

The rain was still whipping about when we left. Donal left the one small light in the vestry lit, as Father Casey had requested. We were all due back in the morning, in preparation for the Good Friday three hours and Stations of the Cross.

It was such a magical kind of night, you see. It had the effect of solidifying both my faith and my love of men at the same time. I had known for some time that I enjoyed the company of other boys, that I liked watching grown men the way I should have enjoyed watching women. But it was that night that led me to where I am now, lying here ready to offer up my arse to you the way Will did to Frankie. It's such a Christian act, you know, to give of one's self. So, Father Thomas, I want to give you my hot, tight arsehole, I want to give you the intensity of coming into my arse as I squeeze you and pump you and stroke your balls, and make every second of it pure pleasure. I want to give you my spunk against your stomach as I come from you fucking me. Then I want you to wipe your cock on your underwear and give it to me to put under my pillow at night, a relic of you, of fucking and sucking you. I want a relic of you, a relic to hold with me after you have left my arms and gone off to prayer and sleep.

That's the story you asked for, then, a good Irish tale of the buggering of a good Irish priest, twenty-odd years in the making. Now, no more talk, if you please. Let's take that lovely, long American cock out of those tight, black briefs and put it to a worthy cause, why don't we. Later you can tell me how a nice American priest like yourself came to have such sinful underwear. And how many pairs you've lost to men like me. . . .

The Pickup

Kyle Stone

It's late, about 4:30, I guess. I'm walking home from Jamie's place, and I'm wasted. Hours of foreplay, heat and panting frustration. Hours spent watching the man dance for me, in nothing but a thong. Sometimes he'd disappear and then come back in a red dance belt or a leather jock. But he didn't want me to take off my jeans or even unzip them. He wanted me dressed and writhing on the pillows of the huge couch while he postured and pranced, the golden light rippling up and down his muscles, his shaved legs and chest, like living marble. I've waited so long to get this close to the guy I've watched on stage so often, only to watch him stroke himself to orgasm and come through the thin material of the dance belt. He did this several times, and at last, he ordered me to peel down my pants and jerk off in front of him. It took a long time. It was painful and strangely humiliating. Jamie seemed barely interested and wandered off to put on a silk gown, leaving me gasping and shaking as I came all over my hands and his velvet cushion.

So now I'm stumbling through the predawn haze, cutting through the parking lot behind my apartment building. I trip over something. At first I think it's wadded up paper, but something makes me look closer. It's a pair of Jockeys! The recognition sends a small jolt of sexual pleasure through me, and I pick them up. I

This story appeared originally in *Canadian Male,* 4 (1997): 30. It appeared again in *MENagerie,* Kyle Stone, 87-92. Toronto: Baskerville Books, 2000. Used with permission of the author.

look around, feeling hot and jumpy, like I expect the guy who was wearing them to be watching me from behind a car or something. The briefs are dirty, as if a car ran over them, but I wad them up and stuff them in the pocket of my jacket and get on home fast. I can't believe just picking up the thing is making me horny again!

When I close my apartment door behind me the first thing I do is take out the briefs and bury my face in them. I can smell the damp outdoors smell of early morning. I can smell a hint of gasoline and the grimy taste of dirt. I close my eyes and feel the thin cotton in my hands, run my fingers along the wide worn elastic, slide my thumb inside the pouch. Where his dick was. Slowly I bring the Jockeys close to my face and draw in my breath. Is it my imagination, or can I smell a tinge of urine?

My eyes fly open, and I feel like a kid caught playing with himself. But I live alone. This is my apartment. I drop my jacket over the back of a chair, pull off my boots, and pad down the hall to the bathroom. As I piss, I hold the Jockeys in my other hand, wipe my cock with them when I'm done. I peel off my T-shirt and jeans and stumble to my bed, still holding the briefs. I fall asleep inhaling the scent of my own piss and the vague sweat smell of a stranger.

Next day is Saturday and I have a lot of errands to run, boring things to do like shopping for food and dropping in to see my old man in the hospital. He's an okay guy, but we never did talk much. We talk even less now, but I know he likes to see me now and then. Sometimes I gaze at him and wonder if I'll look like that when I'm his age. Will I have anyone coming to see me? Afterward, I go into a bar and drink five beers fast, all in a row. Standing against the brick wall, I lean on my elbow and finally take the time to look around.

The afternoon sunlight shows the dust on the floor and tables and on the pictures of muscular guys on the walls. The few drinkers at the bar are older. There's a group of college age kids by the window, laughing and making fools of themselves. They don't interest me. I see what interests me standing alone in the shadows. He doesn't fit in here any more than I do. He's big, broad-shouldered, rough around the edges. He wears a Greek fisherman's cap pushed back on his thick grey-streaked curls. His boots are scuffed and lived-in and so is the rest of him. When our eyes meet, they hold. I feel his interest, watch his mouth begin to smile. I wait until he crosses the room to my side.

"Come here often?" He smirks.

"Let's go."

"Fine by me." He ambles out the door letting me set the pace. I'm suddenly in a hurry to get him back to my place. We start to walk briskly. In the bright light outside, he looks even better. He's not as tall as me, but he's stocky and strong. I can picture me riding his back. I feel the sweat break out on my forehead.

"Warm, isn't it?" he says. His eyes twinkle.

"I live here," I say. I don't want to get to know to him. He's my fantasy man. I know what I want him to do and it isn't talk.

Upstairs on the fifth floor, we go inside and I pull the drapes, keeping out the sun. It's a studio apartment, and my bed fills half of it. He takes off his boots and pulls off his T-shirt.

"Nice place," he says.

I'm holding the old soiled briefs in both hands, balled up. I knead them nervously, wondering how he'll respond to what I want him to do.

"I want you naked," I say, my eyes glued to his broad thighs and solid ass. What's between his legs doesn't interest me so much.

He shrugs and begins to take off his clothes, dropping them on the chair beside the table. I think he's enjoying this, being told what to do, not having to talk. His body emerges into the dimmed light of the room, sturdy and strong, softly furred on his chest and arms and legs. His dick is short and thick. As he turns, I see a tattoo on his shaved ass. The tattoo is old but it looks like an eagle with a heart in its beak.

I can feel my heart begin to trip faster as I undress, too. I leave on my black bikini briefs as I turn to face him. He's waiting, head cocked as he scratches his furry chest.

I pick up the Jockeys and hand them to him. "Put these on."

He frowns, puzzled, and takes the underwear in his hands. He holds them out, studying the thin cotton, the worn elastic and stretched pouch. "A trophy?" he asks.

"Something like that." I'm getting anxious now, afraid he may object to putting on unwashed dirty underwear. I realize suddenly that without the Jockeys, I don't want the man. I watch, my eyes narrowed, almost holding my breath.

"This is important to you."

I nod.

He shrugs and begins to put on the briefs, leaning against the wall to steady himself. I flash back to when I was a kid, standing outside in the flower bed watching my Uncle Leo through the bedroom window. He was younger than my father, played football for his college team. He was blond but he had the same thick thighs as this guy, the same deliberate way of shoving his feet through the leg holes of his BVDs. I snap my mind back to the present.

"They fit," says my visitor. He struts over to the window, back to the wall. He looks good and he knows it. "So, are we going to do anything or is this just a fashion parade of faded glories?" He tugs at his own right nipple, and I feel an instant response.

I remember my frustration with Jamie last night and move in close at once. I can feel the heat from his body even before I touch him. My fingers wander over his chest, down the soft mound of his belly where his waist spreads comfortably under the old elastic of the briefs. He lets out his breath in a sigh and leans back against the wall, letting me explore him.

Slowly I sink to my knees. My eyes are on a level with his crotch, now. The tracks from the tire spread across the filling pouch like skid marks. Already the man's cock is straining the cotton, pushing out the soiled pouch. I can see it through the slit, dark, throbbing with desire. I put my face right against the briefs, breathing in his musk through the material. Closing my eyes, I conjure up the man who bought these briefs, big and handsome and generous with his body. As I press my mouth against the warm cotton, it's as if I'm going down on two men, the sturdy man from the bar and that other shadow man whose memory still lingers around his discarded underwear.

My tongue slides inside the slit, touching the pulsing smoothness of my companion's cock. He catches his breath, and one big hand drops onto my hair. I shake him off. I want to do this completely on my own, allow my fantasies to roam over both the men who quiver and moan at the touch of my tongue.

The front of the briefs is soaked with my saliva, and my mouth is full of the mingled taste of sweat, urine, and the gritty crust of the parking lot. Under the touch of my hands, his massive thighs shudder. He moans and pushes his legs farther apart.

I slide one finger through the leg hole on the right. His cock jumps and I can feel his hairy balls. My own cock swells painfully, pushing against the black nylon of my bikinis. I pull down the thin black strip, releasing my cock. My other hand snakes between his legs, my finger pushing up into the secret heat of his body. He grunts in pleasure.

"Yeah," he growls, twisting himself against my hand.

But the angle is wrong. The leg band restricts any further penetration and I withdraw my hand, put my fingers to my lips and sniff the smell of his ass.

The man moves then, turning towards my only arm chair for support, leaning against it with his back to me. It's clear what he wants, what I want. I push his head down towards the cushions. His broad hairy back curves in submission. His ass is all mine.

Still on my knees, I gaze at the place where the thin cotton is almost translucent across his crack. I can see a faint outline of his tattoo. Saliva gathers as I lean forward and open my mouth, wetting the material until it gives way beneath the sudden thrust of my tongue. My mouth is invaded by the taste of him, tangy and sour. For a moment the taste of both my shadow man and my companion mingle in my mouth. Then my tongue pushes up into his crack, finds the tight rosebud of his ass and slowly forces it to open.

I can hold back no longer. I struggle up and push my bursting cock through the ragged hole I made. He reaches back with both hands, catching each cheek of his ass, opening himself up for me as I thrust inside. The velvet heat of him sucks me in deeper, deeper. We are joined at one spot, yet still separated by the worn grey-tinged cotton of a stranger's briefs.

We are grunting and moaning almost in unison, now. I can feel the pressure build, and I am not able to hold back. I come and collapse against his wide back. A moment later he comes, without even touching himself. We both slide to the floor.

"Fuckin' A," he says. He's grinning. The front of the old Jockeys is slick with come.

I grin and wipe myself off with my black bikinis. I remind myself to get the Jockeys back before he leaves. I am already thinking of the next time, of the third man who will wear them.

Mystery Man

Rachel Kramer Bussel

Out of all the lovers I've had in my life—and believe you me, there have been plenty of them—Jimmy is the one I will truly never forget. Ah, Jimmy. He was the most amazing lover I ever had, even though I never once saw his cock, never got to gaze on what must surely have been one of the most gorgeous cocks in history, but that doesn't really matter. With Jimmy, my mystery man, I felt every glorious inch of him, got to love him with every part of my body.

I saw him appear first in his bright green tightly packed briefs, changing backstage during a show I helped choreograph. That brief glimpse, the bold choice of color, the way he quickly turned away but then flashed me a killer smile that lit up the room, intrigued me. Men at the theater aren't known for their shyness, and it would seem to me to be a liability amongst a crowd of horny, hungry gay men. But Jimmy was a bundle of sexy contradictions that made me want to unlock the layers of his brain, along with a few other things. He was an actor, an exhibitionist, always ready with a witty line and a flirty smile for the camera, always looking like he wanted to devour whoever he was talking to, male or female, friend or enemy. He sank into his roles as if he himself no longer existed; his entire being changing as he said the lines so casually they became part of him.

I followed him around all night after that first show, wondering why I hadn't noticed him earlier (there was a big cast), until he fi-

His Underwear: An Erotic Anthology
© 2007 by The Haworth Press, Inc. All rights reserved.
doi:10.1300/5756_13

nally let me buy him a drink before kissing me blindly, pushing me against the bar and pressing his beer-soaked lips to mine, and literally making the room spin. Behind his casual façade, he'd wanted me, and I wasn't even upset that he'd made me chase him around and fret that he didn't want me back. His cock pressed into me from beneath his thin shorts; I reached for it, but he pushed my hands away. "Not yet, my love," he said in his British accent. No guy had ever made me wait before. They'd always urged me on, letting me do whatever I wanted to with their cocks, and I'd loved every minute of their indulgence. My hands and lips had tasted unknown numbers of thick, manly cocks, had lunged and lusted and stalked and caressed, but never before had I been rebuffed. For a split-second, I was put out, almost turned away with a pout, but he brought his elegant fingers up under my chin and looked me directly in the eyes, making the room stop spinning, the chatter die down, until it was just his eyes boring into mine. I knew at that moment that this wasn't a passing fancy, a trick cock for a single night. No, this was more than that. His eyes drilled into mine as he slowly pressed closer, pushing my back into the bar, practically branding me with his stare. His cock was now hard and firm as I felt it through the shorts but I knew he wanted me to just stay still, to run the show, and as his eyes continued to melt me, I let him.

He offered up his drink, the tiny, red straw dangling towards my mouth, and I sipped it, like a child. It wasn't a belittling gesture so much as a first step, the gateway drug luring me toward his perfect body. With that same sense of youthful innocence, I sipped the sweet cocktail and looked up at him, willing to do anything he wanted. All of a sudden, I wasn't Paul, the self-assured, flamboyant artiste, full of cocky attitude and an ego as large as my cock; I was an eighteen-year-old virgin again, eyes swimming with desire as I gazed all around me at the wondrous bounty of beautiful men surrounding me the minute I hit New York. Yet Jimmy was different than all those pretty boys; he talked and moved with not so much a swagger as an inherent sense of his own worth. The idea that I wouldn't follow him to the ends of the earth, that I wouldn't eagerly suck his straw, never even occurred to him.

I all but crawled on my knees back to his place, trailing behind him in his glory as he stopped to shake countless hands, while I held mine behind me back and was rewarded with his smiles as he turned around. We got back to his place, and he had me kneel down while he teased me, shoving my face into his lap, letting me lick along the edges of his shorts, then pushing me away. Finally, after what seemed an eternity, but was probably only an hour, he took off the belt, using it to secure my hands behind my back. I opened my mouth, not exactly sure why, and nothing came out. My cock was so hard I was almost worried, didn't want to embarrass myself by coming in my pants, but I was also beyond caring as the worn leather pressed against my hairy wrists, tickling and tingling in a way I'd never felt before. He did a slow striptease for me, taking off his shirt, kneeling down and letting me suck on his nipples, then standing above me once again. He lowered the pants to again reveal those gorgeous forest green briefs that hugged every curve of his hard dick as it bulged in front of me, so near and yet so far. I closed my eyes and went to work, licking along the hot, warm fabric, desperate to taste him. I started to peel back the wet cotton with my teeth, but he pushed my head away slowly. "Not yet." I didn't realize that was his way of saying "Never," and simply went back to licking.

I covered those green briefs with my tongue, licked them until they were entirely dark, nuzzled them and bit them, opening my mouth as wide as I could to take in his balls through his underwear. He turned around at one point, and I bit his ass through the cotton, licking along his crack, wanting to taste him for real. I growled and moaned and sighed, waves of lust pushing their way through me as I felt him get harder and harder under my tongue. And just when my own cock was about to betray me, he pulled away again, left the room, then returned moments later. Before I knew what was happening, I was blindfolded. Only then, my vision safely obscured with the fabric, did I get to taste his actual skin, the heat of his cock so bulging and hard. I had only my mouth, my ever-sensitive tongue and lips, no hands to scroll over the protruding veins or fondle the eloquent balls hanging so re-

gally below, no way to truly touch all of him at once. But oh, I did
my best, slurping and sucking, getting him nice and wet before totally letting go and taking his entire cock down my throat.

I missed being able to look up at him as I did so, to see his face,
eyes either open and staring intently or closed in that most beautiful of torturous rapture. Instead I closed my eyes and focused on
the way his cock stretched my mouth, the way I had to position my
already immobilized body just so to take him all the way down
my throat. Sex with Jimmy was always a challenge, one I was
grateful, even hungry for, but it was never easy. It was never the
kind of youthful, simplistic suck-and-fuck I'd previously taken
for quality screwing. There was no cheating, no tricks, no way to
hurry things along, and no desire to. Instead it was pure sensation,
as I rubbed my face all over his cock, lathered myself in his essence, relished being as close to him as he'd allow. When it was all
over and he'd come, shooting his load down my throat, he hurriedly pulled on his underwear before letting me see him. Sometimes he'd shove a used pair into my mouth, make me growl and
bite it, pulling at it as if I were his pet, and I was. I'd have gladly
crawled anywhere for him, eaten from a bowl, barked or mewed
for him.

In all the time that we were together, he never let me see his
cock. I could touch it, fondle it through his endless supply of soft
cotton underwear, all hues and styles, but always soft and delicate,
molding to his cock in the best possible way. And I could suck and
fuck it, but only with my eyes closed. So when I jerked off by myself, it was to his image. It was him and the most glorious cock I'd
ever seen, the outline it made beneath his underwear enough to tell
me that it was as impressive a dick as I'd ever see. His endless
array of bold designer underwear, rivaling any woman's elegantly
appointed panty drawer, served as his armor. He probably spent
more on his underwear than his outer, though he always looked
good.

He told me he was shy, that he had issues that made him want to
keep his most prized possession hidden, but I didn't believe him;
he was too out-there to be timid. When he first told me his reason-

ing, I thought this meant he'd be a shy, neurotic, sexually repressed soul lurking in the body of an Adonis—a shameful, terrible waste. · But no. Jimmy was the hottest lover I've ever had. What I couldn't see, I could touch, taste, smell, and hear, as he or I stroked his magnificent cock underneath that ever-present shield.

He even let me do his laundry. He would come up behind me and ram himself against me, shoving me into the whirring washing machine, simply pinning me there as the cycles spun—lunk, lunk, lunk—with the precious clothes that couched his cock every single day, caressing him in ways I always longed to. Could I be jealous of a piece of cloth? Yes, if it got to nestle all day next to his most special body part, if it got closer to him than he ever let me. Yes, if it got to know the secrets of his cock in ways I could only hope to. Maybe it wasn't jealousy so much as fantasy; I wanted to be the one he let inside, the one he let down his guard with, the one man enough to crack through his defenses, but I forgot all that when he took me in his arms. He made me feel like the most special man in the world, his one and only, perfect in every way. When I was with him, there was nothing to be jealous of, because he gave me everything I needed.

Jimmy's cock should have been a mystery to me, a hidden piece of meat made even more enticing by its absence, but it wasn't like that at all. I felt like I knew Jimmy and his cock better than any other. He fucked me with a raw passion, a kind of animalistic fervor as he spread me out, usually tying me down to his four-poster bed, tapping his cock against my ass before sliding it inside me, always making me wait until that absolute last second when I thought I'd rather die than go without him any longer. And if ever I tried to peek, twisting my head slightly to get just a glimpse, he'd stop and wait until I closed my eyes again, or blindfold me, or simply stop and let me stew in my own stupidity for a while, sometimes letting me overhear him jerk off in the bathroom.

Of course it was a power trip for him, a way to lord over me the one thing I most desired; it worked perfectly. He even let me take endless photos of him in his special collection, a rainbow assortment of hip-huggers that hardly hid anything. I trained my camera on that glorious ass, the cock that stood so proud, sometimes pushing his underwear, straining its durability as his cock leapt forth of its own accord. When I put them up at the gallery, everyone exclaimed over their depth and insight, the reviews treating them not as pornographic works but as classic insights into the male body.

Looking back though, maybe I didn't know him all that well; maybe what he kept hidden was more than the view from inside his underwear. I'll probably never know, as he left one day, leaving nary a trace, not even a stray pair for me to tuck under my pillow. I have these photos, and the memories, and whenever I'm in a locker room, I don't scan it for familiar faces, but familiar outlines, because I'd recognize his cock anywhere. I haven't given up on finding it again. In the meantime, I've acquired quite the underwear collection and have a new boy of my own who gets to lavish my shorts with his tongue, relishing the other side of this complicated erotic equation, enjoying the air of mystery. When I look at my cock now, it seems to have grown. Whether from pride or secrecy or being worshipped with such reverence, I don't know, but I think I understand Jimmy just a little bit better. I may never be able to fill Jimmy's jockeys, but I can certainly try.

Southern Exposure

William Holden

Before he even reached the store front, Jonathan knew they wouldn't have what he was looking for. No one ever did, outside of New York City that is. Atlanta wasn't his first choice as a place to live. Hell, as far as he was concerned it didn't even make the top 100, but his employer had plans for him. Plans that included moving away from New York, the only city he knew and loved, to spend the next two years of his life in the south.

It wasn't that he had anything in particular against the south, well there were a few things lacking in this part of the country—fine dining, wine and martini bars, and, of course, designer clothing stores. As he moved around Atlanta, trying to acclimate himself to the city, the first thing he noticed about southerners was the clothing that people had for some unknown reason decided looked good on them. He was convinced that the people of Atlanta considered Wal-Mart a designer clothing store; his heart went out to them.

If nothing else, please God, let them have something other than Fruit-of-the-Loom underwear on underneath those things. He shook his head at the thought, as he approached the store. He peered in through the window at the underwear display, at what was considered one of the finest male underwear boutiques in the city.

A cold chill went down his spine as he looked at some of the brands they sold. Brands he would never allow to touch his skin. To the left was a portion of a skinny, metallic colored mannequin

His Underwear: An Erotic Anthology
© 2007 by The Haworth Press, Inc. All rights reserved.
doi:10.1300/5756_14

sporting an obvious roll of tissue behind the 2(x)ist briefs. Scattered around its missing legs were other styles: the bikini, the boxer, and the most hideous of them all, the thong.

Standing proudly to the right was yet another brand that Jonathon considered a sin to even think about wearing, the Eros line—which left nothing to the imagination. The style of this line of underwear completely exposes the wearer's front using what appeared to be fish netting.

Jonathan was a true believer in the underwear as art—art that hides the true nature of sensuality and sex appeal. If you could see what your date was packing prior to the sacred removal of the underwear, well that just killed the moment. Even more intolerable were the men who didn't wear any underwear. He just didn't understand it. Jonathan liked nothing more than to explore and caress what his men were hiding from him, to tease and tantalize his men and their urges before removing the last article that revealed it all.

He was tempted not to go in at all. There was nothing in the window display that was remotely acceptable to him. Suddenly he noticed a shadow in the window reflection. He looked behind him then realized the shadow was a man, coming towards him from inside the store.

"I couldn't help notice you eyeing the merchandise," the clerk said as he stuck he head out of the door. "I'm closing in fifteen minutes so if you want to come in, now is your chance." The clerk's eyebrows lifted slightly as he made the invitation then suddenly he was gone—back inside the store.

Oh, what the hell, Jonathan thought to himself. *Maybe this guy can tell me where to go for the real thing.* He turned and walked into the store.

"Let me finish up here and I'll be right with you." The clerk smiled as he returned to the customer at the counter.

Jonathan wandered around the store looking at the displays of half naked mannequins sporting larger than usual packages. He walked over to the 2(x)ist display and rubbed his fingers over the material of one of their t-shirts. "God, how awful," he muttered to himself, as his fingers caressed the ribbed fabric, "and with these prices, you'd think they were selling imported fabric." He rubbed his fingers together as if to clean them after touching something dirty. He jumped as he heard the door shut behind him.

"There, sorry for the wait." The clerk's voiced echoed in the empty store. "Now, what can I help you with?" He walked up behind Jonathan and ran his hand around Jonathan's waist till he was facing him.

"I'm not sure if you can," Jonathan replied, a little agitated by the clerk's closeness. He stepped back to open the space between them. "I've just been transferred to this city, and I'm looking for a place where I can buy some decent underwear."

"Well, look around you; we've got it all."

"Yes, I see." Jonathan cleared his throat. "I don't think you quite understand. You do have a large assortment, but I'm looking for something . . . oh, how should I put this? Higher class." He looked around eyeing the merchandise. He began to suspect that he made a mistake by coming here. "I mean really. Do people actually wear this crap?"

"Well, I do try to provide a full variety of products." The clerk closed the space between them once again. "I'm Chad, by the way. Maybe if you tell me more specifically what you're looking for, I can provide you with what you need."

"Jonathan." He reached out and shook the clerk's hand. Chad's grip was firm, not at all what he would have expected from this serious retail queen. His arms were exposed and covered with black hair. Chad reached up and ran his fingers through his long black hair as the silence continued. Jonathan's eyes glimpsed a small damp spot under Chad's arm. Several strands of dark hair from Chad's armpit poked out of his shirt sleeve. Jonathan's annoyance seemed to falter and then fade away. He took a deep breath before speaking.

"I'm sorry. It's obvious that I've come at a bad time, with you getting ready to close." He looked around the deserted store. "I don't want to waste anymore of your time."

"No, not at all," Chad spoke quickly. "I'm not in any hurry. This is what southern hospitality is all about." He reached up and placed his hand around Jonathan's shoulder. "Now, what can I interest you in?" Chad placed a little pressure on Jonathan's shoulder to get him to follow. "I noticed you were looking at the 2(x)ist display. Did you find anything that interested you?"

"I don't particularly like the way they fit. I much prefer underwear that is slightly more form fitting and that's made of a quality material that allows your skin to breathe." He paused then quickly added, "It also must have a lot of support." With that comment, he noticed Chad's eyes quickly glace at his crotch with a raised eyebrow.

"Well, then. Let's get busy and find you something you like." He winked and then proceeded to walk to the back of the store. "These are some of our more exclusive lines. We keep them back here because most people tend to go for cost rather than comfort or style." He knelt down to pick up a couple of packages lying on the floor.

Jonathan's eyes watched as Chad's shirt pulled up his back exposing his tanned skin. A small patch a black hair covered the area at the center of his waist just above the crack of his ass. Jonathan's finger's twitched at the thought of touching it. Then he noticed the waistband of Jonathan's underwear. His eyes widened as he saw the brand name etched in white against the black fabric—HELMUT LANG. He reached down and tugged on the waistband of Chad's underwear, a small smile crossed his lips. "This, this is what I want."

"Oh." Chad stood up quickly from the surprise touch. His eyes beamed with excitement. "Oh, you mean the brand of underwear, don't you?" He adjusted the waist of his slacks.

"Well, that is what you're selling, isn't it?" He raised his eyebrows as he began to enjoy the playfulness of Chad. He stood there for a moment waiting for Chad to show him what they had available. The room was silent. "Well, do you sell Helmut Lang or not?"

"Of course I do." The tone in his voice was still pleasant. "They're over here in the back corner."

Jonathan followed him over to a smaller section of the store tucked away in the corner. To his left were several cubicles · enclosed by light weight curtains. To the left of the fitting rooms, white plastic torsos displayed the full line of Helmut Lang underwear, including some Jonathan had not seen before. He was immediately impressed by Chad's careful selection.

"Will this do?" Chad questioned with a smirk.

"Wouldn't it have been easier to just show me this area right from the beginning?"

"Easier yes, but not as much fun. So what can I interest you in?" He walked over to first display. "As you can see I have a full range to please the most demanding of tastes." Chad turned and once again closed the space between them.

Jonathan noticed Chad's eyes moving quickly up and down as if mentally taking down his measurement by sight alone. He stood motionless to let Chad admire and size up his body. He enjoyed being admired; after all, he didn't spend all that money at the gym for nothing.

"Okay. Let me check your waistline for proper fit."

"I don't think that will be necessary. I've always been an exact thirty-three."

"Now, now, it doesn't hurt to be sure. If you could just lift up your arms a bit?"

Jonathan decided not to argue and raised his hands as asked. Suddenly, he felt Chad's hands grasp his waist, squeezing gently. "Hmm," Chad mumbled to no one in particular. "Are you sure about that waist size?" I'm reading a thirty-five."

"Yes, I'm positive."

"Well, I'm going to have to ask you to take off your shirt, just to make sure. I don't want to sell you underwear that you will be unhappy with." Chad stood back with a gleam in his eyes.

"You want me to remove my shirt, right here?"

"Sweetheart, we're alone here. No one is going to see you," he paused briefly, "except me."

Jonathan began unbuttoning his shirt and watched Chad's growing interest. He decided it was time to give Chad a taste of his own medicine. *If this southern queen thinks he can out do a New York queen, he's got another thing coming.* A smiled crossed his lips as he pondered the competition. He finished removing his shirt and tossed it to the ground.

"Oh, you do have a nice body," Chad commented as he walked toward Jonathan. "Now, let's try this again." He, once again, placed his hand on Jonathan's waist. "Hmm, gee I guess you were correct after all. A size thirty-three you are, and by the look of the waistband of your underwear, I'd say you were a brief guy. Strange."

"What's strange?"

"I would have pegged you for a boxer man."

"Well, actually, I prefer the boxer brief. As I said before, I like a lot of support, and that style seems to give it to me." Jonathan knew this was his opportunity so he decided to take it. "Is there another style you would recommend for someone who needs that extra support?"

"Well, I'm a brief man myself, always have been. So if it were up to me, I'd be putting those around your waist instead of the combination."

"Is that what you're wearing right now?"

"Yes, but. . . ."

"Why don't you show me what yours looks like, and let me see the kind of support it provides you? Who knows, maybe you'll be the one to change my mind." He paused as a look of discomfort appeared on Chad's face. Then added, "You know, kind of model them for me." A small grin crept across his face. "You do want to make a sale, don't you?"

To Jonathan's surprise, Chad's discomfort seemed to melt away as quickly as it appeared. He didn't hesitate to do what the customer had asked. Jonathan leaned against the edge of the fitting rooms and watched as Chad pulled his black shirt out of his pants, and then up over his head. As Jonathan had seen briefly before, Chad's skin was a light bronze. His upper body was firm, without a lot of muscle. His chest was covered with black hair, obviously recently clipped. His nipples were smaller than what Jonathan would have expected for Chad's body type. As the shirt came up over his head, Jonathan noticed the thick patches of dark hair that covered each armpit. Some of the hairs were damp with perspiration.

He continued to watch as Chad removed his shoes and then began the ritual of removing his skintight pants. Jonathan was sure he would have trouble getting out of them, but they came off as easily as the shirt. Chad's briefs were black and hugged his body beautifully. *Of course,* Jonathan thought to himself, *they're top of the line.* A smile came to his face as he walked over to get a closer look.

"Well?" Chad questioned. "What do you think?"

"I'm not sure." Jonathan rubbed his chin as he walked around Chad's almost naked body. Chad's ass was rounded and firm; dark hair trailed out of the leg bands and continued down his legs. Jonathan stood in front of Chad again and noticed that the bulge in Chad's underwear appeared larger than it did a few minutes ago. Jonathan, too, was aroused as he stood admiring Chad's body. *This,* he thought, *is what the art of underwear is all about.* He walked up next to Chad. He could feel the heat coming off his body. His hand reached down and touched Chad's hip. He felt Chad's body quiver at his touch, as he stroked the smooth material of his underwear. "Hmm. Not bad." He placed his index finger inside the band of Chad's underwear and tugged gently on them. He caught a brief glimpse of the darkness of Chad's crotch. "I'm not really sure about these, the material that is. I prefer something with a little more texture to it. Do you think you could try on a pair of the white ribbed ones for me?"

"Well, I'm not usually in the business of modeling what I sell. Besides, it's a violation of the health code, here in Atlanta, to let anyone try on the underwear."

"Don't worry about the health department I'll make it worth your while." He reached into his wallet and pulled out several one hundred dollar bills. "There are eight of these so I can more than pay for any damages to your merchandise. So, are you going to try on the other pair for me?"

"Sure, whatever you want."

"Good. Now, may I see the white ribbed design please?" He watched as Chad scooted around the display case in nothing but his underwear and socks, looking for what he requested.

Chad approached him with several boxes gathered in his arms. "If you don't mind, I'm just going to slip in this changing room for a minute."

"Not a problem." Jonathan replied while he held the curtain open for him, and then carefully closed it. Jonathan watched the silhouette of Chad's body through the curtain. The large thick shadow of Chad's cock bobbed up and down as he removed his underwear. Within a few seconds Chad was pulling up the underwear Jonathan had requested, but before he could step out of the changing room, Jonathan stepped in.

"I assumed I would come out to you."

"Why bother." Jonathan spoke with a slight edge in his voice. "Besides, this way I can use the mirrors to see you—well, rather the underwear—from various angles." Jonathan peered into the mirror that was facing Chad's back. "Hmm, these do seem to hug the ass firmly. I like that in my underwear." He reached around Chad's body and cupped Chad's left ass check, his thumb moving up and down the thin material. "Yes, very nice." He slipped his index finger under the leg band just over the first knuckle and ran it along the side and up towards the front. He could hear Chad's breathing getting heavy. He slowed is finger down as he began to feel the mass of pubic hair. As he pulled his finger out he brought with it several dark strands, which poked out of the leg band. He stood back and admired the contrast of Chad's jet black pubic hair against the brightness of the crisp, white underwear. He felt himself getting harder and looked around the room at the unopened boxes scattered on the floor. His erection grew. "I'll definitely take two pairs of the one you have on."

"Is that all?" Chad questioned him as he leaned back against the mirror and crossed his arms.

"Well, now that you mention it. No." He knelt down on the floor and began rummaging through the unopened boxes until he found what he was looking for. His heart rate picked up as he held the box in his hand. He pulled the underwear out of the box and held · them up for inspection. They were his favorite—the boxer brief. Solid black, ribbed fabric with the HELMUT LANG name etched in white around the waist band. He held them to his face and took a deep breath of the clean, unsoiled material. He could feel the softness of the cotton against his skin, as if every thread was caressing him. He stood up, ignoring the thickness of his cock in his pants, and handed the new pair of underwear to Chad.

"If you wouldn't mind trying these on for me, I'd really appreciate it."

"No. Not at all." Chad moved his hands down to his waist to begin removing the current pair of underwear.

"What are you doing?" Jonathan's tone was more accusatory than he meant it to be. "You can't just undress in front of me."

"Excuse me?"

"It would spoil everything." He turned his back to Chad and closed his eyes from the mirrors. "There, this will have to do." He could hear Chad directly behind him doing as he was asked, but continued his ranting anyway. "As a boutique owner, you should be better at reading your customers than that." He paused, waiting for a response. "You should know by now, how important the visual effect of the underwear is for me, respect that, and make sure you satisfy me by not exposing yourself—"

"If you're quite finished, you can turn around now."

Jonathan stood silently for a moment, as if shocked that someone would cut him off, and then opened his eyes. His eyes widened as he turned around, his breath stopped as he looked at Chad, in his stunning new pair of underwear. He moved his hand unconsciously to the front of his pants and rubbed the palm of his hand against his cock, which now reached down into the leg of his pants. He felt a chill run through his body as a small amount of precome dampened his underwear and skin.

"Well?"

"They're perfect!" Jonathan looked in the mirror to his left to get a profile view of Chad in the black underwear. His eyes leisurely ran down Chad's body and stopped just above the waist. He turned his head to get a better view and noticed how well the black boxer briefs hid the size of what Chad was carrying. He knew Chad was well-endowed; he could sense it, feel it—and that's exactly what he intended to do.

He knelt down in front of Chad. His eyes focused on the contrast of the black underwear to Chad's skin tone. He could smell Chad's scent, mixing with the clean smell that only new underwear are allowed to have. He reached behind Chad and placed his hands on Chad's ass, feeling the firmness hidden underneath the cotton. He became lost in the softness and comfort of the moment. Chad's voice echoed softly through the air, but his mind couldn't register the words.

He brought his face closer, resting his right cheek on Chad's cock. The heat warmed his skin. He closed his eyes and thought he could hear Chad's heartbeat running through the veins of his hardness. He moved his head up and down, feeling the length of Chad getting longer still. His tongue came out and began running across the fabric leaving a trail of moisture behind.

"Jonathan, your mouth. . . ."

Chad's voice faded in and out of his head as he continued to caress each thread. He began to notice a salty taste to the fabric as his mind began speaking for him.

Yeah, Chad, that's it; get this underwear wet. He began to suck heavily on the damped spot. His words in his mind blended and mixed with Chad's.

"Oh. Yeah. . . ."

Give me more. His mind pleaded

"It feels so. . . ."

I need more. The thoughts ripped through his mind. He opened the fly in the underwear and slid his tongue inside. The scent of Chad's heat rushed into his nose. The moisture was sweet to the taste. His tongue ran through the wet tangles of Chad's pubic hair and along the shaft of his cock. He could feel the body tremble against him as his tongue found the tip of the cock and circled it three or four times. He inhaled deeply and pulled the entire length of Chad into his mouth. He gagged briefly before settling down into long, slow strokes. He could hear Chad gasping and moaning, between words, words which still didn't register with him. His face and chin were becoming wet with spit and precome. He tilted his head to the left and the right to dry them on the underwear, and then stood up.

"Don't stop." Chad's words finally broke through.

"Shh," Jonathan placed his hand over Chad's mouth. "Don't spoil this with needless words." The hot, thick air surrounded his naked torso. He ran his hands over his own chest and felt the dampness of his skin mixing with the hair on his chest. His nipples became erect with his own touch.

Suddenly, he became transfixed on the images in the mirrors, as he realized they were not just two, but eight. He watched himself and his three look-alikes as they removed their pants. He caressed the white briefs feeling his own dampness inside. The look-alikes did the same. Moving in closer he began stroking Chad's cock. The wetness returned at once. He kissed him, their tongues meeting for the first time. Peering out of one eye, he noticed the others in the mirror kissing each other as well. He admired their bodies and wanted each of them.

He reached into his own fly and pulled out his cock. It hung heavily between his legs. Noticing the others staring at it he began playing with it—teasing them. Jonathan became obsessed with the others. He wanted to watch as each of them fucked the other.

Reaching behind him, he grabbed ahold of the material of his underwear and tore a small hole. The sound pierced the silent room. His heart jumped with excitement. He leaned up against the center mirror, facing his twin. They winked at each other.

Jonathan watched as Chad slowly advanced on him, his cock swaying with every step. He could feel the head of Chad's cock rubbing the wetness around his ass, as if oiling a tight door. Jonathan looked directly ahead and watched as his twin grimaced with the initial entrance. He turned and looked to the left as the slow steady moments began. Chad's black underwear wet and sticky clung to his white briefs with each inward thrust. His head turned to the right, and watched as their look-alikes fucked. Black and white, then black on white, then white on black. The contracting colors swarmed around him as the pressure built inside.

The air smelled of sweat and sex as their bodies continued to work together. The images in the mirrors seemed to blur and then regain focus. Jonathan could feel himself getting close to release. The only sounds in the room were their heavy breathing.

Jonathan looked into the eyes of his twin and he began to stroke himself. A smile crossed their lips simultaneously as the sweat dripped off their forehead. They began to pant, Chad and himself, or maybe it was all of them, he couldn't distinguish one from the other. The pressure built to an almost painful point. Jonathan through his head back and released his load into the mirror, it met his twin's come head-on and then dripped down the glass. Suddenly he was filled with a warm rush as Chad came. He felt the weight of Chad's body collapse against his, their hot sweat dampened bodies stuck together.

Chad tried to speak as they dressed, but Jonathan had to quiet him. There were no words to be spoken here. Not now. He quickly gathered up several pairs of underwear and headed for the counter. He stood behind it and pulled a bag out to hold his purchases. He kissed Chad gently on the lips and handed him a hundred dollars. "This should cover it." He left the store without another word. As he turned the corner out onto the sidewalk, he pulled out a black address book. He flipped to the letter *M* and crossed off the name of the store he had just left.

"Well, which store should I visit tomorrow?" He muttered to himself. A smile crossed his face as he looked down inside his shopping bag at Chad's soiled underwear. "That will make a great additional to my collection."

Three Places in New England

Simon Sheppard

Boston

It was the day that same-sex marriage became legal in Massachusetts. When he showed up at my hotel room, the same footage was playing for the umpteenth time on the TV news: happy couples doing their happy couple thing.

"Hello," he said. He was, as advertised online, a handsome, preppy man. Nothing extraordinary: neat blond hair, clean-shaven face, and—as prearranged—nice suit.

"Sit over there," I said.

"Jacket off?"

"Not yet."

He sat down, looking mildly apprehensive. I clicked the remote and got the happy couples the hell out of the room.

I walked over to the seated stranger.

"Spread your legs."

He did. I stood between his thighs, the crotch of my black Levi's just inches from his blandly presentable face.

"Look up at me."

He did—clear gray eyes.

This story appeared originally in *Ultimate Gay Erotica 2005,* ed. Jesse Grant, 106-115. Los Angeles, CA: Alyson Publications, 2004. Used with permission of the author.

I slapped his face. Not hard, just hard enough to gauge how much harder I could go.

His gaze was unwavering.

I reached down and unbuttoned my fly. My cock, when I pulled it out, was already stiff and, as it always is, thick.

"You want this, faggot?"

"Yes, I do."

"I beg your pardon?"

"Yes, I do, Sir."

"That's better. If you want my cock, you'll have to do just exactly what I say."

"Yes, Sir." An even tone of voice, like he was selling insurance. Homeowner's, not life.

I slapped his well-shaved cheek with my cock, just once, and then backed up. "Okay," I said, trying to sound as calm as he did, "stand up and start undressing."

"Yes, Sir." He rose to his feet.

"There's a hanger over there for your suit. Let's not see you making a wrinkled mess."

He removed his suit jacket and placed it carefully over the hanger. When he reached for his tie, I said, "No. Shoes and pants first."

"Sir." He kicked off his highly polished black loafers. Black socks and not, I was happy to see, the sheer sort. He unbuckled his belt, undid the button on his pants, and pulled down the fly.

"What are you waiting for?"

"Sorry, Sir." He pulled his pants off, folded them over, and put them on the hanger with his jacket.

He was wearing, as had been arranged, Brooks Brothers boxer shorts. Nothing fancy, just plain white cotton: banker's boxers. Boring. Perfect.

"Now stand there. Turn around, show me what you got."

In his shirt, tie, shorts, and black socks, he looked faintly ridiculous, the way half-dressed men can. He was obviously excited; the front of his boxers was stretched over a hard dick, his shirttail pushed aside by the bulge.

"Okay, shirt and tie now."

His chest was nice, lean and chiseled, almost hairless, just little thickets around the nipples. He folded the shirt as best he could, fumbling a bit nervously.

"Get back in the chair."

He sat back down.

"Spread your legs."

His cock was just barely restrained by his boxers; I could spot a glimpse of blood-engorged pink through the gapped fly.

"Is this right, Sir?"

"Yes. Don't move."

I walked over to the bedside table and pulled out the drawer. There, next to the Gideon Bible, were the coils of rope I'd placed there, and a pair of scissors.

"Put your hands behind the chair," I said.

He did, making his chest swell out a bit.

I walked behind the chair, coiled rope around his vulnerable wrists, and then tied it off with a square knot.

"What do you say?"

"Thank you, Sir."

"Damn right."

I knelt at his feet, peeling off one sock, then the other. His feet were large. And beautiful, as feet go. I tied one ankle to a chair leg and repeated the operation on the other side.

I stood. He looked up at me, our eyes meeting for one long moment in mutual challenge, desire, surrender. I looked away, went to the drawer, and brought back the scissors.

I knelt down between his spread legs, pair of scissors in my right hand. I drew my left palm over his chest, tweaking a nipple till he moaned in pleasure, then down further, over his lean belly, down to the waistband of his Brooks Brothers boxers. I ran two fingers along the line where flesh met elastic, then over his right hip, careful to avoid touching his straining cock through the cloth. I reached the hem of one leg, sliding my fingers up under the expensive cotton.

I opened the scissors, sliding one blade beneath the cloth, hard steel against soft flesh. I looked up at his face. He was gazing intently down at me. This was the scene, a scene he said he'd never tried before. His hard dick radiated heat.

"Now," I said. I half closed the scissors, sharp edges cutting through the white fabric with ease. Then, with a final decisive stroke, I closed the blades, slicing most of the way up the boxers' leg. I took the scissors away. The cloth fell back, exposing upper thigh, muscular, sprinkled with light blond hair.

I moved to the other side. This time the cut I made was shorter, only partway up. Then a second cut, parallel to the first. I was taking my time, slicing slowly, slowly through the underwear. I went back to the right leg, cut a chunk of fabric off. It fell to the floor. I laid the closed scissors down on his slightly trembling thigh.

"Fucker," I said. "Fucker." I thought about his hard dick, his tender balls, just barely hidden by the tattered, white cotton. "I should feed you my cock," I said, stroking my hard-on. "I really should."

"Whatever you want, Sir."

I stood, looking down at the man, a businessman, a man I would never know, whose name I would never know. He was tied up in a chair, clad only in a sliced up pair of boxer shorts that barely hid his swollen prick. Yes. I would feed him.

"Open."

I guided my hard-on between his lips. He was a decent cocksucker, nothing more. But then, that's not what this scene was about. And I was getting close already. I pounded into his mouth a few more times, then withdrew and got back to business.

Kneeling back down, I opened the scissors and deliberately, so slowly, slid one blade into the fly, the blunt edge rubbing up against the flesh of his cock. When the blade was most of the way in, I closed down the scissors. The double fabric of the fly resisted, then gave way. The middle of his shaft was exposed now, the base and head still covered by fabric. I went back to work on the legs, slicing them both up to the waistband.

Now his crotch was nearly bare, covered merely by shreds of underwear. My dick was drooling. I opened the scissors all the way, laid one blade on the exposed dick flesh, gliding the sharp edge over skin.

"Oh, God," the man said. He shifted slightly, pushing up against the metal, just enough for the cloth to fall away, for the head of his cock to be exposed. It was an average-sized head, an average-sized cock, circumcised, but his piss slit was a big one, nearly bisecting the head. I cut away the rest of the cloth, exposing his balls. His businessman's underwear were in tatters, hanging from the waistband.

I rubbed the edge of the scissors over his balls, up his shaft, taking care not to cut into flesh, but coming close. Closing the blades, I ran the pointed metal down between his thighs, pressing the hard steel into his perineum. Keeping the metal tight against his vulnerable flesh, the point dangerously near his asshole, I bent over and took his clean-cut cock into my mouth, the first time I'd touched it. It took less than ten seconds for him to come. There was a lot of load; either he hadn't come in a very long time, or he was a big shooter.

I leaned back, moved the scissors from between his legs and sawed through the elastic waistband of his shorts. The fabric fell away, and he was completely naked at last. I stood up above him, grabbed at my cock, and jacked off quickly until I spurted sperm over his trim torso. When I recovered, I pulled the tattered boxer shorts from under his butt, using the remnants to wipe my cum off his flesh. Then I knelt, sliced through the ropes around his ankles, and cut through the rope binding his wrists.

"Now, get the fuck out of here." I lay back on the bed and watched him get dressed, hurriedly but precisely. When he was clothed, he looked at the sliced up boxer shorts in my hand. "Should I take those?" he asked.

"Nope," I said, "I'm keeping them. Souvenir."

New Haven

I was in a diner near the Yale campus, having a burger, when
the boy at the other end of the counter caught my eye. He was tall,
even sitting down I could see that. And handsome looking with his
buzz-cut hair, huge mutton-chop sideburns, and a hooded black
sweatshirt—a little hip and a little threatening.

He was hunched over, the way very tall people sometimes sit,
digging into a triple-decker sandwich. I finished my meal and
headed, check in hand, for the register. As I passed him by, he
glanced up at me and smiled. He said, "You've been looking at me,"
but his expression let on that he didn't think that was a bad thing.

He was a musician, not a student, he told me on the way back to
his room. He was, as I'd suspected, really tall—six foot six or
seven, at least—and I had to look up to talk to him. I began to feel
like a youngish father peering up at his basketball-playing son.
Who knows, maybe passersby thought I was just that.

His room was comfortably barren: some bookshelves, a bicycle
propped in one corner, a few band posters on the walls, a placard
lying on the floor that read NO WAR FOR OIL. He caught me looking at it. "There was a demonstration last week," he explained.

I looked up at him. He laid a hand on my shoulder. "Okay?" he
asked. I nodded, and he pulled me toward him. He bent over to
kiss me, his lips soft and yielding. He wasn't, manifestly, as tough
as he looked. I was beginning to think he was, in fact, rather sweet.
I put one hand on his ass, firm through his baggy pants, and slid
the other between us to his basket, a foot higher than my own.

"Let's get in bed," he said. It was a mattress on the floor.

Lying side by side, we explored each other's faces, tugged at
each other's clothes. His newly bared chest was just a little fleshy,
a sprinkling of hair on the pecs, a treasure trail leading down past
his belt line. I fumbled with his pants, got them open, pulled them
halfway down. I was expecting boxers, maybe plaid, but my touch
found briefs instead.

He broke free of my grasp and stood awkwardly so he could un-
tie his boots and pull his pants off. The briefs were utterly ordi-

nary, Fruit of the Loom whites. They'd seen better days; there were a few holes.

Lying there half-naked, I looked up, way up, at his handsome face and felt content. I got to my knees and pressed my face against his briefs, wrapping my arms around his thighs. The briefs weren't too clean, either; they smelled faintly of sweat and pee. I found that sexy. I found him sexy.

"Wait a minute," he said.

I waited.

He turned away from me, folded his long body till he was kneeling, his butt perfection in tattered white briefs. "Want to smoke some grass?" He'd already picked up a bong and was loading it up.

"Sure," I said, though I rarely get stoned with tricks I've just met. He took a big lungful of smoke and passed the bong to me. The dope was good; by the time I exhaled, I started to feel the rush.

He took another hit, then held the bong in my direction. I shook my head, and he placed it and the lighter back down on the floor.

Fuck.

The tall young man sighed and laid down on his back, hands behind his head, stretching out, eyes closed. The white briefs clearly showed the outline of his swollen dick. There was—already—a spreading stain of precum. I extended a stoned hand, laid it on his belly, just above the slightly unraveling elastic waistband. He sighed again. I slid my hand further down, feeling the comforting onrush of senseless lust. At that moment there was nothing I more wanted to do than touch that almost-naked boy. My palm moved down, over the waistband, to his crotch. I pushed against his cotton-clad dick; his hard-on pushed back. I cradled his cock in my hand, feeling the warmth of it burning through the cloth.

"Suck it," he said. "Suck it through the briefs."

"My pleasure." I bent over and rubbed my cheek against his basket, precum damp against my skin. He began to hum something. I turned my head, put my mouth on the bulge of his cock, opened up, took the shaft between my lips. His underwear needed a washing, and I could taste the faint tang of seeping precum; I was in some stoned heaven.

At that moment—you know how your mind wanders when you're having stoned sex—I imagined him carrying that placard and shouting slogans, his head towering above the other demonstrators, the spring sun beating down on his handsome face. I chewed gently on his cloth-wrapped prick.

"Here, let me suck you for a while." His voice was coming from a long, long way away. In a few clumsy moments, I was on my back and he was kneeling over me, my dick in his mouth. I reached over to his butt, stroked his ass, my eager hand against tight cloth. Then I slid a couple of fingers beneath the waistband, stroking the topmost flesh of his naked ass. I maneuvered my whole hand inside. His cocksucking became more intent. I cupped a palm around one ass cheek, the briefs stretched over the back of my hand. His butt was surprisingly hairy.

"Fuck," I said, because his mouth felt good. "Fuck." I tugged down on the back of his briefs until his ass was mostly exposed, then ran a couple of fingers down the crack till I felt the warm pucker of his asshole. He let me play with his cunt for a few moments, but when I began to press inward, he pulled away and scooted around till he was lying facedown between my legs, his mouth still on my dick. From my position, propped up against a wall, I could look down on him, his body so long that half of it was hanging off the foot of the bed, and watch his furry butt pumping up and down as he humped the mattress, his well-worn underwear still half on, still covering, I presumed, his hard dick.

"Take it all the way down your throat," I suggested, though I wanted him in my mouth again, too, this time his cock naked. Actually, I wanted it a *lot*, and when I thought about peeling down his briefs, licking the precum off his wet cock, just the thought of that unexpectedly sent me over the brink. The impulse was unstoppable, that warm itching that says, *I'm gonna come.*

I said just that—"I'm gonna come"—to give him a chance to pull off his mouth, but he didn't, just pumped his ass up and down, harder, faster. It looked so great—the back of his buzz-cut head, his long, lean back, furry ass, line of white cotton across his upper thighs, legs that went on forever, down to his real big feet. And then that familiar warmth shot through my dick and I was, once again, shooting off into a stranger's mouth.

He kept my dick all the way down his throat, milking the last few drops of cum with his throat muscles, showing me what a good cocksucker he was. Then he let my softening dick slide out of his mouth and lay there, his head cuddled against my damp crotch. Sweet. To look at him in that diner, you wouldn't have suspected he'd be that sweet.

"So you want to come, too?" I asked after a minute or so. He didn't say anything, just raised himself to his knees. There, dead center on his white cotton crotch, was a big, wet patch of cum. Fucking hot.

I leaned over, pulled down his briefs. His dick was an ordinary one, medium sized in its deflating state, with a nice, fat foreskin. I leaned over, sniffed at his cum, licked it off his half-soft dick flesh. Yeah, I loved that foreskin. It went with his sideburns, somehow.

When I was done kissing and licking at him, he stood up, all six-foot-seven of him, let the soaked briefs fall to the floor, and stepped out of them. Still very stoned, I reached over and picked them up. The cum was slick against my fingers.

"Mind if I keep them?" I asked.

His handsome face looked puzzled.

"Souvenir," I said.

Montpelier

When I got home, Ken was still awake.

"Hi, honey. How did the trip go?"

"Went fine. I'm just beat, though."

"I know what'll perk you right up." He undid the belt of his bathrobe, let the robe fall to the floor.

He was wearing a bright turquoise thong. "See what I bought while you were away?" He turned around like a model, showing me his smooth, beautiful, gym-built butt.

I liked Ken, loved him. I loved the way that he, a self-proclaimed total top, fucked my ass. We'd been registered domestic partners for about a year. After I told him a few months back that underwear turned me on, he started buying new stuff to wear. I didn't have the heart to tell him that the nylon pouches and brightly colored thongs he brought home—though most people might think them sexy—reminded me more of some Vegas bimbo showgirl than of a guy I'd want to fuck me.

"You like? Glad you like." He ran his hands over his butt, suggestively. I wasn't sure just why a total top would want to show off his ass as much as Ken did. "Give you any ideas?"

I put down my luggage, held him, and kissed him gently on the mouth, his soft, full Eurasian lips. "Sweetie," I said, "I hardly got any sleep last night, and the flight has left me really exhausted. We'll fuck tomorrow, okay?" My hands ran down over his back, down to the waistband of the thong, to his muscular ass.

"Sure, hon. I understand." Ken didn't sound disappointed. At least I think he didn't.

After he padded upstairs to bed, I fished a plastic bag out of my suitcase, went into the downstairs bathroom, and locked the door. There was a paperback Tom Clancy lying on the hamper; Ken liked Tom Clancy. I turned the book facedown.

I pulled down my pants; my dick was already half-hard in anticipation. I opened the plastic bag and pulled out two sets of underwear: the shredded Brooks Brothers boxers, and the tattered briefs, funkier than ever now with its crust of dried-up jizz. With one hand, I rubbed the shredded boxers over my hard-on while my other hand held the briefs to my face, my nose buried deep within the smell.

It didn't take me very long to come.

Not for Long

Jeff Mann

Summer has left before you. A few weeks of drought, a few
cold nights, and between one lovemaking and the next the heat has
receded, the leaves have started to brown. This morning I notice
these deaths as I drive to work. And as I study the mountains, I ask
myself why my love for the land—the comfortable earth that out-
lives and receives us—can be so diffuse, so serene, while my love
for men—ephemera of body hair, beard stubble, biceps and nipple—must be so sharp and maddening.

All about me autumn has arrived: purple tidal pools of iron-
weed, goldenrod's funeral flowers, frowsy road-edge foxtail grass.
By the New River, golden leaves are congregating along the limbs
of sycamore and box elder. Signs of age, like this early silver on
my temples. The sunflowers edging garden plots seem exhausted,
bending their weary necks to earth. I recognize despair. I recognize resignation before the guillotine.

For adulterers, every touch is furtive, hasty. If only I'd met you
first. A few afternoon rendezvous stippled across one summer is
what our timing has allowed. And now all the green we shared de-

---

This story appeared originally in *The Harrington Gay Men's Fiction Quarterly,* 3(1): 127-131. It appeared again in *Best Gay Erotica 2003,* ed. Richard
Labonté, 229-232. San Francisco, CA: Cleis Press, 2003. Used with permission of the author.

generates. The rain's brief pointillism blurs my windshield, medians of redtop grass rush by. Stratus clouds collect, inside and out.

In the office, I check my voice-mail. Nothing. For a week, you have not called. Any day now you and your lover, diplomas in hand, will nail down jobs, load up a U-Haul, and drive off, heading for God knows which city and state. Just when I am convinced that you have finally bolted, that even with you old patterns and new cowards assert themselves, you appear, grinning reprieve in my office doorway.

My officemate, teaching Southern literature this semester, bends over *A Streetcar Named Desire*. I tap on the office next door, which belongs to my friendly colleague Ethel. "May I borrow your office while you teach?" I ask. "I have a confused and upset student, and we really need some privacy." She smiles, nods, and heads off to class. I lead you in, turn off the lights, lock the door.

"Romeo and Juliet, Tristan and Isolde, Edward and Gaveston, Jeff and Thomas," I joke, pulling you to me. On this campus there are, for us, no other safe square feet. Any open touch of ours might heap us with scorn, real and metaphoric stones, the swing of pipes, steel edges that would end your beauty in an instant. All summer I have scrabbled together these rare and risky borrowed spaces, these hasty privacies. Outlawed fusions in secret niches, the double stigma of gay adultery. Only here do our bodies exist, our kisses petal into possibility.

Seconds after the lock clicks, I have your T-shirt tugged up around your neck, your jeans jerked down about your knees. My fingers dig into the hard curves of your biceps. My face nuzzles your chest hair, the cleavage-cloud of fur still moist from the gym shower. I clutch you close as Antaeus did the earth.

Our moustaches mash together, tongues stretched and wrestling to their limits, and still we graze only the shallows, we taste only the surface of each other's darkness and depth. "Priapus," you mutter. "Mephistopheles," I whisper, between mouthfuls of musk and mercy. Soon you will be leaving the room, the town, the state, and I am ravenous in the face of famine, all my frame shaking as you unbutton my pure white professorial dress shirt and touch my chest with what appears to be the silent and studious wonder every inch of you evokes in me. We never know what is mutual, what myths we embody, what myths our lovers stroke.

I want to beg, "Stay, stay!" but instead stifle speech with your cock, with your nipples, with the furry mounds of muscle over your heart. I take as much of your body into mine as I can.

At last we pull back before release. You'll have no chance for another shower before you meet your husband, and he's grown suspicious, having smelt extramarital musk on you before. Seconds after we've buttoned and zipped up, the backwoods janitor, without a knock of warning, unlocks the door and ruckuses in to empty the trash.

I am teaching freshman composition three doors down the hall in half an hour, and you have to head home. In the hallway, just before we part, you say casually, "Oh, I have something you want." Tugging open your backpack, you hand me a package. A quick visit to the men's room to wash my scent from your moustache, a blithe wave at the end of the hall, and then you are gone, dissolving around the corner into memory.

All that denseness of muscle, that softness and ripeness of pubic hair against my cheek, the spill of preseminal sap in my palm like liquid moonstone. One second there, and now suddenly only images stored inside some wrinkle of my brain, the neurons' weak chemical hold on history. How many trysts have we left, I wonder, how many meetings more and more difficult to arrange? When we make love one final time, will we know that touch must be the last?

On my fingers, in my beard, the scent of you still lingers, my lips still sting with stubble-burn. Summoning my usual composed facade, I return to my office, where my officemate continues to re-read *Streetcar*. I borrow the paperback for a moment and, on a whim, read the epigraph out loud—my favorite Hart Crane stanza:

> And so it was I entered the broken world
> To trace the visionary company of love, its voice
> An instant in the wind (I know not whither hurled)
> But not for long to hold each desperate choice.

I return the book, then silently behind his back I open the box you left. Amid gift paper, white jockey shorts. I touch them. Still moist with workout sweat. A few stray hairs. I press the fabric to my face.

It is time for my freshman composition class. While I am teaching, defeated leaves, dry with drought, drop outside my classroom window. As I discuss the fine points of comma splices, the lurking dangers of mixed metaphors, I lift my left hand to my face, ostensibly to smooth my beard, and breathe you in, the vestige of your musk.

Not long after the seedtops of redtop grass comes first frost. You can stay no more than summer could. Back in my desk drawer, from your jockey shorts the sweat evaporates. From my fingers, your aroma fades. *Collect what relics you can,* derides autumn. *You retain nothing.*

Long Johns

Dale Chase

The California gold strike stirred talk in the bunkhouse one night, some of the men ready to give up herding cattle, call themselves miners, and set out for the west. As I listened I began to consider such an adventure but then Tom Call came in and began to undress.

My prick grew hard by the time he had his boots off, because I knew what the undressing would come down to. He would strip of all but his long johns, then unbutton the seat flap, let it drop open, and leave it that way as he took coffee from the pot on the stove in the center of the room. He would linger there, open to the rest of us, and I would wonder again at his reason. Was he truly drying things out, as he said early on when questioned about the practice, or was he one of those men, like me, who appreciates a man's bottom?

At night, when all were abed, there would be sounds among the men, some unmistakable as hands found pricks and muffled grunts told of spewing seed. To the best of my knowledge there was no outright bottom fucking, although Tom Call's display made a man think on it some. I confess that after his showing himself like that I abused my own swollen prick and had a good spend, sometimes two, while recalling that open flap and the pink bottom it framed.

I knew a part of my arousal was born of childhood when I happened upon a cowhand behind the barn in naught but his long

His Underwear: An Erotic Anthology
© 2007 by The Haworth Press, Inc. All rights reserved.
doi:10.1300/5756_17

johns, rear flap down to expose his bare bottom to the fully clothed foreman, who had his pants open to free his cock. And the cock was soon pushing in and out of the cowboy's bottom.

My own young prick stiffened at the sight, and I held it as I watched one man do to another what I had seen bulls do to cows, dogs do to bitches. Boys at the schoolhouse had spoken of a thing called fucking, offering that a man put his prick up a woman to get relief much as the animals did. When it was humans in such acts, it was a fuck.

I had tried to apply this logic to the scene before me but as it was two men, I was not sure it right. But they did seem to be seeking relief, and as I watched them, I sought the same, freeing my boy prick, playing with it the way Pa had forbid. And I felt wonderful urges as I fixed on that dropped flap and the bared bottom.

What begins in childhood often carries forth to adulthood—so I have been told—and I found this true as forever after I became aroused with the sight of a dropped flap. In time, the arousal came when I merely saw the buttoned flap, my imagination alone dropping it down to present the bottom.

By the time I was grown, I had experienced my own flap down, having been taken by a cowboy after being lured to the bunkhouse midday. I was eighteen and ripe, as he said, and I must confess to going willingly into the empty cabin. The first thing I saw was a pair of long johns hanging on a line to dry. The cowboy saw my interest, at which he immediately stripped himself of all but his own pair. I saw the bulge at his front, him drawing me to it as he rubbed the thing. He said I must likewise undress and when I stood as did he, he felt my stiff prick, then unbuttoned me and held it.

I quickly spent on his front and this amused him, the sight of my young squirts while he pulled at me. When I had finished, he turned me around, and I felt him unbutton my flap, dropping it down. "Trap door," he growled as his hands spread my buttocks, and I felt his prick push at me. "Let me in, boy," he said, and his thing began to push into my bottom hole, which caused me much pain but which also got my prick up again.

The cowboy fucked me hard and quick, issuing grunts as he put his cock in and out, then became urgent and cried out while I · felt his spunk flush up into my bowels. When he had finished, he pulled out, and I expected him to dress but instead I felt him kneel, felt his hands pull me open again. And he began to lick me in the way I had seen dogs lick themselves, and it disgusted me as it aroused me. He slurped and grunted as if feeding and then he put his tongue up me. I could feel his mouth pressed to my bottom as the tongue wiggled in my passage. Finally he let go, sat back. "Turn around, boy."

I turned and he fixed his gaze on my prick, which was wet and ready to expel again.

"You got a good one," he said. "You ever have you a fuck?"

"No."

"But you abuse yourself in bed at night, spend into your blanket, do you not?"

"Yes. Many do."

"You are a man now," he said, standing. He reached back and unbuttoned his flap, let it drop, then turned to show me his bottom. I could not help but issue a gasp, such was my excitement at the sight, and I thought back to that early encounter behind the barn where I had watched a cock go up a man. Now, having had it done to me, I was at last being asked to do it to another. I ran a hand down the long johns, felt the coarse wool, then the hot skin as my fingers reached the opening. "Put your cock into me," the cowboy said. When I hesitated, he ordered that I do it. "Put the damn thing up me!"

I did as asked, wetting my cock with spit, poking it at him, then pushing into his passage. Looking down at what I was doing, I took note of the trap door opened to me and felt a shudder rush through my body, gather at my prick, then spurt into him. I became urgent in all this, giving him a hard thrusting which caused him to say all manner of nasty things about fucking.

When I had emptied, I withdrew from him and he bent forward still more, pulling open his buttocks. "Have a lick," he growled. "Go on, get yourself down there and taste it."

This I could not do. When I made no move, he rose and turned. "You are young," he offered. "One day when you have had many a fuck, you will find yourself driven to still more, as am I. It is then you will lick a bottom hole."

With that we dressed and said nothing more of it, although for as long as I stayed on that job he would, when he found me alone, have a fuck. Now, as Tom Call finished his coffee, he set his cup on the table, then stretched his body as one does after a long day in the saddle. He issued a good sigh, as if now satisfied. When he caught me looking, he grinned, turned, and reached his hand down to his bottom where, as he scratched himself, a finger crept between the buttocks.

Tom did not engage in the talk of the gold strike. He declared it folly, said his day was ended, and climbed into his bunk. He made no move to cover himself but lay on his side, bottom bared to all. As I kept my eye fixed on the sight, his arm moved around front, and I knew he had unbuttoned himself to get at his prick. While others declared riches to be had out west, Tom quietly pulled on his cock, and after a time, I saw the buttocks clench and knew he was squirting. After this I sought my own bed, where I did the same.

Debate continued among the men about the gold rush. Opportunity was said to be there for any man willing to take his chance and embark on the great adventure. I thought of this as I sat astride my horse the next day, tending the cattle, but my look at opportunity was colored by the sight of Tom Call nearby. Though clad in his rough trousers and chaps, I could not help but think of him baring himself in the bunkhouse, and I took pleasure in recalling the image which, of course, made my prick stiff.

It was such rumination that led me to be thrown from my horse. Pondering Tom Call's bottom, I failed to see the rattler and my horse reared unexpectedly. With my hands loose on the reins, I was tossed into the air and fell hard on the ground.

For a brief spell, I could not gather a breath and became much agitated. It was Tom Call himself who came to my aid, got me settled enough to take in air. He then prodded my middle and declared my ribs bruised or broken. "He should be taken to his bed," Tom said to the others.

The foreman allowed this, asked Tom to see me back to the ranch. Movement was difficult, as was drawing a breath. We said little, neither the talkative sort, and once inside the bunkhouse, I welcomed my bed. Tom eased me onto it and took off my boots. "You'll recover in a day or two but the soreness will remain a while," he said before he turned and left.

I could not find comfort in my bed, such was the pain, but after a time I managed to make it bearable. It was as I lay hoping for sleep that my eyes looked about the room. All was familiar yet Tom's presence had made it new in some way. As I gazed on a rope strung to hold clothes to dry, I saw long johns I knew to be Tom's. They hung with backside to me, the trapdoor down, and I filled it by imagination.

My prick grew hard and I thought to abuse it, but it then occurred to me I might have more. So with some difficulty I rose from the bed, went to the underwear, put a hand to it, and felt up and down, as would I the man himself. Much aroused by this, I freed my prick and pulled at it while my other hand went into the opening of the long johns.

I could only imagine a man therein, but it sufficed and I stroked my cock with vigor. When I felt a climax near, I wrapped my prick in the flap and squirted into the opening. Thus, in my own mind, I had a fuck with Tom Call and I will say it was a good one.

When evening came and the men returned, it was Tom who saw to me. He brought me a plate of supper, then later helped me undress. As my trousers were set aside and I was left with only my long johns, Tom sat beside me. He assured me once again that I would fully recover, and as he spoke, he put a hand to my thigh.

None of the other men noticed, as all were engaged in a card game at the other end of the room. Tom said once more how I would feel better, and his hand traveled up my thigh to rest on my cock, which now stood hard. He rubbed it a little, which caused me to squirt. He knew well what he was doing and after. When he stood at his own bunk, undressing, baring his bottom as he always did, I wondered if he knew I had soiled his underwear.

I lay beneath my blanket and watched him do as usual, all with trap door open. When he bent down to look for something under his bed—something he failed to find—his bottom was thrust at me, and I'll swear the buttocks clenched as if to speak to me. My hand, already on my prick, had much to do.

When Tom rose from his searching, he looked at me and I saw his prick was up. He then became most bold. As we were back where the bunks sat and all the other men were up front at the table, we went unnoticed. Tom unbuttoned a bit of his front, pulled out his cock, and stood as if to show me. It was a big thing, befitting a man such as he. After he had displayed it for a time, he looked to the others and, finding them busy with their game, came to me with the prick, put it to my face until he got me to open my mouth, at which time he put it into me.

I had never had a cock in my mouth but instinct told me what to do. I seized the thing and began to suck it, and he began to thrust at me, squirming inside my mouth as I pulled on him. He then became urgent, took hold of my head with his hands, and I felt him squirt warm spunk into my throat.

I swallowed what he gave me, and when he was done, he pulled out, held the thing for me to see, squeezed out a few more drops. When he nodded, I knew to lick him. After that, he turned without a word, climbed into his bunk, and slept. Of course he did it without covers, bottom bared, and I was left to abuse my cock once again.

It was four days before I climbed back onto my horse. The foreman would have made it two, but Tom Call convinced him of my need to heal. During those four days, Tom Call continued to bare his bottom to me, and when he had discovered my desire to spend into his long johns, he allowed his extra pair into my bed. I slept with my cock wrapped in them, and when they at last went into the wash, they had many places stiff with dried spunk.

Back on the range I remained sore but was able to work. Tom looked after me and would on occasion ride near me and pass a look that told of his need. And then one day when I had ridden off into a valley some distance away in search strays and stopped to · free my prick for a piss, I turned to find Tom watching, still astride his horse.

"Leave it out, boy," he said. He then dismounted and came to me. "I am in need, and as the others are far away, I mean to have a fuck. Take off your clothes."

With that he removed all but his long johns and I did the same. My cock still poked out the front opening. Once attired in just our underwear, Tom made a show of unbuttoning his trapdoor and letting it drop open. He turned to let me gaze upon his bottom, and he played about it with his fingers until I issued a long moan. Turning back to me, he got behind, opened my flap, and immediately put his prick up me. He began to thrust with urgency, grunting as would an animal, and seconds later he spurted into me in great quantities, crying out as he did so. When he was finished, he remained in me, grinding his prick into my passage until it at last began to lose its stiffness. He then withdrew.

I held my cock, aching for relief. Tom eyed it and grinned. "I'll take your cock," he said. He turned and bent, pulling apart his buttocks. When I hesitated, surprised that he would make such an offer, he commanded, "Fuck me, boy. Give me your prick."

I got in behind him and allowed my cock to play up his hairy crack, looking down at his bottom framed by the underwear. It so aroused me I felt a climax rising and so I relented, looked away, and saw cattle nearby looking at us with curiosity. I then returned my attention to Tom, took hold of my prick, and guided it into his hole.

He welcomed me with a clench of his muscle, and I felt by the ease with which he took me that he was well experienced at being fucked. "Do it boy, give me a rough one!" he called out, and so I set about thrusting very hard, which made the climax arrive all too quickly. "It's coming!" I cried and the squirts began. I allowed myself all manner of sounds as nobody was around to hear, and as I spent inside Tom's passage, I considered it the best I'd ever had.

As he had done with me, I remained inside him until my prick went soft, enjoying the sight of us connected by prick and bottom. I never wanted to forget the sight of him bent to me, taking me as he had. When I pulled out, Tom closed his underwear and I did likewise. We dressed in silence and got back up on the horses. As I sat I felt his warm spunk drip out my hole, and Tom must have felt the same.

Our monthly pay was given us the following day, and all the men rode to town. Tom kept beside me and, after a time, said we should share a room. While others did this to save money, I knew Tom's reasons were different. The other men succumbed to card games and whores, while Tom and I had a bath in our room. My prick grew hard at the sight of him in the tub, but he wouldn't let me put it in him then. He finished washing and stepped out, then I got in and washed myself.

As I washed, Tom took clean underwear from his bag and put it on. He did this slowly, with much deliberation, as if making a show of it. I held my cock while he buttoned up his front but left the trapdoor open. When I was out of the tub and dried off, he told me to get down on my knees and lick him. "Lick my hole," he said, parting his buttocks. "Wet me, play about my bottom. You'll have a fuck, but not just yet."

Still naked, I did as told and when his hands let go, I took hold of his bottom and pulled it open. There was hair at his hole and I knew it to be the dirtiest of places, never mind he'd washed.

"Lick it," he commanded and I did it, running my tongue up the crack then settling onto the puckered thing. This caused him to say base things about the practice.

I found I liked getting my face down there, and the sight of his underwear framing his bottom made it all the better. My cock drooled below, such was my arousal, and as I became more urgent, I did the awful thing; I put my tongue into him.

"That's it!" he called out.

A bitter taste met me but I found this mattered little, as Tom encouraged my efforts and thereby made it most gratifying. "Lick my bottom," he said. "Lick me where your prick will go. Have it up me; lick the dirty hole."

He held his prick while I worked his backside, and at last, breathing hard, he allowed me to stop. "That's enough, boy. Fuck me now. Give me your cock."

I was much relieved to do as asked, because even though I liked having my face at his bottom, I preferred my prick there instead. So once again I had the pleasure of fucking him while standing, gripping him at the waist as he bent to me, bottom alone bared. I called out when I squirted and as soon as I finished, he pulled off, turned, spun me around, and gave me a good fuck in return.

After this we climbed into bed and he took me into his arms. We then slept the night. At dawn, he woke me with a prodding cock. I had remained naked, while he still wore his long johns. I reached back to feel the organ poking out his front.

As he put it up me and began to fuck, he reached around for my prick, which was hard out. "You can have your fuck soon as I'm done," he said, but he took some time to let go, during which I couldn't hold back and spent a fair amount into the bedding. I could not hold my tongue any more than my spend, and I said base things about fucking until he let go a roar and spurted into me. At last we quieted. He withdrew his prick and we fell into a heap. A drowsiness came over me, and when I told Tom I desired sleep, he agreed. But before he settled to it, he turned his back to me, allowing once more the sight of his bare bottom.

I put a hand down there, at which he issued a moan. I then rested my head on the pillow so that my last waking thought would be of his bottom.

We drifted toward slumber then and I thought myself truly happy. Tom spoke softly, "All that talk of the gold fields in California. You have no plans toward them, do you?"

"None at all. Here is where I shall stay."

The Boxer Thief

They arrived at the house in Alabama in the late afternoon. Though Dylan spent many years living with his mother in Texas, he still thought of his father's home in Huntsville as *their* home. This simple two-story brick house was where they lived as a family. Back when they'd spend Saturdays at the space museum or go up to nearby Monte Sano State Park. Back before his mother packed up and left, only getting in touch with his father when she'd secured the services of a lawyer.

Above the house's detached garage was a studio apartment, and since Dylan's junior year of high school, his father let him live up there. Dylan had expected to do the same now, during his summer break from the University of Tennessee. But this year someone else would be living there. During the long drive from Knoxville, Dylan's father told him he'd rented out the apartment.

"But . . . you *promised*," Dylan whined, sounding more like a five-year-old than a college sophomore.

His father, Jerry, exhaled a frustrated breath. "I *know*, but I made that promise before I had to spend six thousand to put a new roof on the house and another fifteen hundred for the truck's transmission." He pounded the old Ford's steering wheel. Dylan could feel his father's anger rising and pressed himself against the passenger door, prepared to jump if necessary. "Top it off," Dylan's father said hotly, "they're starting to lay people off at the plant. I'll be lucky if I have a goddamned job by the end of the summer!"

His Underwear: An Erotic Anthology
© 2007 by The Haworth Press, Inc. All rights reserved.
doi:10.1300/5756_18   *145*

Both men were quiet, Dylan feeling like a selfish bastard, his father staring out the windshield at the unending interstate cutting through the rocky Tennessee mountains. When Jerry spoke again, his voice was soft, his words contrite. "Look, I'm sorry I had to break my promise to you, and sorry I didn't tell you before now. I just got used to you spending summers with me. Afraid if I sprung the news any earlier, you'd change your mind."

The part unspoken: *And stay with your mother.* Dylan's parents got divorced when he was in junior high, yet they still tried to compete for his favor—even more so now that he was past age eighteen, and he, not the courts, decided which parent he spent time with.

Jerry reached across the pickup's cab and gripped Dylan's shoulder affectionately. "But just 'cause you're staying in the house doesn't mean you got to act like you're a little kid. You can come and go as you please, no questions asked. You can even bring girls up there if you want. As long as you're quiet." His dad was wearing sunglasses, but Dylan was sure his father winked at him.

"Yeah, all my women," Dylan snorted, then looked away.

No other vehicle was parked in front of the house or on the driveway when they arrived. "Our tenant's not here, it looks like. Or is he car-less, like me?" Dylan remarked, rancor creeping into his voice.

"Probably not home. Works for a landscaping service, does a lot of weekend work," Jerry replied as he pulled into the driveway. He ignored the car-less remark.

Once parked, the two men set to carrying Dylan's belongings into the house. Hugging a box to his chest, Dylan looked up at the garage's second floor, at the apartment that should've been his. His eyes narrowed into a resentful scowl, as if it were the apartment's fault for allowing itself to be taken by someone else. His resentment intensified when he deposited the box in what was to be his summer home: a bedroom that barely had enough space to contain its furniture. *Like his dorm room at UT,* Dylan thought bitterly. At least he didn't have to share it with a perpetually stoned education major.

Dylan had just set his portable TV on top of his dresser when he heard a car door slam. He stepped out into the hall and heard his father's hearty greeting from outside. Wondering if the new tenant had returned, Dylan went to the window at the end of the second floor hall, the one overlooking the driveway. Although he was inclined to dislike the man who'd displaced him, Dylan was curious to see what he looked like. Jerry had offered few details. "He's a young guy," he said, and left it at that. But then, Dylan couldn't expect a more elaborate physical description. It wasn't like his father would say: "He's cute and you should see his *ass!*"

Out the window he saw another pickup parked beside his dad's—also a Ford, but older and a lot more beat up. Gardening and lawn care equipment—power mower, hoes, shovels, assorted rakes, bags of fertilizer—filled the truck's bed. Standing at the front of the truck was the new tenant, talking with Dylan's father. The trucks obscured the tenant from the waist down, but what Dylan could see more than piqued his interest.

He was shirtless, showing off muscles and a tan cultivated by his profession. The tenant's face was attractive, at least from what Dylan could see from the second floor window, framed by a mane of brown shoulder-length hair, streaked gold by the sun and hanging in sweaty tendrils. Overall, he looked more like a surfer dude than someone who'd waste his time with a mere job.

A closer inspection was necessary. Dylan raced down the stairs, but stopped to compose himself before stepping out the kitchen door. Had to appear casual. Didn't want to seem like some thirteen-year-old girl with a crush, not in front of the tenant and especially not in front of his dad.

When he opened the door, he heard his father say, "Talk to you later." Anxious to get a close-up view of the renter before he disappeared inside the apartment, Dylan walked out of the house in long, purposeful steps.

"*There* he is," Jerry said, as if he'd been searching for his son. "Hey, Preston, let me introduce you to my son."

The tenant was no longer standing in the driveway, but was half-way up the staircase hugging the side of the garage. Dylan got the briefest of views from behind—*cute butt*, he thought—before the renter turned. He cut a nice figure, standing on the steps with the casual grace of a runway model. Even the dirt-stained, olive green cargo shorts he wore hung from his hips *just so*, with the gray waistband of his underwear showing. There was a hole torn in the upper left thigh of the shorts, exposing white cloth under-neath and answering the boxers or briefs question. The cargo shorts fit loosely, but they weren't baggy, showing off a signifi-cant bulge at the crotch.

"Dylan, this is Preston," Jerry introduced, breaking Dylan away from the mound at Preston's crotch. "He's renting the apartment."

"I gathered that," Dylan replied dryly, trying to soften his sar-casm with a tight grin. Giving Preston a more genuine smile, Dylan said, "Nice to meet you."

"Hey, there." Preston raised a hand, giving Dylan a two-fingered salute, twisting his wrist as if pitching a ball. In his other hand, he carried a twelve-pack of Corona. As if suddenly reminded of his manners, he quickly added, "Good to meet you, too." His voice was deep, with an easy-going drawl that suggested that Preston was a laid-back kind of guy. Or that he was a big-time pothead.

Dylan found himself hoping he'd be invited up for a beer. He knew such an invitation was unlikely, but he was still crestfallen when Preston quickly turned his attention back to Jerry and said, "Well, you guys take it easy." Getting to know his landlord's son was low on the renter's list of priorities.

Dylan watched Preston continue his ascent, staring at the rise and fall of his ass, wondering what it looked like bare and feeling his cock tingling as he formed a mental picture. He did not turn away until his father said, "You going to help me finish unloading the truck, or just stand there?"

Dylan hoped his father didn't notice the coloring of his face, or that the front of his shorts poked out. "Sorry," Dylan muttered as he walked over to help his father, tugging the front of his T-shirt in an attempt to hide his protruding crotch. "Lost in thought."

After that first meeting, Dylan devoted much of his time to monitoring Preston's comings and goings. The garage was set back from the house, and Dylan had a perfect view of it from his bedroom window, which faced the backyard. Whenever he heard Preston's truck in the driveway, its engine coughing loudly after the ignition was switched off, Dylan went to his bedroom window. He'd watch Preston—usually shirtless and sweaty—climb the stairs to the studio apartment, admiring the body he had yet to see at a distance less than forty feet.

Dylan's voyeurism was further encouraged by the fact that Preston seldom, if ever, closed his blinds. Most times, though, Dylan would stare out his bedroom window and just see lights on in the garage apartment, or the blue-white glow of the TV, but no Preston. *Not like he'd stand naked at the window, playing with his dick,* Dylan reminded himself mockingly. Still, a guy could dream.

Nearly two full weeks passed before Dylan's persistent spying paid off. The sun was setting and he could see easily into the lit interior of Preston's apartment (Dylan had relinquished his claim on the studio the moment he saw its new resident). First, there was nothing—as usual—but then Preston stepped into view and Dylan nearly squealed with excitement. Preston wasn't nude, but the next best thing: in his underwear, a pair of clinging boxer briefs. He was standing in profile, his arms raised above his head, stretching. Dylan took in the contours of his body, the fullness of Preston's basket, the curve of his ass. He kept staring as Preston turned and walked away from the window, drinking in the sight of the tenant's solid butt encased in gray cotton.

Preston crossed the small studio, almost stepping out of view as he went to the refrigerator in the corner. As he walked back to the other side of the apartment, now with a beer in hand, he paused again in front of the window. This time he faced the window, tilting his head back as he took a swig from his beer. The apartment's jaundiced lighting bounced off his muscled torso. Dylan particularly liked how the light hit the tenant's crotch, creating highlights and shadows that emphasized the weight of Preston's balls and showed where the head of his dick pressed against the fabric. The sight made the head of Dylan's cock fight against its own cotton confines.

Dylan was reaching down to touch himself when he realized Preston was now looking directly out his window. Looking at Dylan looking at him.

Panicked, Dylan dropped to the floor as if dodging gunfire. He crawled over to the desk lamp and switched it off. *Fuck, if he saw me.* . . . As he crawled back to the window Dylan vacillated between worst case scenarios (he'll complain to Dad) to half-hearted assurances he wasn't seen. After all, at night with the indoor lights on it was sometimes difficult to see clearly out your window. Just saw your own reflection a lot of times. But then Dylan reminded himself the light in his room was on, and he'd been able to see out *his* window. His hard-on was quickly melting.

By the time Dylan worked up enough courage to cautiously raise his head above the windowsill, another possibility had entered his mind. What if Preston *wanted* him to watch? What if he was waiting for Dylan to look back out his window, maybe with the underwear off, maybe wanting to put on a *show*.

But the apartment's window was empty.

Dylan sank back into paranoia, imagining Preston was hurriedly getting dressed so he could come over and tell Dylan's dad his faggot son was spying through his window. Dylan sat huddled against the wall in the darkness of his room, feeling the rushed beat of his heart as he waited for the doorbell to ring and to hear Preston's angry complaint.

Five minutes passed. Then ten, then fifteen. After twenty minutes Dylan realized that even if Preston had seen him, he wasn't going to complain about it. At least not tonight.

His fear faded, overridden by the memory of Preston in his skivvies. Dylan's cock stiffened once again, responding to the recalled images. He stood up, drew his curtains and turned on a bedside lamp. He locked the bedroom door; his father was downstairs, and though he was probably asleep in front of the TV, Dylan didn't want to risk any surprises.

From the top drawer of his dresser Dylan took a bottle of moisturizing lotion. Then he removed the dresser's bottom drawer. Here, in the hollow area between the drawer's rail and the dresser's base, he hid his meager porn collection: a shoplifted copy of *Playgirl*, a few gay skin mags ordered over the Internet, and a straight magazine featuring male models in posed pictorials with women. There were also a few old issues of the Undergear catalog, received when his father wound up on the company's mailing list. Dylan had claimed the catalogs when his father tossed them in with other magazines he planned to recycle. The spring issue, with all its skimpy swimwear, was Dylan's favorite, and it was what he chose this evening, with Preston's underwear-clad body still fresh in his mind.

Setting his masturbation supplies on his bedside table, Dylan pulled off his shorts and underwear and settled back on his bed. Before opening the catalog he gave his cock a squeeze, seeing the tiniest drop of precum welling up in the slit, glimmering in the light. Dylan quickly turned his attention away from himself and opened the underwear catalog. The first few pages featured workout wear, most of it loose-fitting and, consequently, basket-concealing. He skipped ahead to swimwear, stroking his dick as his eyes went from one picture to the next, fixating on the packed crotches of the bikinis, wishing the catalog featured rear views of the men modeling the thongs.

Dylan barely took his eyes off the catalog as he grabbed the lotion off his beside table. He was particularly keen on a photo featuring a model reclining on a chaise longue, wearing a robe— open and spilling off the chaise—and a white bikini, what the catalog dubbed The Mediterranean. Dylan squirted lotion onto his cock and rubbed it over the head and shaft while still studying the photo. The model bore no resemblance to Preston, but with his muscular build and savage tan, it was easy to imagine he was the tenant. His pose—one hand resting on his flat belly, legs spread, with one foot resting on the ground—was probably intended to il-

lustrate carefree luxury, but to Dylan the pose was a sexual come-
on. He followed the model's golden brown thighs to their bulging
apex, imagining this was Preston's body and he, Dylan, was
pressing his face against that enticing mound.

Reluctantly, he turned the page. Beachwear followed, lots of
brightly colored outfits made of gauze. A few men captured
Dylan's imagination, but he didn't linger on these pages long. He
skipped ahead to the underwear pages. These photos were even
better than those of the swimwear. Unlike most of the swimsuits,
the underwear didn't have a lining, giving a more shape-defining
outline of the models' cocks and balls. Even the boxers fit just
tight enough so you could make out how the model's dick hung
beneath.

Dylan stroked himself harder as he looked at these pictures,
imagining the protruding crotches belonged to Preston, visualizing the dick creating it. Dylan could see himself slowly pulling
down the UltraLite Brief (or French Contour or Sport Boxer or
whatever featured undergarment his eyes focused on), the dick
falling forward, still soft but thick and longer than average, as all
imagined cocks tended to be. He'd bring his mouth to it, gently
licking the plump, exposed head (Dylan saw few uncut dicks so
all the penises he imagined were cut). Then he would take it into
his mouth, feel Preston's prick harden between his lips. . . .

His cock was throbbing now. Dylan's hand pumped his rod
rhythmically, the sweet-smelling lotion mixing with his own
juices. Each time his fingers moved over his swollen cockhead his
pleasure heightened, and his fantasy became more vivid.

Dylan turned the page. In the bottom left-hand corner of the
right page was a photo of a model wearing a mesh thong. You
couldn't really see through the fabric, but Dylan could make out
the shadow of the model's pubic hair and it was obvious he was
circumcised. Preston's identity soon took over the model's image,
and Dylan had his dick out of that mesh thong and in his mouth.
He'd take Preston's cock deep in his throat, and Preston would run
his fingers through Dylan's sandy-blond hair, telling him it felt
good—

Dylan could feel himself getting closer, each stroke sending a shockwave through his body.

—He'd take his mouth down to Preston's balls, hanging low in their fuzzy sack (Preston didn't seem like someone who'd shave his balls), prodding the cum-heavy orbs with his tongue. Preston would moan, and then Dylan's mouth was back on Preston's stiff cock, taking it all the way down his throat, sucking it until—

Dylan's orgasm hit him with paralyzing force. He clung to his fantasy just a few seconds more. It was Preston who was coming, sending his hot load down Dylan's throat. Dylan could feel Preston's cock pulsing between his lips, just as he felt his own dick pulse in his hand. It was Preston who simultaneously gasped and groaned, though the sounds came from Dylan's mouth. And Dylan could see the expression on his face, a mixture of satisfaction and peace. Dylan closed his eyes, trying to hold on to the feeling a while longer before waking up to the disappointing reality.

Staring out his bedroom window became Dylan's favorite pastime, though it soon proved a frustrating one. If he spied Preston inside his apartment, the tenant was usually wearing shorts or jeans. Dylan was hopeful one evening when he saw Preston saunter by his window with only a towel wrapped around his waist. *Lose the towel!* Dylan urged between clenched teeth, as if he could will it to happen from his darkened bedroom. But the towel remained. Nevertheless, Dylan would jack off (his *other* favorite pastime) after spying on the sexy renter.

Dylan's summer job at a fast food restaurant disrupted his evening voyeurism when the supervisor started scheduling him for the closing shift. Dylan often didn't get back home until after eleven. Not a whole lot of movement in Preston's apartment that time of night, but Dylan checked out his window anyway. Then he got out one of his magazines.

His father awoke him one morning before leaving for work. "Could I get you to do me a favor?"

Dylan, bleary eyed, sat up in bed. "Uh, sure. What?"

"I forgot to go up to the apartment last night and change out the AC filter. Could you do that for me? You know how."

An excuse to go to Preston's apartment. "Yeah, sure." He was wide awake now.

"If he's not home—and he probably won't be—just let yourself in. You know where the key is, on the rack in the kitchen. Left the filter on the kitchen table."

Dylan nodded.

"You're off today?" his father asked.

"Yeah."

"Any plans?"

"Not really. Maybe call Mike." Mike was a friend from high school. He also worked at the fast food place and had a car, so anything Dylan wanted to do that involved traveling more than a mile involved Mike.

"Should do something with your summer besides work and hang around the house," Jerry remarked. "That's what *I* do."

"That's not *all* I do," Dylan said defensively. *Christ, did they have to discuss this at* seven-thirty *in the morning?* "I go over to Mike's, hang out. Went to the movies with some friends from work last week."

"Any of these friends girls?"

Shit, the why-aren't-you-dating rant. "Aren't you going to be late for work?"

"Nice change of subject," Jerry chuckled. "See you tonight."

Dylan didn't go back to sleep after his father left. He was too excited, now that he had a genuine reason to go to Preston's apartment. Yet he postponed doing his assigned chore, hoping to do it when Preston was home. He first decided to wait until noon to go change the air conditioner's filter, hoping Preston would be home for his lunch break.

Noon became one o'clock and that soon became two. No Preston. Maybe wait until four? Dylan wondered. Maybe Preston would arrive home early.

This is how he frittered away his day, checking the clock and out the window every five minutes, and conjuring up far-fetched scenarios when Preston let him into the apartment. ("Gonna take a shower," Preston would say, stepping out of his shorts. "Maybe you can join me.") Not what his father would call "doing something" with one's summer.

By 4:15 p.m., Preston still hadn't come home. Not wanting his father to come home and find the chore undone, Dylan grabbed the filter off the kitchen table and the key off its hook and headed for the garage apartment.

Dylan climbed the stairs slowly, still hoping Preston's battered pickup would pull into the driveway as he made his ascent. He opened the screen door and, even though he knew no one would answer, knocked on the door, just to be sure. Then he put the key in the lock.

The apartment wasn't much bigger than a motel room, and Preston hadn't made much effort to make it any homier than one. The walls were unadorned, save a calendar from an insurance company featuring photos of wildflowers, which Preston hadn't bothered to turn to July even though June was two weeks past. The tenant added no furniture of his own to the shabby pieces already there. Preston's only attempt at personalizing the space was letting the debris of his day-to-day life fall where it may. Dishes were in the sink, empty beer bottles sat on a little Formica dinette set for two, and clothes were strewn about the floor. The air smelled like a bar after closing.

Dylan went to the air-conditioning unit in the kitchen window and changed the filter. The task didn't take five minutes, yet he did not leave the apartment right away. He wanted to know more about Preston, more than just he was a lousy housekeeper.

The bed was at the front of the apartment and Dylan went to it. It was unmade, and Dylan suspected the sheets hadn't been changed since Preston moved in. On the rickety nightstand was a metal ashtray with a couple burned roaches resting in it, a few more empty beer bottles, and a plastic cup with the stagnant remains of a cocktail. The most interesting item on the table, though, was a bottle of Astroglide. Even though it was a given that everyone masturbates, evidence of Preston's self-pleasuring excited Dylan, and he began to search around the bed for more clues to the renter's private activities.

He found a tattered copy of *Penthouse* beneath the bed, a disappointment but not really a surprise. A few wadded up tissues were under the bed, too—tissues that Dylan, wondering if they smelled of Preston's cum, almost brought to his nose before dropping them at the last second when this struck him as pathetic behavior. He wasn't as restrained when he noticed the pair of gray cotton boxer briefs kicked under the nightstand. These he snatched up and inspected closely. Not a designer brand, underwear that would be sold at Target and not in Undergear, yet enticing all the same. These briefs had been in direct contact with Preston's cock and balls and with his ass. Dylan's fingers fairly tingled holding them, and he brought them to his face without a second thought. The pungent smell of dried sweat filled his nose. He rubbed the fly under his nose, trying to pick up the scent of jism, but only detected the faint whiff of piss. When he took the worn boxer briefs away from his face, Dylan's cock was stiff.

Dylan folded up the underwear and stuffed them into the waistband of his shorts.

He had just locked the apartment door and was starting down the stairs when he heard the familiar clacking of Preston's truck, a sound quickly drowned out by the thunderous beat of Dylan's own heart.

"Wassup?" Preston asked as they met in the driveway.

Shit! I hope he doesn't notice the tent I'm pitching. "Uh, just, um . . . Dad wanted me to go ahead and change out your air conditioner filter." Dylan held up the old filter, covered in gray-brown filth, as proof.

Preston nodded. "Cool."

"Ah, well, later." His voice sounded pinched.

"Later," Preston replied, already sauntering toward the stairs to his apartment.

Dylan nearly ran to the back door of his house. He shoved the old AC filter into the trashcan by the back steps and darted inside. Guilt and fear wrestled inside his stomach, not abating until he was in his bedroom and pulled the stolen underwear from his shorts.

He inspected the boxer briefs again, amazed that he held them in his hands, and again he brought them to his face to take in the tenant's musky scent.

Dylan was barely conscious of locking his door and stripping off his clothes; he did these things as if breathing, natural and necessary. Even getting his jack off lotion from the top dresser drawer required no conscious thought.

Naked and on his bed, Dylan held Preston's boxer briefs to his nose while stroking his lubricated dong. He rubbed the underwear across his smooth chest, relishing the feel of the cloth across his erect nipples. Dylan dragged Preston's undies over his flat stomach, then pressed them against his aching cock. He imagined the hot tenant wearing them, laying on top of him, Preston's hard-on rubbing against Dylan's own. Dylan held the pilfered drawers tight against his balls, then pushed them further down between his legs, wanting to feel the cloth against his twitching asshole. He'd never been fucked—his experience was limited to a few drunken blow jobs—but Dylan wanted to feel Preston's dick inside him.

Barely ten minutes had passed and already Dylan felt close to coming. He got up on his knees and arranged the underwear beneath him. Leaning forward, he supported his weight on one hand while his other frantically pulled on his cock. In Dylan's mind, Preston was beneath him, waiting to get splattered.

A loud groan escaped Dylan's throat as he fired his load, his orgasm nearly sapping all the strength from his muscles, causing him to pitch forward. He let out another involuntary grunt as his cock shot its final, thin ribbon of cum. Dylan crumpled onto the bed, falling sideways onto the firm mattress.

As he lay there, panting, Dylan regarded the underwear, his thick, lumpy jism soaking into the fabric. He reached for Preston's boxer briefs, bringing them closer. His intention was to inspect them one more time before hiding them away, but taken by a sudden, lustful urge, Dylan brought the underwear to his mouth and sucked on the fabric, tasting the salt of Preston's sweat the tang of his own cum. He pulled the stolen drawers from his lips just as suddenly, and though alone, he felt his face grow warm with embarrassment.

When Dylan put the underwear away, he hid them with his porn.

In the few days following the underwear theft, Dylan feared a confrontation, even though the likelihood Preston even noticed he was missing a pair of drawers was next to nil, and even if he did, he wouldn't assume they were stolen. He passed Preston in the driveway later in the week—both arrived home from their respective jobs about the same time—and Dylan cringed, expecting Preston to shout, "Hey, faggot, you steal my underwear?" Not to mention he hated to be seen, by Preston of all people, in his polyester work uniform, smelling of grease.

All Preston did was nod in acknowledgment, muttering his usual, "Howzit goin'?"

He jerked off to, with, and frequently on Preston's underwear almost every day, though forced himself to abstain from masturbating a few days; his dick was getting raw and sore. Often Dylan would look at one of his magazines, staring at photos of naked, hard men while rubbing Preston's underwear over his own naked body, imagining the tenant was lying next to him—*on top of him*—in bed.

But Preston's underwear began to lose their appeal after a while. With all the bodily fluids the shorts had absorbed, the boxer briefs were starting to smell funky, becoming less an erotic fetish and more like someone's nasty laundry. Washing them was out of the question. That would make them just another pair of drawers, no different from Dylan's own.

Dylan took the extra key to the garage apartment off the key rack in the kitchen.

Don't, this is stupid.

He stepped outside. It was just after 1 p.m., and the August air · was hot, heavy, and wet. Dylan thought he remembered hearing on the news it was supposed to be near 100 degrees.

Turn around. This is pathetic!

His heart beat faster as he climbed the stairs, holding the apartment key so tightly it cut into the flesh of his fingers.

What are you? A goddamn pervert?

A shaky hand brought the key to the lock. He paused only a moment, giving himself one last chance to reconsider what he was about to do—*It's not worth it!*—before ignoring that inner voice and turning the key.

The apartment's interior looked about the same. A few attempts at housecleaning had been made: the beer bottles on the dinette table were thrown away, the stack of dishes had diminished since Dylan was last up here. The calendar was still on the month of June.

He made a cursory walk around the tiny apartment, trepidation seeming to solidify into a ball in his stomach, making him slightly nauseous. Yet his skin tingled with excitement as he moved about the studio, hoping to see more clues to Preston's private life. He picked up a towel hanging over the back of an easy chair, still damp from Preston's morning shower, then put it back where he found it. Dylan picked up a sci-fi paperback Preston started—the bookmark, a subscription coupon to *Sports Illustrated,* was at page fifty-three—and read the synopsis on the back. Didn't sound very interesting to Dylan and he set the book down. On top of the TV were two rented DVDs, both titles disappointing: a Jim Carrey movie (Dylan *hated* Jim Carrey) and a porno, *Crista's Cooze* (Dylan already knew Preston was straight, but the reminder stung nevertheless).

He quickly moved toward the bed and the area around it. Rolling papers, an orange lighter and a nearly-full glass of water joined the ashtray, beer bottles and Astroglide on the nightstand. The *Penthouse* magazine was still beneath the bed as were the discarded tissues. But there was no underwear.

Dylan was about to check the apartment's claustrophobic bathroom for discarded laundry when something on the bed caught his eye. There, nearly hidden in the tangle of sheets at the center of the bed, was a pair of boxer briefs.

The shorts were in his hands in less than a second. This pair was white with a dark gray waistband, the brightness of the fabric suggesting they were relatively new. He hooked his hands through the leg holes of the underwear, pinching the front pouch of the drawers between fingers. The cloth was slightly stiff and sticky. Could it be . . . ?

Burying his face in the shorts, he inhaled deeply, filling his nostrils with the familiar, yet uniquely personal, scent. The smell of jism. Preston's jism.

Dylan felt like he'd just discovered a suitcase filled with a million dollars, and his excitement went right to his cock. He held the underwear against his nose, taking in the warm, earthy odor cut with a sharp, bleach-like smell.

He removed his clothes quickly. If there was any inner voice cautioning him against this, the rush of blood through Dylan's veins drowned it out. Once nude, he got onto the bed. Dylan rolled onto his stomach, pressed his face into a pillow, and humped the worn mattress that had once been his own. Rolling onto his back, he grabbed the underwear and hoisted his legs into the air, slipping his feet into the boxer briefs and sliding them down his legs. Dylan raised his butt off the bed as he pulled shorts over his hips. The fit was a little loose—Preston was a size larger than Dylan— but his swollen dick took up most of the extra room. He reached between his legs, rubbing his cock through the damp fabric, his precum mixing with Preston's spent load.

Dylan felt like one raw nerve ending, each sensation felt to its greatest intensity. He closed his eyes, and he was with Preston. His imagination whirled with all the visual stimuli he'd taken in over the past two months, and he wove these disparate images into the pornographic thoughts swimming in his head. Preston was wearing his grass-stained cargo shorts, riding low enough that the gray elastic waistband of his underwear were showing, just like the day they first met. Dylan also got a view of those deep-set lines cutting upwards, the upper points of the *V* formed by the muscled · torso meeting the hips, forcing the eyes to consider where these lines intersected. There was the flash of Preston's smile, and the pants were off. He stood there, in the undefined setting of Dylan's lust, in white boxer shorts, his thick cock bulging in the basket, the contours of its head plainly visible. In a jump forward that cock was hard and exposed, offered to Dylan the way the models in the skin magazines offered their hard-ons, like they expected you to drop to your knees and suck it right there. And Dylan did, taking Preston's down his throat easily. His fingers fondled Preston's balls. Dylan reached between the tenant's legs and traced the cleavage of his ass, working his fingers into that sweaty, furry channel. He touched the moist lips of Preston's asshole and got an ecstatic moan for his trouble.

Preston's mouth was on his, his hands sliding down the smooth lines of Dylan's back. He cupped Dylan's ass, each buttock a perfect handful, and squeezed, making Dylan rub his face against Preston's chest and pinch one of his nipples. And suddenly Preston's mouth was at Dylan's cock, licking it, taking it between his lips, sucking him while his hands gripped Dylan's thighs.

He was writhing on the bed now, Preston's underwear pushed down and hooked behind his tightening scrotum. Dylan helped himself to some of the renter's Astroglide. Though he preferred his moisturizing lotion, the lube's slimy, slick consistency felt closer to saliva, making it easier for Dylan to sink deeper into his fantasy. Closing his eyes again, his pumping fist transformed into Preston's slurping mouth. Faintly he heard Preston's voice, telling him he liked Dylan's cock, that he wanted to fuck him.

The fingers of Dylan's free hand crawled beneath the boxer briefs, into the hot valley of his groin. And then further still, until his index and middle fingers were toying with his ass lips, trying to force them apart—giving Preston easy access. Dylan saw him between his legs now, the top of Preston's head peeking above Dylan's throbbing dick. Preston's tongue was at his hole, wiggling inside him. Dylan's pleasure increased, making him gasp aloud: "Fuck me."

The fingers that were digging at his ass were brought to his mouth, moistened, and quickly returned between his legs. Preston was working his way inside him now, first with his fingers, relaxing Dylan's virgin sphincter, then with his cock. He started slow, asking Dylan if he liked it, Dylan saying aloud in breathless whispers, "Oh, yeah." He liked it.

Suddenly, Preston was all the way inside him, his pulsing dick pushing against the walls of Dylan's ass. Getting fucked by Preston was everything he'd hoped, taking Dylan to the heights of ecstasy, and he wanted to go higher. He curled his legs up, bringing his knees up to his chest. Precum crawled down to Dylan's bellybutton, where it collected in a crystalline pool. *So close now.* Dylan didn't want the feeling to end, but he couldn't control himself, not with Preston fucking him hard while stroking his cock.

Dylan's prick exploded, pearly white cream splashing down on his stomach and streaming to his sternum, matting the sparse thatch of hairs there. His body rocked on the bed, his muscles contracting, his orgasm seizing control of his body. For a few seconds, Dylan's mind registered nothing but euphoria.

Had the slamming of his truck door not caused Dylan's crash landing into reality, Preston would have walked into his apartment to discover his landlord's son laying on his sagging mattress, legs in the air, underwear around his thighs, with two fingers poked up his ass and jism coagulating on his torso.

Instead, Preston walked into his apartment to see Dylan, shirtless, his chest looking glazed, frantically zipping his fly. Dylan swung his head toward Preston, also bare-chested, standing just inside the door, holding a small Igloo cooler. His eyes were hidden behind sunglasses, for which Dylan was grateful. Dylan's own eyes were as big as Frisbees and ringed by forming tears.

Preston spoke first. "The fuck?"

Dylan's mouth moved, but he could say nothing.

Preston set the cooler on the floor and took of his shades. Anger and confusion vied for equal time on his face, his eyes narrowed, his brow furrowed.

Dylan stood motionless. When Preston stepped forward, he cringed, fearing the tenant planned to hit him. But Preston moved past him, taking three long strides to his dresser and opening the top drawer. "Better *not* be anything missing," he muttered.

As Preston rustled around the dresser drawer Dylan concentrated his gaze on the floor, not seeing any of the cherished inventory kept in the drawer. Satisfied Dylan hadn't stolen anything stashed in the dresser, Preston slammed the drawer shut.

"So why're you up here?" he asked, turning toward Dylan. Preston didn't shout, but his voice seethed with fury.

"I . . . ," Dylan squeaked. No other words followed.

"Maybe I should take this up with your dad."

A tear spilled out Dylan's eye and rolled down his cheek. "Don't."

In the silence that followed, Dylan stood still, feeling like a convicted criminal awaiting sentencing, praying to be a victim of spontaneous combustion.

Preston let out a long sigh. "Just . . . just get the fuck outta here. Catch you near here again, I *will* tell your dad. Don't need no one up here goin' through my shit, or whatever the hell reason you were up here."

His pardon granted, Dylan snatched his T-shirt off the floor and headed for the door, not daring to look at Preston as he passed him. He doubted he would be able to look at the tenant again. Outside, tears flowed freely as Dylan descended the stairs, turning into sobs by the time his feet landed on the last step. The weeping continued all the way across the driveway, into his house, up the stairs. Only when he was in his own room did he begin to regain his composure, his sobs breaking into laughter as he realized he'd worn Preston's cum-soaked underwear home.

Always Listen to a Good Pair of Underwear

Steve Berman

Steve liked late mornings best. That was when his roommate Mike would crawl out of bed and make his way, first to bathroom, then to kitchen, and finally into the den and slump down on the sofa with a glass of orange juice. Still sleepy, the corners of his brown eyes crusty and heavy, he would wipe his face like a child, the gesture overdone.

Steve liked late mornings best because Mike slept in the most wondrous boxers imaginable. They had to be magic.

Steve kept glancing back and forth, from the television set to the zone of Mike's waist, a flat stomach slightly decorated with a trail of curly hair, thick legs, and, in-between, white boxers studded with full, red lips.

Mike stretched and yawned, oblivious to Steve's gaze. The fly of his boxers stretched wide, allowing a glimpse of something pink and fleshy and wonderful. The mouths on the boxers smirked and a dozen tongues licked those lips. One near the waistband smacked noisily.

Yesterday, Steve had marveled at the school of goldfish that swam around Mike's thighs and almost off the cotton onto the sofa. Another morning, letters spelled out WANT ME WANT ME WANT like a digital marquee from Times Square on his roommate's ass.

His Underwear: An Erotic Anthology
© 2007 by The Haworth Press, Inc. All rights reserved.
doi:10.1300/5756_19

Steve did the laundry—hell, did pretty much all the housework. Italian men liked their mates subservient, Mike always joked, and knowing that he shared the two-bedroom flat with a gay guy seemed to cast Steve in the role of the little woman. When he lifted the magic boxers from the clothes hamper, they were a dead white, often still warm from Mike's body. Before he handwashed them in the sink, he would bring them to his face, sniffing once and smiling if he caught sight of any small, curly hairs left in the crotch. He once nibbled on one, but it had no taste.

So what if I'm insane, Steve thought, *at least I'm in love.* He had written to the twink behind a help column on a gay youth site, admitting his crush on his roommate, how every day he was mesmerized by Mike's boxers, and signed it with his real name (he never cared for the corny noms de plume, like Lost in Love or Smeared Second, that people used). The peroxide addict responded with a suggestion that Steve start taking Thorazine.

"Psst," whispered one of the mouths on Mike's underwear. "Psst."

Steve turned from the commercial promising all the flavor of beef in an aerosol spray to make your vegetables taste like they were grown at a Texas ranch. Mike had fallen back asleep, his head supported by one muscular arm. Autumn sunlight from the window turned his skin to bronze.

"C'mere. Come closer." The voice was low and breathless.

"Aww, he's a shy one."

Another mouth muttered, "Loser."

Steve knew he should be getting to class. But without really meaning to, he inched closer to Mike on the sofa.

"That's it." One of the mouths talked like a tipsy drag queen. "Just move on over an' get some of what you been aching for." A cloth tongue pulled at the edges of the fly, allowing more of Mike's cock to be seen.

Steve felt his mouth grow dry. He envied all the spit the ones on Mike's magic boxers must have. Some even drooled.

"He knows you snort his shorts."

Several of them giggled like school girls.

"Mmmmhmmm. Boy's got it bad for this one."

"Doesn't know what's what, what is, and what could be."

Steve didn't like being razzed. Not by the kids back in high school, not by the old fart with the bad hairpiece at his last summer job, and certainly not by underwear, no matter how sexy. He started to get up.

"Now don't be running off so fast."

"We have something to show you."

The mouths began licking Mike's dick, which responded to the massage by growing larger and larger.

"Oooh, look at that."

"Seven—"

"Shit, that's eight if I ever saw it." The mouth kissed the reddish tip which began to leak sticky fluid. "Sweet sap too."

Steve stood there, his own crotch suddenly active and feeling a little constrained. He wanted nothing more than to unzip and begin playing. The only thing that stopped him was pure envy, along with the notion that he needed to buy his underwear from some place other than Kmart.

Why are they being such a tease? What could a pair of boxers possibly want, Steve wondered. *A lavender sachet in the drawer? Just brushing Mike's skin should be enough. Maybe they're growing greedy? Or rebellious?*

"We're lonely, babe."

Steve took a step closer. The floorboards under his foot creaked and Mike shifted in his sleep.

"Not for you." One tongue stuck out and gave him a rude raspberry.

"We want a mate." A chorus of "mate" followed for several seconds.

Steve scratched his head. "So, umm, like you want me to buy him another pair? A thong?" Mike's stiff penis momentarily bobbed, distracting him.

"Think, fool. Aren't we bottoms?"

He shrugged. Honestly, he had never given it much thought, though it did make sense.

"Shit, you think Miss Thing would know another of her kind."
"Loser."

"Now listen here," said the mouth that had been lucky enough to give Mike the most intimate of kisses. Its lips still gleamed with precum.

Steve could not believe what he was hearing. He shook his head after a moment. "No way, his chest is my favorite part." Indeed it was the perfect map, with typography of smooth skin, taught layers of firm muscle over bone.

"Then guess you'll never be seeing *this* again." The mouths began pinching at the fly as Mike's penis, abandoned of attention, began to wilt.

"Wait," Steve hissed. He could not turn back, not after catching sight of something so breathtaking. "Can you do more?"

Several chuckles erupted from the underwear. "Maybe. Treat us right and you'll be in for a treat yourself."

That was all Steve needed to hear. . . .

Late the next morning, Mike stumbled into the living room, sipping from a glass of fresh-squeezed. With his free hand he lightly tugged at the shoulder strap of the white, ribbed tank top. Steve had bought it yesterday and half-expected Mike to take one look at the gift and make some nasty remark, but instead he had greeted both present and Steve with a wide grin.

Steve smiled at the tiny red hearts that rose up like champagne bubbles from the boxers, up onto the tank top to pop, exploding in pink fireworks. A larger red heart beat with a disco staccato over the covered spot of Mike's left pectoral.

As Mike passed by him on the sofa, his roommate lifted a hand and roughly yet fondly swept it through Steve's hair. The touch was electric, sending shivers down his body.

All it needed was a good top, Steve thought. *Like me. Love was definitely a magical thing.*

Y

Lukas Scott

Electric.

That's my memory of him, of it all. Some kind of energy, some kind of vibe. Donna feeling love, Chic freaking, Sylvester feeling mighty, mighty real, and Gloria surviving.

And him. *Stevie.* Tank tops and corduroys, browns and creams, suede jackets and shoes. Flares you could use for sails.

Electricity everywhere. Static. Nylon clothes, nylon sheets . . . nylon underwear. Every touch electric, every movement crackling, bursting with energy.

I thought he was superman, some kind of superhuman; every time Stevie was near, he bristled with electricity. Sun kissed, light brown hair, grey eyes that lit up a whole room, the sort of tan American exchange students from the West Coast always seemed to have when they come over to England. His accent, his way of saying "neat" about everything.

We were what he called roommates, what I called flatmates. He was a sporty jock, talking about baseball or American football, while I could only mention cricket or Shakespeare.

I remember him in the early mornings most. Uninhibited, walking round the flat in nothing but his underwear.

His underwear.

It wasn't, like, *sexy* underwear. Looking back, it's embarrassing because—well, no one wears that sort of thing. It's cartoons or superhero comics (ahh, but he was, you see, a superhero). Or

His Underwear: An Erotic Anthology
doi:10.1300/5756_20

cringey pictures of friends at the beach caught without trunks, or
jumble sales, or boxes of old clothes in the attic that need getting
rid of.

But on Stevie, they were the tops. Not jock straps, not boxers,
not thongs, not banana hammocks. Nothing sophisticated, nothing
couture, nothing fashionable. Nothing much.

Y-fronts.

Blue, mostly, with that strong white Y inverted right down the
middle. Stevie walked round the flat in the morning wearing nothing but, munching toast and *jelly*, tousling his hair. The electricity
as he sat on the sofa, scratching himself. Occasional heart-stopping instances when I realized he wasn't only hanging to the left,
but that that most intimate, most *electric* part of him was making a
bid for freedom. His sheepish grin as he readjusted himself, then
leaving his hand stuck down his pants as a comforter. Trying not
to glance over, trying not to see what his hand might be holding,
not daring to see if the mound was growing, rising, hardening. . . .

That sense of loss when he shucked on his jeans, the disappointment as I heard him zzzzzip up and buckle. The door closing with
Stevie—gone, clothed, superman camouflaged in student civvies.

Only rarely did they make an appearance outside those waking
moments. The times they did, I remember them clearly, kaleidoscopic visions where blue and white whirl round and round in my
head. Most frequently, they appeared on those trips to the launderette. Coin-operated, always the smell of detergent from tiny little
boxes and of damp but clean clothes. Blue fluff in the air from the
dryer filters. Furtive and embarrassed fumbles from solitary souls
trying to race their intimate clothing into empty machines without
revealing anything. Towels full of intimacies, all bundled together
so as not to show, my own private ruse to ease the discomfort.

Not Stevie, no, he took delight in popping each pair (A pair? A
pair of what?) into the machines. He'd single them out, hold them
out to inspect. Sometimes, I recall clearly, he'd sniff the pairs before putting them in the machine. My mouth must have dropped
open; he caught me looking. The wily grin, his underhand pass as

he threw them at me. No feint dodge from me, transfixed, electrified as Stevie's blue Ys came straight at me.

SPLATT! Like the comic books, like the THWACK of a superhero in his tights and underwear.

Stuttering, spluttering, blinded, flailing, feigning horror, revulsion, incandescent rage. Stevie's soundtrack of laughter. An eternity, smelling Stevie on my face, suffocating on his musky masculinity. Secretly relishing every second, wishing he was inside them, there, in my face, there even in the launderette, even at home, even in bed.

I couldn't make the moment last forever. I had to give them up. Holding them at arm's reach, pretending to be disgusted by his odor, by such sudden and unwelcome intimacy.

Oh, I'd never been a sniffer. I never crept into his room and went through his laundry. I won't deny this: I'd thought about it. Fantasised, even. Sometimes my dreams were full of acres of Stevie's blue Y-fronts, like chamomile lawns or poppy fields in summer.

His room smelt of the same musk, that warm male odor of sleep, sweat, and testosterone. His was a room where the door was always open, where there was a certain half-light from curtains never drawn, never closed. Sometimes, I could peek in at night. I'd see him half sleeping, blankets thrown off. Just the merest glimpse of his blue Y-fronts, the merest hint of a satisfied smile on his face.

Glorious mornings. One in particular, Stevie overslept. A night out and us due for an early lecture. Bouncing into his room when his alarm hadn't gone off, calling his name. Hearing the stalled snoring of his slumber, the slow arousal from deep sleep.

Transfixed. Looking at him spread eagle on the bed, his jeans and shirt tossed over the bottom of the sheets. His lithe body spread out on top of them. Stevie in his blue nylon Y-fronts. Morning wood.

He was half erect. I could see the stiff tension of his cock against the material, straining in the blue tent. Attempting to uncurl, to rise up out of the material, but only lazily large. I took in the panorama of his restrained cock nestled between Stevie's out-stretched legs, noting even the damp bead at the tip.

Stevie moaning slightly, his hand reaching down into his Y-fronts. I watched him lazily fumble, the morning ministrations of a man not yet awake. Slow, teasing movements, not enough to mastur-bate, more to comfort, to reassure. Simple morning stretches to greet the day.

Replaying the scene, he wakes and sees me watching him. His sleepy eyes meet mine. He stretches fully on the bed. One arm stays behind his head. The other drops back down to his pants and nestles over his fleshy parcel. He grabs his cock; he looks at me. His hand moves inside. Our eyes still locked, he begins to stroke himself. I watch him grow, watch the tent of nylon peak until he is forced to unleash his cock, to flick it out of its prison.

I watch as Stevie wanks. Sometimes, when I think it through again, I join him on the bed. I feel myself close to his warm body. I feel him moving beside me, stroking himself. Sometimes I imag-ine putting my hand out, feeling the flesh and his Y-fronts, joining him on his erotic journey. My hand cups his balls, pulling down his Y-fronts so he has absolute access the expanse of his tanned flesh.

He never kisses me but never has to. I can feel his body shaking, can hear his breathing quicken, can hear his heart beating. We're mates, we're roomies, we're jerk buddies. I can feel him getting ready, feel his body spasm, hear his throaty grunt and then feel the warm spatter over me. Looking down, I can see his whoer falling onto the blue of his pants, settling in white puddles. Staining.

Things move on. Stevie moved on. Underwear moved on. It's fancy and pricey and showy these days. But there's still some-thing about the blue nylon Y-fronts on Stevie.

Something electric.

Stroking Midnight

Hank Edwards

Cameron swallowed hard past the lump in his throat as he came to a stop a few feet away from the group of men gathered at his front door. He wore only an old pair of Jockey boxer briefs, the front comfortably soft as it cradled his cock and balls. One of the group stood slightly ahead of the rest, a firm, deep purple pillow in his hands. On the pillow rested a gleaming glass codpiece. The man holding the pillow lifted to hand to him.

Taking the codpiece, Cameron raised his eyes to the handsome man standing behind the pillow bearer, his blue locking with the man's deep brown, then Cameron slowly lowered his underwear to expose himself. He held the narrow end of the codpiece beneath his balls as his mind raced back over the two days leading up to this moment, trying to pinpoint when everything had started to change. If he could remember correctly, at that time he had been standing in the basement surrounded by all that underwear. . . .

He stood ankle deep in a pile of men's underwear, sorting the soiled garments by material before he started the washer. Across the room, his large black cat, Gabrielle, lay in a faded old easy chair, her bright green eyes half closed.

"For God's sake," Cameron said as he tossed jockstraps and tighty whities in one pile, silk and lame in another. All of them

His Underwear: An Erotic Anthology
© 2007 by The Haworth Press, Inc. All rights reserved.
doi:10.1300/5756_21

sported suspicious stains. "How many pair of fucking underwear do these assholes have to wear every night?"

As if to answer his question, a handful of damp, fragrant underwear fell out of the laundry chute above him and landed on his head and shoulders. A floor above he could hear the moronic giggling of Rodolfo's houseboys Avie and Ty, or Avalanche and Typhoon when were on stage stripping.

"Idiots," Cameron muttered, tossing the new arrivals in the appropriate piles.

"Hey, move your ass, slowpoke!" Avie called down the chute. "We need pedicures before we head to the club."

"What?" Cameron said and raised his face to yell back up the chute, "I just gave you pedicures two days ago!"

"So?" Avie shot back. "We went to the beach today, and the sand ruined them. Now hurry the fuck up and get up here. We have to be at the club by nine." And then he dropped a final article of clothing, a gold lamé thong crusted with old cum and sweat. Cameron was still looking up the chute when the thong came down, and as Avie had undoubtedly planned, the soiled garment landed directly on his face. Cameron let out a cry of disgust and shot the ceiling the finger as a floor above he heard Avie and Ty roar with laughter.

While he completed sorting, Cameron began to grow hard. He loved men's underwear, either on a man's body or warm and damp with sweat from having just been worn by a man. And Avie and Ty, obnoxious houseboys though they were, both were handsome and well-built and wore a lot of underwear each week during their strip routines down at the Roundabout Nightclub.

Cameron held a pair of boxers to his nose and took a deep breath, inhaling the unmistakable scent of Avie's cologne (something woodsy and expensive) as well as the cool, damp smell of the man's sweat. Cameron's cock sprang up to full alert and he moaned, reaching down to squeeze his long, hard length through his jeans. He pressed the boxers more firmly against his face and unzipped his jeans, then reached into the straining pouch of his comfortable old jockstrap. Precum had already seeped into the pouch of his jock, and it coated the back of his hand as he stroked himself.

Several moments later, the rush of orgasm flooded his system, and Cameron leaned forward, the boxers pressed tight against his face, unleashing his load across the piles of dirty underwear at his feet. He squeezed the final few drops from the red, swollen head of his cock and used the boxers he had been sniffing to clean himself off.

Just as he had tucked himself away and zipped his jeans, Rodolfo came clomping down the basement steps in a pair of Japanese-style flip-flops made from bamboo or wicker or some other shit. His caftan flowed behind him like a cape. Rodolfo was not what Cameron would call young. The man was in his fifties and attractive in a George Hamilton way-too-tan-to-be-healthy kind of way, but Rodolfo was not a good person. How and why Cameron's father Albert had hooked up with Rodolfo on that gay cruise for older single men Cameron had sent him on for his birthday he could only guess at. All Cameron knew was Albert came home from his week on the cruise, tan and relaxed, and a week later Rodolfo and his two houseboys, the aforementioned Avalanche and Typhoon, moved in and Cameron's quiet, dignified life changed forever.

Albert traveled a great deal for his business, and so the three newcomers had made Cameron their indentured servant, demanding he cook for them, clean up after them, perform hideous personal upkeeps (cleaning out fungus from beneath Avie's toenails had been one of the worst), and basically wait on them hand and foot. And though he was miserable, Cameron could not bear to tell his father about the situation on those rare occasions Albert actually got to spend a night at home. His father always looked so tired and Rodolfo, undoubtedly knowing what side his bread was buttered on, pandered to Albert every minute he was in the house, never leaving his side and making it impossible for Cameron to talk with his father alone.

And so Cameron clenched his teeth and dealt with the cruel comments, never-ending chores, and overall unpleasantness of the three men who had invaded his home.

"Why aren't these clothes in the washer yet?" Rodolfo demanded as he came to a halt on the bottom riser of the steps. He sneered down at the underwear-littered basement floor then raised his head to sneer at Cameron.

"Because I've been sorting them all by material," Cameron said. "I wouldn't want to ruin Avie's best thong or Ty's favorite flannel boxers by washing them all together."

Rodolfo narrowed his eyes and put his fists on his bony hips. "Don't get smart with me, Cameron. I am the master of this house while your father is gone, and I won't put up with lip from you the way he does. Now, get this laundry started and get upstairs. We need pedicures before dinner."

Cameron's jaw dropped. "All three of you? Before dinner?"

Rodolfo nodded once then turned and, lifting his caftan so as not to trip over the hem, ascended the steps.

"Fuckers," Cameron muttered but bent to resume his sorting.

That was when he found the flyer stuck to one of Avie or Ty's leopard-print thongs. He unfolded it, careful to avoid the slightly sticky parts, and gasped quietly. Godfrey Prinze, the handsome young millionaire who lived in a huge stone mansion up on the hill, was holding a go-go boy contest tomorrow night. According to the flyer, Godfrey was holding open auditions in a search for the best male stripper in the city to live in his mansion and dance for him.

Cameron's eyes went wide as he read the flyer. He could imagine himself as a male stripper living in Godfrey's mansion and being waited on by two or three of his own houseboys. He'd always been a bit of an exhibitionist, and if Avalanche and Typhoon could do it. . . . Cameron's mind spun at the thought of it.

Then he heard stomping footsteps cross the floor above, and he hurriedly bent back to work, stuffing the flyer in his back pocket as he resumed tossing underwear into the washer. Ty stuck his head around the corner at the top of the stairs and bellowed,

"Cameron! Get your musty ass up here and get to work! Christ, how long does it take to sort stupid, fucking underwear?" There was a moment of silence, then Ty added, "And no starch this time, bitch!"

Cameron grinned to himself as he stuffed the washer full of clothes, thinking about Avie and Ty stripping. Undoubtedly they were planning on auditioning for Godfrey Prinze. Cameron had never pole danced before, but he had watched plenty of times from his bedroom window as they practiced on the clothesline pole in the backyard. Pole dancing didn't look too hard, really, and neither of them was very coordinated, he had no idea how they kept from being fired.

As the washer tub filled, Cameron lost himself in a fantasy of flashing lights, a heavy bass beat, and the cool, slick feel of a stripper pole in his hand. He wore only a silver lamé thong, the multi-colored lights reflecting off the material as he twisted and spun around the brass pole. He danced on a slightly raised stage, and directly in front of him sat Godfrey Prinze. He had seen pictures of the man in the local gay paper and always thought he was handsome. Godfrey was Hispanic, his dark hair swept back from his forehead, broad shoulders barely contained by a cream-colored silk shirt. Cameron could feel Godfrey's keen, dark eyes moving along his sweaty body as he spun and undulated, touching on his chest, lingering on the ridges of his abs, before moving down to the glistening bulge of his thong.

And then Godfrey stood before him, reaching up and hooking his fingers beneath the silver lamé waist band and easing it down, down, down to allow Cameron's long, hardening length of cock to unfurl and his smooth, heavy balls to swing free. Godfrey held the thong to his handsome face, closed his beautiful eyes, and inhaled the scent of Cameron's sweat, reaching down to grab the outline of his own hardened cock through his linen pants.

"CAMERON!" Rodolfo screamed down the steps. Cameron jumped, blinking back to reality; his erection wilted immediately. "Get up here, now!"

Cameron dumped detergent in the washer and, taking a breath to steel himself for the next horrific chore, trudged up the steps.

The next day Cameron cleaned and pressed Avie and Ty's best stripping outfits and prepared a light but filling meal for them all, in preparation for Godfrey Prinze's party. The three danced out the front door at 9:00 p.m. as Cameron stood scrubbing pots at the sink, and Rodolfo had the nerve to say over his shoulder, "Don't even think about coming to this party. We'll want something to eat when we get home, so make sure it's ready."

Cameron waited until the door slammed shut before muttering beneath his breath, "Bitch," then returned his attention to the pots.

A little later, Gabrielle followed Cameron out the side door to the dark backyard as he carried a bag of trash to the cans behind the garage. Light from the backdoor light and streetlamps did not reach back here and the shadows were deep, a fact that always made Cameron a little nervous when doing this chore. He lifted the lids on the aluminum cans until he found some room in one of them and had just secured the top when someone directly behind him cleared his throat.

Cameron gasped and whirled, his heart pounding and adrenaline spiking through his system. A tall man stood blocking his way. He wore an oversized leather motorcycle jacket, heavy motorcycle boots, and faded jeans torn at the knees. Sharp cheekbones and a strong Roman nose were revealed in the orange glow of his cigarette as he took a deep drag.

The man nodded then flicked the cigarette over the back fence into the alley beyond. He looked down at Cameron and said in a rough voice, "Evenin', Cameron."

"How—how do you know my name?" Cameron asked.

"Oh, I know all 'bout you," the man replied with a grin. "I've been watchin' you for a long time now."

"S-stalking me?" Cameron said, slightly alarmed.

"What? Oh, no no," the man said hurriedly. "Nothin' like that. As a protector of sorts. I'm your fairy god-daddy. I watch over you."

"Fairy god-daddy?" Cameron said slowly. "Okayyyy." He began to back slowly away from the man. "Well, thanks for all the protection and stuff, but I need to be heading inside to finish cleaning—"

The stranger sighed and said, "You want to go to Godfrey Prinze's party tonight and dance for him but Rodolfo forbade you to go, and besides you have nothing to wear." Cameron stopped in his tracks. "There, you see? Am I right?"

Cameron was at a loss for words; he simply nodded.

"I've been keepin' an eye on you for a long time," the man said. "Like a guardian angel if you will."

"Really?" Cameron said, wanting desperately to believe someone, somewhere was watching over him.

"Yeah, really. And tonight, I'm gonna make your wish come true. I'm gonna get you all duded up and get you to that party."

Cameron felt himself swoon. "You are?"

"Yep. Now, come over here into the light and let me take a closer look at you." The man moved back, and Gabrielle followed Cameron out into the wash of the backdoor light.

"Do you have a name?" Cameron asked as he got his first clear look at the burly man before him who, he decided, was handsome in a rough sort of way.

The man smirked self-consciously. "Yeah, I do. It's Norbert."

"Norbert?" Cameron repeated, eying the leather jacket, black T-shirt, faded denim jeans and heavy boots. "You don't look like a Norbert."

"Yeah, well, it's a family name." Norbert looked him up and down. "You look good, Cameron. Very handsome."

"Thanks. So, how does this work? Is it like in that fairy tale where you wave your wand and turn a pumpkin into a coach and mice into horses?"

Norbert raised his eyebrows. "Er, well, not exactly. I actually use a different kind of magic, see. I don't really have a wand, at least, not in the classic sense of the word."

"Oh?" Cameron said, suddenly nervous.

"Yeah. See, I can change objects, kind of like you said, but since there are no pumpkins or mice around here, we'll have to improvise." Norbert looked around then stepped into the shadows behind the garage, and Cameron jumped at a sudden barrage of banging and clanging. A moment later Norbert reappeared carrying an empty garbage can. "Here we go." He brushed past Cameron and walked to the driveway where he laid the trash can on its side. Gabrielle trotted after the man and Cameron followed the cat to watch as she sniffed the inside of the trash can then edged inside, tail twitching.

"Okay, and what's that?" Cameron asked.

"That's your ride!" Norbert said with a smile as he stepped up beside Cameron. "Now, we just need some magic."

"Great. How do you do that?" Cameron asked.

"Well . . . ," Norbert took a breath. "Like I said, I don't have a typical wand. My magic is in my cock. I have to fuck you, and when I come, I can grant your wish."

Cameron crossed his arms and gave him a doubtful look. "Really. You fuck me and suddenly, I'll be able to get to Godfrey Prinze's party and dance for him."

"Yep," Norbert said with a nod, then more quietly, "I'll be real gentle."

"You know," Cameron began backing away, "I think I'll just go back inside. . . ."

Norbert rolled his eyes. "You cry yourself to sleep almost every night and secretly hate your father for bringing Rodolfo into the house."

Cameron stopped and turned back. "Good guess."

"Cameron, it's the only way I can help you." Norbert shrugged. "I don't make the rules."

Cameron sighed and bit his lip. "Let me see it."

Norbert looked startled. "What?"

"I want to see your cock. It's kind of a funny rule I have; I like to see what's going up my ass before it's stuck in there."

Norbert nodded then unzipped his jeans and let them hang open. He wore white Calvin Klein briefs, which surprised Cameron.

"I wouldn't have taken you for a tighty whities kind of guy," Cameron said.

"Yeah, not many people do. But I like how clean they look." Norbert pulled the elastic down and let his cock hang out. It was thick with a meaty, heart shaped head and a wiry patch of dark brown pubic hair framing the base. Cameron felt his own cock respond at the sight and let out a breath.

"How big does it get?" Cameron asked.

"Seven inches." Norbert smiled. "Just right."

Cameron sighed. "All right. Come on inside."

"Oh, no," Norbert said. "We have to do it out here in the yard. We need to be close to the trash can to make the magic work."

Cameron rolled his eyes but walked up to Norbert, looked him in the eye for a moment, then turned his back and pulled down his pants to expose the pale round globes of his ass. He bent forward, fingers around his ankles, and said, "All right then, go ahead."

Norbert cleared his throat and Cameron felt a hand on his left ass cheek, surprisingly smooth for such a rough looking man. Norbert squeezed each cheek then slid his hand slowly along the canyon of Cameron's ass, pausing to rub gently at his twitching, puckered hole.

"You've got a real nice body, Cameron," Norbert said, his voice thick with lust. "A nice, tight little ass."

Cameron heard the click and burp of a tube of lube as Norbert drizzled the stuff on his growing cock. A moment later, a lubed, slick finger slid into him and Cameron gasped. Norbert pushed more lube deep into him, slipped two fingers inside, then three, and all the while Cameron gasped and grunted.

"You need to be quiet, Cameron," Norbert whispered. "You don't want the neighbors to hear us, do you?"

"Sorry, it's just been so long," Cameron gasped.

"Here, use these." There was a tearing sound and then Norbert handed up his warm, damp pair of tighty whities, which Cameron placed between his teeth. He could taste the man's sweat and moaned as quietly as possible.

"Okay, ready for the magic?" Norbert asked and Cameron grunted, "Mm hmm." Norbert's fingers slipped out of Cameron's asshole, and a moment later he felt the wide, blunt head of the man's cock press against the threshold of his body. The fat, bulging tip slipped past the tiny ring of his sphincter and burrowed up into him. The shaft followed after, spreading the muscle wider as Norbert penetrated him completely.

The man paused a moment, fingers digging hard into Cameron's ass cheeks as he stood buried in him to the hilt.

"Oh, God," Norbert sighed and leaned down to rest his head on Cameron's spine, his beard brushing along his skin. "You are tight."

Cameron bit down on the man's underwear and gripped his ankles harder as Norbert began to move within him. The length of Norbert's cock slid out then pushed back in, feeling as if it went deeper each time, until the man was drilling him hard, his thighs banging against Cameron's ass cheeks.

A few minutes later, Cameron heard Norbert gasp and the man said, "Okay, here it comes. Get ready. Oh, God. Oh, fuck yeah."

Cameron felt a tingle spread through his body as Norbert came inside him. He reached up and grabbed his own hard on as it oozed what felt like gallons of precum; two strokes was all it took to bring him to climax. His cum spurted out across the grass, and he grunted around the underwear held between his teeth.

"Oh magic power mine, let Cameron be seen, arriving at the party, in a fine stretch limousine," Norbert chanted as his balls pumped their load into Cameron's ass.

The trash can resting on the driveway shook then levitated. Cameron raised his head and opened his mouth, Norbert's underwear falling to the ground as he watched the trash can begin to spin. A flash of light followed, so bright he had to close his eyes, and when he opened them a long, gleaming Hummer limousine sat in the driveway.

Then his body was thrumming and he felt Norbert pull out of him as Cameron himself began to spin around. There was a flash of light, and he found himself standing in the yard wearing a retro cool mesh tank top, tear away track pants, gleaming black jack boots, · and a pair of expensively understated sunglasses. Pulling the pants down a little, Cameron found a fitted, glass codpiece covering his cock and balls, held up by strands of pearls that circled his waist and ran down the crack of his ass and between his legs.

"Like it?" Norbert asked and Cameron looked up to where the man stood with his arms crossed, jeans around his ankles, and his softening cock drooling cum onto the lawn. "I sort of like the look, you know? The goods are on display but untouchable."

Cameron looked back down at the elaborate codpiece and nodded. "I like it."

Norbert pulled up his jeans and tucked his cock inside. "Okay, here's how it works. The magic lasts until the final stroke of midnight. No extensions. Everything reverts back to its original state at midnight, got it?"

"Got it," Cameron said with a nod. "Thanks so much, Norbert."

"My pleasure," Norbert said with a grin, then looked at his watch. "Holy crap, it's already ten o'clock. You'd better get moving." Norbert nodded to the limo and Cameron turned to see a tall, beautiful black woman dressed in a tuxedo step from the driver's seat. She had bright green eyes and moved with feline grace as she walked to the passenger door and opened it for him.

"Gabrielle?" Cameron said and the driver smiled at him. "Wow, you're gorgeous."

"Of course she is!" Norbert said. "Now, get your ass moving!"

Cameron settled into the soft leather seat, the pearls rubbing pleasantly along the loosened lips of his asshole. A moment later the Hummer's engine purred to life, and the car eased down the driveway and into the street.

The limousine pulled up in front of Godfrey Prinze's large, ornate house, and Cameron peered out the window at the many guests standing on the steps. The people all wore feathered masks and stood staring at the circular driveway with bored expressions as more guests arrived. Colored lights flashed along the three story stone face of the house, and Cameron could hear the heavy bass line of dance music thumping out the wide open front doors.

A short, lithe valet stepped up to the Hummer's back door, but Gabrielle was beside him in a flash, hissing so loud the man jumped back. She gave the valet a cool look as she opened the door and Cameron stepped out, smiling self consciously at the crowd of people staring down at him.

"Sir?" the valet said, nervously watching Gabrielle. "Please wear this." He handed Cameron a dark blue Mardi Gras mask decorated with blue and red feathers, which covered the top half of his face. On it was a piece of plastic with the number eighty-eight. "You are number eighty-eight. Wait inside until your number is called, and when you dance, please face the throne."

Cameron blinked. "There's a throne?"

"Yes, sir," the valet replied with a smile. "Mr. Prinze had it built especially for this occasion. Good luck."

"Thanks." Cameron took off his sunglasses and smiled when Gabrielle took them from his hand, purring deep in her throat. He slipped the mask over his head and took a breath before he climbed the stairs to the main doors.

The massive entry hall was packed with people, all of them wearing masks, some of them dancers wearing numbers. A few were coated with sweat and stood in groups talking about how well they thought they had done. Cameron recognized Rodolfo, wearing a ridiculous parrot mask, who was flanked by Avie and Ty, both shirtless and both wearing masks. Cameron reached back to adjust the strand of pearls running along the crack of his ass then moved into the main room of the house.

This room was even more crowded. The onlookers surrounded a raised platform from which a shining brass pole rose to the tall ceiling. At the far end of the room, Godfrey Prinze sat on a heavy gold throne looking bored. Attendants stood around him, some with cell phones pressed against their ears, others holding various drinks on trays.

"Attention please," an amplified voice announced and Cameron jumped. "Number eighty-six please approach the stage. Number eighty-six."

Cameron watched as Typhoon strutted through the crowd. The man wore a gold mask decorated with white feathers and vaulted onto the stage then turned to wave to everyone. The people stared blankly back at him, drinks in one hand, cigarettes in the other. The music started, a heavy bass thumping beneath a light, energetic synthesizer, and Ty began to move. He danced well, though uninspired, and Cameron caught Godfrey yawning more than once during Ty's routine and felt his heart soar. For all his slutty, urban streetwise moves, Typhoon had not made much of an impression on Godfrey. During the final few spins of his routine, Ty stripped down to the silver lamé jock strap Cameron knew so well from the washing, pressing, and mending he had performed on the garment the last few months. The man hung upside down, arms outstretched, legs wrapped around the pole as he lowered himself slowly to the stage.

The music faded out and silence reigned as all heads in the audience turned to look expectantly up at Godfrey Prinze. The man took a breath, held out his hand with his palm turned down to the floor, then teetered it back and forth, shrugging as if to say, "Eh, no big deal."

There were murmurs but no applause as Ty gathered his clothes and left the stage in a huff, one of the feathers in his mask hanging down to his chest, having broken during his routine. Avalanche was next and fared no better. Their moves, Cameron decided, were bland and rote, lacking originality and spirit. They were all bulk and no flex.

And then it hit him. Cameron himself did not have a routine. He had never danced in front of anyone but Gabrielle before, and then it had been without a stripper pole. His stomach knotted and a clammy sweat broke out all over his body. Oh God, what had he gotten himself into? He was no dancer, he was a college student and an indentured servant to Rodolfo and his houseboys. What the hell had he been thinking, wishing he could come to this party and dance for Godfrey Prinze? He was going to be the laughing stock of the night.

"Attention please," the amplified voice boomed and Cameron jumped again. "Number eighty-eight please approach the stage. Number eighty-eight."

Cameron's bladder shrank and seemed to fill with urine as his stomach collapsed in fear. All heads in the crowd turned to face him, cool eyes staring out from behind feathered masks and for a moment, he couldn't move or breathe.

Someone behind him gave him a gentle push and his feet began to move. Looking over his shoulder, he saw Gabrielle standing behind him. She wore a cat mask with green feathers and gave him a small smile.

Cameron reached the chest high stage, tried to vault up onto it as Ty and Avie had done, but his arms were shaking too much to support his weight. Instead he walked around to a set of steps, tripping on the top one and stumbling across the platform to the brass pole. He stood up and smiled nervously at the expressionless eyes all around him, then gave a small wave. Gabrielle was the only one who waved back.

The music boomed to life and Cameron jumped. He took a breath, shrugged the tension from his shoulders, and started to move. His hips swayed and his arms rose over his head. And, suddenly, he knew just what to do. He closed his eyes and lost himself in the rhythm of the music, forgetting about the crowd, Avie and Ty, and Godfrey Prinze. He spun around the pole, his fingers finding the perfect place as he lifted his legs and hung upside down. The mesh tank top came off without ruffling a single feather on his mask. He moved like a person who had never heard of gravity, doing handstands and back flips. At just the right moment he reached down, grabbed fistfuls of his track pants, and tore them away to reveal the molded glass codpiece; over the thump of the music he heard a gasp from the crowd.

As the music ended Cameron did the splits, arms overhead, and his eyes went to the throne, searching for Godfrey Prinze. But the throne was empty; Godfrey Prinze had walked out on Cameron's routine! And then Cameron looked down to find Godfrey standing at the edge of the stage, his dark eyes intense as he stared up into Cameron's face. There was a moment of absolute silence then the room exploded into cheers and applause. Godfrey's attendants ran up and began to whisper to their boss, who wasn't responding to them; he refused to take his eyes off of Cameron.

Cameron stood up and waved to the crowd. The applause continued as he gathered his clothes and made his way to the steps at the side of the stage. From the corner of his eye he could see Godfrey shouldering his way through the crowd to meet him, bumping Rodolfo, Avie, and Ty out of his way and, from the expression on Rodolfo's face, stomping on the man's foot in the process. Seconds later Godfrey Prinze stood before him, his eyes traveling over Cameron's body and lingering on the glass codpiece before moving back to his face.

"You were exquisite," Godfrey said.

"Thank you," Cameron replied as someone pawed at his arm. He turned to find Gabrielle standing beside him. "Hi, Gabrielle," he said, then turned back to Godfrey.

But Gabrielle was insistent. She dug her nails into his arm to get his attention once again.

"Hey!" he yelped, rubbing at the red marks. "What was that for?"

Gabrielle turned to look over her shoulder and Cameron followed her gaze. Just inside the door to the main hall stood a large, ornate grandfather clock. As Cameron fixed his eyes on the clock's face, the hour and minute hands came together over the twelve and deep chimes began to reverberate through the room, loud enough to be heard even over the music.

"Oh God, it's midnight," Cameron gasped and turned to Godfrey. "I have to go."

"What? No, stay just a little longer," Godfrey said.

"I'm sorry, I can't. I . . . I have to go. I'm sorry." Cameron turned to run. Godfrey reached out to stop him but his reach fell short, and his fingers brushed Cameron's shoulder before falling lower to hook beneath the string of pearls around Cameron's waist. The delicate string snapped, and the pearls bounced away across the floor of the room, some of the crowd slipping on them and falling with surprised cries, spilling their drinks and losing their cigarettes. Cameron felt the fitted glass codpiece fall away and turned back, his eyes locking with Godfrey's for a moment before Gabrielle grabbed his hand and dragged him away.

They ran out the front door and down the steps as the clock continued to boom out its chimes. Cameron dove naked into the back of the limousine, and Gabrielle leaped agilely over the hood to duck into the driver's door. She maneuvered the long vehicle down the winding driveway to the street and burned rubber to the next corner, which she took on two wheels. A familiar tingle started in his gut, the same one he had felt when he had been transformed by Norbert's magic cum. There was a bright flash and a moment of weightlessness. Suddenly, he was crammed inside a trash can, his arms wrapped around Gabrielle's furry, struggling body as they rolled over and over. Finally, the can bumped into a curb, and they came to a head-knocking stop.

Cameron let Gabrielle go and the cat ran off down the street as he climbed stiffly out of the trash can. He pulled off the feathered mask to find he wore the clothes he had on prior to his magical makeover. He tossed the trash can and mask into the ditch then turned to run after Gabrielle, who sat at the top of a slight rise licking her fur.

The next day the gay population was all aflutter over the identity of the mystery go-go boy who had captured Godfrey Prinze's heart before fleeing the scene at the stroke of midnight, leaving behind only a formfitting, glass codpiece. Cameron heard the excited whispers in the halls between his classes, at the campus café, in the music store as he priced and stocked CDs, and even around the table in his own home as he served Avie and Ty dinner and listened to them grumble about the previous evening's events.

And then a flyer was passed around the town, and the whispers grew more urgent. Godfrey Prinze was coming down from his house on the hill to make his way through the town, visiting all the strip clubs, gay bars, and houses of known gay men. He was going to bring with him the fitted, glass codpiece and would ask each man to try it on until he found the one it fit perfectly—the man he wanted to come to his house on the hill and live and dance with him forever after.

"Oh, come on," Avie said that night, his voice drifting up to Cameron's third floor bedroom through the heat ducts. "What was so special about that dancer? Just because he did handstands and the splits. I bet that codpiece will fit me."

"That beer can cock of yours fit inside that fitted, glass codpiece?" Ty replied. "Good luck."

"Jealous?" Avie shot back.

"Not as jealous as you're going to be when I put that thing on and dance my way out of this run-down shack," Ty said. "Oh, dammit, there's a stain on this jock strap. What is this?"

"As if you don't know," Avie said.

"Oh, fuck off," Ty replied. Then Cameron heard him bellow, "Cameron! Get down here and clean my jock strap!"

But Cameron stayed where he was, lying on his back across the bed with Gabrielle perched on his chest, purring as he dug his fingers into the fur on her neck.

The following day Avie and Ty spent all morning in the bathroom, primping and rubbing bronzer on each other. Late in the morning, Ty had an idea and demanded Cameron highlight their hair. As he brushed the dye over their foil wrapped heads, both men talked about him as if he weren't even in the room. Cameron bore all this with more patience than he could have imagined, smiling as he caught sight of Gabrielle spraying piss on each of their beds in the next room.

Late in the afternoon, just as Cameron left the bathroom and started back upstairs in his underwear, the doorbell rang and Rodolfo twittered with excitement as he danced to the door, favoring his toe which still ached from when Godfrey's stepped on it the night before. He took a moment to collect himself then smiled and pulled the door open. Godfrey stood on the porch wearing a bored expression. He was flanked by several assistants, two of which wore cell phone ear pieces and murmured occasionally into the dangling vocal pickups. A third assistant carried a deep purple pillow on which rested the polished glass codpiece. Rodolfo took a breath at the sight of the accessory and held his hand to his chest then waved all the men inside.

Cameron stood in his faded old boxer briefs at the bottom of the stairs and watched from around the corner as Avie stomped up and immediately dropped his pants. His long cock fell out and he snatched the codpiece off the pillow, causing the man holding it to jump back in surprise. Avie smirked with self confidence at Godfrey Prinze then settled the codpiece over his cock and balls. He shifted it around a little before reaching down to tuck his balls up higher. No matter how he arranged himself, however, he couldn't make himself fit inside the inflexible glass codpiece. The attendant tentatively reached out to take it back, finally prying it from Avie's fingers and glaring at him with narrowed eyes.

Ty was next and tried to fit the codpiece against his longer, thinner, uncut cock. After a few moments of finagling himself, he ended up mashing the codpiece against his balls so hard he collapsed on the floor moaning, and the attendant retrieved the accessory, curling his lip a little as he wiped it clean.

"Anyone else in the house?" the attendant asked.

Rodolfo smiled coquettishly. "Just me, Mr. Prinze."

Godfrey and his attendants looked at Rodolfo a moment then turned to go as Cameron opened his mouth, but no sound came out. What was the use?

"What about Cameron?" a familiar voice asked and everyone jumped, turning to the kitchen.

Cameron gasped quietly as his father strode into the living room with a suitcase in his hand; his face drawn from too much travel. "Did Cameron try it on yet?"

"Oh, I don't think stripping is really Cameron's thing," Rodolfo said as he fluttered to Albert's side. "I wasn't expecting you home until later. You're just full of surprises!"

"I caught an earlier flight," Albert said. He turned to Godfrey Prinze. "I believe you wanted every gay man to try on the codpiece?"

Godfrey nodded. "Yes, I did."

"Then my son should try it on as well," Albert said. "Let me call him down."

Cameron stepped off the stairs into the hall, his heart in his throat. "No need, I'm here." His eyes locked with Godfrey's as he walked up, then he turned to smile at his father. "Hi, Dad. I'm glad you're home."

"So am I, Cam."

The attendant nodded to Cameron and handed over the codpiece. Cameron held it in his palm for a moment, feeling the familiar smooth, cool curves and weight of it, then took a breath and lowered his boxer briefs to the floor. He held the codpiece low to catch his balls and cock in it, then slowly raised it until it fit snugly over his groin, and pressed tight against his flat stomach. His cock curled perfectly into the indentation as his balls settled into their own places.

Rodolfo, Avie, and Ty gasped, and the assistant holding the pillow stepped back, his eyes going wide. Cameron looked up to find his father beaming proudly then turned to find Godfrey Prinze smiling at him, white teeth flashing as he stepped forward and extended his hand.

"Cameron, come live with me," Godfrey said, his voice deep and eyes serious. "Will you come dance for me?"

"Yes," Cameron said with a smile. "Oh, yes."

Now, as Godfrey flicked his tongue across the clenched wrinkle of Cameron's anus, a sigh escaped Cameron's lips where he lay stretched across the king-sized bed, his cock straining beneath the glass codpiece.

"Oh yeah," Cameron said, "that feels really good."

Godfrey rimmed him a few minutes longer, slicking Cameron's asshole with spit, before he straightened up and climbed on the bed to walk on his knees up the length of Cameron's torso until he straddled Cameron's chest. Godfrey wore a pair of pale yellow silk boxers, his erection tenting out the material and exposing the bottom curve of his left ball. Cameron reached up to run his hand through the hair covering Godfrey's flat stomach and firm chest, pausing to pinch his nipples into hard brown points.

Lowering his hand, Cameron grasped the solid length of Godfrey's cock through the silk material of the man's boxers and slowly began to stroke him. Godfrey tipped his head back and groaned as Cameron worked his cock faster. A spot of precum bloomed on the material pressing against the tip of Godfrey's prick, and Cameron's mouth watered at the sight.

Snaking his left hand up the leg of Godfrey's underwear, Cameron wrapped his fingers around the base of the man's balls and tugged firmly. Godfrey groaned louder and fisted his hands on his thighs as a bead of sweat tracked down his torso. Cameron adjusted the position of Godfrey's cock so that just the big, fleshy head poked out the fly of his boxers. He wrapped the silky material around the shaft and continued to stroke the man, faster and faster as, hidden within the underwear, he tugged on Godfrey's balls.

"Oh, fuck," Godfrey gasped and suddenly unleashed a flood of cum that spurted across Cameron's face, dousing his cheeks and chin and dribbling down onto his throat. Cameron continued to stroke through Godfrey's underwear until the final remnants of cum had oozed from his softening dick, then smiled up at him.

"That was hot," Cameron said.

"Not as hot as it will be," Godfrey replied and leaned down to lick the cum off Cameron's chin. When he had cleaned Cameron's face, Godfrey slid down his torso, nipping at the tall points of his nipples and running his tongue over the smooth surface of the glass codpiece until he stepped off the bed and stood at its edge. Godfrey pulled Cameron closer to the edge of the mattress then, still wearing his silk boxers, began to rub the cum slick head of his cock up and down along the crack of Cameron's ass.

"Oh, God," Cameron gasped then grunted as Godfrey slipped his rapidly swelling cock between the lips of Cameron's anus. "Oh, fuck me!"

Godfrey's dick seemed to grow longer as he pulled back, so that to Cameron it felt as if the man would never withdraw. Just as Cameron felt the cool vacancy left by Godfrey's extraction, the man pressed forward to fill his ass again with his cock.

Cameron could feel the slick tickle of Godfrey's silk boxers as the man fucked him. Godfrey dove deep each time, pulling back and driving hard into him so that Cameron grunted with each penetration as the man's cock pressed against his prostate. It didn't take long for Cameron to tumble over the edge into orgasm, and he raised his head to watch as the glass codpiece flipped off his erupting cock to land beside him on the mattress. Cum spewed up along his belly and he felt Godfrey's fingers tighten around his ankles as the man reached his own crescendo and, with a final strong push, emptied himself deep inside Cameron.

Godfrey fell atop Cameron and they lay sweaty and entwined for a moment, both men catching their breath. Then Godfrey raised his head to kiss Cameron softly on the lips and asked, "Shall we dance?"

Wired

Mark Wildyr

I did it out of utter frustration . . . and because I had the skills to do it. Dave Albano has been the object of my desire, the genesis of my dreams, the inspiration for masturbating buckets of cum, and the likely reason I am a closet gay. It all started when we jerked off together after one of Lannie Lou Hilderman's wild parties when we were fifteen. I remember little about the party, but everything about the jerk off session.

Dave cornered Lannie Lou in the cabana, figuring he was going to get his first real piece. All he got was groped, and was about to pop his cork by the time we left the party. Naturally, he confided all to his best friend, Nicholas Nix . . . that's me, Nick Nix. When we were in an appropriately dark stretch of the park on the way to our respective houses, I suggested he get rid of his problem. And just like that, he plopped down on a low wall sheltered by thick shrubbery, pulled it out, and started grunting over it. In a flash, I was beside him, my pants around my ankles, working on what I called my Dave Bone. I got harder and hotter with that good-looking fucker than with all the girls in school . . . in town . . . fuck, in the state!

What I saw intimidated me; he was maturing faster than I was. His shoulders were so wide and his waist so slender, it almost didn't look natural. And his belly was flat . . . mine still had that little-boy bow to it. But it was his cock that really got to me. As long and thick and straight and hard as any fully grown man's, it looked

His Underwear: An Erotic Anthology
© 2007 by The Haworth Press, Inc. All rights reserved.
doi:10.1300/5756_22

dangerous. Mine got stone-hard all right, but it was shorter and milk white. Looked like something to play with, not something for doing business. Still, I got there faster than he did, shooting a lot of stuff all over me. Of course, I had the sight of his exciting body and dark, Mediterranean features to get me there. Then I just held my shriveling dick in my hand, cum dripping back into my lap, while he jerked his big cock and came like a real man. The gunk shot up and hit him on the cheek. He lay back on the wall, breathing heavily while I fought to keep my hands off him. In a minute, he sat up and looked embarrassed as he cleaned himself off and got dressed.

I remained his best friend even though he went football while I went soccer. He got tangled up with a bunch of girls at school, but I only fooled around half-heartedly for appearances sake. We never got together like that again, although I thought it was going to happen at the bachelor party I gave him a week before he married Charlotte Leeper. He was so soused when the stripper came out of the fake cake that he reeled backwards and grabbed something to steady himself. What he grabbed was my king-sized erection—I'd matured in the six years since the jack off party. He just howled and told the other guys I was hot for the blonde's body. I wasn't . . . I was hot for his dark, hunky, athletic physique, but of course, I didn't let on. I stood beside him as best man when he married Charlotte and waved them off on their fucking honeymoon . . . and to hear him tell it when they got back, that's about all they did.

I became his confessor when he started having marital trouble, sitting at his side and listening to his litany of woes. I was there the night he got drunk and raised hell to the point that she called the cops. He never raised a hand to her, but he sure tore up their house. They released him into my custody. As he slept away the spell of Madam Alcohol beside me in my bed that night, I exposed him and felt him . . . and even licked him briefly. Then I went into the bathroom and jerked off yet again, picturing him passed out in my bed.

After four unsettled years of marriage, I was there when he went to court and got the divorce. He was finished with that part of his life and should have looked to me for consolation. He did, but as a buddy, a pal, a confident. The thing that moved me to action *now* was the three-day hunting trip Dave and I had taken with a couple of other buddies. We shared a two-man pop-up tent, and I saw more of that dark, gleaming flesh than I'd seen in ten years. When I was a kid panting after the good-looking fucker, I always thought that being Mediterranean he'd gross up as he got older: he'd get thicker in the limbs and sprout dark, coarse body hair. Well, he didn't. He took after his mother, I guess, because he was still slim and smooth at twenty-five.

As soon as I got back to the house after the hunting trip, I stripped, got in the bathtub, and played with myself until I clouded the water with cum. Lying there panting, I realized it couldn't go on like this. I had to do something . . . *anything.*

I had no idea of what that something would be until I sorted out my dirty hunting clothes in the laundry room. There, wadded up with my stuff, were two of his shorts. I examined, felt, and inhaled the colored briefs, their cloying, sweaty, musky smell about driving me crazy. I buried my face in the scrap of cloth that covered his cock, held the balls, and clad his smooth buns and got hard. The briefs had wide, white elastic bands, but the rest of the material was soft cotton. One was baby blue; the other, dove gray.

These two skimpy cradles for the part of him I coveted gave me the idea. Hell, I could do it! I was an electronics engineer, wasn't I? I tossed all the dirty clothing in the washer and headed out the door to get what I needed. It took three stops, but by the time I was back home to put everything in the drier, I had it pretty well figured out.

It took two hours to weave an invisible web of fine wires among the cotton fibers. Making certain there were no exposed ends to scratch his flesh, I attached a microchip. Finally satisfied with the job, I slipped on the baby blue pair and grabbed the small rheostat dial that excited the wiring . . . and hopefully, Dave Albano. Dialing up the rheostat, I sighed in pleasure as a comfortable warmth suffused my genitalia. I eased the control higher; my flesh began to react to tiny electrical impulses. In record time, I had an erection. Then the nerve endings in my cockhead began to tingle. I slipped the elastic waistband down my thighs and jerked off right there in my laundry room. It was a whopper! I was still leaking cum when the phone rang. I managed to grab it on the fourth ring.

"You sound funny," Dave said when I answered.

"Ran up from the basement to catch the phone," I puffed, watching my half turgid cock drip semen onto my carpet.

"Hey, man, I can't find my underwear. Did I get them mixed up with yours?"

"Yeah, they're in the laundry as we speak. You'll get them back cleaner than you left them."

"Great! I'll be right over. Since the divorce, I'm down to three pair."

"Shit, did Charlotte take you for your shorts, too?"

"Damned near," he said with a sour laugh. "We had a fight one night, and she starched every fucking pair I owned. I ripped them up and bought me a three-pack, and that's all I've got left. You've got two-thirds of my entire supply of underwear in your washer right now."

I thought quickly. The thing I had rigged up wouldn't survive more than one washing, if that. But if I got him another three pair, I'd have over eighty percent of his shorts rigged for action. If I couldn't attain my goal with those odds, then it wasn't going to happen.

"Uh, I was on the way out the door. Wash out your one pair for tomorrow. Come over after work and we'll have a pizza. You can pick them up then. Okay?"

"Sounds like a plan. But I'll just go *au natural* tomorrow. About six okay?"

"Yeah," I answered, giddy at the thought of him parading around his real estate office without underwear. "But put on a pair when you get here. I don't want you sitting around with your balls hanging out," I joked feebly . . . and hopefully.

"I'm not making any promises," he laughed and hung up.

Faced with a full evening of work, I raced to the mall and prowled around until I found the brand he wore—expensive fuckers for such tiny rags—and bought three of them. Back home again, I threw the new underwear in the washer and waited impatiently until they were clean and dried. Then I wired them up, seriously considering writing *Intel Inside* on them. I didn't, of course; they weren't computer chips, just small, controllable power supplies.

Maybe it was my imagination, but the thing lurking behind Dave's fly seemed a little more obvious as he sprawled underwearless on my couch the next evening, devouring his half of the pizza. Damn, I loved being around that guy. Talk was easy, and even the short stretches of silence were so fucking comfortable I never wanted our visits to end. He told me about the four-bedroom he sold that day and claimed it was because his privates were hanging out there for the woman to see. He scared me when he said he thought he'd switch to boxers so he'd feel loose and free all the time, but he was only joking. We'd both worn jockeys and athletic supports all our lives and weren't about to change now.

Dave let his surprise show when I brought out five pairs of shorts and tossed them in his lap. "Damn, did they mate and multiply?"

"I felt sorry for your wretched ass being so poor and raggedy, so I picked up some more for you." It was an acceptable crack because he made more in real estate than I did at my job. Charlotte had cleaned his clock but only temporarily. There were no children, and she hadn't asked for alimony, just all of his accumulated assets.

"These are brand new?" he asked, holding up a pair.

"Brand spanking," I answered.

"Then how come they aren't in the store wrappers?"

"I don't like to wear my shorts until they've been washed. I assumed you felt the same way. Anyway, they've been through the washer and dryer."

"Thanks, bro. I'll take you to dinner for being so thoughtful. How about Chez Charles Friday night?"

"Can't," I lied. "Have a date. But I'm free tomorrow night." I had to strike while the iron was hot.

"Okay. Meet you there at six," he said, getting to his feet and cleaning up his part of the mess we'd made.

"Aren't you going to get decent?" Shit! I wanted to see if the fucking contraptions worked.

"Naw. I'll go on home bare assed. But I promise that tomorrow night my privates will be snugly covered."

I didn't get more than two hours of sleep that night thinking about those privates.

The next evening, I waited until we finished dinner before nervously slipping my hand inside my coat and fingering the control mechanism. While he ordered the aperitifs, I twisted the dial a fraction.

"Enjoyed that," Dave said, leaning back and patting his flat belly. "Haven't had a good steak since the divorce."

"You okay, financially?" I asked, hoping that he wouldn't notice I'd started sweating. Nervous, I guess.

"Yeah. Had to take that cheap-ass apartment, but in a couple of months I'll recover and move up some."

"You can move in with me. I'm all alone in that big house since my folks died."

Dave reached under the table and adjusted himself. "Naw. But thanks. A single guy oughta have some privacy. I'll hang on where I am. I've got three closings scheduled this month, so I'll be okay." He shifted in the booth. "Man, I'm getting horny as hell. I need to find me something."

Here it is, right here! I didn't say it, of course, but man, my mind was shouting it. He gave me a peculiar look.

"I've been living like a monk for the last few months. Didn't want to give Charlotte any more ammunition than she already had, and it didn't bother me. But tonight, I think old Davy's ready for some action. I mean *really* ready."

"Well, there's always what we did when we were fifteen," I sort of mumbled, but I don't believe he even heard me. His eyes went straight over my shoulder and sort of glazed.

"Like with that," he breathed, giving a nod.

Turning in my seat, I saw a big, busty blond in a tight sweater and short skirt approach the cashier. It was Karen Washbourne, a girl he'd chased our senior year in high school for half a semester before he caught her.

"My friend," Dave said with a loopy grin. "You'll have to excuse me. Call you tomorrow night." He tossed some bills on the table to cover the tab and gave me a friendly pat on the shoulder as he rushed off to give the erection I'd generated to a fucking woman! Well, at least my contraption worked; I'd seen a hard lump of flesh straining against his slacks as he rushed to catch up with Karen.

I ran around the next day pissed as hell. I'm sure Dave got a piece of ass because of the wired underwear, and all I got was another jerk off job in my cold, lonely bed. Even my secretary commented on how grouchy I was . . . except she put it more tactfully. Touchy.

Dave confirmed my fears when he called that night. Wildest time since the honeymoon, he claimed. Fucked for an hour. He put it down to Karen's enthusiasm, but I knew better. I'd stimulated his balls so much that he fucked like a wild man.

Needing to get him alone again before he washed all of his shorts, I claimed my date Friday night canceled and suggested we do something. The big, dumb, handsome shit accepted the fib, and we decided to swing by the Corner Pocket, our favorite watering hole, for a few drinks and then go home to watch a ball game. There had to be a ball game on TV somewhere.

I kept my hands off the rheostat in my pocket until we were on our last drink. Then I set him to squirming in his seat like crazy. When he started looking over the crowd, I chugged my glass and declared it was time to go.

"Maybe we oughta stay a while. I'm feeling like some action again. We oughta pick up a couple of girls and take them with us. Shit, Nick, I feel like a teenager again. I've got a hard-on over here you wouldn't believe," he whispered conspiratorially.

Oh, yes I would. I was counting on it, but I couldn't say it out loud. "Well, cover it with your jacket, and let's get out of here."

He grumbled some, but I got us out of there in about two minutes flat. Man, I was home free! I turned up the control a little and saw him dig at himself. Maybe I was pushing it. I eased off the power.

Home free, my ass! We turned the corner of the building and walked right into the arms of a couple of girls—working girls. We'd seen them at the bar several times and never taken a second look. But old Dave's pump was primed, and he wasn't about to waste a water bucket. He started negotiating right away, and by the time my head stopped spinning, we were loaded in his convertible and headed for my house. Well, at least I wouldn't masturbate tonight.

We stayed in the living room, so I had the pleasure of watching Dave fuck his redhead on the rug in front of the fireplace. I shagged the brunette, all the while wishing we could switch partners. He came with a roar and rolled off the hooker, his impossibly-big, condom-sheathed cock slick with their juices and beginning to flag a little. The sight of his broad, smooth chest and flat belly and thick, black cock hair shoved me right over the edge of the cliff. I filled up my rubber to the point I had trouble pulling it out of the whore. Shit, I guess it was better than jacking off . . . a little.

Dave called Saturday afternoon, and we smirked over fucking the working girls. Tomorrow would be the fifth day since I wired his shorts, and I was getting desperate. Albano, a clean-freak, wouldn't wear his underwear more than once before throwing them in the · washer. I had to make a move—excuse me, *another* move—soon. I suggested he come over later and watch a game. He countered with a suggestion that we go bowling and then watch the game. Reluctantly, I accepted; wasn't much else I could do.

Fortunately, most of the people bowling were guys. I got one scare when he went into a huddle with an old girlfriend who sauntered by. She was with somebody, so that didn't develop into anything, thank goodness. I kept my hands off the rheostat in my pocket until the last frame. Then I couldn't resist it; I gave him a shot as he went for a spare . . . and the lead. I must have overdone it because he step-stuttered and rolled a gutter ball.

"Shit!" he yelped, digging at himself.

Since I had no way to confess my unintentional sabotage, I accepted the ten dollars we'd waged and offered to buy the beer. He was literally squirming in his seat by the time we finished and went out to the parking lot.

"Man, I don't know what's the matter with me. I walk around with a hard-on all the time. Guess it's the new freedom." Concentrating my energy in getting him loaded in my car, I merely mumbled a reply. About halfway home, he slapped the dash. "Man, I can't go sit in front of a television. I need some action!"

"You're going to wear it down to a nub if you don't slow down some. You've had more nookey this week than you had all last month."

He giggled. "All last *year*. Nick, I'm turning into a nymphomaniac. Do they have male nymphos? Anyway, I can't get enough. I need to shoot my balls!"

Surreptitiously, I fingered the dial and turned up the power slightly. Tonight was the night my investment in wired underwear would pay off in spades. Well, in mattresses, anyway.

"Stop!" he yelped. Startled, I stood on the brakes. He bolted out the door and headed off into the trees.

It took a minute to realize this was the park . . . *our* park. The place where we whipped out the fiddles and played tunes ten years ago. The son of a gun remembered. I caught up with him when he came to a halt and hunched over, hands on his knees.

"What's the matter?"

"Shit, I don't know. I got so antsy, I had to get out and move. Fuck, Nick, I gotta walk or something." Trusting me to follow, he set off at a half-trot.

Man, he was heading for the wall . . . *our* wall. The place we sat while we jerked off ten years ago. He *did* remember. Dave slowed and allowed me to catch up. I wondered if I should take his hand or something. No, of course not; he was horny, not in love.

"Somebody's coming," he said, motioning with his head toward two shadowy figures.

"That's okay. They'll pass us by."

As they drew closer, it was apparent they were kids from the college a few blocks away. Two young guys out looking for something. One of them, a towhead, smiled as we approached.

"Hi! What's up?" Shit, it looked like his eyes were glued to Dave's prominent crotch. I couldn't be sure in the darkness, but it sure seemed that way.

"Out for a walk. Got itchy feet . . . or something"

"Looks like you're carrying a load. What're you looking for?"

Whoa . . . wait a minute! What was going on? I opened my mouth, but Dave beat me to it. Except, he didn't say what I was going to.

"Relief, man. Just relief."

"How about a good blow job?"

Panicked, I blurted out the first thing that came to mind. "If you want to blow somebody, do your buddy. He's a hunky looking guy."

The hunky buddy spread his hands and shrugged. "We aren't really queer. We're just college men looking to augment our scholarship money."

"How about that!" Dave said. "Getting blown by two straight guys! What more could you ask? How much?"

Just like last time, lightning negotiations were concluded while I stood there with my mouth open. The next thing I knew they turned off path between some bushes. When I caught up, I found somebody had thoughtfully provided an ornate iron bench for the cocksuckers' convenience. The two college kids sat down beside one another. The towhead grabbed Dave's belt and pulled him forward. The brunette reached for me.

"Come on, Nix. Don't be a wet blanket," Dave said, grinning at me broadly as the kid unzipped him and pulled out his big dong.

"Man, you weren't lying!" Towhead exclaimed. "You're leaking already."

I thought my handsome buddy was going to come when his servicing agent rolled a condom over his big dickhead. Then I felt fresh air and realized my cocksucker was doing the same.

"This guy's ready, too!" Hunky Buddy said.

Dave gave me a wink as his cock disappeared in the college kid's mouth. "Different, huh?"

"You might say that," I said sourly. "Uhhh!" The little fucker knew how to suck cock. For a moment, he took me back to my college days when Dave was far away at another campus on a football scholarship. I'd indulged in a little homo action in those days. Got my first blow job there. And took my junior-year roommate's cock up my ass for two whole semesters. Learned to suck him, too. I had closed my eyes and dreamed of Dave Albano each and every time. I did the same thing now.

I about lost it when Dave slung his arm around my shoulders. Then the towhead came up off Dave's dick and made a comment that put me off. "Man, your balls are *hot*! You been in a monastery or something?"

"Shut up and suck!" Dave said good-naturedly. So the kid did.

We both cracked our nuts at about the same time. It was good, I guess, if I could have gotten over feeling cheated because some college hustler was taking advantage of the erection I was responsible for. Dave's wired shorts were getting action for everyone in town except *me*.

A phone call saved my Sunday from total desolation. A phone call from Dave Albano. Sounding as cheerful as ever, he reminded me we hadn't gotten around to watching any of the ball games and proposed that he bring over burgers for Monday Night Football. I clutched at the offer like a drowning man grabs flotsam. After we hung up, I came down to earth. Would he have on the right underwear? If so, that meant he had washed it at least once. Would it still work?

The next thirty hours were agonizing. I looked at the clock and my watch so much I swear the dials faded from overuse. Nonetheless, I endured, coming alive when I heard his car in the drive Monday evening. I rushed to the door, half afraid he'd have a woman on his arm . . . or worse yet, one of those college kids. But there he was, all by himself, with a happy, sloppy grin plastered on his handsome mug. I got weak in the knees when I noticed he wore cutoffs. He'd ripped out the sleeves of an old sweatshirt, which showed a lot of bronzed skin. Wish I'd thought of my cutoffs and muscle shirt. Why? He wouldn't have noticed.

We finished our burgers and polished off a six pack before the first quarter was over. By halftime, the game was a boring blow away. We criticized the quarterback, the defensive line, wobbly passes, and the coaches until we were sick of it. When Dave professed disgust and turned off the set, I twisted the rheostat and waited to see if anything happened.

After a couple more criticisms of the losing team, we sat comfortably and worked on some more beer. He leaned back on my sofa, adjusted himself, and looked at me through lazy eyes.

"We've spent more time together lately than we have since high school. We used to be inseparable, remember?"

"Except when you were on the gridiron, and I was on the soccer field," I observed.

"Yeah, but you were always there cheering me on, and I went to a lot of your games."

"When some girl didn't get in your way."

"True." He paused. "I'm glad. It's good to have my best friend back."

"You never lost him."

"Yeah, I did. It was one more thing Charlotte took from me." He winked broadly. "But we fooled her, didn't we? We got back together again." He fell silent a moment and fidgeted nervously. "I'm beginning to think it's you."

"Me what?" I asked, startled.

"Man, I've been hornier the last couple of weeks than I have been since my honeymoon. I'm beginning to think it's you." Hoping this was true provided no comeback, so I kept my big mouth shut. "You know," he went on, "your lifestyle. Single. Always ready and able to go. Bet you got a lot of poontang in this house since your folks died." His eyes fixed on my crotch. "You go around half-hard like I do, did you know that?"

I grinned; the wired shorts were still working. "One of the hazards of a single man's life."

"Come on. Let's go down to the Corner Pocket and find a couple of women."

My growing elation collapsed in a heap at my feet. All that trouble . . . for nothing! Worse than nothing, because I'd had all those expectations. I couldn't take it any more.

"No!" I exploded, hardly aware of what I was saying. "I don't want to go find any women. I don't want any old girlfriends. I don't want hookers. I don't want college hustlers. Fuck, Dave, I want *you!*" Stunned at my own outburst, I sat there like a dummy and turned red as a beet. Dave stared at me, wide-eyed.

"Well, shit, Nick, why didn't you say so?"

My mouth dropped open. Be damned! The fucking wired shorts worked! He was so turned on, he'd screw anything . . . even me.

"But what do you wanta do?" he kept on, that maddening, lazy smile splitting his lips. "You remember that time . . . how old were we, fourteen, fifteen?"

"Fifteen," I mumbled.

"We went to the park and jerked off. That what you had in mind?"

Before I knew it, I was on my feet. "No! That's *not* what I had in mind!"

I fell on him, his legs between mine, our chests mated to one another, groins caressing. Oblivious to the fact I might turn him off, I pulled his head to me and planted my lips on his astonished mouth. In a moment, he relaxed, and I forced my way inside, twisting my tongue around his. Something tickled my balls, the electricity from his shorts or the pure joy of touching him, I don't know which. Effortlessly, I ripped his old sweatshirt right down the middle and attacked his nipples, pinching one and sucking on the other with a little chewing motion.

Dave squirmed beneath me and laughed aloud. "Man, you weren't kidding, were you?"

"Fuck no," I took the time to growl before I stuck my tongue in his belly button.

When I fumbled with his fly, he put his hand under my chin and lifted my head. "Don't you think we'd be more comfortable in the bedroom?"

Marching lock-step behind him, I couldn't keep my hands off his ass. When we arrived at the bed, he turned, and I walked right into him. His arms went around me. This time, *he* kissed *me*. Fucker was good at it. My balls tingled again. Then he pushed me away and stripped. I tore off my clothes and fell on the bed beside him.

"Oh, Dave," was all I could say before I bent to him. His cock was as big as I thought, more than I could take, but I tried it anyway. He gasped when I took the head into my mouth. For one frantic moment, I wondered what he thought about his best friend, the cocksucker, but then I didn't care. This was what I wanted, schemed for, went high-tech to get; now it was mine. I sucked as much of his thick rod into me as possible and slowly came out to the end, doing things with my tongue my college roommate had taught me. They worked. Dave groaned aloud.

After five minutes, I slid down the bottom of his big sausage and feasted on wrinkled, hairless nutsack. He danced a horizontal jig on the mattress.

"Shit, Nick! What you doing to me?" I didn't bother to answer; I just wormed my way deeper, attacking the flesh behind the sack. "Oh, fuck!" was his response.

Then those strong arms pulled me atop him once again. "That what you wanted, sport?"

"No," I wheezed, sitting up on his belly and reaching behind me for the pulsing rod jabbing me in the back. I lifted myself and sat down on him.

Dave's eyebrows reached for his hairline and his hazel eyes bugged out. His mouth came open, the tip of his tongue touched his upper lip. Then his eyes slowly closed as I slid down the length of his cock. He was bigger than my college roommate—lots bigger. But that just meant he filled me up more. After a momentary pain, the pleasure of his thick prick penetrating my bowels almost made me pop my cork.

"Damn, Nick! That's incredible! Didn't know it was possible. Well, knew it was—"

"Shut up, Dave, and fuck me."

That damnable grin reappeared. "Hot for it, aren't you? Well, you better look out because here it comes!"

He rolled over on top of me. That big, good-looking, athletic stud used all the tricks he'd learned from Charlotte and Karen and all the others I didn't know about to give me a fucking I'd remember all the days of my life. I just *thought* my college buddy had fucked me. He merely diddled; Dave Albano fucked . . . like a man. Like a sex machine. Like a champion.

When he was getting close, he reared above me. "Get yourself off; I want to see you come," he wheezed. My nerve ends were so excited it didn't take long. And when the first spurt of jism shot out of my red, raw cock, he let out a whoop. My rectal muscles grabbed him, massaged him, tried to expel him, and brought him to climax. He jabbed hard half a dozen times, and then lifted his head to let out a howl. Hot cum sprayed my insides. The handsome fucker came . . . and came. . . and came! Then he surprised me by laying his body over my torso and squirming around in the semen covering my chest. He amazed me again with a deep-throat kiss. He was still in the throes of his orgasm, I realized.

Worries about postcoital regret eased when he whispered into my mouth. "Nick, Nicky, that was fucking great! Why didn't you tell me you were such a great piece of ass? Shit, you're better than most of the women I've fucked. All of them."

With another groan, he rolled off of me and looked down at himself. "Crap! I'm a mess."

"Use the shower," I managed to force through my exhausted lungs.

I lay with my cum drying on my chest and belly, in the grip of euphoria and fighting a small, niggling fear he'd eventually work around to feelings of revulsion and shame. I never had, but then I've already admitted I'm gay.

Then I heard something from the bathroom that sent my heart soaring. Singing! He was singing—loud, off-key, and hokey—but he was singing. Then he stopped.

"Hey, Nicky! Come on in here, and I'll show you what *I've* fantasized about for years!"

Stumbling out of bed, already half-hard again, I tripped over his abandoned clothing. I looked, paused, and took another look. Reaching down, I lifted his shorts . . . his cranberry red shorts. Shit, this wasn't a pair I wired. I smiled broadly, dropped the little bit of cotton and elastic, and rushed to the bathroom.

It wasn't a pair of wired shorts that got him hot tonight. It wasn't a dirty trick I'd pulled to get him into bed. He *wanted* me! Handsome, hunky, manly David Armstrong Albano wanted *me,* like I wanted *him.* Bless his Mediterranean heart . . . and balls and cock and ass.

www.menschangingroom.com

Sean Meriwether

"What kind of underwear are you wearing?" the handsome man behind me asked. Not an unusual question, but not something you were normally asked while standing in line for the changing room—not even in Chelsea. I turned to him; his brown eyes lit up with some mischievous piece of information he seemed eager to share. He looked me over, that quick head-to-toe evaluation of cruising, then pronounced, "Boxers, right?"

"Excuse me?" I sputtered, not certain if this was just his way of entertaining himself or if it was his patented flirtatious icebreaker. I worried that if I told him he was completely wrong that there might be a later opportunity for him to uncover the truth and catch me in a lie.

"I mean, poor choice. He doesn't use guys in boxers, only if their cock head pops out of that little slitty thing. Jocks are what he likes, so that's what I have on. White one, makes everything look *bigger*." He smirked in such a way that made me want to slap, then kiss him.

"I don't know what you're talking about," I said, my imagination suddenly overwhelmed by the idea of what he looked like in a white jock—the dark bulge of him straining the fabric, his bare ass open for exploration. I held a pair of jeans that I was going to try on, dampening the stiff denim with wet fingers.

"You've got that naïveté down cold. It's very endearing," White Jock added with a cheeky wink. "Come on, everyone knows what's

His Underwear: An Erotic Anthology
doi:10.1300/5756_23

in there." He pointed to the solid wood door in front of us. "This is the changing room. *The changing room.*" He squeezed my biceps in a very familiar way, as if I were his slow friend who needed to have everything repeated twice; only, he was the one not making sense.

"Yeah, and sometimes it's called a fitting room," I countered lamely. "What's your point?"

The brown-eyed man behind me laughed contagiously, causing the two men behind him to look over at us. They smiled and whispered to each other. Behind them I noticed the line for the changing room had grown incredibly long, snaking to the front of the store. It was stocked with a large ratio of attractive men. Ripped demigods in sleeveless shirts with their hair cut short in a disturbingly similar fashion. The crème de la Chelsea.

I whispered to the man behind me, "What's going on?"

"You really don't know?" he asked, incredulous, tapping my chest with his outstretched fingers. "I thought everyone knew. Everyone gay, that is. You are gay, aren't you?"

"Yes," I snorted. "What the hell is this, one of those reality shows or something?"

"In a manner of speaking, yeah." The man laughed, and the two men behind him joined in on the joke. White Jock rubbed his bristly jaw and contemplated the situation; a glint in his eyes warned me to tread cautiously.

A tall man emerged from the changing room, a wide smile riding his face. He wasn't holding any clothes that we would have tried on. We all moved up one.

"Boxers, definitely boxers," the brunet behind me confirmed. The broad-shouldered man behind him shook his head, "Never get on. With boxers and that . . . ," he made a convex sweep of his hand over his stomach. I flushed red.

"But there was that one, Black 2(x)ist Thong. He's as cute as him, no?" White Jock draped his arm around my shoulders and presented me to the couple behind us.

"I don't look at their faces," the broad-shouldered man replied, "just their baskets." The couple laughed together, sharing their · own joke; it seemed that everyone was in on it except me.

I turned away, the blood in my head ready to boil over, searing the tops of my ears scarlet. I stared at the Celtic tattoo on the neck of the man in front of me. He was next; I was after him.

"Isn't this cute. You really don't know, do you?" White Jock's warm breath feathered across my cheek, his chin perched on my shoulder. "This is the changing room," he insisted. "From menschangingroom.com."

"A website?" I kept my eyes on the tattoo, followed the complex design, wondering how much it must have hurt, wanting above all else to distract myself from feeling humiliated.

"A website? It's *the* website. In there," White Jock said, his powerful hand on my shoulder. His other hand pointed straight ahead, beyond the tattooed man, "is a webcam. The guy who runs the site takes footage of men changing and then posts it online. Members get to vote on the hottest one. The only rule is no nudity . . . and no boxers." I could feel him smile against the side of my head.

"He's right you know," the broad-shouldered man concurred. My guide tightened his grip on me and turned us to face the couple behind us. "I think out of all the mpegs online, there are only three in boxers. No offense, honey, but they were a lot hotter than you."

I had stumbled into some gay *Twilight Zone.* "So what you're telling me is that some guy films other guys undressing, in there," I pointed to the changing room that was now directly behind me, the tattooed neck guy having disappeared within, "and he posts this on the internet. Isn't that illegal?"

All three men behind me laughed. The broad-shouldered man said, "Honey, it's harder to get on that site than it is to get into Warhol after midnight. These boys would do anything to get online."

I asked them why and they all smiled again. "For the sex, stupid," the broad-shouldered man's friend quipped. "The top rated guys

on that site can fuck anyone they choose. Amateurs are so *now*."
He finished with a Norma Desmond flair of hands.

We stood quietly together, listening to the tattooed-neck man
moaning. "Nope. Jerking off. He won't post that either."

"Just jockstraps?" I asked.

"Primarily jocks," the brown-eyed man said. "Like mine." He
dipped the front of his jeans down to expose the white elastic
of his jock. I followed his fingers, hoping for a more southern
exposure.

The changing room door opened. The tattooed-neck man
emerged, stared down at his shoes, and stumbled away. The
broad-shouldered man tsk-tsked. "Too bad. He was hot."

The brown-eyed man gave me an encouraging little push forward, and I slipped into the small room, closing the door with damp
hands. It was slightly larger than a walk-in closet, but unlike most
fitting rooms there was nowhere to sit down. One complete wall
was a mirror. I stared at it wondering if that's where the camera
was; I swore I saw a blinking red light in the glass.

I stood there holding the jeans I had planned to try on, wanting
to be told what to do, waiting to be given some direction. Then I
thought of White Jock just beyond the door—worried he would be
disappointed in me if I didn't even disrobe for the camera. If I
wimped out, I wouldn't be able to face him. I closed my eyes,
swallowed down the nervous tickle in my throat and made the de-
cision to just do it.

I bent down to undo my shoes, untying them slowly, studying
the white laces with an unwavering focus. I slipped off my shoes
and braved myself for the next step, but an alarm went off in my
head. I had on an old pair of socks. The right one had a hole, which
my big toe was poking through, and they had stripes—*straight
boy socks*. How could I take off my pants while wearing those
socks? I removed them quickly, tucking them into my shoes
where no one would be able to see them. I stood, looking at everything but the mirror, trying to pretend that this was just like any
other changing room I'd been in, and not one with a webcam that

might be broadcasting my image to all the guys logged on right now, jacking off while I undressed on their monitors.

My hands were shaking as I fumbled with the button-fly, and I inadvertently popped them all open in one jerk. I stared straight ahead as I lowered my pants, thinking of all those guys out there, maybe even an ex-boyfriend or two, watching me do this. Hundreds, even thousands of men downloading my three minute movie; electronic voyeurs with their eyes darting along my legs to the lump of my crotch.

I was hard before my jeans hit my ankles; not just in-the-mood-to-fuck hard, but hard enough to break through walls—like when you're nineteen. I shyly pulled the front of my T-shirt over my erection, which threatened to escape through the slit, remembering what White Jock had said about the guys on the site who wore boxers.

I squatted down ungracefully and yanked off first one pant leg, then the other, falling against the door with a bang. Titters from outside, and I imagined the broad-shouldered man and his partner whispering to each other about me. I hoped the brown-eyed man was not a party to my ridicule.

When I stood up, my cock popped well beyond the slit and tugged free of my shirt. I watched it emerge in the mirror, a pearl of precum glistening in the reflection. I wiped it off and licked my fingers without thinking of the camera capturing my every movement, thinking only of White Jock, and how I wanted him in here with me. I tucked my dick back into my striped boxers and then stepped back against the wall, staring straight ahead at the floor-to-ceiling reflection of myself.

My eyes swept over the figure standing a few feet away, arms crossed girlishly over his midsection. His T-shirt draped over his limpening dick, striped, wrinkled boxers flared out over thin legs. The potent image of thousands of men jerking off in the blue light of their monitors evaporated and was replaced by the single man standing opposite me. It was not an image I wanted to identify with; the scrawny teenage boy who masturbated in secret to work-out magazines, fearful of his own body and unfulfilled desires. I thought I'd left him behind when I moved to New York, when I'd become an independent gay man, but there he was, as awkward and gangling as ever. How did he ever think he could compete with the demigods of Chelsea?

I struggled back into my own pants and shoes, leaving behind the jeans I was going to try on. My face flushed as I pushed the door open and stared straight into the soulful brown eyes of White Jock. A confident and welcoming smile graced his lips as he said, "Wait up, boxer boy," before gliding past me, his body brushing mine, firing a million nerve endings simultaneously. I quickly imagined the swell of his dick filling his jock, filling me. . . . The door closed, and I was left with the suspiciously quiet couple that stood next in line, staring right through me as if I weren't there.

I moved forward in a daze, my body ringing with White Jock's heat, my head in a fog of adolescent trauma. My eyes turned away from the line of near-perfect men snaking their way toward an audition for localized celebrity and sought the burning light of the street. I burst out of the door, gasping for breath like a claustrophobic, dragging in fumes from the slow Chelsea traffic.

Weekend errands forgotten, I went straight home and climbed into bed, fully clothed. My mind echoed my reflection back to me; the memory of my old body merging with the reality of my current one. That insecure boy in striped boxers stared back at me through the years, accused me of letting him grow soft and unfuckable in my late twenties. He encouraged the gnawing belief that White Jock had only been interested in me as a supplicant to worship him, to feed his engorged ego with my own. It was all my fault, he sneered; I'd failed that frail boy of my youth, denying him the sex and adventure that moving to New York had once promised.

My eyes burned closed and I slipped into a fitful nap of denial— the dead, dreamless sleep numbed me, leaving me more drained than refreshed.

When I woke up, I remained on the bed for hours, staring at the ceiling while trying to banish the image in the mirror. The idea of it possibly being broadcast over the internet, for other men to disparage, held me in check but finally forced me to rise, wanting to take some disturbed satisfaction in seeing just how bad I looked. I moped through the dark apartment, dragging my feet with a dramatic lethargy, and plopped down in front of the computer. I pecked out the URL www.menschangingroom.com; the sharp report of the keys blasted the bare walls of my empty apartment. The site flashed up, all perfect bodies in perfect jocks, tempting the unwary into becoming a member. I entered my credit card info blindly, certain I would find the embarrassing image of me in rumpled shirt and swollen belly with those awful boxers left over from a failed relationship. Having to pay $19.95 for that humiliation added a whole new edge to my angst.

I quickly scrolled past the links to International Jock and used undie sites, scanned over the meaty image of Hot Daily Jock, and clicked on the current images gallery. I waited impatiently as dozens of thumbnails loaded, each labeled with a number and the ability to rate them on a scale from 10 to 1—hot or not. I scanned the gallery quickly, my blood rioting for a fight. I was ready to call whomever ran this voyeur circus and threaten liable, or some more appropriate legal term; I was thankfully disappointed that none of the images were mine. It only confirmed that I hadn't measured up, allowing me to wallow in my body's flaws.

Half of the parade of men I'd been in line with were there, including the broad-shouldered man in a black pouch of a thong, but I was happy to note his catty partner was absent, as well as the Celtic tattooed man. I sought out the miniature photo of White Jock, the strong muscles of his thighs, flat plateau of his stomach, and the rise of his pecs clearly defined despite the small black and white image. The message CLICK HERE TO LAUNCH MPEG taunted me in little letters as I outlined his body with the arrow of my mouse.

I clicked on the image, against my better judgment, wanting to rub the salt of a lost opportunity into a deepening wound. A second window appeared, warning that the movie was downloading and would take some time depending on my internet connection. It offered a DVD of the top men from the site for the low-low price of $39.95. Then he was there, staring directly into my blue eyes from the screen, just as he had at the store. I felt the tingle of his body as it brushed past mine on the way into the changing room, a climbing chill that dashed up my spine and fanned out over my scalp.

The volume was turned way up, and beneath the chronic pop and hiss from my speakers I could hear him breathing—the steady intake of breath, confident exhalation. I matched my breathing to his; he watched me from the safe vantage of the monitor. He removed his shirt first, stretching it over his head, revealing inch-by-inch the hair-trail that led up his lean stomach to the spread of his chest, to his quarter-sized beige nipples, and finally to his lean shoulders. Not the overdeveloped Chelsea body, but a lean and tight swimmer's build reminiscent of northern Italian and French men. Hands on hips he stood, waiting for the viewer to get an eyeful, building the moment with the skill of a natural performer.

I swore I heard the metallic release of his top button and the long sigh of his zipper. White Jock slipped his fingers inside the waistband of his jeans, the bulging curve of his hands working forward toward the open crevice of his zipper. He cupped himself, dropped his head to let a curtain of long dark hair spill forward over his face, then smiled up through the veil of hair. His hands parted and slid the faded denim down his thighs. His immaculate jock appeared, followed by brown, furry legs; turning his back to the camera, he bent over and stepped out of his pants, the perfect globes and shaded cleft of his asshole holding the shot.

I slipped my own pants off, remembering the intense moment of all those presumed men staring at the rise in my underwear. My hand worked my cock slowly; my blue eyes locked on White Jock as he turned back to me. He eased the elastic of the waistband against his tanned skin with a wayward hand, giving me a glimpse of a fiery patch of bush. Another minor adjustment, a hand on the pouch of his jock, massaging his dick and balls into perfect symmetry, like sculpture. His hand on his cock, my hand on mine beating erratically while he slipped two fingers along the side of his jock and teased out his growing erection.

Quite unexpectedly he folded over, revealing the lean expanse of his back, and worked a pair of jeans up his furry legs, carefully fondling his package into the *V* of the zipper before closing up. He left the top button undone. The jeans he now wore, I realized, my own dick swelling, were the ones I'd brought in to try on. The waist was too large, and the pants slipped down his hips, revealing the top of his jock. He did an about face, showing the rise of his ass over the top of the blue denim horizon, then ran his hands beneath the fabric, cupping his cheeks as if sizing himself up. Again he turned towards the camera, slipping his hands inside the pants to arrange himself, pulling at his cock with a playful smile, brown eyes begging me to help him out. Then the jeans were gone, a magician's trick, revealing the full expanse of his jock pulled taut by his swollen erection. The head twisted like a demon to escape, a wet spot forming a perfect, dark circle on the white fabric.

I mentally knelt before him and ran my tongue along the nubbly fabric of his jock. I tasted that salty wet spot, made it larger, wetter, and grazed my teeth over the sensitive head of his dick. I ran my hands along his hairy thighs, beneath the elastic straps running up either side of his ass, trapping my arms as my hands sought out the dark crevice behind him, dipping my fingers into his heated gorge. My mouth on his jock, tongue bathing that restless demon in layers of spit. White Jock's hand captured the back of my head and pushed forward until my face was filled with him; the rich funk of his sweat in my nose. Separating his ass with my hands, my face pummeled by his sheathed dragon, my lips tightening over his thick shaft, pulling him into me as his shot burst through the fabric into my hungry mouth.

I exploded, filling my own hand with wasted spunk and baptizing my rumpled shirt with splashes of sticky white. On the monitor White Jock ended his show; the last image of him standing with an errant erection and a sexy scowl shaping his lips. I touched my cum-wetted fingers to his face and body, smudging the monitor with my sacrifice to him.

After six months of regimented diet and gym routines, I returned for a second chance at Internet celebrity and to recapture what I had lost in that room. I nodded curtly to the members of the gay elite who were beginning to accept me as one of their own, men I'd recently fucked and brunched with on my way into their exclusive community. I'd soon be worthy of White Jock, my muse and inspiration for the metamorphosis of my body, and this was to be my testament to him.

I moved forward in that quiet line, holding the same size and style of jeans I had originally planned to purchase, amazed that they would have fit snuggly on the physically awkward boy I had banished with free-weights and yoga. Now, twenty-six pounds lighter, the jeans would slide right off my lean hips, just like the brown-eyed man, exposing me on cue. This time I would make the cut. I had to, I *must* make it online, if for no other reason than to honor White Jock, who had been relegated to the archives.

Inside the changing room, so familiar from watching hundreds of other men audition here, I began my homage to White Jock. I'd studied his every movement, practiced over the intervening months to replicate his routine, and manhandled my white-jocked cock with the same playfulness he'd inspired. I went through the motions, over-rehearsed and slightly rushed, but performing for him. I imagined the brown-eyed man out there in the light of his monitor, watching me as I had watched him, touching his cock as I touched mine. I massaged my erection beneath the stiff denim as he had hundreds of times in the mpeg loop. The knowing smile as the jeans disappeared and my jock is pulled out tight, filled with my offering to White Jock. I incanted his name, fingering the wet spot at the end of my dick, standing tall in the body he was responsible for transforming. *This is for you.*

Enlightenment

Dominic Santi

I wasn't looking for enlightenment. My dick and I were looking for an orgasm, preferably one induced by someone else's hand. My own would do in a pinch.

No matter how much fun I had at tonight's JO party, this particular Cinderella's ball needed to be over well before midnight. The crew boss had promised he'd dock my wages if I was late again. My dick had to be comfortably quiescent in time for me to get my beauty rest and get to work in the morning.

The loft was packed by the time I got there. Brad and Scott had already stripped down to their designer undies. We made a good threesome—smooth, buff, stylish. I was an inch taller than their matching six feet even. Together, we were definite eye candy. Brad had short, straight auburn hair and a thick, stocky dick that made a respectable bulge in his boxer briefs. He and Scott were both into designer sneakers, though Scott had a blond buzz, a long, thin cock, and a preference for silky, European-type bikini slips. Me, I have dark brown curls and a perfectly proportioned six-inch dick; I'm into combat boots and wear a jock strap, which I like to lose early in the evening.

They greeted me with grins as I scoped out the room. In the far corner, a skinny Asian guy with blond dreadlocks definitely had

This story appeared originally in *Kerle im Lustrausch,* Dominic Santi, 179-192. Berlin: Bruno Gmunder, 2004. Used with permission of the author.

potential. I'm into unusual. Brad slipped his arm over my shoulder and rubbed my tit while I blatantly stared.

"Hope you guys don't mind that I brought a friend."

"No problem," I said, turning to meet the guy. I knew one of Brad's former Army buddies was in town for the week.

I was glad I'd spoken before I turned. Tom was a troll. I don't mean he was just not an Adonis. I mean his face could have stopped a clock, or at least my wristwatch. His nose had obviously stopped more than one fist in its time, and he was at least ten years older than the rest of us. He was short and squat, and fuck, he was ugly.

"Hi," I forced a smile and stuck out my hand. "I'm Mick." As we shook, I frantically tried to remember what Brad had said about him, about why they were such good friends—something about Tom's being an artillery sergeant and their being buffed up fags in the military together and fantastic hand jobs. Hand jobs at a JO party. Okay, I could work with that. Tom was still holding my hand. His grip was firm and warm. I squeezed back and made myself notice the guy had a nice enough bod, not gym hard, just firm all over, with washboard abs, actually. The discount store plaid boxers made me cringe though. His black hair was cropped short. I couldn't remember if Brad had said Tom was still in the service. His silvery blue eyes sparkled kind of nicely when he smiled, which, I found out quickly, he did a lot. Still, that face. . . .

Tom turned our hands and rubbed his thumb over the back of my wrist. "Nice grip. Long, strong fingers, and your skin's sensitive." His thumb brushed farther up, just enough to make the hair on my arm raise up. My shiver surprised me. "I like a responsive man," he grinned.

As Brad laughed, Scott leaned over and gave Brad a kiss. Then Scott kissed me and grabbed a tit on Brad and Tom—Scott's an inclusive kind of guy. It wasn't long before the four of us were swallowing each other's tongues and rubbing each other's chests and shoulders. Tom still hadn't let go of my hand. I didn't mind, even though I was really aware of the contact between us. I'd never thought much about hand-holding before. Hands on dicks, yes. But hand to hand, well, I'd never been much into PDAs. Still, the way he moved his fingers on mine and the different pressures he used felt good, in an odd sort of way. When I closed my eyes, I could concentrate on kissing and the feel of skin on skin as the four of us pressed together. It didn't matter that we weren't paying attention to anyone else in the room. I didn't have to think too much about whose lips were whose, or whose hands, or whose tit I was squeezing—or what Tom looked like.

As the action got more frenzied, Scott's moans got louder. He's noisier than hell when he gets turned on, and he's watched way too much porn. Before long, his guttural demands to, "chew that tit!" let me know every time I was kissing him. Tom quietly settled our clasped hands between where our thighs now touched. His movement was slow and unhurried, just a gentle placement, then his thumb was stroking again. Just the edges of our hands touched our legs, below the edges of his boxers. Every once in a while, an extra tingle on my lips or skin had me guessing it was him I was touching. I rubbed down sweaty abs, recognizing Scott's outie belly button. I grinned and slid my hand lower, splaying my palm over the hard-on stretching past the low-riding waistband of his precome soaked slip. Scott jerked and thrust up his hips.

"Fuck, man! Jerk that cock!"

Scott always matches his motions to the latest video he's watched. I opened my eyes to see what he'd do this time. He had one hand draped over Brad's shoulder. Scott's other hand was on his own butt, like he was pushing it up to make his dick meet my hand. His head was thrown back and his body glistened with sweat. He looked so fucking hot as he watched himself fuck his dick against my hand. Beneath my fingers, the wet stain on his silky bikini clearly defined the outline of his cock.

"Jerk that cock, man!" he growled, grinding his dick into my hand.

I glanced up to see how Tom was reacting to our one-man porn act. Damn, that face! His eyes were shining, though, so brightly they were almost shimmering. Like whatever he was looking at had his absolute attention. And he wasn't looking at Scott. Tom was watching Brad. Holy fuck, it was easy to see why.

Brad stood frozen in place, his head thrown back, his eyes closed, his arm braced motionless on my shoulder as a soft moan escaped his lips. His hips were arched up, but he wasn't thrusting them the way Scott was. Instead, Brad was taking deep, even breaths, trembling ever so slightly as Tom's hand stroked slowly and rhythmically up the dark red, fiercely erect cock protruding through Brad's open fly. On the next downstroke, Tom twisted his hand. When he pulled up again, he squeezed just hard enough to pull another clear, heavy drop of precome free. Brad shivered and pressed against my shoulder.

Milking. That was the only word I could think of. Tom was milking the precome from Brad's cock, and it was driving Brad nuts.

It was making me harder than fuck, too. I tried to move our joined hands to my dick, but Tom resisted. His eyes flicked to mine. "Later," he said. Then he was looking back at Brad.

"Fuck, dudes. It is time to take off our fucking shorts!"

Scott stepped back to strip off his slip. I started to follow his lead, but again, Tom stopped me. "Later," he said again. His smile made his eyes so silvery, almost molten, as he turned our hands just enough to stroke the tips of fingers across my thigh. He nodded towards Brad. "Take his off instead."

I don't think Brad could have moved if his life depended on it. Tom still didn't release my hand, so I turned to take Brad's boxer briefs off one-handed.

"Fuck, man! Look at him jerk that dick!"

Scott squatted down, his hard-on bobbing between his legs as he alternately jacked himself and helped me work Brad's shorts over his sneakers. As Brad's dick slid free, Tom's hand moved over the fly so smoothly, it seemed like he hadn't even really let go of the hard flesh he'd been holding. Then he was milking Brad's dick again. This time, Brad moaned out loud.

"That is so fucking hot, dudes!" Scott stepped back to the shelf nearest us and pumped out a handful of lotion from an industrial-sized bottle. He slathered the creamy lube over his dick, jerking himself quickly as once more Brad shakily balanced himself against us. Scott thrust his dick out at me again. My hand glided downward, heating the thick, slick lotion covering his shaft. Scott reached for me, but Tom's arm came up and blocked him. Tom shook his head firmly.

"No, please. I'm going to do him later."

I couldn't help the shudder that ran through me. Scott laughed and instead let his hand drop back to pull on his balls.

"So," Scott cocked his head at me. "You going to do me like that, too?"

I was more than willing to give it my best shot.

Scott groaned as I slowly twisted up. "Fuck, man."

"Each dick is different," Tom said quietly. His hand was moving differently on Brad now, a thumb and finger squeeze that had Brad barely breathing. "Each man jacks himself off differently. The trick is to first find out what he likes, what feels good to that particular dick. Find out what he usually does and copy it. Then you add something new, something that builds on what he likes, but has him pleading for what only you can give him, not just what he can give himself."

Tom had obviously already found all of those things on Brad. Brad was leaking like a sieve, his shaft arched up so red and hard it looked like a fire hose, ready to shoot. Tom set his fingers on the top of Brad's dick, his thumb on the bottom, and squeezed lightly. Brad's hips bucked as a whispered, "Please!" slipped past his lips. Just looking at him, I wanted my dick touched so badly I couldn't help trying to turn into where my hand meshed with Tom's. I wanted to cry at the gentle but deliberate resistance that held our hands firmly between our thighs.

To distract myself, I concentrated on giving Scott what I already knew he liked. Gripping him lightly, I pistoned my hand hard and fast over the entire length of his shaft. The friction made his skin hot as his hips started to buck wildly.

"Fuck, yeah! Jerk that dick. Jerk that dick, dude!"

Where our hands joined, I felt Tom's body shift as he changed strokes on Brad. I couldn't see exactly what he was doing, because at exactly that moment, I slowed my hand and tightened my grip on Scott's dick, twisting my hand and turning it as I pulled up and over the leaking head. Since Brad had liked the movement when Tom did it, I figured Scott would probably like it, too. I didn't realize he'd like it enough to come.

He did. Oh, fuck, did he ever. He gritted his teeth and bucked into my hand, forgetting all about his porn star commentary as his warm come gorped out onto both of us, mingling with the creamy white ropes suddenly spurting from Brad's dick. Scott fucked my fist through his entire come. He was shaking as hard as Brad while they both leaned, panting and gasping for breath, into Tom and me.

I was rubbing Scott's lotiony come on the side of my hip when Tom turned and kissed my forehead. Glancing down, I saw he'd shoved his boxers below his balls. His pole was half-hard, the crown hiding back in the hooded cowl of his foreskin. He was too close for me to see his face, so I closed my eyes and kissed him back. His lips were soft and warm and his spit was sweet. He was sucking my tongue when he finally pulled our joined hands to my crotch. He rubbed our hands over my cock. My face heated as I realized just how wet my jock was.

I was only vaguely aware of Brad moving in back of me. Then he pulled me up against him, sucking the back of my neck as he tipped me back to lean against his chest. His sticky, soft cock rested against my hip. I wiggled, and he laughed.

"Relax and enjoy it, Mick," he whispered in my ear. "I promise Tom will make you feel good."

Tom's low chuckle had me blushing all over again. His thumb was stroking my wrist again. Then the warm, strong fingers of his other hand covered my groin, cupping and squeezing as he learned the shape and feel of my dick. I couldn't help the shiver as my cock reached up for him.

"Nice shape, nice length—just the right heft for some serious stroking." He leaned over and nipped my tit. I jumped and moaned. "And very sensitive nipples," he laughed. "Scott, will you do the honors up here?"

"With pleasure," Scott growled, using his best porn star voice as he slid his palms over my pecs. "I know just what Mick likes done to his perky young nipples." He pinched and twisted. I arched up into Tom's hand. He was squeezing my shaft, up and · down, like it was a long, fat sausage he was plumping up for his dinner. As my cock stretched out into my jock, he covered it with his palm and rubbed hard and fast, until the friction of my skin against the wet cotton had me panting and thrusting against him.

"Take his jock off," Tom said quietly. Brad tipped me further back while Scott worked the straps down and over my boots. Tom's hand tipped and rolled over me the same way it had when we'd removed Brad's underwear, and even with feeling what he was doing, I still couldn't figure out exactly how he'd done it.

"Lube," Tom ordered. As always, Scott was right on the ball, but again, Tom didn't let him touch me. Tom opened our joined hands enough for Scott to pour the creamy lotion onto our palms. Then Scott's slippery fingers were back on my nipples. Instead of closing our hands, Tom stepped forward, so close Brad had to tip me further back to give Scott access to my nipples. Cloth moved against my thighs as Tom shoved his boxers the rest of the way off. Then he wrapped our joined hands around both of our dicks, rubbing against me as he squeezed our fingers together.

The cry that left my lips was embarrassingly inarticulate.

"Fuck, dudes," Scott whispered, his fingers twisting my nipples as Tom slowly jerked us off. The feeling was exquisite. Our joined hands glided over our dicks, the heat of his shaft sliding against mine as Scott milked sensation from my tits.

"Brad said you like having your balls tugged when you come," Tom said softly.

"Unh, huh," I nodded, my head moving against Brad's shoulder. Tom laughed.

"Tell me which things you like. Slow squeezes?"

I groaned, nodding as he squeezed my fingers against us, up, then back down again. "Squeezes with massaging just below the head? Maybe with a pause, rubbing that real sweet spot just below the V?" Brad kissed the back of my neck as Tom rubbed. My knees buckled.

"I'll take that as a *yes*." His voice vibrated against my chest. "You have to tell me what you like, so I know which things you want me to do again."

"'S'all good," I moaned, leaning heavily on Brad, but not really giving a shit as Tom pumped our hands quickly over our shafts. Then he suddenly slowed.

"Oh, yeah!" I panted.

"You like it slow?" He murmured, stroking in long, lazy glides.

"S-slow is good," I gasped, arching into the juncture of our hands as he squeezed again. "Th-that, too!"

"Slow, with squeezing," he said quietly. His hands matching his words as our dicks again slipped together. I moaned as Scott poured more lube over us. "Do you like it when I squeeze the precome up your dick tube?"

"Fuck, yes!" I gasped, shaking as he did exactly that. Again, he squeezed and stroked. I realized that at the end of each stroke, I was waiting for him to rub the *Vs* of our dicks together. When it didn't happen, I thrust my hips forward.

"If you want it different, you have to ask for it," Brad said quietly into my ear. I looked up into Tom's eyes. They were almost glowing with lust. Our hands glided together and, once more, he squeezed just below the head. I licked my lips and blurted out. "The *V* thing. You know, where you rub that spot just below the *Vs* on our dicks together . . . oh FUCK!"

I bucked up, shaking and thrusting my hips wildly as Tom rubbed just the way I'd asked him to.

"Oh, yeah," he panted. For the first time, I could feel the heat and sweat on his body where we rubbed together. "I like up and over with a twist sometimes. You want to try that?"

I nodded, but his hand was already moving. Tom may have been seemed cool and detached before, but the over with a twist was getting to him in a big way.

"Again," I demanded, pushing against his hand as he pulled our joined fists over our dicks again. Our dicks were so hard against each other, I knew he was as close as I was. Our wrists twisted, and my balls pulled up. "Gonna come!" My voice echoed into Tom's.

As Brad worked my nipples, Scott reached down to pull on both our ballsacks.

"Fucking aye, you're both going to come," Scott laughed. "Jerk those dicks!"

Tom shook his head vehemently. "No!" He gasped, grabbing my other hand and wrapping that over our dicks as well. "Jerk my dick!" he choked. "Mine!"

I tried to say "mine," too. But I was too fucking far gone to spit it out. Tom and I once more squeezed our hands over our dicks. I stiffened, arching up onto my toes as an ocean of come spurted through my dick. The creamy juice ran down over us, and Tom bucked against me. His dick jerked, then his hot, musky juice joined mine as we pumped each other through orgasms that left us both shaking.

It was a while before I could stand on my own again. Even then, I left my come-covered hand resting in Tom's.

"Dinner tomorrow night? I know a great Thai restaurant by the mall." Tom's eyes sparkled as his thumb once more stroked my wrist. I was starting to get really used to the feeling.

"I'd like that," I smiled. "I'd like that a lot." I looked over at Brad and Scott, who were smirking blatantly at us. "You two can join us for dessert, if you ask nicely."

"You fucking aye, I'll ask," Scott laughed, flipping his key between his fingers as we headed back towards the clothes check. "In the meanwhile, Cinderella, you best get your ass home so you get your beauty rest. It's almost eleven, and you need your job. You're treating all of us tomorrow."

I was too blissed out to bother arguing with them. Tomorrow night's dinner was bound to be interesting. In fact, I couldn't wait to check out dessert.

The Boy in the Boxers

Tim Bergling

The scene replaying in my mind's eye is just as vivid, just as
clear, as the playback from any video or DVD, maybe more so; I
can almost feel the cold night air on my skin, feel the utter stillness
of the dark . . . until it's broken by a cacophony of light and sound.

The car pulls around the steep curve of the road, headlights flar-
ing, stereo inside throbbing deep bass lines. Brakes and tires
squeal to a stop, a chorus of competing male voices sound—
young male voices—and bodies tumble out. They're college kids,
most likely students at the small university a few miles away in
the smallish town where I live. But what brings them so far outside that tiny oasis of light and cheap beer, into this empty rural
countryside on a Saturday night?

The answer comes quickly, as figures move into the headlights.
One of the young bodies shuffling around in those twin beams
isn't a willing player; he's being roughed up a bit and shoved
around by the others, bigger and stronger than he is. . . . Suddenly
he is stripped down to his underwear, and his arms wrap around
his upper body against the cold. I can see he's barely more than a
boy, pale, smooth skin shining white in the harsh light, nipples
shrunk to tiny dots by the near-freezing temperatures. His face
would be something close to beautiful if he wasn't so terrified and
trembling, standing there facing his tormentors; one of them steps
forward to deliver another shove, and as the poor youth falls,

His Underwear: An Erotic Anthology
© 2007 by The Haworth Press, Inc. All rights reserved.
doi:10.1300/5756_25

others reach in to strip away his last bit of clothing: some reddish plaid boxers may be a half-size too big for him.

Is this some sort of fraternity initiation rite? Could be, though it seems rather brutal even for that crew. Maybe this youngster pissed off his buddies somehow and it's time for a payback, or perhaps they've discovered he's gay . . . that thought chills me, and I pray the drama I'm watching won't become something tragic. Yet even in the midst of the scene I can't help but admire the youth's naked smoothness as he struggles to his feet, his well-formed chest and mid-section, his ample ass and taught athletic legs. He looks like he could be a swimmer, or maybe a gymnast. My eyes travel over him. I don't want to stare at his dick and balls, it just feels wrong, somehow—but I'm helpless *not* to look. The boy has a perfect package, especially factoring in the shrinkage doubtlessly induced by his fear and the god-awful cold.

The naked youth tries a few times to make for the car. Clearly he's no weakling, but the others have him outweighed by several pounds—they look to be about football-player size—and they keep pushing him back until he's simply standing there, shivering in the headlights, as they pile back in and leave him there in the road. His clothes are nowhere about; they must have taken them with them into the car, which is now slowing backing away. I can hear him pleading above the engine noise and stereo sounds: "At least let me have my underwear!" That's when the car stops for a moment, and one of the youths inside steps out. "Here ya go!" he cries, and gives the wadded-up boxers a mighty toss upward. They land in the branches of a tree, about fifteen or so feet above the ground, far out of the naked boy's reach. That's when he looks down, whimpering at his fate, as the car drives off and disappears into the night, leaving him alone in the dark. . . .

At least, that's what I imagine he'd do, just as I've imagined the whole sequence of what *might* have happened at some point, on some imagined night not too long ago. Sure enough there *is* a steep curve of road, and a college town just a few miles away across the rural countryside. The rest is just a fantasy, a mental movie I like to play in my head sometimes . . . it's all a product of too much time on my hands, too little real excitement of the carnal variety, and my overwrought imagination.

Except the boxers. Those are quite real.

It's going on five years now that I've moved out here—make that *way* out here—just another refugee from all that overcrowded urban and suburban DC sprawl, and its gay scene filled with people whose charms were growing evermore elusive over time. The endless fucking around, STDs aplenty, and all that bitchy backbiting from caustic queens just got far too tiresome for yours truly, and having been fortunate enough to have some money set aside, I took an early retirement, sold my house, and got the fuck outta Dodge. First I found a loft above a used bookstore, then said "what the hell?" and went ahead and bought the whole building. Now I work on my meager writings by night, and by day, I do my best to cater to the needs of the students here at Backwater U.

Unfortunately I'm only catering to their book-buying needs, 'cause I have to tell you, this student body—accent on *body*—is beyond fabulous. It feels like I landed at one of the schools where they shoot the Abercrombie & Fitch catalog; I have never seen so many handsome faces and fit young physiques in one place at one time, not since my Army days, at any rate. Now it's those students—the male ones—who often people my wilder fantasies, though I am very careful not to let on when I'm observing them as they walk the stacks, looking for a *Paradise Lost* or *Waiting for Godot*. Even with today's baggier styles of clothing, I can detect the firm shapes beneath their T-shirts and board shorts—or their jerseys and jeans—as they stoop for the lower shelves or perch on a stool to reach for the upper racks; that's when I catch the occasional glimpse of fine tender skin riding above their loose waistbands. Even more titillating, those moments when I spy them standing and perusing a dusty old novel, hands reaching idly inside shirts to rub their young bodies absentmindedly, as they silently mouth the words to themselves.

Most compelling are the athletes who populate our modest but
apparently rather successful sports programs. They often descend
on my store in groups of twos and threes, some still wearing their
practice basketball, track, or lacrosse shorts that do precious little
to hide their ample endowments. The jocks here *do* seem to require the most help finding whatever it is they need for class, and I
am only too happy to oblige. I try not to be too obvious when I'm,
well, checking them out, so to speak, but if there is anything more
perfect on this planet than an athletic male youth swinging to and
fro within his gym shorts, I have yet to encounter it. The daily exposure I get during the academic year is like a tonic. I cannot tell
you how many times I've pictured spiriting one of those fine young
specimens up to my loft, to see if the reality matches my imagin-
ings. But though once in a while I have caught one of them actually looking at me with what seems to be more than a passing glance,
I've never yet mustered the courage to do anything about it.

Don't get me wrong, now, I'm not just some lonely old voyeur;
I've had *real* relationships in the past, of every kind imaginable,
from one-night stands with near-total strangers to long-term part-
nerships measured in several years. But when the last one ended
seven years ago, it nearly took me with it. Since then I've been
content to go solo, and on the vast majority of nights, it's a soli-
tude I treasure. One day the city may well pull me back in; or
maybe one day I will actually find myself meeting a kindred soul
out here in the boonies . . . but for now, as long as I have one hand
and an imagination, I am a happy camper. I use that imagination
quite frequently up in my loft, more and more these days it seems.
Which brings us back to the boxers. . . .

I long ago stopped wondering why I still bother to try to keep
myself in shape, I just do, okay? Even if I have become the well-
appointed home that no one really visits anymore. Military training dies hard and so do love handles. I use the gym on campus
whenever I can—there's certainly an eye candy factor there, but I
try to contain myself—and about a month ago when the snows finally melted it was time to start up my daily runs again. Several
times a week now I drive my little car out past the edge of town,

park it on the side of the road, throw on my shoes, and go. I find the stillness and the still-chilly air quite bracing . . . my mind just goes on a sort of autopilot, and I enter what can almost be described as a dreamlike state. Sometimes I am not even sure how far I've run or for how long.

It was on one of those runs that the previously mentioned boxers came to my attention. They caught my eye as a splash of unlikely color, high up in the branches of a tree dangling over the road, just before it makes a steep turn and heads back toward town. The sight of them snapped me out of my reverie and brought me to a halt, and I walked around taking a breather, glancing upward occasionally, eventually just standing there gazing at them before slowly moving on.

My next several runs brought me back to that same spot in the road, and every time I found myself looking upward as the boxers flapped forlornly above me in the breeze. It's not everyday one sees under shorts in such unlikely circumstances, and I started envisioning various scenarios as to how they might have come to be there, out here in farm country miles from the nearest house. One such scenario you know already, and as my favorite, it's a scene I've built up and embellished up in the privacy of my loft. I am sure there are more likely explanations—they might have just blown out of the bed of a passing pickup rolling down the highway, and somehow wafted high enough to be captured by the tree branches—but for some reason my poor tortured lad drama just *feels* true. It has a power and a clarity that's helped me to the Promised Land dozens of time.

I doubt I'll ever know the true story, and maybe that's why those silly little boxers with their bright colors and their mysterious origin have me fascinated. Boxers, I suppose, have *always* fascinated me, ever since I first traded in my snug, ball-hugging briefs some years ago in favor of the looser fit that boxers afford. I can still remember the first time I tried them out, the sensual feeling of being naked inside my clothes, like I was free-balling it. (In all honesty, it was hard not to *get* hard wearing them for the first few months.)

And not to sound like I have a fetish or anything—not that there's anything wrong with that—but I have over the years often talked a young man or two out of his boxers, after finding a way into his pants. I don't think of them as trophies exactly; they're more like fond mementoes of old relationships, of random hot afternoons, and languid mornings after. Now it seems whenever I do my wash these days I can spot a pair that takes me back to some far-away time and place. Those green Old Navy plaids? He was a hot young man I spotted in a gym locker room in Manhattan, then struck up a conversation with out on the street. That led to coffee, and then a drink . . . and not long after I was slipping those shorts off of him slowly as he lay back on my bed, eagerly following his happy trail as the waistband drew further south into his nicely trimmed bush and past his slowly hardening cock. The two American Eagle flannels? They both came from former partners, one of them a sweet boy with a huge dick that I dated for just six months before he got a job on the West Coast—we still e-mail each other from time to time—the other a clinging, crystal queen in Philadelphia whose evil clutches it took me over a year to escape. He was always horny but never able to come. (At least he had good taste in underwear.)

There are lots of others to speak of—I could go on forever about the pale yellow A&F number I found on my old balcony, after I sobered up from a three-day bender over DC's Pride Weekend in 1997, and the semi-conscious boy I found under them—but you get my drift. And now it's occurring to me more and more that the boxers in the tree are becoming a must have for my collection; the spring rains haven't come yet, and preserved by our late winter cold snap, they still look to be in pretty good shape. Now all I have to do is figure out how to liberate them from their lonely perch.

But how am I going to do that, exactly? It's not like it's a kitten stuck up there, and there's a local fire department standing by to come to the rescue. I don't own a ladder, and it's hard to picture renting one; I'm obsessed, but not *that* obsessed. Standing beneath the sadly flapping boxers late one afternoon, my car idling nearby, I am sizing up their location, debating internally the strength of that branch, pondering whether I even still remember how to climb a tree.

Before it gets to that, I consider some alternatives. I could try a fishing rod, I suppose. Though since I've never actually used one, I can't imagine I'd be very effective casting about in the trees. (And I have no idea where one gets a fishing rod out here, anyway.) For the moment I adopt the simple approach; I grab a handful of small stones from the roadway shoulder and toss a few up into the branches. It's been a while since I've tried to hit a target with a rock, and it takes me several throws to get the range and altitude; most sail right by without even coming close. The boxers continue flapping in the breeze. It begins to feel like they're mocking me.

Eventually my aim starts to improve, and one decent-sized stone hits the plaid pattern dead center and catches there. Now the boxers are no longer flapping. They've become a pouch of sorts, swinging back and forth now with my rock inside. It occurs to me that with a few more lucky shots I could land enough stones in there that the weight will pull the boxers free. Alas, I am not that lucky. I continue tossing stones until the sun is sinking beneath the tree line, and I fail to land even a second one on target. I resolve to return tomorrow.

Life gets in the way of my plan. A shipment of books I've been waiting for is late, and I spend half of the following afternoon cussing out the shipping clerk responsible. The sun is a memory before I get disentangled from the telephone. (But at least I'm getting my bill cut in half.) The next day I'm getting ready to close up my shop when no less than a half-dozen desperate freshmen show up, all looking for the same Psych 101 text; I have to dig through four different crates before I can find enough books.

Now three days after my first retrieval attempt, I'm finally headed back to get my prize. I pull to a stop on the grassy patch where I usually park, get out, and gather a handful of stones, limbering up my throwing arm as I approach the middle of the road. The boxers are still hanging there, and after a few wild throws I hit the bull's eye; my stony missile makes solid contact with the rock already suspended inside, and the impact knocks the shorts free.

They fall into the road with a little plopping sound, none the worse
for wear.

I walk over, almost wary about touching them, wondering for a
second if the boxers will give off some kind of mental image when
I do, like something out of a Stephen King novel. *Now you're just
being silly,* I think to myself, as if this whole exercise wasn't silly
enough to begin with. I bend over and pick them up for a close ex-
amination: medium size A&F, red plaid pattern, gray waist band.
Nothing about them gives a clue as to who might have owned
them, let alone how they got up in the tree in the first place. A little
self-consciously, I bring them close to my nose, wondering if there'll
be some kind of residual scent there, some latent musty aroma
from the unknown owner's nether regions, but apparently they've
been airing out far too long for that. I'm sorry to report I get no
mental image, except the sudden realization that I'm standing in
the middle of a road holding a pair of boxers that don't belong to
me. And I am also suddenly realizing that I am no longer alone. . . .

I don't know how long the young man has been standing there
by the road; he seems to have crept up silent as a cat. He looks to
be about nineteen or twenty and maybe five-nine or -ten; by his
clothes—some khakis, a sweater, a heavy leather jacket—I'd
judge him to be a student. There's nothing at all threatening about
his manner, he looks far too clean-cut to be looking for trouble.
He's simply standing there, watching me with a quizzical expression on his face. And a rather cute face it is, at that. *He could
almost be the boy in my boxer fantasy.*

"Hey there," I say, rather stupidly, but nothing else occurs to me
in my surprise.

"Hi," he says back with a faint smile, and now I'm wondering if
he saw me sniffing the boxers, wondering if I look to him like
some kind of major league pervert. (How long will people keep
coming to my store if *that* gets out?)

"Are you heading back to town?" he asks, surprising me yet again.
(He must have missed the sniffing scene, otherwise he wouldn't
be so eager to get in the car with me; either that or he doesn't object to perverts.)

"Sure," I say without thinking, now realizing as my heart settles down that it's pretty strange he'd be out here without a car or bike. It's more than an hour back to town on foot. *What's that all about?*

"I'm Mike," he says, as we start toward my car.

"Barry," I say, and he shakes my hand. That's when his eyes go to the boxers I am trying to wad up and stuff in my jacket pocket.

"What's that?" he asks, innocently enough, though his eyes seem to betray more than a passing interest.

"Just something I found in the road," I say simply, and honestly, if you leave out a few facts.

"Cool," he says, as we climb in.

"So you're that bookstore guy, right?" he asks a few minutes into the ride. "You gave me a good deal on a book once when I didn't have enough cash."

"I did?" I say, a little surprised that I wouldn't have immediately recognized such a handsome young face. Then again there *have* been thousands of those running through my store.

"Yeah, it was really nice of you, too." *His smile is totally intoxicating.*

"Well, I do what I can," I say, not knowing what else to say. "So what brought you out here without a ride?" I ask, trying to sound like I'm just making small talk.

"Just looking for something," he says, and his eyes seem to dart for a second to my jacket before shifting back to the road ahead. "Didn't find it, though," he adds, smile fading a little.

"Sorry to hear that," I say. "Was it something important? Anything I can do to help?"

"Nah, it's okay," he answers, then adding quickly, "you're helping me out enough already with the ride."

Of course by now I'm wondering if he came all the way out here for the red boxers, though the chance coincidence in our timing seems impossibly remote—that he would show up *just* as I was getting them out of the tree. Stranger things have happened, I guess, and I feel a little guilty that I've been so intent on keeping something that might well have some kind of sentimental value for him. But somehow even broaching the subject seems like it would betray more about me than I care to right now.

We make a little more small talk as the edges of town creep closer. He's a junior and an English major; he wants to be a teacher and maybe to write a novel one day. I tell him I've dabbled in a little writing from time to time, and perhaps I'll actually finish my own novel someday, too. Soon we're riding past the old stone walls that run alongside campus, and I find myself slowing down a little, realizing how much I'm enjoying his company and not looking forward to saying goodbye. Other than the fast exchanges with customers over the cash register, I don't have much contact with youngsters—or anyone else, really—and this break in routine is waking up some long-dormant social yearnings.

"Damn," he says suddenly. "I missed the dining hall hours."

"Oh, that's too bad," I say, somewhat lamely.

"It's okay," he says, then looks as me with a broad smile again. "You can always get something in town."

That comment seems to carry an extra meaning in it, something in his tone that almost has an invitation within it. Is he *flirting* with me? The idea feels preposterous; what could he possibly want with me, I'm just a helpful stranger giving a kid a ride. *Or maybe he just wants me to give him back his underwear and doesn't know quite how to ask me yet.*

"Where do you want me to drop you?" I ask, trying to sound nonchalant as we approach the row of cozy eating joints just outside the school gates.

"I don't know . . . ," he says absently, then more firmly, "wanna grab a burger or something?"

"Sure," I say, now almost past the point of surprise. This boy is just amazing.

It's an hour or so later, and we're sitting in Willy's Pub. The sun has set—we had a great view through the bay window—the burgers are history, and we're well into our third or fourth beers. I'm trying not to let his devastating smile or bright eyes distract me from what he's talking about, which at the moment is his last relationship, one that apparently didn't end well. His words are giving me a little flashback of sorts; I notice he's been using carefully constructed sentences that don't use "she" or "hers," but rather "they" and "theirs." It was the same device I once used, more years back than I care to remember, in those long ago days when I felt a need to be honest, but not exactly open, yet.

"So what about you, Barry? Any heartbreaks in your past?"

"More than a few," I answer, feeling my head buzzing with all that beer; it's been a while since I pounded so many down so fast. "The last one pretty much landed me out here."

That's when Mike drops his biggest surprise so far, raising his beer mug in a toast. "Then here's to heartbreaks. Was he a young guy, like me?"

Thank God for the alcohol I've got in me, because stone cold sober I think I might have had a stroke. "Um . . . he was a few years older," I say, after a pause that feels just short of eternal. Then I slam the rest of my drink, quickly signaling the waiter for two more.

"Easy tiger, you should pace yourself," Mike says, smiling.

"Was I that obvious?" I venture, now that just about everything seems to be on the table.

"Not really," he says. "It's something in your eyes, the way you look at me. Oh, and the way I've seen you checking out some of the boys in your store."

Now that throws me a bit—that reputation thing, again—and the concern is obviously showing. "Relax, Barry," Mike says, reaching out to quickly touch my hand in reassurance. "Your secret is safe with me, and I'm pretty sure only another gay guy would notice."

"Like you?" I ask, quite unnecessarily now. Things have certainly moved on since *I* was twenty-one; I would have never had the balls to do what Mike is doing now.

"Sure, like me," he says, that smile somehow growing even more dazzling. "So I wanna ask you two questions, and now that we're sharing secrets, I hope you won't mind."

Right now he could ask me anything and I wouldn't give a shit; I am totally in the tank for this beautiful boy who just dropped into my life out of nowhere. I'm assuming at this point he's going to ask for his underwear back, and my hand moves inside my jacket pocket. "Go ahead," I say.

"Well . . . ," he starts, coyly. "Would you ever hook up with someone who went to school here?"

Holy shit, I almost say aloud. *Didn't see that one coming.*

"It hasn't happened yet," I reply, regaining a little of my footing. *Maybe he thinks he'll have to get me alone before I'll give the boxers back.* "Which is not to say it never would, if the moment was right."

"Fair enough," he says, then drains about half his beer before sitting his mug down, and beaming that smile at me again.

"What's the second question?" *This is where he asks for the boxers*—I'm certain now. I get ready to pull them out with a flourish.

"Do you ever have company up in your loft?"

"Haven't yet," I say, and now it's my turn to smile at him. "Which is not to say I wouldn't." *He must really want them bad.*

I may have talked a good game in the pub, but walking back to my loft with Mike, my stomach is tied up in knots. It's been years—literally years—since I embarked on a sexual escapade with anyone approaching his level of personality and looks, and I don't want to disappoint him. (I'm thinking that all that beer may sabotage my best hydraulic efforts, even though my spirits could not have been more willing.) And all this might still be some kind of ruse to talk me out the boxers, though really by now all he would have to do is ask and I would hand them over gladly. Part of me, in fact, *wants* him to do just that, so we can go our separate ways and I can get back to my familiar, solitary territory. This is almost terrifying.

But my fears and suspicions look to be unfounded. Just as we get to the alley where the stairs lead up to my loft above the store, Mike pulls me into the shadows for a brief but intense kiss, and I can feel myself growing extremely hard, almost painfully so. (Performance, as they say, does not appear it will be a problem.)

Then rather stupidly—much of what I've said to him today seems to have had a lot of stupidity in it—I can't help but ask him something. "Why me?" He pauses, just as he was coming in for another kiss. (See what I mean? Stupid!)

"If you'd rather not. . . ."

"Of course I want to," I say quickly. "I just mean . . . you're such an attractive kid, and there have to be other, younger gay guys around here you could be with." I kick myself instantly. Am I *trying* to scare him away with a last-second display of low self-esteem and internalized ageism?

But he rescues me. "You must not own a mirror, Barry. You're a really sexy guy. Older, yes. Which is just what I always liked, what I always wanted to be with. So, you gonna invite me in now, or what?"

Up in my loft, he makes himself comfortable immediately, kicking off his shoes and stripping off his coat. It's not a big space, but it's got a certain kind of rustic charm. Looking around and nodding his head, Mike seems to like it. "Cool place," he says simply.

"Thanks," I say, lighting up a few lanterns I keep around the room, noting how, if possible, he seems to glow even more by firelight. "Can I get you something?"

"Nah," he says. "So where do you sleep?"

"In there," I point to the darkened bedroom.

"Let's go chill," he says standing up, taking a lantern in one hand and gripping my fingers lightly with the other. I follow, my nervousness completely consumed now by a deep, simmering lust. If it was in fact the boxers that keyed his interest, he seems to have forgotten them now.

The flickering lamps aren't very bright, but they give off more than enough light to illuminate Mike's fine young body as he slips off his shirt and jeans—I see he's not wearing any underwear at *all*. It's thrilling just to see him standing there in a pose, naked at the edge of my bed. I'm taken again by how much he resembles my fantasy boy. He has the same athletic form I envisioned: smooth hairless chest, firm rounded musculature, a deeply rippled midsection, like a gymnast or well-toned swimmer, powerful legs, and a ridiculously fine ass. And his package is just the way I saw it in my masturbatory longings, except in the warm here and now his cock is well on the way to full hardness, not diminished by my imagined winter air.

I can see he's enjoying the way my eyes travel over him, that he likes to be admired. With some guys that would be a turnoff, but with him it feels right, somehow. I almost can't believe this is actually happening—I'm getting a weird feeling it's only a dream I'm going to wake up from at any moment—then Mike reaches out and pulls me into another long kiss, and we fall onto the bed together.

Time stretches, fades, then seems to stop entirely. I'm drifting now, only seeing images, feeling sensations; there's little sense of conscious thought . . . only an impression of being here and nowhere at the same time. I'm lying with him, my hands running over his fine chest and stomach, then gripping his fully hard cock sliding in and out of my hand . . . ; I am buried in his crotch, inhaling his young smell, tasting him on the end of my tongue, consuming him inside my mouth. He's above me suddenly, performing his own acts of tasting and consumption, and I am teased with hints of pleasures I have almost forgotten.

And then I am inside him, and Mike is moaning and writhing in the air astride me, his strong, smooth legs encasing my body. His form glows above me and casts multiple shadows on my walls. His head is tossed back, and I can sense his urgency growing along with my own. There's a rumbling deep inside my own groin, building, building, then releasing as he releases, and it's like a shower on my stomach, chest, and face. . . . In all my years I have never climaxed with someone at the same moment. This being the singular most momentous act of lovemaking I have ever experienced, it only feels right. He subsides slowly, and I can feel his softening cock nestle itself close to me as he leans forward, keeping me inside him, locking my lips in a deep, deep kiss.

"Sleep, now," he says. And his smile is the last thing I see as I instantly drift off.

"Hey sir, are you okay?"

Mike is jostling me now, as we seem to have slept the night away in my bed. Except it's not my bed; it's the front seat of my car I'm sitting in, parked on the side of the road just at the point where it makes its bend up toward town. Neither is it Mike jostling me; it's a state police trooper. Nor is it the next morning. By the angle of sunlight still streaming through the trees, it appears to be afternoon.

Which afternoon, I'm not quite sure.

"Do you need a doctor?" The state trooper is talking to me through the car door; despite the temperature outside, it appears to have been open, with the window rolled down, for . . . exactly how long? I try hard to focus on the trooper.

"Um . . . what day is it?"

"Look, I am going to call you an ambulance. You just sit tight."

"No, I'm okay," I tell him, though okay is really the last thing I am right now, so confused and disconnected from reality am I. "What day is it?" I ask again.

"It's Thursday," he tells me, which was the same day I set off on my mission. But how could it be? There was a sunset, there was a night . . . and there was Mike. Wasn't there?

"Do you have a medical condition I should know about?" the trooper asks, and there's real concern on his face.

"I'm just a little tired," I lie to him, trying to smile, but it's a weak attempt. "I guess I just dozed off here, instead of trying to drive." With the car door open and the window rolled down. Yeah, right.

But the explanation seems to settle him down, though he's clearly not going anywhere yet. "Mind if see your license and registration?" he asks, politely but firmly.

"No problem," I reply, knowing he'll run my tag and grateful for the several minutes it will take him to find out that I'm not a fugitive. I reach for my wallet, fish out my license, and hand it to him. Then I open my glove compartment. Inside my hand brushes against the red boxers, folded neatly and tucked away; my heart freezes a little at the sight.

But the trooper doesn't seem to notice, he just nods after I hand him the registration card, and walks back to his cruiser.

Calm down, I admonish myself. *This will all make sense soon.*

But I don't know how it can. I can see Mike's face so clearly in my mind, still feel his lips, his touch, still smell his scent. *Am I going insane?* How could I have possibly imagined it all, so fully and richly detailed, more vivid than any dream could ever be?

The trooper is taking his time, which allows me a moment to reach back into the glove compartment. The boxers are still there—of course I don't remember putting them there, but that seems the least of my worries—and I take them out carefully, thinking that perhaps touching them again might conjure up an explanation.

Nothing happens. If they had some mystical powers before, those powers appear to be exhausted. Or dormant, or whatever the fuck happens to charms and talismans after they rearrange your world. I put the boxers on the seat beside me, pondering and collecting myself. *It* must *have been a dream, a wondrous, glorious dream; nothing else makes sense.*

Suddenly the trooper is back at my window, handing me back my cards. "Sir, I really think we need to get you checked out. You look pale as a ghost."

If he had kicked me in the ass I couldn't have jolted any harder. "What . . . what did you say?"

"I said you're looking pale. Like a ghost." Now he begins to look at me very strangely, straightens up, looks around the car, then out in the road, then back at me. "Sir . . . did you see some-thing out here? Something strange?"

I am shaking a bit now, and all of sudden an ambulance is be-ginning to sound like a very good idea. "Please tell me what the hell you're talking about."

The trooper looks down at the ground, then back up at me. When he does, I'm not seeing an officer in a uniform anymore; he just looks like someone from town, like anyone else who might have grown up out here. "There was an incident, right over there," he gestures with his chin over toward the grass by the side of the road. "One of the kids from school. Sort of an accident."

"Was it a car crash or something?" I ask, knowing already it was not, feeling that cold hand on my heart again.

"Nothing like that," he tells me, huddling up closer to the car now, like a neighbor spinning out gossip over the backyard fence. "Started out as some kind of prank . . . bunch of kids came out here, left one of their buddies stranded without his drawers on in the middle of the night."

"That's awful," I say, gripping the steering wheel now so hard my knuckles whiten.

"They said they were going to come back for him. They weren't going to let him freeze to death or anything; it was just a big joke. . . . But the shitty thing is, they tossed his shorts up in that tree, and the poor kid tried to climb up after them in the dark. Looks like he fell and broke his neck. . . . They found his body naked beside the road when they came back. Really messed *them* up, too. One of them killed himself; the others all quit school. Kid was from a rich family around here. They kept it quiet, out of the papers . . . but we've gotten some reports from folks coming down the road; peo-ple seeing strange sights."

"Strange sights," I say, sweat rolling down my back, past all the little hairs that are completely standing on end from my neck to my ass. *I could tell you about some strange sights.*

"Sure it's just folks imagining things; people calling saying there was a kid, sometimes a naked kid, standing by the road, looking up in the trees in the middle of the night. You hadn't heard anything about this?"

"Not a word," I say, and that's the God's honest truth. I hadn't heard anything about this at all. *And yet I know the story. I've seen it in my mind. What the fuck is going on?*

The trooper straightens back up, all business again. "Well, if you're going to be okay, I'll let you get back to town. Taking a nap beside the road out here probably isn't a good idea."

"Thanks, officer," I say. I start the engine, head still swirling, but I want to get out of here now. *Right now.* Still, I call out to him one more time, and he halts just beside his cruiser. *I have to know something.*

"Officer . . . the kid had a name? And when was this accident?"

The trooper calls back. "About ten years back . . . and the kid's name was Mike. You have a good day now."

That's funny, I almost say out loud as he pulls out, and I follow him up and around the bend toward town. I'm glad to see him occasionally glancing back at me in his rear view mirror; it makes me focus harder on the road, keeps me from sinking into utter hysteria. Almost in imitation I glance in my own rear view mirror . . . and that's when I drive right off the road into the woods. I hit something, from the feel of it, a very large tree.

I don't see the officer's lights ahead of me come on in a blast of red and blue, or see his cruiser wheel around in a cloud of dust and come to rest beside my car. But I hear his siren wailing, and before I collapse on the seat next to me, I can see him on his radio. I know he's calling that ambulance, and it's all fine with me. I don't think I'm injured all that badly, but I want every drug they can pump into me. I don't want to remember any of this . . . not the dinner with Mike, not the sweet conversation, not even the warm love-making. I want it all erased from my mind, gone . . . just as the red plaid boxers are gone, vanished from the front seat of my car as if they were never there.

But at least I know where they went. I saw Mike wearing them, just now . . . when he was standing on the road behind me, waving goodbye.

Shoot

Tom Bacchus

THOMAS: Do you remember last time when I asked if you were
   a sex toy, what kind would you be?
TONY: And what did I say?
THOMAS: You said, "The biggest dildo ever!"
TONY: Did you get me a dildo?
THOMAS: No, I'm sorry to disappoint you. Do you wish I had?
TONY: What would I do with it?

> from a *Flow* magazine interview
> with Tony Saturday, underwear model

Off the Record

It was then that he asked me to stop the tape recorder, in the
midst of our second interview. I was following his rise over
the period of another historic photo shoot for another historic
fashion magazine.

So, my career was in the shits. At least I got to chat up empty-
headed cute guys.

But he had to stop the tape recorder. There was more to this guy
than I thought.

"Tell me. What would you do, Thomas?"

I sat across from him, in an expensively quiet and discreet restaurant. Fortunately the magazine was paying for it, and I told

him. Him, the latest manufactured prince of fashion. In person, though, he simply radiated a warm sexual charm.

"First of all, I'd rip off those underpants. The underpants go."

He smiled the widest grin. His mouth seemed ready for a lot of anything.

"I mean, you're a great model and all, but we really wanna see the parts. I mean, you're a monument to the tease, your gray-toned image looming from billboards like a constant reminder of your imperial fame and our perpetually unrequited desire. I'd say it's about time we all got to see the parts."

"You think so? Is that what you want? I could do that."

"Really?"

"Sure. But we are just . . . how you say, ejecturing, yes?"

"Conjecturing. Yes. Something like that." I sipped my wine and signaled the waiter for another bottle.

"Do you know the day I decided to seek you out for an interview, Antonio?"

"Tony. Please."

"Tony." I sighed, feeling flush, but embarrassed to be exposing myself to him, when it was supposed to be the other way around. But I was honest. That was my first mistake.

"I don't imagine your ass has been tried out," I said. "Women don't know what to do with a man's ass, what pleasure is there."

"Really?"

"I imagine you possibly giving it up to say, a producer, once or twice, as a favor for this extensive fame. I imagine the underwear man didn't know how to treat you properly, how to respect your ass, before plowing into it with the power and force and girth of the bus that nearly ran me down one day on my bike."

"What?" He looked a bit more nervous now, not so cocky.

"A week ago, after my people called your people."

"Right."

"I'm all happy and thrilled, and I go for a ride in the park and wham! or near-wham. The last thing I might have seen, had I been killed in that near accident, would have been you, in your underwear, lying down. If only I could be assured that such a vision would greet me in heaven, I would have gladly ridden in front of that bus."

He laughed with me over the absurdity of the story, but it wasn't fiction.

"I am not sure there's a reservation for us up there," Tony smirked.

"Perhaps not. But if beauty like yours is forbidden, I don't want to go."

"Very well, then. What does . . . a gay man like you think? What do you, or even any of these people who want my autograph on their shorts, what do they think? Tell me."

"I don't know what they think. I don't know if they *do* think. I know for me, always, what I can never remember after a great lover, is the taste. That's what they should sell, the taste of your skin, which they will never touch."

"Most won't." His eyes glowed. He grinned.

"I imagine it tasted different in your younger years, say a few years back, when you were thinner, and more innocent, and eager. The Enrico Fortuna shoots."

He seemed genuinely surprised. "You do your homework."

"Thanks," I smiled.

"So, what would a gay man like to do with me? Just your opinion."

"Your arms would wrap around me as we lean in close together, away from the cameras, away from the stylists, away from the girls you flirt with, and fuck, one after the other, night after night."

"I wish."

"We talk close, and your breath is of toothpaste, as you are considerate, but your tongue is salty from the lasagna you wolfed down at the catering table for the shoot. You need release. You need more attention. You are a junkie for love, Tony."

"It's the price of fame."

"You ask me if I see how you've been working out. I concur and fondle your biceps. I graze my hand down to your belly. You contract, not because you're ticklish, but to show off the abdominal muscles that you so love to exercise in sit ups. You love your body, don't you?"

"Yes!"

"You love it so much you want to share it with the world."

"Well, you've convinced me."

"Excuse me?"

"Sex. You wanted sex?"

"But—"

"Here." He grabbed my hand, forcing me to feel the thick protrusion along the thigh of his pants. "Before the shoot tomorrow? You are coming, yes?"

"Yup." I was suddenly almost ready to, in my pants.

"You buy a dildo. Afterward, you show me a thing or two, eh?"

"You're serious."

"Why not?"

I sat in the back as they fussed. It was hours before they did even a test print. When an assistant made a move to pick up my backpack, I almost jumped out of my seat, fearful that he would discover its contents, that it was all a hoax.

Of course, Tony was being fawned over and loved it. But every now and then, I noticed him glancing at me and at the photographer, a long-haired woman who seemed perturbed by my presence. It seemed as if he were drawing lustful energy from us.

I envied the stylist. Everyone envied the stylist. She got to nudge and buff the contents of his shorts, pinning them in the back to achieve just the right discreet bulge that will sell millions of units. His balls and cock had to be arranged just so—teasing but not revealing—so as not to upset the suits, the ones who run the show.

But now that bulge pressed upward, not at all styled, in fact. I crept closer to see the bulge become a rod pushing at his white shorts. Click. Click. So it is true. He is hard at work.

I reached down into my pants to adjust my erection, grasping it through the fabric, as I'd done with my cousin years ago—as I'd done with straight roommates as well—on those nights when we had to share a bed, his brother having returned too soon from a trip. I longed to grasp the cock of Tony Saturday, the unseen truth behind the sale of all those units, since Marky left for greener pastures; the same pastures on which Tony hopes to prance.

The tension in the room was broken by music. There was a moment, though, before someone opened a window, before a cigarette was lit, that I swear everyone felt it. Everyone wanted him.

A break was called. Another pair of shorts was to be prepared.

Tony sauntered easily toward me.

"How are you doing, my friend?" He patted my shoulder. Oddly, his touch relaxed me.

"Fine. You're beautiful."

"I hope this is not too boring for you."

"Not at all."

Tony leaned close, making sure no one else could hear. "You brought it?"

"Of course."

He smiled, no teeth this time, a conspiratorial smirk.

"What is it you want, right now, Thomas?" he whispered.

"To tug those undies down enough to release your browned, uncut, immense penis and take it into my mouth. No, wait, no . . . first just marvel at it in its dry, pulsing state, this snake that aims at me, another warm body, and as I tug them further down, the balls, graced with wisps of hair, pubes neatly patterned. I soak in the scent of your musk, your smell, and I let the shorts gird the base of your balls, cushioning them, pushing them up, jewels, eggs to behold, fleshy toys."

"You should stop selling yourself cheap to those magazines and write poetry."

"If you'll be my muse."

Another grin, with teeth that time, and a snap. For just a moment, he pulled the shorts open, and I truly saw the meaning of the term *basket*. Nestled in there was exactly what I'd hoped for. Sausage and eggs, Italian-style. The sound of that snap as the elastic hid his tools was the slap of gym class towels, swimmers' victorious butt spanks.

But what I was thinking, I knew was my lust betraying me. Even though true joy would be to greet him any night in bed, or anywhere, and that no matter how he teased, or even used me, as he would, I knew that he would never be the great actor he wishes to be, because he was just too damn beautiful.

As he chased everyone out, saying we are doing "more for the interview," I panted nervously as the room quieted.

"You said you wanted to be the biggest dildo ever, Tony? You are. A nation of boys and men and women dream of impaling themselves with you.

"And I'm gonna fuck you now.

"Your thighs will quiver as the bolts of sperm seep into your shorts. I'll clutch your balls through the fabric. You'll grunt and gasp, shoving against me with a probing kiss. You slurp my chin and bite my neck. I'll smell the spurts of your living juice, soak it up in the world's most famous underpants.

"Tony, take off the underwear.

"Roll over.

"Spread your legs.

"I'm going to show you what to do."

Toy Time

Tony looks worried. He lies on a warm floor, sheets and blankets in a rumpled yet comfortable mess. We grabbed them from the side bedroom of the studio loft, where only an hour ago his form was being immortalized yet again for millions to enjoy, to sell millions of "units." Underwear for a nation of sexually repressed men and women.

We are alone in the room. I hadn't even brought a tape recorder. Wish I had.

I hold a large, eight-inch dildo upright. It wobbles. We giggle. He's nervous. I'm not, although I was on the ride here, wondering what the EMS squad would think if I'd crashed my Honda and had been found with a dildo in my backpack.

Tony fakes shock. He is not a great actor.

"You don't think I'm going to take that, do you?"

"I think we'll start small."

"Good."

He relaxes. He doesn't want to get hurt. Wouldn't want to damage the merchandise.

Tony spreads his legs and turns back. He lies on the floor; his firm muscled legs spread out before me like a human cross. He hunkers up on his elbows and turns back to watch me ponder my great fortune. Tony lies naked before me. When he tossed his designer undershorts, they flew off to a corner of the studio.

Tony wants to figure out what to do with a dildo. Or be shown.

Somehow, I don't think Tony is that naive, but I am willing to play along. So is he.

His ass strikes me in its solidity. His gluts are firm and large. It's not a cute butt. It's a powerful butt, a big, solid, muscled butt. This is a man who uses his body, who could hike up a mountain with me. I imagine us there, under a brisk breeze and the hot sun, instead of in this hot, stuffy photo studio.

"You better be nice," Tony flirts as he feels my hands caress his cheeks, not even feeling him, just passing my hand over him, less than an eighteenth of an inch above his skin. I just feel the fuzz, the pale hairs around the outer areas of his skin, and down his thighs, until the chill bumps rise, and I know I've got him. He hums into his arms. He's dropped his head, relaxed, ready.

The darker hairs of Tony's ass lay nestled between the two large mounds of muscle. I explore them; close them up, and let them part to reveal the tiny little bit that astounds and repulses. I begin with a playful bite, then a smack, then soften to licks and swirls of kisses.

Every movement, I know, is just a tease, urging me closer to the center, the scary, tangy opening.

I part the hairs with my tongue, swirling them outward.

"Mmnn," Tony groans. First entry is always a shocker. Then, when you get down to it, they never want you to stop.

I reach up toward his face, stick a few fingers in his mouth. He wets them, sucks on them like a lime after a shot of tequila.

But that's not enough. I want his ass coated in my spit. I open my mouth, droplets of myself falling on him like salty honey. It's getting warm. Sweat droplets fall from my forehead and onto the cleft at his lower back, the delicate place where I could rest my head forever.

But I'm not resting.

How can one politely and accurately describe the flavor of a young god's ass? Like salt? Like an ocean of flesh? Like shit? No. It's . . . aw, fuck it.

"You like it?" Tony purrs.

"Like? Love." I sigh. "Love is not even strong enough."

I dive in again, fondling the little flesh folds, the circular, almost purple entrance. I dart my tongue in and out. The puckered area reminds me of a sea anemone, a pulsating, delicate, liquid creature. I begin to understand how a straight guy can fall in love with a woman's pussy. There is such delicacy in this flesh, such strength as well. As I slide my fuck finger in again, nestling it around to tickle Tony's prostate, he clenches, and I feel a grip I know will make my cock choke and pulse.

But that will wait. First is his ass, first is worship of him.

I only brought one dildo, which is too bad. I had wanted to take my time, to introduce Tony to an array of possibilities. But that will come.

I go into the bathroom off the studio while he stretches. I wash the dildo. Although it's clean, I like to moisten it, to warm it up.

"Hurry up!" he calls out, giggling.

When I return, he has a small bit of pot. He lights up. We smoke it together.

"Relaxes me," he says, and I know. This is not his first time. No way. But that's good. That means I'll get further inside.

Tony gasps, reaches back for my crotch, and grabs the tent between my legs that is my erection. He wants to reciprocate. I don't want that yet. I want to just be a sensation taking place inside his body.

"Please, lemme suck it." He reaches for my pants.

"No, Tony. This is about you, not me."

"Well, *me* wants to suck it!"

He grabs my belt buckle, nearly ripping the button off my jeans. · The dildo falls with a wet plop.

He nudges around and shoves his head into my lap. My cock sproings up like a small diving board, bapping him in the face. I don't even get to see my own cock for more than a moment before it's surrounded by velvety wetness, hungry lips, and the tongue of a Saint Bernard.

He slurps it hungrily, impaling his head with my dick. He doesn't want me this much, I think. He's just horny. It's not me he's slurping, just attention. Beautiful people are often very insecure, I remind myself, while secretly wishing I could die in this position.

Tony squats before me, then with one strong muscled arm, shoves me down to my back. I fall, lie back, and admire the ceiling lights, the instruments of fame.

How many people will ever believe this, I wonder?

No one.

I resist the urge to reach over for a camera, to document every moment; believing the myth of his fame, that every moment of Tony's sexuality, of his body movement, every gesture, is worthy of immortality.

Fuck that, I realize, as he scrapes a few teeth against my cock. He's just a model.

"Come on, big boy. Let's finish what we started."

"Mmn." Tony peels my pants down to my ankles, forcefully. I have to admit, I love it. I scoot around after pulling my shirt off, which clings to my chest from the heat of this room, a remnant of the shoot. The water bottles lie dormant over along the blue background. Empty.

His underwear. Where? I must remember to grab them. They will be my only souvenir, make-up stains and all.

We nestle in a loose 69. He's half-hard. I'm worried he's going to bail if I don't fulfill some weird exhibitionist fantasy he's got going. I look around for a peeping voyeur.

Whatever it is, it's working. Ah, the joy of feeling a man's cock inflate to steely strength in your mouth.

His insistent male impulse takes over. He shoves it in and out of my mouth, past my lips, humping me sideways while his balls jiggle around and above my nose.

Ah, the smell of it.

I can't see it, so I feel around for it, feigning interest in fondling his immense thighs, which I do, but what I really want is that dildo. He said he wanted it, damn it, and I do, too.

I want to see his ass getting fucked, and now, it seems, we're going to have a multimedia attack; sucking each other and fucking each other, or Tony's attempt at finger-fucking. He needs a few pointers there. I clench my ass tight like a vise. He retracts a very thick thumb. No, I'll let him fuck me with his cock, later. That's probably where he's better skilled.

But now, I've found the rubber dong and retracted his erection from my mouth, since I tasted a good bit of near-jizz. I admire a string of drool that connects the tip of his cock to my lower lip.

"Like a small bridge of a dew-dropped spider web," I admire, then burst out laughing.

"What?" He thinks I'm laughing at his dick. I am apologetic and a fool.

"No, no, the, the string of your, our, on my lips, it. . . ."

"What?"

"It reminded me of the first time I saw you on televison."

"No. Not the—"

"It was on one of those blooper shows, and you were on that soap opera. . . ."

"Oh god, yes."

"And you'd just kissed a girl and that string of drool came out!"

"So embarrassing!"

"It was so sexy!"

We sigh and giggle, our legs now entwined like wrestlers in a match called on exhaustion.

"So much for fucking," he mutters.

"Oh, no, we're not done."

I grab the dildo, rip open another ampoule of lube with my teeth, slather it on the fake dick, and head right for the zone.

Tony squirms away, but I know he wants it. He wants to resist. That feels good too, sometimes. He's already loosened up, so I aim, and hit, letting the rubber dick nudge his opening for a while.

We kiss the longest, wettest, drooliest kiss ever not caught on a blooper show. He lets me inside and licks around my teeth. Down below, he spreads his ass a bit, rearing up like a dog about to piss, and then helps me lodge it in.

"Agh! Oh!"

It's in.

He pants a few times, recovering from it, but I can tell he's in heaven. The dick parks completely up his ass. He gasps as if shot, then nestles back down to sideways, parks his mouth on my cock, and I do the same for him.

I slather more lube on all sides of the dildo as it slides out. I lean in and lick the ring of flesh that clings tight around the edges of the glistening pole. Tony's grunting harder but shoving back.

Then I really start to fuck him, sliding the dildo in and out. The lips of his bunghole retract with it. I can't keep this up much longer. This is too beautiful, my head between the legs of the world's most popular model, his groin my dinner table. I continue sliding the cock into him. He deep-throats my cock, smacks my ass a few times, then I feel him insert two fingers into his mouth. He fingers the tip of my cock as it lies on his tongue. I feel almost electrocuted with pleasure. He's jacking me off inside his mouth! But then he extracts the wet fingers from his mouth, trails them down my back, and inserts them roughly into my butthole.

The humming, groaning sounds reverberate through his mouth and into my cock. I can tell by the clenching of his thighs that he's close. I want this to last longer, but he's just found my button—motherfucker—proving he's obviously got pussy-experience.

I retract his cock from my mouth, pull back the skin, admire the sopping wet spit-coated ruby beauty, and while shoving the dildo in and out—just halfway now—I jack his cock with my other hand. I'm choosing views, since this is definitely going to be an eyes-wide-open orgasm.

"Mnffm," he groans, not content to release my cock, which I wrench out at the last moment as my spillage swirls over his face and neck. We both gasp aloud, faces coated in spit and sweat. I think about licking off the glob on his eyebrow first, just as soon as he comes.

Tony reaches down to retract the dildo. I allow him and grab his cock with both hands. When he comes, I see the quivering legs and feel a sense of total control over him. I feel his lack of control, his release, as the sperm oozes out, not shooting, but pulsing out, dribbling over my fists, a slow, thick, pulsing gush of life juice.

I fight the incredible urge to lick it, to taste him. He is a product after all, and I am the consumer.

But I know better. Guys like him, omnivorous, you never know where they've been. I settle for rubbing it all over me; I lie back, entangled in him, as we heave, panting, finished for now.

"We're really late for that dinner party," Tony says.

"So?"

"So, everyone'll be there."

I scoot around to face him. We are a mess. No stylist could even deal with how we look—sperm- and sweat-coated rats.

"So what?"

"So let's go, reeking of sex."

He leans forward, licking his own self off of my face and my hands.

Dressed in dark coats, curbside, the night greets us with the fresh yet slightly squalid scent of Manhattan. Tony raises his arm, fly-fishing into the river of taxis.

Without Reservations

The cab ride from the studio was strange and lovely. It created the sort of lulling superiority one feels in any cab in New York City on a warm autumn night at the end of a century. The people on the street are all our extras. Even deli signs take on a shrine-like beauty. Neon hums.

Tony lazily spread his legs wide, ensuring that our thighs rubbed with each bump as the cabbie silently guided us out of the · photo district and uptown toward Lexington Avenue, where a fabulous dinner, at the underwear guy's expense, awaited us.

Tony sat to my left, looking forward, feigning indifference to my presence, while his hand crept over to my thigh. I dared to bring my hand closer. I wondered about his willingness to be even this privately public with his affection, even after I had so thoroughly plowed him with the dildo, which lay hidden in my backpack.

My body still tingled. I was completely caught by this guy. I would never print a bad word about him, and yet my magazine wanted a critical look, "the buffoonery of machismo," my editor called it.

This was no buffoon. This was a demigod.

Absurd? Yes. I am absurd. I interview celebrities, sometimes become involved with them, less often become friends.

And yet, I felt hope with Tony. When he asked me to bring the dildo, jokingly, I thought, *no, he is toying with me.* But no, it was he who wanted the toys. And, as thanks, he became my toy.

In the cab, I was still sweating from our exploits. Tony seemed cool as ever, though. He took one of my fingers, then another, and we were holding hands, then slightly fondling each other's fingers. Tony's hands are gloriously manly: thick, well-maintained, yet slightly callused from daily gym workouts. "I am," he has often said of his regimen, "a fanatic."

"Hi," I said. He winked. This is what I love about the regality of a cab. You pay someone for the privacy, for this elite space. I fondled Tony's fingers, recalling what he had done with those fingers only minutes before: the funky traces of our sex trailed out the half-open cab window as we hit an open patch up Third Avenue.

There are times where you can hit all the green lights, and it's a glorious bumpy ride. I was more than riding high. I felt immortal. I was in love with the world.

"She's going to be so pissed," Tony smirked. He was either referring to Carmella the photographer (yes, she worked with Almodovar, but she doesn't like to talk about it), Ivaldo the producer

("Fashion! Fashion! Fashion! Nothing else matters!"), or the underwear man himself. Fortunately he was in Europe, so at least everyone was not as incredibly edgy, or as falsely professional as they behaved with him around. Some said this wasn't as important a shoot since he wasn't present. He was there for the other events. Whatever.

Anyway, all of them had hoped for a grand entrance with Tony, no doubt, and here I was, "his friend, the magazine writer" delaying their fabulism, their glory. I would pay for it by being duly eaten alive at the dinner.

But I didn't mind. I'd already dined on the main course. In fact, I could still taste him if I chewed a fingernail.

"Whad ze address?" the cabbie stuttered.

"Jean Georges on Fifty-Ninth Street," Tony said.

The cabbie nodded. "Oh. Oui, bon."

I glanced down at my baggy jeans and less-than-hip jacket, wondering if I would be denied entry. Jean George was the kind of restaurant that only admitted the utterly famous, or those who acted like they were. To get a reservation you had to plan it in your post-millennial calendar, or be as famous as the underwear guy.

"Oui," Tony joked. He said it, "Wheee," like, what a lark.

Tony smirked at me, holding back his wide toothy smile. He saved those now, it seemed. From that night forward we shared a remarkable secret, one that everyone would know, or suspect, but which none would dare mention.

As the cab driver pulled over, I made a move to pull away and get my wallet. Tony grabbed my hand, pretended to lean down behind the driver's seat, and gently took two of my fingers into his mouth, then released them like a Popsicle. It was as if he wanted another taste of me, for strength, before facing the crowd. The feeling of my fingers grazing those gorgeous teeth, his lips, his tongue, gave me shivers. I would have to make an appointment to swoon later.

I smirked this time as my cock stiffened in my jeans. I took out my wallet, avoiding using the two wet fingers. I wanted them to dry out with his spit on them.

Tony watched, noticed the swell in my jeans, and grabbed for it as I leaned forward. I let him squeeze as the cabbie counted out my change. The tip was large.

As we walked the few yards along the sidewalk, Tony hung close, as if I were his bodyguard. An elderly uptown woman walked by with her tiny dog, a sniveling creature that darted away, but then so did the woman on seeing the large bulge in both our jeans. Two walking boners heading into a fashionable restaurant, not unusual for New York. I've often bumped into fucks-in-transit, and not just on the piers.

I realized the reason for Tony's odd behavior. As famous as he was, as purportedly straight, or maybe bisexual as he is, some instinct in him had to show off, to show me off, to display my desire for him.

"You are too much," I muttered to him as we entered the foyer of the restaurant. I made a feeble attempt to adjust my cock to a less obscene position; a problem, since neither of us was wearing underwear.

The underwear.

I'd left his come-seeped, worn-just-once, soon-to-be-immortal-ized-on-billboards-worldwide, fresh undies lying on the floor of that photo studio.

"Damn." Since I didn't really collect items, it was no wonder I forgot.

"What is it? You look fine." He instinctively ran a hand through his own hair, which seemed to have styled itself with the breeze of the cab ride.

"I . . . I . . . nothing." What could I say? That I'd just developed an undie fetish and wanted to collect his shorts? Maybe sell them to the highest bidder? Save it as a token of our love? It wasn't as if I could steal another pair. And I couldn't ask for him to give me the ones he was wearing. Here's the scoop I pondered for my story: the world's leading underwear model never wears them.

"I left something at the studio."

"Oh. What?"

"My keys." Fortunately they were actually hidden away in the small side right pocket of my coat, for Tony jokingly made a move for my hips, patted my pockets front and back, then pulled back.

"Well, we get them from Carmella."

Carmella. Worldwide fashion photographer. Gorgeous, with long tresses of black hair, which she was known to tie in a bun tighter than Martha Graham's. When her hair was up, so was she, when she let it hang down, so did she.

Carmella had made it quite clear that she resented the presence of me, a wr-r-r-iter (she rolled her r's excessively in what I took as distaste) in the midst of what would be her most commercial, and popular, photo shoot ever. She was touchy enough when we'd asked to stay late. I was sure she'd resent my presence but not Tony's. I knew, however, that following dinner there would be further invitations for him, others who wanted to "get closer to Tony," to wine him, to dine him, to consume him. I would not regain admittance without the power of Tony's presence.

"You have a reservation, I hope," the rail-thin hostess inquired. Her tresses were tied up in a way that made you wish she could be the actress she aspired to become.

Tony turned to me, as if even speaking to someone of her sort were beneath him, or as if he were letting me take control, act as manager, top. It was at moments like that that I became torn. Should I hug him or slap him?

I explained that we were expected with Carmella's party.

"Oh, yes. Right this way." She extracted two menus from her podium and began leading us through the restaurant in a manner that could only be described as bad catwalk.

If you've seen the dinner scene in *I Shot Andy Warhol,* or any scene where a court of any era is in session, you will understand my nervousness with facing this . . . entourage. During the shoot, I'd sat in a corner. Afterward, Tony and I wrecked any trace of their power and pomposity with our sex. But this was a court: the queen, her courtiers, and other pals. I could make a great deal from this dinner, or be banished from several magazines with one wrong comment.

I could feel Tony getting nervous as we were led past huddled groups at tables. All of a sudden, as we rounded the corner to the private back room, Tony reached out, lightly touching the hostess's shoulder.

"Excuse me, where is the rest room?"

"Oh, that way. Do you . . . ?"

"We'll find our way in."

Tony left her, grabbed my arm, and led me down a hallway past a phone and into the men's room. He locked the door, pushed me against it, and pressed his face against mine. His tongue began making looping trails around my lips, face, neck, and chin. His hand dug into my jeans, grabbing my cock like a dock worker yanking a rope.

"Mmfnm," I mumbled an escape. He pulled away.

"Except for Carmella, whom I love dearly, I hate those people. I wish we could just. . . ." He tore away from me, unzipped his pants, led me to the urinal, where, as he nudged to me, I realized what he wanted. I unzipped, fighting the erection from his kiss and from the sight of his cock hanging out of his pants as he pulled back his foreskin and unleashed a gush of piss.

I swayed, a bit dizzy from it all. Finally, only by closing my eyes was I able to piss. Tony seemed pleased to watch me, as I was him. It's a strange sort of kink, but I felt like a little boy with him.

We giggled as we crossed streams, and at one moment, which I knew he only meant as a joke, or so I thought, he ran a finger under my stream and brought it to his lips, as if testing a recipe. I did the same, then knelt forward, taking his penis in my mouth, tasting the last bitter drops of him. He shoved himself into me, grew stiff in a few seconds and wagged it about.

We both marveled at it: wet, stiff, just a rod of flesh and blood protruding from the pants of an Italian man in the bathroom of a restaurant in the greatest city in America.

Pulling back his foreskin to suck only made his cock jut higher. Tony grabbed his pants and belt, shoving them abruptly down as he stood, legs apart. Above his pants, white shorts. No, not quite white anymore. I reached for them.

"I put the ones from the shoot back on. They smell good."

My mouth clamped around his cock; my fingers slipped around the cotton of his shorts as I shoved them lower. In a moment of acrobatic wonder inspired by the urgency of swiftness needed, Tony managed to slip his pants down each leg, and then the shorts, and put his pants back on all while I crouched, my mouth following his bobbing erection, never once releasing it. Once stable again, Tony held my head steady and face fucked me with force. The back of my throat filled wide. To keep the string of drool and impending spurt of cum from dripping onto his pants, Tony cupped his balls with the bunched up shorts, holding them under my chin like a bib.

Someone knocked.

"Just a minute," Tony called out.

He then bent over, jamming his cock faster in and out of my mouth. His legs quivered. "Oh, god. I wanna get caught. I want the door to swing open and a thousand cameras to capture us."

One grunt from my choked mouth in agreement, and he went over the edge. A blast, then more, salty sweet, mixed with my snot. He held himself in me, then slowly pulled out, wiping his cock and my face with the underwear.

Stunned silence, followed by panting and giggles. Bashful glances in the mirror as we rinsed off.

We zipped up.

"You ready?" He kissed me.

"Ready as I'll ever be."

"Um . . . ," Tony looked at my hand.

The shorts. I shoved them in a pocket.

We wiped our mouths, adjusted our pants, opened the door, and walked past a very stunned waiter. At dinner, I didn't eat much. Nothing could outdo the meal I'd already been served.

About the Editor

Todd Gregory has published numerous stories in anthologies such as the *Best Gay Erotica* series, *A View to a Thrill, Latin Boys,* and various Web sites. His first anthology as an editor, *Blood Lust,* was published by Alyson Books in 2005.

His Underwear: An Erotic Anthology
© 2007 by The Haworth Press, Inc. All rights reserved.
doi:10.1300/5756_27

Contributors

Jonathan Asche has been writing erotic fiction for more than ten years. His work has appeared in *Playguy, Inches, Torso, Men, In Touch for Men, Indulge,* and *Mandate,* as well as the anthologies *Friction 3, Three the Hard Way, Manhandled, Best Gay Erotica 2004,* and *Buttmen 2* and *3.* In 2003, Asche published his first novel *Mindjacker,* an erotic thriller, with STARbooks Press. He lives in Atlanta with his husband, Tomé, and their emotionally unbalanced pets. Asche is currently at work on his second novel.

Tom Bacchus is the author of *Q-FAQ,* published by The Haworth Press (2007). His short fiction has been published in more than thirty anthologies and magazines, and his artwork and videos have been shown at various locations, illicit and licit, in the United States and Europe. His two first books are *Bone* and *Rahm* (also published in Spanish as *Sueños de Hombre* and in German as *Seiter vollen Lust*). Visit his blog at tombacchus.blogspot.com/.

Tim Bergling is the author of *Sissyphobia, Reeling in the Years,* and *Chasing Adonis.*

Steve Berman has sold over sixty short stories and articles since he started writing with stories sold to *Gay Best Erotica 2005, The Faery Reel,* and other noted anthologies. His career could be broken down into three periods: The Early Years or Tight Whities Time, College Days or Boxers are Keen, and Current Era or Boxer-Briefs with Unbuttoned Flies. His specialty is queer and weird fiction and more can be found about Steve at his Web site (www.steveberman.com).

Rachel Kramer Bussel serves as senior editor at *Penthouse Variations.* She is the reviser of *The Lesbian Sex Book (2nd edition)* and editor of *Up All Night: Adventures in Lesbian Sex, Glamour Girls: Femme/ Femme Erotica, Naughty Spanking Stories from A to Z,* and *A Spanking Good Time.* Her writing has been published in over forty anthologies in-

His Underwear: An Erotic Anthology
© 2007 by The Haworth Press, Inc. All rights reserved.
doi:10.1300/5756_28

cluding *Best American Erotica 2004, Best Women's Erotica 2003* and *2004, Best Lesbian Erotica 2001* and *2004, Best Bondage Erotica, Quickies 3,* and *Juicy Erotica,* as well as *AVN, Bust, Cleansheets, Curve, Diva, Girlfriends, On Our Backs,* Oxygen.com, *Playgirl, Velvetpark,* and *The Village Voice.* Visit her at www.rachelkramerbussel.com and lustylady.blogspot.com.

Dale Chase has been writing gay erotica for eight years with over 100 stories published in various magazines and anthologies including translation into German. His collection of Victorian erotica, *The Company He Keeps,* will be published soon.

Jordan M. Coffey is the pseudonym of someone who always wanted to be a writer, but who took a divergent twenty-year path into computers and accounting. After rediscovering the obsessive joy of putting words to paper, Jordan took the plunge into professional publishing and is pleased to have found haven in *Wet Nightmares, Wet Dreams, Best Gay Love Stories 2005,* and *Daddy's Boyz.*

Hank Edwards is the author of the novel *Fluffers, Inc.* Find his stories in *Honcho, Mandate,* and *American Bear,* as well as the anthologies *Full Body Contact* and *Just the Sex.* He lives in a suburb of Detroit with his partner of many years. Visit his Web site at www.hankedwards books.com.

Trebor Healey's debut novel, *Through It Came Bright Colors,* won both the Ferro-Grumley and Violet Quill awards. A poet, essayist, and writer, Trebor has published in numerous anthologies, collections and magazines. For more information go to www.treborhealey.com.

Greg Herren is the author of four novels *(Murder in the Rue Dauphine, Bourbon Street Blues, Jackson Square Jazz,* and *Murder in the Rue St. Ann)* and the editor of the anthologies *Full Body Contact, Shadows of the Night, FRATSEX,* and *Upon a Midnight Clear.* He has also published a collection of his erotic short fiction, *Wanna Wrestle?* He lives in New Orleans with his partner of nine years, Paul Willis. Check him out at www.gregwrites.com.

William Holden is a native of Detroit but now lives in Atlanta with his partner of seven years. He is currently attending graduate school at Florida State University, School of Information Studies and is employed as a librarian at Emory University. He contributes the start of his writing to his partner Mark, who encouraged him to take the ultimate leap of faith. He has published stories in numerous anthologies including *Sex Buddies, Slow Grind, View to a Thrill,* and *Bad Boys,* among others.

Jeff Mann is a highly respected poet and essayist whose work has appeared in, among many other places, *The Spoon River Poetry Review, Prairie Schooner,* and *Journal of Appalachian Studies.* His collection of essays, *Edge,* was published by The Haworth Press in 2003. He also published the novella "Devoured" in the Kensington Books collection *Masters of Midnight.* His three chapbooks, *Bliss, Mountain Fireflies,* and *Flint Shards from Sussex,* were nominated for numerous awards. He also published a full length collection of poetry, *Bones Washed with Wine.*

Adam McCabe is the pen name of a well-known author and reviewer. His erotic work has appeared in a variety of magazine and anthologies, including Susie Bright's *Best American Erotic 2000.*

Sean Meriwether's fiction has been defined as dark realism, his subjects rooted in the peculiar nature of everyday life. His work has or will be published in *Lodestar Quarterly, Out of Control: Erotic Wild Rides,* and *Quickies 3.* He is currently working on a collection of short stories and a novel. In addition to writing, he has the pleasure of editing two online magazines, *Outsider Ink* (outsiderink.com) and *Velvet Mafia: Dangerous Queer Fiction* (velvetmafia.com). Sean lives in New York with his partner, photographer Jack Slomovits, and their two dogs. If you are interested in reading more of his work, stalk him online at seanmeriwether.com.

The erotic fiction of **Christopher Pierce** has been published most recently in *Bound & Gagged, Freshmen, Men, Honcho, Inches, In Touch, Indulge, Torso,* and in the anthologies *Men Amplified, FRATSEX,* and *Friction 7: Best Gay Erotic Fiction.* He is currently co-editing the new collection *Men on the Edge* with Michael Huxley for STARbooks Press. Write to him at chris@christopherpierceerotica.com and visit his world online at www.ChristopherPierceErotica.com.

Max Pierce is a survivor of class reunions, wishing they could be more like Martin's. Living in Hollywood, California, he writes on film history and gay life for numerous national publications. His fiction also appears in the STARbooks Press anthology *Dangerous Liaisons.*

Max Reynolds is the pseudonym of a well-published East Coast queer journalist.

Dominic Santi is a former technical editor turned rogue whose latest erotic work is the German collection *Kerle Im Lustrauch (Guys In Lust Frenzy)*. Santi's fiction is available in English in *Best American Erotica 2004*, *Best Gay Erotica 2000* and *2004*, various volumes of *Friction* and *Best Bisexual Erotica*, as well as in *Best Transgender Erotica*, *Tough Guys*, *Latin Boys*, *Sex Buddies*, *Kink*, and many dozens of other smutty anthologies and magazines.

Lukas Scott puts the MAN into Roman with his latest queerotica novel *Legion of Lust* (Zipper Books, 2004), making *Gladiator* look like *Mary Poppins*. His first novel, *Hot On The Trail* (Idol, 2000), put the Wild back into the Wild Wild West. He's published numerous short stories, several nonfiction books and articles, and, rather mysteriously, a romantic novel. Over what seems numerous lifetimes, he has been a university lecturer, theatre director, television and film extra, model, counselor, and even used to hang around toilets for a living. You can open his portal at www.lukasscott.com, where he'd love you to probe him further.

Simon Sheppard is the author of *In Deep: Erotic Stories*, *Kinkorama: Dispatches from the Front Lines of Perversion*, and *Sex Parties 101*. His work has appeared in over 125 books, including five editions of *Best American Erotica* and ten editions of *Best Gay Erotica*. He also writes two columns, "Sex Talk" and "Perv," which can be found in queer newspapers and online at gay.com and planetout.com. He lives in San Francisco and loiters at www.simonsheppard.com.

Troy Ygnacio Soriano released his debut novel, *The Beginning*, this year. It is an allegory of a man who actually gets his boyfriend pregnant. "The idea of a gay male union resulting in life, after so much death, is very attractive to me." He writes in San Francisco and Boston. He recently moved from San Francisco to Nebraska to write a book called *My Blue Year in a Red State*. His website is www.troysoriano.com.

From Vancouver, Canada, **Jay Starre** has written for numerous gay men's magazines including *Men*, *Honcho*, *Torso*, *Mandate*, *Indulge*, and *American Bear*. His stories have been included in over twenty-five gay anthologies including *Full Body Contact*, *Kink*, *View to a Thrill*, and *Wired Hard 3*. His short story *The Four Doors* was nominated for a 2003 Spectrum Award.

Kyle Stone first appeared as the author of the scorching SM/SF erotic adventure novel *The Initiation of PB500*, which has since been labeled a cult classic. Four other novels soon followed. Stone's short stories have appeared in many gay magazines and anthologies. The latest are collected in *MENagerie,* which received much attention.

Aaron Travis is the pen name of novelist Steven Saylor. His first erotic story appeared in 1979 on *Drummer* magazine, which he later edited. Travis retired from writing erotica in the early 1990s but his work continues to find an audience; in 2003, the readers of Susie Bright's *Best American Erotica* voted his story "The Hit" their all time favorite. His Web site is at stevensaylor.com/aarontravis.

Born and raised an Okie, **Mark Wildyr** now lives in New Mexico, the setting for most of his stories. He has sold over thirty five short stories and novellas to The Haworth Press, Alyson Books, STARbooks Press, Arsenal Pulp Press, and Companion Press. Two of his novels finished in the top twenty-five of the recent Project: QueerLit contest.

Order a copy of this book with this form or online at:
http://www.haworthpress.com/store/product.asp?sku=5756

HIS UNDERWEAR
An Erotic Anthology

_____in softbound at $17.95 (ISBN: 978-1-56023-624-5)

273 pages

Or order online and use special offer code HEC25 in the shopping cart.

COST OF BOOKS_____

☐ **BILL ME LATER:** (Bill-me option is good on US/Canada/Mexico orders only; not good to jobbers, wholesalers, or subscription agencies.)

☐ Check here if billing address is different from shipping address and attach purchase order and billing address information.

POSTAGE & HANDLING_____
(US: $4.00 for first book & $1.50 for each additional book)
(Outside US: $5.00 for first book & $2.00 for each additional book)

Signature_____

SUBTOTAL_____

☐ **PAYMENT ENCLOSED: $**_____

IN CANADA: ADD 6% GST_____

☐ **PLEASE CHARGE TO MY CREDIT CARD.**

STATE TAX_____
(NJ, NY, OH, MN, CA, IL, IN, PA, & SD residents, add appropriate local sales tax)

☐ Visa ☐ MasterCard ☐ AmEx ☐ Discover
☐ Diner's Club ☐ Eurocard ☐ JCB

Account # _____

FINAL TOTAL_____
(If paying in Canadian funds, convert using the current exchange rate, UNESCO coupons welcome)

Exp. Date_____

Signature_____

Prices in US dollars and subject to change without notice.

NAME_____

INSTITUTION_____

ADDRESS_____

CITY_____

STATE/ZIP_____

COUNTRY_____ COUNTY (NY residents only)_____

TEL_____ FAX_____

E-MAIL_____

May we use your e-mail address for confirmations and other types of information? ☐ Yes ☐ No
We appreciate receiving your e-mail address and fax number. Haworth would like to e-mail or fax special discount offers to you, as a preferred customer. **We will never share, rent, or exchange your e-mail address or fax number.** We regard such actions as an invasion of your privacy.

Order From Your Local Bookstore or Directly From
The Haworth Press, Inc.
10 Alice Street, Binghamton, New York 13904-1580 • USA
TELEPHONE: 1-800-HAWORTH (1-800-429-6784) / Outside US/Canada: (607) 722-5857
FAX: 1-800-895-0582 / Outside US/Canada: (607) 771-0012
E-mail to: orders@haworthpress.com

For orders outside US and Canada, you may wish to order through your local sales representative, distributor, or bookseller.
For information, see http://haworthpress.com/distributors

(Discounts are available for individual orders in US and Canada only, not booksellers/distributors.)

PLEASE PHOTOCOPY THIS FORM FOR YOUR PERSONAL USE.
http://www.HaworthPress.com   BOF07

Dear Customer:

Please fill out & return this form to receive special deals & publishing opportunities for you! These include:
- availability of new books in your local bookstore or online
- one-time prepublication discounts
- free or heavily discounted related titles
- free samples of related Haworth Press periodicals
- publishing opportunities in our periodicals or Book Division

❏ OK! Please keep me on your regular mailing list and/or e-mailing list for new announcements!

Name _____

Address_____

STAPLE OR TAPE YOUR BUSINESS CARD HERE!

_____

*E-mail address _____
*Your e-mail address will never be rented, shared, exchanged, sold, or divested. You may "opt-out" at any time.
May we use your e-mail address for confirmations and other types of information? ❏ Yes ❏ No

Special needs:
Describe below any special information you would like:
- Forthcoming professional/textbooks
- New popular books
- Publishing opportunities in academic periodicals
- Free samples of periodicals in my area(s)

Special needs/Special areas of interest:

_____

_____

_____

_____

Please contact me as soon as possible. I have a special requirement/project:

_____

_____

_____

_____

The Haworth Press Inc.

PLEASE COMPLETE THE FORM ABOVE AND MAIL TO:
Donna Barnes, Marketing Dept., The Haworth Press, Inc.
10 Alice Street, Binghamton, NY 13904–1580 USA
Tel: 1–800–429–6784 • Outside US/Canada Tel: (607) 722–5857
Fax: 1–800–895–0582 • Outside US/Canada Fax: (607) 771–0012
E-mail: orders@HaworthPress.com

GBIC07